EVERY SHADE

A COLLECTION OF NOVELLAS AND SHORTS

NORA PHOENIX

NOTE FROM NORA

This collection of novellas and shorts contains five stories. Four of these have been published before as part of an anthology or as a free story, but *Waiting for Alexander* is a brand new story.

Happy reading!

UN-STUCK

1

Samuel Norris rushed through the three blocks between his office and his boyfriend's law firm, taking care not to slip on the gray, sopping mush on the pavement. It had once been pristine white snow, but the combination of salting and too many people walking on it had transformed it into a slippery, dirty mess.

That was February for you. Even worse, it could stay like that till halfway through April. New York City in the winter, always a joy. It was a good thing he loved this city so much. Still, he should've taken a cab. Three blocks didn't sound like much, but they were three blocks more than was fun in this weather.

He checked his watch to make sure he was still on time, then caught himself. He *had* been on time, waiting for Evan to pick him up for their date, only to get a text that he was still at work and could Samuel please come to him? Rationally, it meant he could slow down, but mentally, he was still trying to get there as soon as possible. They did have reservations at seven thirty, after all, and it was already close to seven.

He was looking forward to trying out the place where Evan had made a reservation, an up-and-coming French restaurant that was rumored to be receiving its first Michelin star this year. Evan had said they'd better try it out before everyone else discovered it, and Samuel thought he had a point. Personally, he was just as happy eating a good burger, but he knew fine cuisine was something Evan valued.

Plus, it was Valentine's Day, so all the more reason for a more romantic location. Samuel wasn't gonna jinx anything by spending too much time thinking about it, but if he wanted Evan to take the next step—and god knew he did— it wasn't gonna happen at a burger place. Evan had *standards*, so he liked to tell Samuel. Even though Samuel thought those standards a bit pompous and snobby at times —and that was saying a lot coming from him, what with his background and all—this restaurant could be an excellent opportunity for Evan to pop the big question. At least, that's what Samuel had quietly reasoned in the back of his mind, too scared to allow that thought too much space in his head. That could only lead to disappointment.

But it was Valentine's Day, so today of all days, he allowed himself a little more leeway to dream about what could be. They had been together for two years now, so it wasn't too crazy to expect more, right? Of course, Evan hadn't even *officially* moved in with Samuel, but the reality was that most of his clothes were at Samuel's Upper East Side apartment. That's where Evan spent all his nights as well, mostly renting out his own studio through Airbnb. That was a clear signal he was invested in this relationship, Samuel reasoned.

Sure, their relationship wasn't perfect, but that was life.

None of his friends had the perfect relationship either—hell, both of his brothers were making a mess of the whole dating thing—though he had a few that came pretty damn close. He and Evan were well-matched, he had felt from the beginning. They had similar interests, never lacked anything to talk about, and they rarely had a fight. Okay, maybe that was also because Samuel tended to give in, but he hated confrontations.

The only thing Samuel would love to change was how much Evan worked, but that was kind of unavoidable with how focused he was on his career. Samuel cared a lot about his own career as a graphic designer, but his didn't require the same amount of hours. Or maybe, if he was honest, he was simply better at striking that right balance between work and life, but that was something Evan could learn.

Plus, he was well aware it was different for him. Samuel didn't *need* to work, not for money anyway, whereas Evan still had student loans and whatnot to pay off.

And maybe, if he was completely honest, their sex life could be a little more fulfilling. It used to be, when they'd first met, with Evan open to Samuel's ideas. So he loved to try new stuff, sue him. Evan had been into it at first, but that had quickly changed. Samuel had tried to bring it up, but that had not gone over well. Evan had accused him of being too demanding and had made it clear that he was too busy to fulfill that need for Samuel. Silly games, he'd called them, and that had *hurt*.

There had been the suggestion that maybe Samuel was a little too needy in that department, and maybe Evan had a point there. From what he could gather from their friends, none of them had as much of a drive for sex as he did. And none of them loved to experiment and *play* the way he liked.

Oh well, good thing Amazon sold a wide variety of toys. And even better that he could make up all kinds of scenarios in his head as he used them. It wasn't the same, but it did quench some of that need.

But something needed to happen, because it felt like they were stuck, somehow. Not moving forward, not moving backward, but not in a place that was fully satisfying either. Was Evan not ready for more commitment? Or was Samuel naive to believe that getting married was the solution to getting unstuck? That thought was unsettling. But what else could help them move on?

He kept mulling it over in his head, happy when he finally reached Evan's building and quickly made his way inside through the revolving door, stamping off the remainders of the slush from his shoes before he walked up to the receptionist.

"I'm here to see Evan McLeod with Nash, Bunter, and Brookfield," he told the professionally smiling brunette who clearly wasn't concentrating fully on her job, judging by the phone she reluctantly put down. Maybe she had exciting dinner plans for this special day as well. Samuel could only hope they would be as amazing as his.

"Can I see some ID, please?" she asked.

Samuel already had his wallet in his hand, knowing the drill by now. It was a shame the building, which housed many companies spread out over thirty floors, couldn't seem to hold on to their receptionist. He practically saw a new face every time he came here, which in general was about once every two weeks or so. It would save him the trouble of having to identify himself all the time. Still, it was a small price to pay, he supposed.

He showed her his driver's license, and her eyes widened

as she recognized his name. To her credit, she didn't say anything, only wrote his name on a visitor's badge and handed it to him.

"Thank you," he said as he stuck it to his chest with the little magnet.

As he made his way to the elevators, another guy came in. Samuel only caught a glimpse of him, but he smiled inwardly at the contrast between his own snazzy suit and the stained cargo pants and work boots this guy was sporting. Samuel might look a bit more classy, but this guy clearly had the better choice of outfits when it came to this weather. Samuel knew for a fact he would not only have to remove the slush from his pants, but from his shoes as well to prevent permanent salt stains.

He whipped out his phone as he waited for the elevator to arrive, something that always took forever in this building. Too many floors and only two elevators, a clear design mistake if he'd ever seen one. He checked his email, his face turning into a smile when he saw the positive feedback from his boss on his mockup for a new campaign for a well-known diaper brand. The idea for that had come to him late last night and he'd worked till two in the morning to create something. Clearly, that had been time well spent.

A loud ding announced the elevator had finally arrived, and he put his phone back into his pocket. He pressed the button for the twelfth floor where Evan's office was, and the doors were already closing when he heard a voice call out, "Hold the elevator, please!"

On reflex, Samuel held his hand between the doors and they reopened. The guy he had spotted coming in after him shot him a grateful look. "Thank you. These elevators always take forever."

Samuel nodded. "I know. Glad to be of help. What floor?"
"Twelfth."

Samuel lowered his gaze a little, then studied him through his eyelashes. The guy was ruggedly handsome with his messy dark hair, a beard that needed a bit of trimming, and an outfit that indicated he was used to working outside and getting dirty. Samuel held back a giggle at that last word, amused at where his own thoughts were going with the word *dirty*. But the guy was one hell of a hot bear, and Samuel appreciated the view as they rode up.

Then the lights in the elevator flickered, a screeching sound erupted that hurt his ears, and the elevator came to a sudden halt, throwing them into complete darkness. As if on cue, Samuel let out a scream, grabbing the handrail inside the elevator with both hands. What the hell had happened?

His heart rate sped up and his lungs suddenly felt constricted, making it hard to breathe. Why weren't the lights coming back on? Had the power been disrupted? Oh god, what would happen to the elevator without power? It should have a backup generator, right? If not, they could plummet to...

"You okay?" A low voice interrupted his thoughts.

Samuel wanted to answer him, but it turned out talking was hard when your body had forgotten how to breathe. He gasped for air, his body trembling with the sensation of the darkness attacking him. Why was there no light? What was going on?

"You're breathing a little fast there, Samuel," that low, steady voice spoke.

What did he mean Samuel was breathing fast? He felt like he wasn't breathing at all, like his body was gasping for oxygen. But when he focused enough to listen, it turned out the man was right, as the sounds of his raspy, quick breaths filled the elevator. He was hyperventilating, Samuel realized, while at the same time unable to stop it.

"Don't pass out on me now," the guy said. "There's nothing to worry about. I'm sure that whatever is wrong with the elevator, they'll fix it soon enough. We're not gonna plummet to our death, if that's what you're scared of. An elevator like this is attached to strong, metal cables, and they have nothing to do with power. They'll get us out of here, don't worry."

Samuel liked his voice, he decided. It was low, rich, and with just the right amount of authority to reassure him. He focused on it, allowed the deep timbre to roll through him. Still, he was getting a little light-headed.

"Samuel, I'm starting to worry about you. You need to slow down your breathing."

"I can't," Samuel managed to get out, wavering a little.

"I'm going to touch you now, okay? Don't panic, I'm going to help you breathe."

Seconds later, a strong, gentle hand found his neck. "We're gonna sit down on the floor so you can put your head between your knees. I'll hold on to you, no worries."

For one second, Samuel thought of the devastating effects of that dirty floor on his crisp suit, but then he allowed himself to be pushed down. Breathing trumped a clean suit. He was lowered to the floor, two strong arms holding him, until he sat down between the man's legs, that big body behind him.

The guy gently pushed his head forward, and Samuel went with the movement, bending forward until his head was between his knees. After twenty seconds or so, his breathing finally slowed down, and the airy, dizzy sensation in his head disappeared.

"That's so much better," the man said. "You're doing great, Samuel."

The guy kept using his name, and Samuel only registered it now. How did he know it? Oh, right, he was wearing a name tag. The guy must've spotted it before the lights went out.

"What's your name?" he asked between gasps, and he didn't even know why that was the first thing out of his mouth.

A low chuckle rumbled in the chest behind him. "I'm Tris. It's a pleasure to meet you, even if the circumstances could've been better."

Tris. Samuel let that unusual name roll around in his head. He liked it. It was short, punchy, and it fit what he'd seen from the guy.

He stayed seated with his head between his knees until he felt like he was breathing normally again. Tris must have agreed with that assessment, because he allowed Samuel to sit up.

"I would like for you to stay seated for a little longer, just to make sure you're okay," he said, gently pulling Samuel backward until he was resting with his back against the guy's chest.

It was an intimate position to be in with a stranger, and yet Samuel felt safe. "Thank you," he said.

"You're welcome."

Tris had barely sounded out the last syllable when a buzzing sounded, followed by a canned voice that echoed through the elevator. "Attention, please. We are experiencing technical difficulties with the elevators. Please know that we are working on fixing them as soon as possible. At this point, all elevators have been shut down while we await the arrival of our elevator technicians to diagnose and fix the problem. Please stay calm. If there are any urgent medical needs, let us know by pressing the intercom button."

The arms around Samuel tightened as if to reassure him. "Well, fuck it," Tris said. "We're stuck."

2

Tris didn't object at all to the cute guy leaning against him, his back pressed against Tris's chest. It was a damn shame the lights in the elevator were out, because he wouldn't have minded feasting his eyes a little longer on that appealing face. His dark hair had been styled to perfection, not a strand out of place, and it completely fit his neatly trimmed beard and his eyebrows that looked like he waxed them regularly.

The only reason Tris paid attention to things like that was because Cara had once railed about not having her eyebrows done in so long she'd acquired a unibrow. She'd had to explain that one to him, and ever since, he'd paid attention to eyebrows for some odd reason. Not a particularly helpful skill on a construction site, but it provided some amusement every now and then.

But it wasn't Samuel's eyebrows that had made Tris notice him or even the cute beard and the gorgeous, dark blue eyes, nor the suit that had to be custom-made, since it hugged his slender body so perfectly. No, it was a pair of full lips that were just begging to be kissed. Tris rarely had such a physical reaction to people he met, but this time, his whole body had shown attention, his dick most of all. That had to be the first time he could remember that he'd gotten a hard-on because of a guy's lips.

"How are you doing, Samuel? Or would you prefer to be called Sam?"

"Either is fine," came the soft response.

Tris still detected stress in his voice, which didn't surprise him after that announcement. He had zero fear of small places and wasn't afraid of the dark, but he couldn't deny this experience was a little unnerving.

He moved his leg sideways so he could reach his phone, then took it out and turned the flashlight feature on. "How about I put this right here so we have at least a bit of light?"

Samuel let out a little sigh. "Thank you."

"You didn't answer my question," Tris said, keeping his voice light. "Which do you actually prefer, Samuel or Sam?"

"My boyfriend always calls me Sam," Samuel said, and Tris's first reaction was a deep disappointment that he was taken, followed by a thrill at the good news that at least he was interested in men. Not that Tris would ever poach a boyfriend off another man. That was something you just didn't do, not even to strangers.

"I'm sure he does, but technically, that's still not an answer to my question," Tris said.

"Huh," Samuel said, and that one expression packed a lot of surprise. "I guess you're right. I prefer Samuel, actually."

"Samuel it is," Tris said. "Since we're going to be stuck here for a while, let's chat and keep our minds off the fact that we can think of a million places we'd rather be right now. So, tell me about yourself. What do you do for a living?"

It was the most mundane of opening questions, obviously, but considering Samuel's stress, Tris figured it was a safe enough place to start.

"I'm a graphic designer at an advertising agency," Samuel said.

"Cool. Or at least, it sounds cool. What does that entail, exactly?"

Samuel let out a cute giggle. "It means that other people come up with creative ideas for ad campaigns, and I make whatever graphics they need, like designs for ads in magazines, newspapers, or even billboards. I also do branding for ad campaigns or companies, so developing a new logo or a house style for a company."

"Gotcha. I take it you spend most of your days behind a screen then, creating beautiful things that didn't exist before," Tris said.

"I love that description," Samuel said, and Tris could hear the smile in his voice. "It's accurate, though not everything I create can be labeled beautiful. But yeah, I create what wasn't before. What do you do? Judging by your appearance, you don't look like you spend all day indoors."

Tris weighed his words for a few seconds, then decided it was a neutral observation and not a judgment on his appearance. He'd been there before, some urban professional judging him for being a guy who worked with his hands. As if they had zero understanding that both of their jobs were needed, since they wouldn't have a place to live without guys like Tris.

"I own a construction company," he said, allowing his pride for his achievements to ring through in his voice. "I started it about ten years ago, and it's grown from being just me to employing about twenty guys full time and countless per diem workers."

"What kind of things do you build?" Samuel asked.

"We mostly do remodeling and renovation, but we have scored a few new construction projects as well. They're hard to snag for a small company like mine. I can't be as competitive on pricing as the bigger guys."

Samuel's body, which had still been a little tense, relaxed against Tris's, and it almost felt like he was snuggling against him. There was absolutely no need for Tris to still have his arms wrapped around Samuel, but he couldn't seem to let go of him. Still, no harm done, as long as Samuel didn't push him away or give any indication he was getting uncomfortable, right?

"So what you're saying is you're creating beautiful things that didn't exist as well," Samuel said.

"I guess so," Tris said, feeling strangely happy at hearing his own words echoed back to him.

He'd better remember this guy was taken, he told himself. "And you have a boyfriend, I understand?" he asked, just to help himself focus on that crucially important tidbit.

"Yes," Samuel said. "We've been dating for two years now."

"And he calls you Sam," Tris said, not knowing why that was so important for him to mention.

"He does. I don't mind from him, I guess," Samuel said, and there was a hint of an edge to his voice that alerted Tris there might be some trouble brewing in paradise.

Still, he wasn't the kind of man to capitalize on that. There were few things he hated more than cheating. "Is he taking you out for dinner tonight?" he asked.

"Yes, he made reservations at *Quatre*, an exclusive French restaurant," Samuel said, and now there was a happiness in his voice that hadn't been there before.

Tris had never heard of the restaurant but since going

out for dinner usually meant fast food for him with the occasional chain restaurant thrown in, that didn't surprise him. "Sounds like you have a wonderful evening planned."

"If we ever get out of this damn elevator," Samuel mumbled.

Funny, a few minutes ago, Tris had been just as impatient but now he was fine spending some more time with Samuel. Maybe it was for the better that he was delayed, since he'd been hot-headed when he'd stormed into the building. Some time to cool off might prevent him from doing something stupid, like using his fists rather than his words to communicate his displeasure with the letter he'd received from that asshole lawyer. That two-timing bastard totally deserved to get his face smashed in, but getting arrested wasn't gonna help Tris's case. Or his company.

"How about you?" Samuel asked, interrupting Tris's thoughts. "Are you in a relationship?"

He'd carefully avoided naming a gender, Tris noted, which amused him. His sexual orientation was hard to read for most people, and he usually got pegged as straight, especially when he had his kids with him. "I'm divorced, now single."

"Oh. Newly divorced?"

"Nah, three years ago. We met in high school, got married when we found out she was pregnant in our senior year. We stayed together for a long time, but we'd grown apart long before then. We're still good friends, though, and we share custody of our kids, two teenage boys."

"Oh," Samuel said again, but this time there was a little edge to his voice. "That's great that you're still such good friends, especially for your kids."

"It is. She's in a new relationship now, and her new boyfriend, Colin, is a cool guy who fits her perfectly."

"But you're not dating?" Samuel asked.

Tris shrugged. "I've dated a bit but nothing serious. I wanted to focus on my company and on my kids, and I figured that with all the changes the divorce brought, some stability for them would be good. But maybe it's time to get back into it, I don't know. It seems like such a hassle, you know?"

"It can be. I dated for years before I met my boyfriend. But you know what they say about having to kiss a lot of frogs before you find your prince. Or *princess*, in your case?"

It was cute, the way he'd subtly framed that as a question, and Tris smiled. "Either. All," he said. "I'm pansexual, so gender is not something I focus on, if that makes sense."

The relief from Samuel was audible in a little sigh as well as obvious in the tension that left his body. "I thought you were gay because you were so comfortable with touching another man, but then you mentioned your ex-wife and I figured I'd maybe gotten it wrong. Then I considered you might be bi, but it seemed like a rather personal question to ask."

Tris's smile transformed into a chuckle. "So you figured you'd drop a little passive-aggressive suggestive question, huh?"

Samuel pulled his right shoulder up in a shrug. "It worked."

It sure had, and Tris had to admire his devious tactic. "So what brings you to this office building?"

"My boyfriend works here. He was supposed to pick me up, but he texted me he was running late and asked me to come here," Samuel explained.

Tris frowned. A guy who was late because he had to work on Valentine's Day clearly had an issue getting his priorities straight. There was no way in hell he would keep a cutie like Samuel waiting. A man like that deserved to be pampered and taken care of.

"Well, at least you're going out together in a little bit. I'm sure it won't be long now."

"God, I hope so. He will be so pissed when we lose our reservation. He made it, like, two months ago. Anyway, what brings you here?"

Even thinking about it brought his simmering anger back in full force, and Tris couldn't keep the venom from his voice as he spoke. "I'm here to see if I can get a one-on-one with a lawyer who's fucking my company over. It's a long story, but basically, I did a job for a real estate developer who turned out to be a shady motherfucker—pardon my French—and tried to get out of paying me by suing me for incompetence. I thought everything was settled, but I got a letter today from his asshole lawyer that he's decided to go ahead and take it to court. They damn well know I can't afford the lawyer fees for a trial."

For the first time since they'd sat down, Samuel pushed against Tris's arms, and he let him go immediately. Samuel scrambled to turn around and face him, and even in the dim light his phone produced, Tris could see his indignity. "That's horrible!"

The pure emotion on his face wrapped around Tris's heart like a warm embrace, softening his anger. "It is. They're taking advantage of a small company like mine because I can't afford expensive lawyers. So I figured I'd come over and try to talk some reason into this asshole, though I doubt it'll do me any good. The guy is a massive dick anyway, and not the good kind."

He got a chuckle for that lame-ass joke. "Just because he's doing this to you, or do you know more about him?" Samuel asked.

"Oh, I know more about him than I care to. The guy is a cheater, and there are few things I despise more than that. Apparently, he has a husband or boyfriend or something, but he cheats on him like every week or so. My ex, Cara, owns a cleaning company and she cleans the studio he still keeps, even though he lives with his partner. She's run into him on more than one occasion when he was just done fucking some hookup. Seriously, he's a total douchebag."

He stopped talking when he noticed Samuel's body going rigid. What was the matter? Was he triggering bad memories? Maybe his boyfriend had cheated on him and Tris had made him relive that?

Then it dawned on him. Oh god. Samuel had mentioned he was here to see his boyfriend. It couldn't be, could it? Then again, how many gay lawyers could work on the same floor? Fucking hell, he'd gone and done it now, hadn't he?

"Samuel," he said, more a plea than anything else, and even in the weak light the terror in Samuel's eyes was stark. He *knew*. "I'm..."

What could he say? That he was sorry? He was, for causing him pain, but the truth was that it wasn't his fault. But would Samuel see it that way?

"The asshole lawyer, what's his name?" Samuel asked, his voice barely audible.

"Samuel," Tris tried again, not wanting to hurt him even more by confirming what they both knew was true.

"What's. His. Name."

Samuel's ice-cold tone would be a damn turn-on if it didn't break Tris's heart. He forced the words out. "Evan McLeod."

3

As much as Samuel wanted to tell himself that it couldn't be true, deep inside he knew it was. He'd known it when Tris had started talking about the cheating lawyer with the studio where he fucked other men. Maybe he'd even known it when Tris had mentioned the asshole lawyer who was trying to screw him over.

It was like his subconscious and his conscious had repaired a connection that had been malfunctioning, because now he was aware of all these subtle signs he should've have seen, should've picked up on, that should've made him suspicious. And now that he allowed his subconscious in, it was screaming at him that it *had* seen it, *had* picked it up, but Samuel hadn't allowed those instincts to surface to his conscious mind.

His boyfriend of two years was a cheater. The man he'd hoped would ask him to marry him tonight had cheated on him. Everything he had clung to as the truth turned out to be a lie.

"Samuel," Tris said again, his voice now pleading.

"You'll have to give me a minute," Samuel said, noting how detached his own voice sounded.

"I'm worried about you."

Samuel lifted his eyes from the floor he'd been looking at, not seeing anything else but the endless stream of images and memories in his mind. Snapshots of the past two years that made it crystal clear how big of an idiot he had been. All these signals, all these signs, he'd ignored them. What a fool he'd been. He slowly refocused, spotting the look of deep concern on Tris's face.

"Dude, you *should* be worried about me. I just found out the last two years of my life have been a total lie," Samuel said, still with that weird detachment.

Then something occurred to him. Maybe he'd been wrong. Maybe Evan hadn't cheated on him the whole time they were together and it had only been the last few weeks or months. Maybe he'd done it because Samuel had become too needy in bed? No, that didn't even make sense. Why the hell would he have sex with someone else when he didn't want to have sex with Samuel?

He was crazy to even go there. Did it really matter? Did he really want to know how long and how often he'd been made a fool of? He discovered that yes, he did. He wanted to know it all, like one of those disgusting pimple-popping videos that grossed you out yet you couldn't stop watching. He was witnessing his own life turning into a train wreck, and he couldn't look away.

"Your ex, when did she first mention this to you?" he asked.

Tris visibly cringed. "Do you really need to...? Over a year ago," he said when Samuel's eyes narrowed.

Not something recent then. Samuel sighed. "And you

know for a fact it's been multiple men? Like hookups? Not like an affair with one guy?"

"Different men," Tris said. "She saw three of them, but she noticed signs of frequent sex all the time."

Motherfucking asshole. Telling Samuel he was too demanding and needy in bed and then fucking around on him? What a complete dick.

"How are you feeling?" Tris asked, and Samuel had to admire his guts to even ask that.

"I think I'm moving straight onto the anger phase of grief," Samuel said. "I can't believe he cheated on me not once, but all the time. What the fuck is wrong with him?"

But just as quick as his anger had flared up, it fizzled out, and a wave of defeat rolled over him. "What the fuck is wrong with me?" he said, much softer now. "Why would he do this? I don't understand."

"Samuel, I hate to say this, but Evan McLeod is not a good man. He's a nasty, backstabbing asshole, and he's quite proud of that reputation, too. His client list is a veritable who's-who of high rollers who are known for shady deals and tactics that fall on the wrong side of the law."

Samuel had to close his eyes for a second as a wave of nausea hit him. "I thought that was just his job," he said weakly, hearing how stupid that argument sounded even to his own ears. "Kinda like I have to make designs I don't like sometimes because they're what the client prefers."

Tris's face showed sympathy and it made Samuel feel like the biggest fool ever. "He doesn't do it because it's his job. He does it because he enjoys the kill, because he wants their business, because on some level, he gets a perverse satisfaction out of screwing people over. What he's doing to me, that's not business. That's doing something because you *can*. That's being a bully, knowing you can get away with it."

Every word stabbed Samuel in his heart. How could he have been with Evan for two years and not seen that side of him? He and Evan had rarely discussed his work, Evan always citing attorney-client privilege. And since Samuel wasn't all that interested in the law anyway, he'd found it convenient to not have to discuss it.

"I didn't know," he said, his head reeling.

"I understand. But now you do."

There was a slight edge to that tone, as if Tris wanted to suggest that knowing the truth had consequences. Well, it did, didn't it? Samuel could never go back to being the naive person he'd been before, completely blind to Evan's dealings. This had consequences, maybe even more for him than for others because of his background.

"What do I do now?" Samuel asked, as much to himself as to Tris. "What do you do when you think you're gonna get a proposal and instead you discover your boyfriend has been cheating on you?"

Much to his own dismay, his voice broke on the last few words. He didn't want to cry, didn't want Tris to witness his humiliation and embarrassment any more than he already had.

Just then, the intercom crackled again. "We're happy to inform you that our elevator technician has arrived and determined the cause of the problem. We're hoping to have the elevators running again in about fifteen minutes. Please do let us know if there are any medical emergencies, and we will try to get to you with priority."

Samuel released a sad sigh. "I wish I could go down instead of up and walk out and never see Evan again. I guess that doesn't really qualify as a medical emergency, does it?"

The corners of Tris's mouth tipped up in a hint of a smile. "I'm afraid not. But is that really what you want?"

"I'm not the confrontational type," Samuel said defensively.

"Are you scared of him?" Tris asked.

Samuel considered it, something that had never even occurred to him before. "Should I be after what you told me?"

"I'd love to say no, but honestly, I don't know him well enough to reassure you either way. But if I were you, I'd be careful. And whatever you do, you should definitely consider not mentioning what you've learned about his shady dealings."

Samuel's stomach rolled uncomfortably, even as he appreciated Tris's careful wording. The man wasn't putting any pressure on him but was rather allowing him to make up his own mind. That was something Samuel could appreciate. His parents had always been the same, giving him and his brothers a lot of freedom and responsibility even within their privileged life—something he'd always appreciated them for.

What Tris said made sense. If Evan was as deep into illegal stuff as Tris suggested, there was no telling what he would do if he found out Samuel was aware. And how fucked up was that, to suddenly be afraid of the man he thought loved him? Plus, he had to keep him at a distance, if this was the case, to protect himself and his family's reputation. God, he should've done that background check on Evan his father had recommended when they'd started dating, but it had seemed so cold and distrustful. That joke was on him now.

"I have to break up with him," Samuel said, that part at least being crystal clear to him.

The rest, that was the question. What reason should he give him for breaking up? If he admitted knowing about the cheating, Evan might want to know how, and Samuel didn't want to drag Tris's ex into this. Hell, he didn't want to drag Tris himself into it.

"Obviously, I can't tell you what to do, but that sounds like a smart decision. I'm so sorry, Samuel."

Samuel let out another sad sigh. "I know. And I do appreciate you telling me, even if it was by accident. As much as I hate knowing it, it would've been far worse had I discovered this a year from now."

"What reason are you going to give him for breaking up?" Tris asked.

"Yeah, that's what I'm debating right now. Should I tell him the truth? He would want to know how I found out, and I don't want to drag you or your ex into this."

Tris cocked his head, his face kind. "Looking back, can you think of any other hints of what was going on? Is there anything you could use as a reason to have discovered his infidelity?"

Samuel thought about it for a few seconds. "Lots of late-night text messages, which I assumed were from clients. Some business trips that I now question. Him guarding his phone with his life. He even takes it into the bathroom when he showers, you know? But nothing that could have easily given me a clue. Suspicious, maybe."

"So don't tell him how you discovered. You owe him shit. Just tell him you found out he's been cheating on you this whole time and leave it at that."

Samuel considered it, then decided that was actually a pretty smart strategy. All he needed was to hold his line when Evan started pushing him. Because there would be pushing, that he was certain of. But what would happen if Evan didn't take no for an answer?

With what he knew now, Samuel didn't understand

what Evan saw in him, why he'd wanted to continue their relationship in the first place, but he clearly had. He could've broken up with Samuel easily months ago if he preferred the hookups, but he hadn't. There could only be one obvious reason, but that was so cold-hearted he didn't even want to go there.

"If you want to, I can stay when you tell him," Tris offered, and Samuel's head jerked up from staring at the floor again.

"Are you serious?"

"Yeah. I'm not comfortable letting you handle this on your own. Not because I think you're weak or anything, but with what I know about your soon-to-be ex-boyfriend, I'm hesitant to leave you alone with him when you deliver news like this. I don't know why he decided to stay with you, but he has to have a reason, so I can only assume he's not gonna be too happy when you show him the door."

Samuel stared at him for a few seconds. The man clearly hadn't recognized him, but he'd still offered his support and protection. That said a lot about his character. "Thank you. From the bottom of my heart, thank you."

Tris nodded at him, a soft smile playing on his lips. "You're welcome. I've always felt comfortable in the role of white knight, you know?" he joked.

"I could use one right now," Samuel mumbled, deeply grateful he wouldn't have to face Evan on his own.

He shivered, the anxiety of what he was about to do getting to him. This had to be by far the scariest thing he'd ever done, and how fucked up was that? Out of all the scenarios he'd considered of him and Evan maybe not working things out, he'd never imagined being scared of him, but he sure as hell was right now.

"You cold?" Tris asked.

Samuel shook his head. "Nervous. Terrified."

Tris's face softened. "If you want to, you can sit with me until the elevator starts moving again. Draw some strength from me, maybe? Or is that weird?"

Samuel didn't even think, just crawled over the floor back to the safe spot between Tris's legs. He couldn't help a sigh of relief escaping from his lips when those strong arms wrapped around him again, and he allowed himself to be pulled backward against that broad chest.

"I don't care if it's weird. I'll take all the strength I can get. Thank you."

4
_____

They sat like that, lost in their own thoughts it seemed, until the intercom switched on again and that same metallic voice announced the elevators were fixed and would start moving any second. The intercom had barely turned off when the lights flickered back on. Tris blinked a few times to adjust his eyes, then reached for his phone to turn the flashlight off. His battery was down to eleven percent, so he'd have to charge it soon.

"You okay now?" he asked Samuel.

Samuel scrambled to his feet, and Tris saw with regret that his gorgeous suit now had stains all over his butt and knees. He hauled himself up, then without thinking, started patting down Samuel to get the worst of the stains off.

When he was done, he raised his head and met Samuel's eyes, which were dancing with laughter. "That was such a dad-thing for you to do," he said. "But so freaking sweet. Thank you."

Tris groaned with embarrassment. "I'm so sorry. I didn't even think about it or ask for permission to touch you. I saw the stains on your suit and wanted to see if I could make them a little better."

Samuel placed a finger on his lips, preventing him from saying more. "I mean it, thank you. It was super sweet. "

With a jerk, the elevator started moving, slowly bringing them to the twelfth floor. Samuel let go of Tris's mouth, and Tris put a soft hand on Samuel's shoulder, meeting his eyes. "Are you ready? You can do this. Don't let him intimidate you. And don't forget that I'm here to step in if needed. I won't let you face him alone."

He heard and saw Samuel suck in a deep breath, and then the man nodded. "Yes. And thank you."

Tris had somehow expected Evan to be waiting for them when they got out of the elevator, considering he had to have been expecting Samuel about an hour ago. But when they stepped into the hallway, it was empty. Samuel's shoulders dropped, and Tris realized he must've had the same expectation. It drove a fresh stab of anger through him. A cute, sweet guy like Samuel deserved so much better than this asshole.

He followed Samuel as he made his way to the lobby of the law firm, where a receptionist gave him a friendly smile. "Samuel, how nice to see you again. Evan has been expecting you."

Then her eyes switched to Tris. "Can I help you?"

For a second, Tris hesitated, but then Samuel said, "He's with me."

Her eyes widened a fraction, but Tris had to give her major props for not losing her professional smile. "Go on in then," she said.

Samuel's posture was stiff as he preceded Tris into an office, opening the door with slightly more force than necessary. Tris had been to the firm twice before but always in a conference room, not in Evan's personal office.

"Where the hell have you been?" Evan said, swiveling his chair to face them across from his desk. The guy didn't even bother to get up to properly to greet his boyfriend, Tris thought. "I called you maybe ten times." Then he spotted Tris. "What's *he* doing here?"

It took Samuel a second or two to react, and all that time, Tris was holding his breath, hoping that he wouldn't lose his courage.

"I was stuck on the elevator, which, as you know, doesn't have cell reception. It would've been easy for you to find out, if you had bothered to call to the lobby downstairs, since I had already signed in."

A tingle danced down Tris's spine at Samuel's arctic tone. He was off to a good start.

"Oh, well, I was busy working, so I didn't notice until a few minutes ago. It's a damn shame, because we're too late now to make our reservation. But that still doesn't explain what he's doing here?"

Tris was curious how Samuel would explain his presence, but the man chose a surprisingly effective strategy. "I have no idea. He followed me here. But we have far more important things to discuss."

Tris saw Evan's attitude change, the man apparently picking up the first signal that there was trouble in paradise. "What's going on?" he asked, his tone suddenly much softer, and his face losing some of its sharpness.

Samuel straightened his shoulders and balled his hands into fists. "What's going on is that I discovered you've been cheating on me, sleeping around with fuck knows how many guys."

Evan did get up from his chair now, quickly making his

way around his large, mahogany desk that Tris thought looked preposterous for a guy his age. "Who told you that? Where did you even get that idea?"

He wasn't denying it, Tris thought. That made sense from his point of view. He wanted Samuel to share details first, of course, so he wouldn't cop to more than he had to.

"Does it matter how I found out? The bottom line is that it's true. You've been cheating on me, and not just once, but many times. How could you, Evan? Did I mean so little to you?"

Samuel's voice broke again, and Tris had to force himself to stick to his role of observer and not try to help him or comfort him, as he so desperately wanted to.

"How can you say that? You know how much I love you. I thought we were happy together," Evan said, and dammit, he was one hell of an actor.

"You're not denying it," Samuel said, his voice dropping even more in temperature. If his tone got any icier, the windows would start showing frost patterns. "So I'm asking you straight out, Evan: Is it true? Is it true that you cheated on me?"

Something flashed over Evan's face that was so fast Tris wondered if he had imagined it. But what he had spotted had been so dark that his subconscious was putting his body on full alert. Something was wrong, something far beyond a simple lovers' spat.

"It didn't mean anything, Sam. It was maybe once or twice, and I never meant to hurt you. It was just blowing off some steam, nothing important. You know I love you."

Before Samuel could even react, Evan reached into the pocket of his pinstriped suit, pulling out a little velvet box. It seemed Samuel would've gotten his wish, had he not discovered the cheating. As much as he hated having wounded him unintentionally with his remarks, Tris was so glad he'd found out now, before Evan had asked him to marry him.

"I had plans for us tonight, honey," Evan said, his voice dropping to a soft, seductive whisper. "Please, don't let a little mistake from me ruin our future together."

Tris took a little step to the right to make sure he could see what happened. Samuel seemed frozen to the spot as Evan flipped open the little box, revealing an undoubtedly expensive ring that flashed brightly.

"Please, honey," Evan said in a pleading tone that made Tris almost throw up in his mouth.

At the same time, he held his breath, waiting anxiously to see how Samuel would react. He'd seemed so angry in the elevator, so convinced he was ending things. But what if Evan got to him? Tris wasn't sure if their relationship could be categorized as abusive, but the psychology had to be the same with how hard it could be for people to believe bad things about a person they loved.

Then Samuel spoke. "I don't know what's more insult-ing: that you call cheating on me a *little mistake*, that you lie to me and say it was only once or twice when we both know it was way more than that, or that you think that knowing all of this, I would still marry you. Fuck you, Evan. Fuck you, fuck your ring, and fuck your lies. We're done."

God, that should not be as hot and sexy as it was. Tris was not only tempted to break out in applause for that abso-lutely phenomenal speech, but also physically aroused, which had to be the weirdest thing ever. Then Evan's hand flashed, grabbing Samuel's wrist in what looked to be a painful grip, judging by the wince on Samuel's face.

"You don't mean that," Evan said, all the sexiness gone from his voice, replaced by menacing steel.

"Ow, you're hurting me," Samuel said, his voice rising in

pitch. "Evan, let go of my arm." He tried to break himself free from Evan's grip, but the lawyer wouldn't let go.

Tris stepped forward. "Let him go."

Evan's eyes flashed toward him. "Stay the fuck out of this, Gabelman."

Tris took another step forward until he was standing shoulder to shoulder with Samuel, Evan still holding on to his wrist. "Too late now. I'm already involved. Let go of his wrist."

Evan's eyes narrowed. "If you think that you've seen the worst of what I can do with that lawsuit against your pathetic company, think again. You have five seconds to walk out of this office and forget what you saw, or I promise you, I will come after you with everything I've got, and your company will be done for."

He seemed to have forgotten Samuel was still in the room, despite holding on to the man. Tris could see it, the sheer horror on Samuel's face, and then the reaction on Evan's as he realized he'd shown too much of his true nature to his now ex-boyfriend.

"Evan!" Samuel cried out, and that one word was stuffed with repulsion.

Tris was done being patient with Evan. He feigned a move to the right, and when Evan reacted, Tris clamped down on the wrist holding Samuel and turned it upward. Evan had no choice but to let go, and he did so with a loud curse. Tris didn't let go of him, but bent his arm backward until the man let out a grunt of pain.

"You really need to learn the meaning of the word *no*," Tris said, forcing himself to keep his voice level. He looked over to Samuel, who was rubbing his wrist, tears in his eyes. "You okay?" he asked.

"Yeah," Samuel said. "Thank you for stepping in, sir."

Tris had to applaud him for keeping a cool head and continuing the pretense of not knowing each other. "You're welcome. If you're ready to leave, I'll walk you out to make sure you're safe."

If looks could kill, the deadly glare Evan sent him would've incinerated him on the spot. Good thing Tris didn't give a flying fuck what the man thought of him.

"Oh, I'm more than ready to go. Thank you. I would appreciate your escort," Samuel said.

"All right, let's go," Tris said, letting go of Evan's wrist.

He'd known the man would come after him. It was so predictable, it was almost funny. But the lawyer, no matter how smart and cunning he was, was no match for Tris, who made his living working with his hands. He'd been involved in more than a few brawls and had broken up quite a few between his men as well. Construction guys weren't known for solving arguments with words, after all.

So when Evan's fist came for him, he ducked, then swiped his right foot against the man's legs, sending him crashing to the floor. Evan went down with a loud grunt, which was music to Tris's ears. He didn't even give him a second look, but instead nodded at Samuel. "As I said, time to go."

Once they were in the hallway, Tris signaled to Samuel they should hurry, and luck was on their side, as the elevator arrived almost instantly for once. They didn't say a word until they had rushed through the downstairs lobby, outside into the street. Tris wasn't ready to let Samuel go just yet, and judging by the look of panic on the other man's face, he felt the same.

On impulse, Tris grabbed his hand, then pulled him close to him. "Let's get out of this neighborhood."

They walked three blocks before Tris realized that

Samuel was crying. Not big, violent sobs, but sad, silent tears that streamed down his face. One look at him and Tris was a goner. All he wanted was to make him feel better, to take away the pain. And so he pulled him close, then hugged him, drawing that slender body against his and burying his face in Samuel's hair.

"You were so brave in there," he said. "I'm so proud of you."

Samuel didn't respond for maybe a minute, quietly sobbing against Tris's chest. And so Tris held him, as people all around them hurried to their destinations, barely sparing them a glance.

"What do you want to do?" Tris asked Samuel when the sobs quieted down. Samuel was still hidden against his chest, but Tris could feel some of the tension leave his body. "How about we get some food into you, hmm? You must be starving right now, and food always makes you feel better."

"I'd love that."

Samuel's voice was barely above a whisper, but it had no trouble reaching Tris's ears. "Sounds good. I know a great burger restaurant. Nothing fancy, but they make the best burgers in the city."

For some reason, Samuel let out laugh at that. "I'd love a good burger. Thank you."

Tris grabbed his neck and tilted Samuel's head back. "How about you stop with thanking me now? It's my pleasure, so forget about it, okay?"

Samuel nodded.

"Okay, burgers it is."

5

Fifteen minutes later, Tris ushered Samuel into a restaurant that looked from the outside like it was closed. But once the door opened, it revealed a cozy-looking, if somewhat rundown, burger place. The smell of grease and bacon wrapped itself around Samuel, and his stomach rumbled in response.

"I know it doesn't look like much, but they have the best burgers in town," Tris said, and Samuel realized he was nervous about bringing him here.

That made sense, considering how Samuel was dressed and what he had told Tris about the restaurant Evan had planned to take him to. And Tris didn't even know the truth about him yet. That would've probably intimidated him even more, which Samuel hated.

"I love burgers," he told him. "And I'm far hungrier than I realized, so thank you."

A sharp look from Tris had him cracking a smile. "Oops, didn't mean to thank you again."

Tris smiled back. "You're learning."

They were brought to their table by a fifty-something

woman who took her time to welcome them with a genuine smile, despite the fact that every table in the place was full. She handed them menus, which were surprisingly simple, and said she'd be back in a few minutes to take their order.

"They don't have a lot of choices, but what they have is phenomenal," Tris said.

Samuel looked up from the menu he'd been studying. "How about I stop saying thank you and you stop defending your choice for this place? It's fine, Tris. I'm happy to be here, I swear."

Tris sent him an apologetic smile. "I'm sorry. I feel like you might've expected more, what with what you and Evan are probably used to. I mean, look at how you're dressed. That's not the attire of a man who is used to a place like this."

For a second, Samuel had been worried Tris had recognized him after all. That wouldn't have been a big deal, but he felt relieved when he realized Tris had merely drawn conclusions from his suit and the mention of the restaurant. He lifted an eyebrow. "And here I was thinking that I asked you not to defend yourself anymore. Those restaurants, that was mostly Evan's choice. I won't deny I appreciate exquisite food, but I love a good burger just as much. Besides, do you have any idea how long it's been since I had greasy food like this?"

As if on cue, his stomach rumbled so loud that Tris chuckled. "Okay, point taken."

Samuel decided on a classic bacon cheeseburger, while Tris ordered a double one. After a slight hesitation, Samuel asked for unsweetened iced tea. He would've loved to order a beer, but after everything that had happened, adding alcohol to the mix didn't seem smart.

"You can order a drink if you want to," Tris said, apparently picking up on his hesitation.

Samuel shot a quick look at the server who was patiently waiting for them to hash this out. "I'm not sure if alcohol is a smart idea right now."

"I promise you I won't drink, okay? You deserve a beer right now or whatever you want to order. I'll stay sober and make sure you get home safe."

Tris's face changed at that last word, as if he had realized something. Samuel frowned.

"Order your beer," Tris said. "I'll explain after."

Samuel stopped debating and gave in, ordering some craft beer he'd never heard of on recommendation from the server. "What was that look on your face?" he asked as soon as she had moved on.

"You and Evan, you were living together, right? Was that in his place or yours?" Tris asked, his face frighteningly serious.

"It's my apartment. I bought it when I moved out of my parents' home Evan moved in with me. Why?"

Tris leaned forward. "So his name isn't on the deed?"

Samuel didn't know why, but something cold raced down his spine. What was Tris getting at? "No. I own it free and clear. He has a key, obviously." And then it hit him, and he gasped. "You think he's going to go home and do something to the apartment?"

"Look, I don't know. But considering what I know about Evan and how angry he was with you, I wouldn't rule it out. Do you have anything of value in there?"

Samuel felt the blood drain out of his face. Evan could walk right in. He had the key and the doorman knew him, would let him through without a second thought. He was on the approved visitors list, had been since shortly after they'd started dating.

"Oh god. You have no idea. I work from home a lot. My computer setup alone is a couple of grand, but I have much more. What do I do? I need to go home."

He was about to rise from his seat when Tris gently held his wrist. "I have an idea. You'll need new locks now that he's out, right?"

Samuel slowly nodded.

"I have a guy I work with all the time. I trust him completely. How about I call him and ask him to replace all the locks right now? Would that be okay with you? That way, if Evan shows up, you won't have to face him. Trust me, he won't mess with Law. That guy is six foot five of solid muscle."

"Law?"

Tris smiled. "Lawrence, but everybody calls him Law."

Samuel considered it, then decided it was a much better plan than going home himself and maybe facing a furious Evan. "I'd appreciate that." He barely held back the *thank you*, but Tris's quick smile showed he'd picked up on it.

"Let me make a quick call," Tris said. Within seconds, he had placed the call, and Samuel experienced a strange nervousness as he waited for it to connect. What if this guy didn't have time? Should he call the cops? They would never come, would they? Not without knowing for certain Evan had something planned. Well, maybe if he dropped his name. He hated doing that, but it usually worked. Luckily, he wouldn't have to make that choice, because Tris started talking.

Within minutes, he had arranged for Law to stop by the burger place to get Samuel's keys, then head over to his apartment and change the locks. Samuel agreed to all of it, happily providing him with the address.

"Law, you may want to bring your brother. You may run into trouble with an angry ex-boyfriend."

Samuel couldn't hear Law's reaction, but Tris snickered. "Glad to provide the entertainment, dude. Thank you."

Samuel raised his eyebrows in a wordless question. "Law said he had a shitty day and was itching for some trouble," Tris explained. "I think he's hoping Evan will show up. Law is one of those guys who can fix anything, and his brother Rab is a football coach. Between the two of them, Evan doesn't stand a chance."

Samuel wondered for a few seconds what would happen if Evan did try something with these two brothers, then decided that he really didn't give a shit. If he were honest, he was hoping Evan would show up as much as Law, probably.

"I need to call the doorman and let him know not to let Evan in anymore. It won't keep him out completely, as the doorman is on a schedule that Evan knows, but he needs to be informed anyway," he said.

Tris nodded. "Go ahead. Smart thinking. Tell him to let Law in as well."

Samuel's call was done in under a minute, the doorman responding with nothing but professional courtesy. No wonder, they paid a fortune for that service. He ended the call, determined to focus on something else.

"Tell me about your current project," he said to Tris. "What are you building right now?"

When their burgers came, Tris was still talking about the renovation of a former orphanage in Queens that was being transformed into apartments. It was easy to hear his enthusiasm for this project, and after seeing some pictures on his phone, Samuel could totally understand why.

Conversation flowed easily as they ate, only interrupted when a towering giant of a man popped up next to their table. Tris hadn't been kidding about Law. The man looked like he could wrestle in the WWE. Samuel quickly handed off his keys, and Law promised he would text them as soon as he got to Samuel's place.

The food was delicious, and Samuel was nursing the last few swallows of his second beer as he pushed the plate back, leaving only a few fries. "Oh my god, you weren't kidding about the food. Best burger ever. I'm so stuffed."

That made Tris beam, a strangely endearing expression on a man his size. He was such a bear, all big on the outside but with a soft inside, Samuel was discovering. "Glad you liked it."

Samuel emptied his beer, enjoying the slight buzz in his head. He didn't usually drink a lot, since it tended to affect him, but if there ever was a day to get absolutely plastered, it would be today. He looked around the restaurant, spotting several couples who were holding hands. Of course, it was still Valentine's Day.

God, what a clusterfuck this day had turned out to be. Instead of a proposal, he was sitting here with a guy he'd met only hours before. Still, he had to admit that dinner had been a resounding success. Obviously not in the category of a romantic proposal, but then again, after what he had learned about how Evan had pulled the wool over his eyes, he doubted he would ever think about proposals the same way again. Fool me once and all that shit.

"Do you want another beer?" Tris asked.

"I really shouldn't. I'm a lightweight when it comes to alcohol," Samuel said with a laugh.

Tris's phone rang, and he picked up after a glance at the screen. "What's up?"

He listened for a little bit, then held out the phone to Samuel. "The cops need to talk to you," he said, sending him an encouraging look.

The cops? What the hell had happened? With a trembling hand, Samuel accepted the phone. "This is Samuel Norris."

"This is Officer Daniels from the NYPD. Can you confirm you're the owner of the apartment on East 66th Street?"

"Yes, sir, that's my apartment."

"Your locksmith called 911 because someone was trying to force entry into the apartment while he was replacing the locks. The intruder claims he lives here, but your doorman says you've removed him from the visitors list. According to his driver's license, his name is Evan McLeod. Do you know this person?"

Samuel grabbed Tris's hand, somehow needing the reassurance. God, he was regretting that second beer now. "Yes, sir. That's my ex-boyfriend. We broke up, and I had the locks changed."

"I understand. Mr. McLeod claims he still has your permission to access the apartment. Is that correct?"

"No, sir. He does not. He needs to pick up his stuff at some point, but not unannounced," Samuel said, not knowing where he got the balls to be this resolute.

"Okay. Hang on one minute while I talk to him."

The call was muted and Samuel waited with bated breath to see what would happen next. With the cops there, there really wasn't much that Evan could do. Then again, today had taught him that he really didn't know Evan all that well, so there was no predicting what he would or wouldn't try.

It took a few minutes before the cop returned to the

phone. "Mr. McLeod claims he has personal belongings in the apartment that he needs right now. He says the breakup was unexpected for him, and that according to the law, he should be allowed to pick up his belongings."

Samuel rolled his eyes. Of course he would cite the law, ever the lawyer. His eyes met Tris's, and an idea popped into his head. "He has permission, but I want him supervised at all times. He is not to take anything that doesn't belong to him."

"That sounds like a smart strategy," the cop said, and Samuel couldn't help but feel the man was on his side.

No wonder, since cops and lawyers didn't exactly get along. Plus, Evan had been caught trying to force his way into the apartment, apparently. That had to set some bad blood with the cops in the first place. Then there was Samuel's last name, of course, which the cop had no doubt recognized by now. With the generous donations his parents made every year to several NYPD charities, that had to count for something as well. Tris might not know who Samuel was, but that cop sure did.

"You need to give us some guidance on what he can take, then," the cop said.

And Samuel didn't know why he had never realized it, but it sank in that everything in that apartment was his. How had he never noticed that Evan hadn't contributed at all? Sure, he had pitched in for groceries or takeout every now and then, but not for any purchases like furniture or even something as small as towels or kitchen utensils. Every single thing in that apartment was Samuel's, and that was sobering as much as sad. How had he not seen how unhealthy and weird that was? It wasn't normal when two people lived together.

"Mr. Norris?" the cop asked, and Samuel realized he'd been lost in thought.

"I'm sorry. He's only to take his own clothes and toiletries. The books on the nightstand are his, and he can clear out the fridge and take all the food from the cupboards for all I care. But all the furniture, all the equipment, including everything electronic, is mine. Please do not allow him to touch the computer setup in my work room."

"Crystal clear. Do you want to stay on the line while we do the walk-through with him?"

Samuel opened his mouth to answer, but then he waited because he heard voices in the background.

"Your locksmith is offering to stay here until Mr. McLeod is done grabbing all his stuff. That way, you wouldn't have to stay on the line. Would that work for you?"

Samuel breathed out with relief. "That works for me very well. Thank you, officer. I apologize for the inconvenience."

"You're welcome. Life would be so much easier if people respected the word no, right?" the officer said, and if that didn't sum up the whole situation perfectly, Samuel didn't know what did.

He ended the call and then looked at Tris. "On second thought, I want to get blindly drunk."

6

A sober Samuel was cute, but a drunk Samuel was irresistible, Tris discovered. He'd taken him to a bar around the corner from the burger restaurant, more than willing to accommodate Samuel's wish to get drunk. Hell, the guy had every reason to after what he'd survived today.

Tris was so grateful he'd thought of changing Samuel's locks in time. That could've been a disastrous mistake, had Evan managed to get into the apartment. His gut instinct had been spot-on that Evan would try to gain access. Tris wasn't sure why, but he had a nagging suspicion that Evan had been after more than just Samuel's personal belongings. It could've been revenge that he'd wanted, but the whole thing didn't sit right with Tris.

Why was the man so hell-bent on staying in a relationship with Samuel when he clearly had zero intention of being faithful? Why marry him if it was obvious it was never going to work? Tris had kept wondering this, until Samuel had provided his address. Upper East Side. If he could afford an apartment there, he had money. Big-time money.

And that would explain Evan's motives. From anyone else, Tris would've thought twice before accusing them of being such a cold, money-grabbing piece of shit, but it fit everything else he'd learned about Evan.

He hadn't discussed it with Samuel, not wanting to add to his already considerable grief on this day. The man had endured enough hits. Tris was surprised he was still standing after being confronted with what Evan had tried to do. It showed how trusting Samuel still was. It had never even occurred to him that Evan would try to steal from him or whatever he'd been up to until Tris had brought it up. And even now, the fact that he trusted a complete stranger enough to get this drunk, it said a lot about him.

Tris found it endearing. Irresistibly so, in fact. But that could also be because the more Samuel drank, the more touchy he got. And not touchy as in short-tempered, but touchy as in having his hands all over Tris. He didn't even seem to realize it, how he kept reaching out to Tris to pet his arm, caress his leg, bump his shoulder, hold his hand. It seemed to come completely natural to him, and Tris found himself enraptured.

Samuel pulled on his sleeve. "I love this song," he said, his eyes going dreamy.

Tris cocked his head, trying to recognize the song over the sounds of bar patrons chatting. It was "(Everything I Do) I Do It for You" by Bryan Adams. "A classic ballad."

"Kevin Costner was *hot* in that movie," Samuel said.

Tris chuckled. "You're way too young to remember that movie. That's from the nineties."

Samuel hummed a few notes from the song. "I'm a bit of a movie geek," he said. "I've made it a mission to watch the most popular movies from every decade. *Robin Hood: Prince of Thieves* was a perfect movie. Well, it would've been even better had Robin turned out to be gay, but all things considered, I really liked it."

He'd put his head against Tris's shoulder, and he smiled at the intimate gesture. For years, he had told himself that he wasn't ready for a new relationship. When he had married Cara, he had never expected them to divorce. It had hit him hard, feeling like a failure, even though they had parted on the best of terms. So when the divorce had become final, he had thrown himself into his work, determined to grow his company into a solid success, while at the same time prioritizing spending time with his boys.

He'd had a few hookups over the years, but they had been few and far between. He'd dated once or twice, but it had never moved beyond a second date. He kept telling himself that he wasn't in the market, but right now, with Samuel's head resting on his shoulder, he questioned the truth of that. Maybe he was in the market, but he just hadn't met the right person yet. A person like Samuel.

It didn't make sense, this instant connection he felt with him, but he couldn't deny it. It was a tad inappropriate, considering the guy had literally come out of a two-year relationship hours before. The last thing he needed was another relationship, and yet Tris had already considered several ways of keeping in touch with him.

He could be his friend, he decided. Be there for him, support him, and then hopefully, take it from there. He'd have to be patient, as Samuel clearly wasn't ready for more. He would have to give him time, but he could do that. He'd been single for years now, and a few months more wouldn't hurt.

"Dance with me," Samuel said, and Tris was shocked.

"What?" he asked.

Samuel lifted his head from Tris's shoulder and pointed

toward the corner where the bar had created a small dance space. There were a few couples slow dancing to the music, creating an atmosphere far more romantic than was usually the case in this bar. Right, *Valentine's Day*, Tris reminded himself. He'd tuned out the overabundance of red hearts in the tacky decorations as soon as they'd walked in.

Samuel slid off the barstool and held out his hand. "Come on, big guy. Dance with me."

How did he say no to that? It turned out he couldn't, and Tris allowed himself to be pulled toward the dance floor, where Samuel nestled himself in Tris's arms without a second doubt. He wrapped his arms around Tris's torso, resting his head against his shoulder, his mouth pressed against Tris's neck.

Oh god, holding Samuel again was everything he remembered from the elevator and the long hug they'd shared outside. His body fit so perfectly against Tris's, despite their difference in height. It made Tris feel so big and strong, and as caveman-like as that sounded, it did something to him inside. Like he was Samuel's protector, and he *liked* it.

Bryan Adams's timeless classic made way for another slow song, and Tris gave up pretending he didn't want to dance. As far as you could call this dancing in the first place, since it was more coordinated swaying to the music, their bodies so close you couldn't fit a sheet of paper between them.

Samuel's breath danced across the skin of his neck, and with every breath, Tris grew harder. He had to bite his tongue not to tell Samuel how much he wanted him, but then Samuel whispered against his neck, "You're so fucking hot, and you feel so good against me."

It was the alcohol talking, Tris knew, but still his body

responded with fervor. "Right back atcha," he said, allowing himself to at least be truthful about that.

"I'm really horny," Samuel said, and Tris almost choked on his own breath.

"W-what?" he asked, thinking that he must've misunderstood.

"Evan always complained I was too needy. In case you missed the memo, that's a code word for wanting to have sex, which according to my asshole ex, is a bad thing. When we started dating, he was in for some fun and games in bed, but after that, he didn't want to do anything experimental. Hell, I had trouble even getting him to fuck me properly. Don't ask me how, but I managed to find the one guy who doesn't like to get laid. I'll add it to the long list of reasons why I should've known better. Wait, what was I saying?" Samuel rambled, stuttering on his consonants several times.

Tris swallowed. "Something about you being horny," he helpfully supplied.

"Right. I haven't been fucked in a week, and I desperately need a good fuck. Wanna head to the bathroom?"

Tris felt like all of his blood had accumulated in his dick, which really was hard enough to pound nails, as the expression went. He should know, having swung a hammer more than enough times. Was Samuel making things up when he was drunk? Because how could that asshole ex of his have complained about Samuel wanting sex? God, Tris would kill right now to sink inside him. Except he couldn't. No fucking way.

"You're drunk," he said, reminding Samuel as much as himself.

"Yeah, so?"

"So you can't give consent."

Samuel let out an adorable grumble. "Leave it to me to proposition the one guy with morals."

Tris grabbed his neck and gently pulled his head back so he could look him straight into his eyes. "We both know you would regret this tomorrow, and so would I."

Disappointment flashed in Samuel's eyes, but then he pulled his mouth into a pout so cute that Tris wanted to kiss it off his lips instantly. "And if I weren't drunk?"

Tris put one hand on Samuel's ass and pressed their bodies even closer together. "If you weren't drunk, I would be balls deep inside you right now."

Samuel's mouth sprang open in a little O of surprise, and before he thought better of it, Tris bent forward and took his mouth. The connection was instant, like he'd been shocked by an electric charge. A soft little moan felt from his lips, straight into Samuel's mouth. Tris shivered at the intimacy of it, this first exploration.

It took Samuel two seconds to catch up, but when he did, he went all in. He opened up for Tris, and Tris swept inside his mouth, not satisfied until their slick tongues brushed against each other. His right hand was still on Samuel's ass, and he squeezed it, causing Samuel to gasp into his mouth.

Tris found a rhythm, thrusting into Samuel's mouth while kneading his ass at the same pace, flexing his hips every now and then to grind into him. He was delighted to notice that Samuel was doing the same to him, unabashedly rubbing against his body, like a cat seeking friction.

When he broke off the kiss, they were both panting, and Tris's cock was leaking in his pants. He'd better stay plastered against Samuel until he had cooled off a little, because stepping away right now would definitely expose the other bar patrons to something they might not want to see.

Then Samuel looked up at him with those dark blue eyes and said, "I don't want to go home tonight."

Tris shook his head at him. "Nothing can happen. Not today and not while you're drunk."

Samuel's smile was an equal mix of sweet and sexy. He rose to his toes and pressed a soft, wet kiss on Tris's lips. "I understand, and while I regret the hell out of it, I'll respect it. But I still don't want to go home tonight."

Tris's mouth opened of its own accord and words came tumbling out. "You can come home with me."

7

W hen Samuel woke up, he blinked a few times when he was confronted with a room he didn't recognize. Where the hell was he? He blinked again, then turned his head, wincing when that sent a stab of pain through his head. Oh god, what was wrong with him?

His mouth tasted like garbage, and his stomach swirled uncomfortably, even as his bladder alerted him to the fact that he needed to pee badly. But all of that was secondary to his utter confusion of where he was. He closed his eyes, frowning, trying to remember. What was today? Right, Saturday. Yesterday had been...

His eyes flew open as memories hit him. *Valentine's Day.* Evan cheated on him. *Tris.* That's where he was, Tris's guest bedroom. Though he could've sworn he hadn't fallen asleep here, vaguely remembering something about wanting to sleep in Tris's bed. He groaned as distant recollections hit him, probably unreliable because of the insane amount of alcohol he had consumed. How much had he had? Two full pints of beer in the restaurant, and in the bar, hell, he couldn't even remember. He'd started on those fruity vodka drinks, and after two of those, things had gotten a little hazy.

He scrunched his face, trying to picture how they had gotten home. Well, not home, but to Tris's house. A wave of shame rolled over him as he realized he didn't even know where he was. Where did Tris even live? They'd taken the subway and then another one, maybe? The ride had been quite long, but he'd fallen asleep a few minutes in, only waking up again when they had changed trains. He could barely remember stumbling into the house, and after that, everything was fuzzy.

This had to be one of the craziest things he'd ever done. Not that that was saying much, as he'd never been much of a party animal, but he'd taken a huge risk and could only be grateful that his instincts had proven to be spot-on with Tris, even if they had failed them miserably with Evan.

After debating with himself for a minute or two about the all-too-tempting possibility of just pretending he was asleep for a few more hours, he slowly pushed himself upright. His head pounded, but his stomach stayed at that slightly nauseous level, which was good. Not nauseous would be better, but he'd settle for not throwing up right now.

With slow, careful movements, he dragged himself to the adjoining bathroom, letting out a sigh of relief as he emptied his bladder. When he went to wash his hands, he found a glass of water, some Tylenol, and a toothbrush and toothpaste. God bless Tris. He took two Tylenol, the cold water a wonderful sensation on his raw throat, then brushed his teth. So much better.

He saw that he was wearing a T-shirt and his underwear, so at some point, Tris must've undressed him partially, because Samuel was pretty sure he couldn't have managed that himself in the state he'd been in.

When he walked back into the bedroom, he spotted his suit neatly draped over a chair, and he couldn't help smiling. Tris had turned out not only to be a gentleman but a rather caring gentlemen as well. Not what he would've expected from a construction guy. It only showed that looks could deceive, because Evan *had* appeared to be a gentleman and look how that had turned out.

Samuel found his phone on the nightstand and powered it on, his eyes widening when he saw a barrage of missed calls and texts from Evan. He'd turned it off last night after the first two texts from Evan had come in, not wanting to hear from him.

He debated listening to his voicemail and reading the texts, then thought better of it. The day had just started, no need to get upset this early. Early being relative, as he saw it was almost noon, much to his shock. Well, they hadn't made it to Tris's until probably three in the morning, so there was that.

The house was still quiet, but considering the time, he couldn't imagine Tris still being in bed. He was probably downstairs somewhere, and it was time to face to music. Despite the cold outside, the house was comfortably warm when he opened the door, so Samuel went downstairs in his T-shirt and boxer briefs. He followed the smell of coffee to a large kitchen, where he found Tris at a messy kitchen table, surrounded by stacks of paperwork. Bills, by the looks of it, and he was peering at the screen of the laptop with an angry frown that disappeared as soon as he spotted Samuel.

"Hey, you're up," he said with an enthusiasm that made Samuel realize Evan hadn't shown that kind of joy about his presence for a long time, if ever.

"Good morning," he offered, then cleared his throat when it came out rather raspy.

"Coffee?" Tris asked.

"God, yes please. Black."

"Man after my heart," Tris said with a smile as he got up and poured a tall mug of dark coffee. He gestured at the table as he put it on an empty spot. "Find yourself a seat. I'll get my paperwork out of your way."

Samuel waved him off. "It doesn't bother me. I'll just sit here quietly and mainline caffeine."

Tris chuckled. "How's your head? You look a sight better than I expected considering the amount of alcohol you consumed last night. I was kind of counting on you getting closely acquainted with the toilet bowl."

Samuel's stomach definitely didn't appreciate that visual, but he managed to swallow it back. "Don't call it a success just yet, the jury is still out."

Tris poured himself another coffee as well and sat down across from Samuel. "Just out of curiosity, how much do you remember from last night?"

Samuel sighed. "Enough to be embarrassed, not so much I'm mortified. Is there anything I need to know?"

Tris studied him for a few seconds. "You fell asleep in my bed," he then said, his voice quiet. "I tried to put you in the guest room right away, but you didn't want to be alone. The alcohol made you sad, and I didn't want to leave you by yourself crying, so I helped you fall asleep and then I carried you to the guest room."

Samuel saw nothing but kindness on his face. "Why didn't you let me sleep with you the whole night?" he asked, curious.

"You were quite...touchy, and I didn't trust myself

enough not to respond to that, especially being barely awake myself."

Samuel felt his cheeks heat up. "I'm sorry. I didn't mean to make you feel uncomfortable."

"You didn't. You made me feel horny, which apparently, was how you were feeling as well, or so you told me. Repeatedly."

Samuel carefully swallowed the sip of coffee he had just taken, wanting to avoid choking on the hot liquid. "Alcohol really lowers my sexual inhibitions," he said, his cheeks on fire.

"That's a normal reaction," Tris said, his voice level.

Samuel played with the handle of his mug, swirling his index finger around in the half circle. "That doesn't make it less embarrassing to hear."

Tris shrugged. "No need to feel embarrassed. It was clear you needed an outlet, and I was happy to provide a safe space for you to do that."

"Anybody ever accuse you of having a bit of a *knight in shining armor* complex? Because your behavior so far is pretty damn knight-like," Samuel said, meaning every word.

Tris's face split open in a wide smile. "That's what Cara says all the time as well, even in high school. I guess it's ingrained in me."

"I can't believe you're still single."

Tris gave one of his one-shoulder shrugs again. "I haven't dated much since my divorce. You'd be surprised how many people are just looking for a hookup, for fun. I like sex as much as the next guy, but I guess I'm a little different in that I prefer to have an emotional connection with someone. I've done anonymous sex in bathrooms, but it's really not my style."

That comment popped Samuel's words during their

dance back into his mind, when he had suggested Tris fuck him in a bathroom. He held back a groan. "It seems I once again have to apologize for making you feel uncomfortable by propositioning you for sex."

Tris put down his coffee, then leaned forward and looked straight into Samuel's eyes. "My sweet Samuel, I don't think you're hearing me. You didn't make me feel uncomfortable yesterday, unless you count the discomfort of being highly aroused for hours. That, however, is not something you should apologize for. I think we need a new rule. No more thank you and no more apologizing."

Samuel's hand shook as he, too, put his mug down on the table. "You're very open and direct."

Tris grinned. "So were you yesterday. I seem to remember a little rambling about you being needy or something to that order."

Samuel refused to look away, especially since Tris's eyes sparked with something deeper. "I am. Needy, that is. An ex-boyfriend of mine nicknamed me hungry hippo, though hungry hole would be more accurate, I guess."

He couldn't believe he had just said that, but after a short moment where his eyes widened, Tris's grin broadened. "Don't tell me he thought that was a bad thing."

"He didn't seem to mind so much, and it had nothing to do with why we broke up, which was more because he had a nasty habit of wasting money I took issue with. My money, more specifically."

As soon as he said it, he knew Tris would ask. In fact, he'd been somewhat surprised the man hadn't brought it up so far. There had been plenty of opportunities for him, and Samuel had no doubt whatsoever he hadn't picked up on the truth.

"I googled you this morning," Tris said, his face sobering.

Samuel picked up his mug again and emptied it. "I don't blame you."

"Some things yesterday didn't add up for me, like you owning a crazy expensive apartment at your age. I didn't recognize your name. I guess that only goes to show I don't really follow that kind of news very much."

"Trust me, I'm grateful every day for people like you who don't instantly recognize me or my family's name. But yeah, that's me, the rich heir to the legendary fortune. Not much I can add to what you found online, I suppose."

Tris pursed his lips before responding. "No, but it does clear up why Evan didn't want to break up with you."

Samuel frowned. "The thought crossed my mind, but I don't spend all that much on him. Hell, I don't spend that much in general. I know I'm worth quite a bit on paper, but I try to lead a pretty normal life."

"You own an apartment on the Upper East Side. You allowed Evan to live there rent-free without contributing. I'd say that in itself was worth it for him. This is a guy who gets off on status, and that's what you brought to the table. Money, status, and connections, more than he could've ever hoped to achieve on his own."

Samuel let that thought sink in, and it didn't sit right with him at all. Shortly after his twenty-first birthday, when he had gained access to his trust fund, he'd been super suspicious of men approaching him. The press had never made a secret of the fact that he was gay, and he knew he'd been approached by more than a few guys trying to take advantage of him. He'd turned them all down, but Evan had been different. Hadn't he?

Tris was quiet as Samuel tried to piece it together, allowing himself to look at the past two years without the rosy glasses he'd been wearing. Evan insisting on accompanying him to all events he attended in his family's name. Evan wanting him to host more parties himself, inviting the rich and powerful his family was connected to, like investors, politicians, media moguls. Evan suggesting investments for Samuel, who used the same investment banker his father had used for years and paid him handsomely to never have to spend more than the bare minimum of time on his portfolio. He had to admit the picture that emerged didn't look good.

"I'll have to meet with my lawyer," he said softly. "Let her have a thorough look at my finances and see if anything is amiss. I've been careful with allowing Evan access to my financial information, and he certainly didn't have my passwords, but I can't help but think now that he may have profited in some way that I haven't been aware of."

"I'm sorry," Tris said, and the genuine empathy in his voice was easy to spot.

"So am I," Samuel said from the bottom of his heart. "Trust me, I'm now in the phase of I wish I never met him. This whole thing is like some horrid nightmare I can't wait to wake up from."

Tris was quiet for a few moments, but then he said, "I can't even imagine how you must feel about everything that has happened. You deserve so much better. All I can say is that even amid these unfortunate circumstances, I can't help but be glad that we met."

8

Cara had always called Tris a softy, saying that underneath that tough-guy exterior beat a mushy heart. Maybe she was right, because right now, Tris was feeling anything but tough as he watched Samuel struggle with confronting the truth about Evan. How he wished Samuel could have been spared this pain and disillusion, but he had to know.

Tris was glad Samuel had brought up the topic of having a lawyer look into his finances himself, because if he hadn't, Tris would've suggested it. He'd been jaw-droppingly surprised at finding out Samuel was one of the richest men in the city, courtesy of a family legacy of being financial wizards. He and his two brothers were featured in more gossip-style pieces on the internet than Tris had ever thought possible.

The Norris family had survived the great stock market crash of 1929, Tris had discovered, had avoided the dot-com crash by pulling out of bad companies on time, and in general, had managed to keep adding to their wealth with smart

investments. Luckily, the family was also known for their phil-
anthropy, supporting dozens of local and national charities.
He'd heard of them, obviously, but he hadn't made the
connection with Samuel, even when hearing his last name.

Tris had felt stupid for a minute or two for not realizing
Samuel was sort of a celebrity, but then he had shrugged it
off. No one could fault him for not reading the gossip magazines, right? Plus, from what he'd read online, Samuel was
known for keeping a low profile, unlike some other
members of his family who seemed to appreciate the spot-
light much more.

One thing was for certain: it did answer the question
why Evan had been so interested in Samuel, and even more,
why he had wanted to hang onto the relationship at all
costs. It was a sad testament to how much people were
willing to do for money, and Tris's heart broke a little for
Samuel, who had truly believed Evan loved him. That
money of his, that was going to be a big obstacle for him in
finding a new partner. He needed someone who didn't care
about money at all, but that was a tough challenge.

"I'm glad we met as well," Samuel said, bringing Tris out
of his thoughts back to reality. "And I would thank you for
taking care of me, if I wasn't sure that you would once again
scold me for uttering the forbidden words."

Tris smiled at him. "Smart boy."

Samuel's head shot up, his eyes widening in surprise at
that word. Tris wasn't sure why he'd said it. Instinct, maybe?
There was something so vulnerable about Samuel, despite
the fact that they couldn't be that much apart in age. Maybe
it was his build, since he was more of a twink compared to
Tris who could definitely claim to be a bear.

"That was unexpected," Samuel said slowly.

The surprise was still on his face, but Tris saw something else as well. Curiosity. "Objections?" he asked.

"No. It raises a lot of questions."

"Why don't I make you some food and we can talk about whatever you want," Tris said. "What would you like to eat?"

"Whatever you have. I'm the easiest eater ever. Eggs, bacon, pancakes, toast, cereal, yogurt, fresh fruit, I'm down with anything. No allergies, no preferences."

Tris chuckled. "Low maintenance, huh? I can appreciate that."

Samuel was quiet while Tris fixed him some toast, two scrambled eggs, and a banana. He felt Samuel's eyes on him the whole time, studying him, but he didn't call him out. The man could look all he wanted, for all he cared.

He made himself some scrambled eggs and toast as well. He'd already had breakfast earlier, but he was feeling *snacky*, as his kids would say. For the first minute or so after he put the food on the table, having stacked his paperwork to the side, neither of them spoke.

"Are you into daddy kink?" Samuel then asked.

It was a reasonable question, but not one that was so easy to answer, Tris discovered. "Not so far, but I have to admit I am feeling somewhat protective toward you."

"Dude, we're not even dating," Samuel said, but Tris didn't take that in a negative way.

It was almost as if Samuel was trying to convince himself of it rather than Tris. That was understandable, considering he was coming out of a two-year relationship. Not only that, but the way his relationship had ended had to cause some trust issues. He was probably telling himself that the very last thing he needed to do was jump right into the next relationship, especially with a man he barely knew.

Still, Tris took the jump. "We *could* be."

Samuel's hand stopped halfway to his mouth with a bite of toast. "You want to date me?"

Tris couldn't help but smile at that question, which was said with way too much surprise considering the signals he thought he'd been emitting. "To mirror your words, *dude*, if that wasn't clear by now, I either need to work on my flirting game or you need to learn how to pick up signals."

Samuel lowered his hand back to the table, still clinging to that piece of toast. "I thought you wanted to fuck me. That's different from dating."

Tris's amusement heightened. "I'm well aware, but thank you for clearing that up. And for the record: yes, I do want to fuck you. In fact, there's a long list of things I would like to do to you and with you, but in order to do those things, I would definitely need to see you more than once, hence the dating suggestion."

A lovely blush spread across Samuel's cheeks as he finally nibbled on that piece of toast. "You're very direct," he commented.

"I'm of Dutch heritage, way back when New York was still New Amsterdam. We have a long and proud tradition of being Dutch direct, as we call it."

"It's quite the change from Evan's lawyer language," Samuel said, looking pensive. "Getting him to answer a question in clear, uncertain terms was like pulling teeth."

Tris knew he shouldn't be surprised Samuel would compare him to his ex, but it still stung a little. "You'll find that I am nothing like him in many, many ways."

"So I'm discovering. How do you envision that, us dating?"

"What do you mean? Isn't dating pretty much a well-known concept? You know, taking you out to dinner, watching a movie, hanging out on the couch, making out on said couch, maybe visit some exhibitions you're interested in, I don't know."

"That all sounds nice and lovely, but I'm way more interested in hearing about that list of yours and how you plan to work your way through it," Samuel said, and his eyes sparkled, even if his body language showed some tension as well.

Ah, Tris understood now. *Sex.* He wanted to talk about sex. Well, that could be arranged. "Do you want me to write down the list so you can approve it?" he teased.

"I may add a few things of my own," Samuel fired right back at him.

"I'm always open to suggestions. What did you have in mind?"

Samuel shook his head, laughing. "You were the one with the list, so why don't you start sharing?"

There was something more going on, Tris realized. There was a reason why Samuel was focused on that list, which had been more of a metaphorical thing for Tris. What was it about that concept that intrigued Samuel? He'd reacted strongly to that simple word *boy* as well. Was he interested in daddy kink? It seemed more than that, but he couldn't figure it out.

"Well, sex on every surface in the house sounds pretty appealing to me," he said, deciding to go with his gut and continue the conversation. "Combined with the fact that you look like you're pretty flexible, that should keep us busy for a while."

Samuel leaned forward now, his eyes burning. He was still invested in the conversation, but he seemed to be waiting for something else. Tris was racking his brain trying to figure out what he was after.

"Keep going," Samuel said, as if to underscore Tris's point.

"You seemed to like it when I called you *boy*, so we could see if we both liked some daddy role play," Tris said, latching on to what he knew had gotten a reaction.

And yes, there it was again, a little hitch in Samuel's breathing. "You'd be up for something like that?" Samuel asked.

Tris's first instinct was to respond with a resounding *hell, yes*, but then the phrasing struck him. Samuel hadn't asked if Tris was up for that, meaning daddy kink specifically, but for something *like* that, which encompassed more. But what was he going for?

"Sure. I love experimenting in the bedroom," he said, figuring he'd word it as broadly as possible.

"You do?"

This was it, Tris felt it. He was close to Samuel revealing what he really wanted. All he needed was a little more assurance that it would be well-received. "Hell yeah. Look, Cara and I grew apart, but our sex life was never the issue. Both of us loved to try new things, so we experimented with a lot of different stuff."

"Like what?"

"Oh jeez, what not? Toys, a little bondage, anal, she used a strap-on with me a few times, some role play..."

All that time, he was watching Samuel closely, and when he said that last word, his eyes had widened. It clicked. It wasn't the daddy kink specifically Samuel was after. It was the *role play*. That was what he wanted, what got his blood pumping.

A wave of emotions rolled over Tris. Exhilaration over this little verbal match they had going, but it was much more than that. Anticipation. Excitement over how well they connected. An unexpected tenderness for this sweet guy, who had gotten burned badly with that douchebag ex of his. And an unrivaled thrill at the images his brain produced of how they would look together.

Samuel's slim body under his own broad one. His big hands holding that narrow waist as the boy rode his cock. Those pretty, plump lips taking his dick in till he choked on it. And the role play possibilities were endless as well. Him as a cop and Samuel getting arrested. Or a principal with a naughty student. A house owner catching a burglar. A dungeon master with his slave. God, they would have so much fun.

"That sounds good to me," Samuel said, and Tris understood he wasn't quite ready to show his hand. Understandable, but they had time. Maybe it would help if they did a test drive—though he cringed inwardly at his own expression—to see if they were as sexually compatible as he thought.

He took a deep breath. "How are you feeling right now?"

Samuel frowned. "What do you mean?"

"Are you clearheaded? No headache? Not feeling sick in any way? Overly emotional?"

Samuel's frown intensified. "What are you, my doctor all of a sudden?"

"Just answer the damn questions," Tris said, allowing a bit of dominance to slip into his voice.

Much to his surprise, Samuel reacted almost instantly. His body shot up into a straight position. "Sorry. I'm fine. No hangover anymore. Emotionally, I'm not sure, since I'm perfectly happy pushing my rage at Evan deep, deep inside me until I'm ready to deal with it. But seriously, why are you asking?"

Tris leaned forward, waiting until Samuel met his eyes.

"Because I want to make sure you're in the right frame of mind to give consent."

Samuel finally seemed to catch on, as he licked his lips in a gesture that shot straight to Tris's balls. "Consent for what?"

Tris held out his hand. "Consent to start working on that list."

9

I t didn't happen very often that Samuel was speechless. His brain usually worked fast enough to come up with some smart reply, but this time, it failed him completely. It was like when he tried to speak French, his brain always needing a little time to translate the words he heard into something he could understand. Right now, he was scrambling to make sense of that expression. *Working on that list.*

Sex. Oh god, Tris was asking him for consent for sex. Holy hell to the yes, please. He didn't even need to think about that one. Not after Tris had made it clear he was more than open to experimenting and had mentioned role play. Samuel wasn't ready to tell him just how much that thought excited him, but he was definitely feeling optimistic about their sexual compatibility. And Tris wanting to get started right away? So fucking hot.

"Yes," he said, a little louder than he had intended to, which made Tris laugh.

"You sure about this? Considering you just broke up?" Tris checked, and Samuel had to respect him for that.

"Oh hell yes. Absolutely. Haven't you ever heard of revenge sex? Apparently, it's the best."

"I have no personal experience, but I'm definitely willing to offer myself up as a volunteer if you want to test that theory," Tris said with a big grin.

"How selfless of you," Samuel said. "I accept that offer."

For two, maybe three seconds, they stared at each other, and then they moved at the same time, jumping to their feet. Samuel's neck was enveloped in a strong grip that yanked him toward Tris, and he allowed it, tumbling against that big body. His mouth was caught in a searing kiss, Tris's tongue capturing his, then starting an intricate cat and mouse game.

Samuel shivered at all the sensations thundering through his body, almost dizzy with how deep it hit him, his need for this man. He arched his back, pressing his groin against him, seeking fiction. Just when his neck started to hurt a little from craning it, Tris lifted him up and planted his ass on the table, stepping between Samuel's legs. Ah, much better.

Dressed in boxer briefs, there was no denying his erection, as it threatened to peep out from under his waistband. Samuel placed his hand against Tris's dick as their tongues kept tangling, curious how big he was. He gasped into Tris's mouth when he discovered he couldn't even wrap his hand around it, what with how thick it was.

"Dude!" he let out.

The look in Tris's eyes was absolutely feral as they stared at each other, chests heaving. "You like?"

Samuel licked his lips. "How sturdy is this table?"

"I built it myself."

"Good." He whipped his T-shirt over his head. "Please

tell me that somewhere on that list of yours is to fuck me senseless on the kitchen table?"

"It just jumped to the top of the list," Tris said, his voice lower than ever.

"Even better." Samuel reached for Tris's belt. "Show me what you got. I have a feeling it's gonna make me very happy."

Samuel unbuckled Tris's belt, then reached inside his jeans and found the thickest cock he'd ever seen outside of porn. Hell, even now he couldn't wrap his hand completely around it.

"Strip," he told Tris.

"Are you going power bottom on me now?" Tris said with a laugh.

"I'll do whatever it takes to get that thing inside me, preferably in the next few minutes."

"Fuck, that's hot," Tris growled, dragging his shirt over his head and kicking off his jeans.

This was what Evan had hated, when Samuel had gotten this needy and bossy and vocal about what he wanted in bed. In the beginning, he'd played along, but subtle hints at first and then not so subtle reprimands over time had taught Samuel to rein himself in. Now, for the first time in two years, he wouldn't have to. He could be as vocal and demanding as he wanted to, because Tris seemed to lap it up.

"You have condoms?" he asked. "Lube?"

"Yeah, upstairs. Gimme a sec."

Tris dashed upstairs, wearing only his underwear, and Samuel figured he'd have time to admire his body later. Right now, the fire inside him was burning too hard and too fast to slow down. He needed to be taken hard, filled until he stopped feeling so damn empty inside.

He got out of his underwear, figuring he might as well help move things along. He cleared the table of their plates and put Tris's laptop on the kitchen counter, just to be safe. By the time Tris came hurrying down the stairs again, Samuel had positioned himself on the table, his upper body resting on the surface, his ass sticking back in a blatant invitation.

"Oh wow," Tris said, coming to a full stop. Samuel looked over his shoulder, smiling at the look of pure want on the man's face. "Now there's an appealing visual."

His hands shook a little as he placed lube on the table, followed by two condoms. Samuel couldn't resist teasing him a little. "Two? Feeling optimistic?"

Tris made quick work of his underwear, and that thick cock sprang free, causing Samuel to lose his train of thought. It wasn't that long, but god, it was thick. Much thicker than the biggest toy he owned and that was saying something. It would split him open in the best way possible.

"Pessimistic, rather. I doubt I'll last long once I'm inside you," Tris said, and it took Samuel a few seconds to realize he was answering his earlier question.

"Now that I've seen the size of your cock, I don't think two will be enough, but we'll see."

That made Tris break out in a smile that gave Samuel butterflies in his stomach. He stepped up and let his right hand trail down Samuel's back, a smooth glide all the way from his neck to his ass.

"You're stunning," he said, his voice low, and Samuel couldn't remember if anyone had ever looked at him like that. "That list just got a hell of a lot longer." He repeated his move, this time gently squeezing his ass cheek, then slapping it, just hard enough so it bounced. "I could do this for hours."

"You're more than welcome to...some other time," Samuel said, pushing his ass back even farther.

"I think I may actually have to tie you up and gag you if I ever want to do that, or there's no way you'll let me," Tris said, and the thought alone made Samuel shiver in the best way. "Oh, you like that idea, huh? At this rate, we'll need eighty years to finish that list."

It was meant as a joke, but it hung between them, loaded with something heavy and meaningful Samuel couldn't even put into words. All he knew was that the idea of spending eighty years with this man didn't sound nearly as terrifying as it should after the way Evan had fucked him over. He pushed it back for another time.

Before he could start begging Tris to please, for the love of everything holy, put that cock in him, Tris reached for the bottle of lube and slicked up his fingers. He didn't say a word as he went straight for his target this time, circling Samuel's hole until it softened a little and let him in. Samuel let out a little moan and turned his head forward so he could rest it on his arms on the table.

He fucked himself with a toy every day, often more than once, but it was so much better when someone else did it. That first sensation, that first slight burn, there was nothing like it. And Tris knew what he was doing because he added that second finger right before it got too comfortable, so it still stung a little. So good. Samuel closed his eyes, focusing on the slick sounds of the two fingers slowly pumping his ass.

Then two became three, and where he'd normally declare himself ready, he allowed himself a little more prep time. Taking a dick that girth, he'd need it. He loved having his hole stretched wide. Fisting was something that had been on his to-try list forever, but Evan had not been interested, and before him, he'd never had a partner he trusted enough to do it. Maybe with Tris, he thought, amazing himself with how natural that thought felt.

"Think you're ready?" Tris asked, the first words he'd spoken since he'd started to prep him.

"Yeah," Samuel answered. "I love a good burn."

"Good, because I'm told you'll feel this," Tris said as he reached for the condom and rolled it on. "You have to communicate with me, Samuel, because I can't see your face, so tell me to slow down or stop if need be."

"Or go harder and faster and deeper," Samuel said, thinking that there could be no earthly reason why he'd want Tris to slow down.

"Or that," Tris said, amusement lacing his voice.

Then he pressed the fat head of his cock against Samuel's entrance, and he stopped talking. Stopped thinking too. He pushed back, allowing himself to be breached. His breath turned into a low grunt as the burn spread, circling his ass before traveling both outward and inward. Oh, that thing was big, forcing him wide open until his eyes watered. But so, so good.

He breathed out again, relaxing as much as possible, and Tris slid in a little deeper. Samuel's moan mingled with one from Tris. "God, you feel amazing."

Samuel couldn't even talk, too focused on letting him in. He bore down, his mind going blank as his body's needs took over. All he could do was breathe out in little puffs as that thick cock split him open inch by inch until he felt Tris's pubic hair tickle his ass. Tris gave a few shallow thrusts and Samuel moaned. This man was gonna be the death of him, he knew it.

"Please tell me you know how to work that beauty," he said.

In lieu of answering, Tris pulled out almost entirely, then slid right back in, pushing the air from Samuel's lungs.

"Oh god, yes. Like that," Samuel moaned.

After the next two thrusts, he spread his arms wide and held on to the table for leverage. Tris was careful at first, tuned into Samuel's reactions, it seemed. But when Samuel started pushing back, he sped up. The sensation of that impossible fat cock inside him was amazing, sending sparks throughout his entire body. He tried to reach underneath to wrap a hand around his cock, but his position wouldn't allow it.

He groaned with frustration, and Tris stilled inside him for a second before pulling out. "On your back," he told him. "Wait, let me grab a towel."

Samuel slid off the table while Tris grabbed a thick towel from a cabinet and placed it on the table, then lifted Samuel up as if he weighed nothing and lowered him. He slid downward until his ass was on the edge of the table, almost whimpering with impatience until Tris leaned over him and slid back inside him.

"Much better," Tris said. "Now I can see your beautiful face as I make you soar."

The man was a damn poet, Samuel thought, sighing with happiness as he was filled to the max once again. And Tris was right, this position was better, because he could pull up his legs, which allowed Tris to get even deeper and holy fuck, *yes,* that was his prostate.

"Your eyes rolled back," Tris said with distinct pride.

"Do that again." He did, and Samuel couldn't hold back the loud moan that erupted from his lips. "God, yes, there. Exactly there."

Tris was clearly not in the category of tops who resented getting instructions, because his face broke open in a wide smile and he slammed back in, hitting the exact same spot. Samuel's hand wound around his dick, and he fisted his crown a few times to spread the precum. This was gonna be a good one, he could already feel it building up inside him, one of those orgasms that seemed to come from your toes, slowly rising in intensity until you wanted to cry and shout and scream with the force of it.

"Hands-free orgasm just went on the list," Tris panted as he sped up his thrusts. "I wanna fuck an orgasm out of you without you ever touching yourself."

"I'm game," Samuel said between his own heaved breaths, his muscles tensing in anticipation. He increased the pressure on his cock, his orgasm so close he was getting desperate.

"I hope you're fucking close…" Tris grunted. "Because I don't have much left."

His thrusts grew faster, more uncoordinated as the man chased his own release, and Samuel closed his eyes, allowing his body to take over. Then Tris slammed into him, so hard and so spot-on to his prostate that his balls exploded before he had felt them releasing, sending jets of thick cum through his cock, coating his hands and his stomach.

Tris came seconds after him, jerking a few times before freezing balls-deep inside him, letting out a long, low grunt of pleasure. As soon as his muscles relaxed, he reached for Samuel to pull him up and kiss him in an encounter that lacked finesse but more than made up for it in enthusiasm.

Finally, they rested with their foreheads against each other. "Great start of that list," Tris said.

Samuel's body felt loose, well-fucked. God, he loved this. "I couldn't agree more. What's the next item?"

10

Before Tris could react to that statement, his ears perked up at the faint sound of a car. Was that...? Oh god.

"We have to get dressed. Now."

As carefully as he could, he pulled out of Samuel, quickly getting rid of the condom by dumping it in the kitchen trash can, making sure it was buried under some other trash. When he turned around, Samuel was still on the kitchen table, looking at him with a dazed expression.

"I'm so sorry, but that's my ex-wife in the driveway, with my boys. She has a key, and you have about thirty seconds before they walk in the door."

That did get a reaction out of Samuel, as his eyes widened in shock before he scrambled off the table, then hurried out of the kitchen up the stairs. Tris frantically grabbed his own clothes, putting them on as quick as possible, then realized Samuel's shirt and boxers were still in the kitchen as well. He heard the back door and knew he had no time to take them upstairs, so instead, he hid them in a cupboard behind a few boxes of cereal.

He dragged two hands through his hair to get rid of the worst of the just-fucked look and spread his papers back out on the kitchen table before putting his laptop back. He had just turned it on when his oldest son, Dean, walked in.

"Hey, Dad."

He was followed on his heels by his brother, Paul. "Hi, Dad, what were you doing?"

They were too old for hugs and kisses, they had told him a few years ago It was something Tris usually lamented, but now he was grateful. He was certain they would've smelled the sex on him.

"Nothing much. Paying bills. Boring adult stuff."

Cara came into the kitchen and of course, she did give him a hug. "How have you been, big guy? The boys wanted to pick up the new Nintendo game they got from you last week."

"That's fine," Tris said, almost holding his breath in the hopes Cara wouldn't notice anything out of the ordinary.

Alas, he had no such luck. He spotted it at the same time as she did, the condom and lube that were still prominently displayed on the kitchen table. Her hand flew to her mouth, but he had to give her props for not showing anything to the boys. In fact, she handily moved toward the table, half-hiding behind Tris as she pocketed the condom and slid the lube quickly toward Tris so he could grab it and put it in his pocket.

Thank you, he mouthed to her, and he got a cheeky grin in return that told him he would have to explain later. That was a small price to pay for his boys not finding out their dad had just had sex on the kitchen table, he supposed.

"So get the game," Dean told Paul. He always liked to boss his younger brother around. Good thing Paul had a mouth on him and wasn't afraid to use it.

"Go get it yourself," Paul said. "You're the one who wanted to play it so badly Mom had to drive over here to get it."

"Dude, that thing is buried somewhere in the unholy mess of your room. I'm not digging through your dirty underwear to find it."

Tris was about to tell Paul Dean had a point, when he realized the problem. Dean's room was, of course, upstairs. That was also where Samuel was. The last thing he wanted was for his kids to meet him like this.

"Jeez, don't the two of you ever get tired of bickering all the time?" he said. "You're lucky I'm in a good mood. I'll go get it. You just stay downstairs with Mom."

Cara's grin told him she was seeing straight through his ruse, but he didn't care. Anything to make sure Samuel was okay. "I'll make sure they stay with me," she said, affirming his suspicion.

"Never mind, Dad. I'll get it. I wanted to pick up some of my comics for a project I'm doing for English lit," Paul said.

Tris shot a look of pure panic at Cara. What reason could he possibly give why his son couldn't go into his own bedroom?

"You can get that Monday, when you're going back to your dad's," Cara said. "Your dad is busy right now, and we shouldn't interrupt his day any further. Let your dad get the game and we'll go."

Paul looked from one parent to the other, a frown furrowing his brows. "The two of you are acting strange," he said.

"We're adults," Tris said. "That's our prerogative. Listen to your mom now."

Before his son could protest, Tris hurried out the kitchen and up the stairs. He grabbed the game first, which fortu-

nately for him wasn't hiding underneath dirty underwear—
though he did have to give Dean credit for calling the state
of Paul's room correctly. Definitely something he should pay
attention to more.

With the game in his hand, he softly opened the door to
the guest bedroom, where he found Samuel hiding under
the covers. "It's just me," he whispered. "I'm so sorry. They
came by unannounced. They'll be out of here in a few
minutes, I promise."

Samuel had appeared from under the covers. "Okay. I
didn't think you wanted me to meet them, so I figured I'd
stay here and not make a sound."

Tris's heart softened. "I do want you to meet them, but
not like this. Properly. Okay?"

Samuel rewarded him with a big smile. "Okay."

Tris sent him a meaningful look, then closed the door
behind him again and hurried downstairs. Apparently, their
kids had been badgering Cara the whole time for more
insight into what was going on, but she was standing her
ground. She was good like that, supporting Tris. She always
had been, just like he had kept her relationship with Colin a
secret until she'd been ready to introduce him to the kids.

"Okay, boys, let's go," she said, her voice leaving no room
for interpretation.

With a last, somewhat accusing look at Tris, his sons
filed out behind their mother. "See you guys Monday," he
called after them, sighing with relief when he heard the
back door close. Damn, that had been a close call.

He waited until he heard the car pull out of the driveway,
then rushed back upstairs. Samuel hadn't left the bed,
which made sense, considering he was naked. Tris couldn't
deny the sight of him in that bed was an appealing one, and
he had to resist the urge to crawl in next to him for round

two. But if the unexpected encounter with Cara and his kids had shown him anything, it was that they were moving at a breakneck speed. Slowing down was probably a good idea to avoid crashing.

"I'm so sorry about that," he told Samuel, lowering himself on the bed next to him on his side so he could look at him.

"Don't be. They're your kids. You shouldn't apologize for the place they have in your life."

His easy acceptance of how important his boys were to him flowed over him like a warm shower. At that moment, Tris realized that he was already halfway in love with Samuel. It was crazy fast and it didn't make much sense, but they were so perfect together. Still, slowing down was necessary.

"It means a lot to me that you recognize that," he said.

"This is moving fast, isn't it?" Samuel asked, turning on his side as well so they were face-to-face.

"It is," Tris confirmed. "It feels good, but we may want to slow down a little."

"You mean you don't think it's wise to meet your kids after we've known each other for not even twenty-four hours?" Samuel joked, and Tris appreciated he could see the humor in the whole thing.

"It seemed kind of fast," he said with a laugh, but then grew more serious. "But I think you need a little time to process everything that has happened. Maybe talk to your lawyer, find out if there are any unwanted consequences of Evan's presence in your life. Then take some time to consider if you're ready for a new relationship."

"That sounds wise." Samuel bit his lip. "What if I come to the conclusion that I'm not ready yet?"

Tris reached for his hand and enveloped it in his much bigger hand. "Then we'll wait until you're ready."

"That's a big promise to make to a man you only met yesterday," Samuel said, but Tris had no trouble detecting the hope in his voice.

He brought Samuel's hand to his lips and kissed it. "I know, but I stand by it. Look, I met Cara after her family moved to Jersey from upstate New York. We were sixteen, and she sat in front of me in math. I fell in love with her on sight, and I asked her for a date two days later. When you know, you know, and I've always been a man who goes by his gut. Right now, my gut is telling me that I am willing to wait until you're ready."

Samuel shot him a look that made Tris think of those cartoons where the character had little red hearts instead of eyes. "You said you and Cara grew apart. What happened?" Samuel asked.

"Honestly, I think we were too young when we started dating. We both changed a lot since high school, and we lost that magic connection. I think if she hadn't gotten pregnant, we would've broken up a long, long time ago, but I never regretted marrying her. We're just better off as friends. She is a loving mom and a fantastic woman, but just not the right fit for me and vice versa."

"She sounds like a wonderful person," Samuel said. "I'm so happy you guys still get along and that you can co-parent your kids. I'm sure that makes a big difference for them as well."

"It does, but it helps that we parted on such amicable terms. It's a whole different scenario when one of the parents cheats, I can tell you that from experience."

Samuel frowned. "You've mentioned your hatred for

cheating a few times now. I'm assuming you have personal experience in some way?"

"Close friends of ours, he cheated on her while she was pregnant, then left her days after the baby was born. That divorce turned ugly, as he refused to pay child support and it broke her. She was never the same and it was devastating to see."

"People suck sometimes," Samuel said, and Tris could only imagine what was going through his head.

"They do...but not all of them. Every now and then, you strike gold."

Samuel's look changed, softened. "Are you saying I struck gold with you?"

Tris leaned in for a soft kiss. "No, I did."

11

A few hours later, Samuel walked in the front door of his building.

"Mr. Norris," Ben, the doorman, greeted him. "Your locksmith left new keys for you here."

"Thank you," Samuel said. "I do apologize for the disruption with Mr. McLeod."

Ben's face showed nothing but kindness, but then again, it always did. The man had held this job as long as Samuel had lived here and probably far before that. He excelled at his job, knowing when to pretend he didn't see something and when to pay attention.

"No need, Mr. Norris. It was most fortunate that your locksmith was still here, as Mr. McLeod must've slipped past me when I was taking a quick break. Because he still had a key, he could access the elevator."

Samuel sent him a tense smile. "That was an oversight on my part. I assumed that breaking up meant Mr. McLeod understood he was no longer welcome here and invited, but in hindsight, I should've made that more clear to him."

Ben's smile at him was fatherly. "I'm sorry to hear that. A

most unfortunate turn of events considering yesterday's date."

Samuel sighed. "Yeah, it wasn't what I had expected either."

The elevator ride up was short, but Samuel smiled as he thought of being stuck on that elevator with Tris. That had turned out well, all things considered. Who could've predicted that? They had such crazy chemistry, and he'd been elated to find out it hadn't been only from his side. God, the sex they'd had had been explosive, his hole clenching in fond memory. He'd been glad Tris had suggested slowing down a little as well. It had been oh-so tempting to stay. But he had to face the mess his break up had caused, and Tris had stuff to do as well, he'd indicated.

So Samuel had taken an Uber back to Manhattan...from New Jersey. Because that's where Tris lived, in Jersey. It was a little frightening to admit that Samuel had been so out of it he'd never realized they'd gone that far. It made sense, as the house Tris lived in would be impossible for him to afford on Manhattan, or even in the other boroughs. It was a nice enough neighborhood where he lived, though a sharp contrast with Samuel's apartment.

Still, his apartment had been home for him for the last few years, and he could only hope it would feel the same without Evan. He wasn't sure what he had expected to experience when he walked in the door, but it wasn't the relief that surged through him. Everything was still in order, nothing out of place. He checked his computer setup first, even though he had no doubt Tris's friend Law had kept a close eye on Evan. Nothing was amiss, and he exhaled slowly.

The kitchen cupboards were closed, but a quick peek revealed that Evan had indeed taken some of the more luxurious food items they'd had there. It was hard not to judge a man who would be that petty after living there rent free for over a year and a half. Well, he could add it to the growing list of everything that was wrong about Evan McLeod.

In the bedroom, Evan's closet was empty, and so was his nightstand and his shelf in the bathroom cabinet. He'd taken the expensive aftershave Samuel had bought for him a week or so ago, an impulse gift in a long list of things he'd bought for him.

It was like he'd never even been there, like every trace of his existence had been wiped, and it was a strange feeling. The only thing that reminded Samuel of the two of them were some pictures he had framed and put on a dresser. They looked strangely out of place now, two smiling faces that looked like strangers.

He picked up one of the pictures, a shot that had been taken at the wedding of friends of his parents. Samuel had been invited, as the bride was his godmother. Her husband had passed away from cancer and she had found a new love with a widower, which delighted everyone seeing as she was a wonderful, warm person. Evan had insisted on coming along, even though Samuel had warned him there would be little for him there, seeing as how he didn't know any of the other guests. Samuel had caved, reasoning that it was normal to bring your significant other to events like that. And it was, so looking back, Samuel wondered why he had felt reluctance.

He studied the picture, those two smiling faces that seemed so in love with each other. He remembered when the photographer had asked them to pose, thinking at the time that it would make a perfect picture for him to frame. How weird was that, that he'd thought of the visual rather than the emotion? Studying the picture now, it was like looking at two strangers.

Alas, he had priorities other than reminiscing about the past. He'd better call his mother, because considering how well-informed she was and how fast gossip tended to reach her, he was pretty sure she knew already. And if not, he really preferred it when she heard from him.

She picked up on the second ring, which told him she knew already. "Mom," he simply said.

"Samuel, sweetheart, what happened? I heard you and Evan broke up?"

He smiled. Just as expected. Her network rarely failed her. "We did, and it was rather nasty." His intention to stay cool and collected went out the window as soon as he started talking, his voice breaking up at the last word.

"Oh, sweetheart, I'm so sorry. What happened?"

He sat down on the couch, then snuggled under a twenty-dollar velvety soft blanket he'd once bought at Walmart. Evan had always made fun of it, insisting it clashed with his expensive couch, but Samuel didn't care. "He cheated on me, Mom," he said, tears filling his eyes. "Not once, but repeatedly. I didn't know till yesterday, but when I found out, I broke up with him."

"That is horrible," she said, and Samuel heard the judgment in her voice loud and clear. "And of course you did when you found out. You deserve better than that."

Something in those last words triggered him. "Mom, be honest with me, did you and Dad like Evan?"

The time it took her to answer told Samuel everything already. Still, his heart clenched painfully when she said, "I'm sorry, but no. But we never said anything, because he was your choice. You know we learned our lesson with your brother about interfering in his love life. We had hoped you would find out sooner, though."

The tears came faster now, and Samuel had to close his eyes because he couldn't see anything anymore. "I was hoping he would propose yesterday," he said, half-sobbing. "And he would have, had I not confronted him about the cheating. He tried to, even after I confronted him. He had the ring and everything."

"I'm so sorry," his mom said. "It takes a special kind of man who can propose knowing he's screwing around on you. You deserve better, sweetheart."

Samuel took a minute to compose himself, as well as to gather the courage to ask the next question. "Mom, do you think Evan was after my money?"

This time, the answer came fast. "Yes. Your father and I agreed from the beginning. That's why we asked Clark to keep a close eye on your finances." Clark was his investment banker, the one he shared with his parents. "We asked him to alert you if he spotted any suspicious activity. Obviously, we couldn't ask him to contact us out of client privilege. And we made the same request with Sharon, your accountant. Again, all we asked was that she kept an eye out for anything out of the ordinary and alert you if that was the case. We just wanted to look out for you."

Samuel let it sink in, the careful way his parents had tried to have his back. "Thank you, Mom. I haven't heard anything from Clark or Sharon, so I should assume everything is okay, right?"

"It would seem so, but it can't hurt to reach out to them now that you're aware and ask them specifically. Do you have any reason to believe he took money from you? And by the way, sweetheart, I'm so sorry. I had hoped we were wrong about him."

All Samuel could do was let out another deep sigh that seemed to come from his toes. "No, no specific indications, just a general sense that he used me. Hell, he lived here rent free, so there's that. But I never gave him money for anything other than the occasional gift. A watch. Some expensive fountain pen he really wanted. A pair of sunglasses. Some trips we took together."

As he listed it for his mom, he did the math in his head, concluding that together, it added up. That was worth another sigh. "Dammit, I guess he *did* get money from me after all."

"Now, Samuel, shake that feeling off. You're a generous person by nature, and you don't need that money. Those things were not personal. That's just money. Let him have it. It would've been far worse had he taken something from you that meant something to you or had damaged your reputation."

His mom, as usual, was right. It was one of her strengths, his father had once pointed out to Samuel, the fact that she rarely lost her calm and had a way of helping you see things in the right perspective.

"Someone suggested he might have tried to use my contacts, act on my behalf," Samuel said.

"That's definitely a possibility. Contact your lawyer and have her be on the lookout. Maybe even let her do a little investigative digging to make sure. Better to spend a little money now and uncover everything there is to know than be faced with nasty consequences later."

"You know what sucks about being rich?" Samuel said, allowing a little whine in his voice. "That even when you discover your boyfriend of two years has cheated on you, you can't just be mad like everybody else. There's always the financial and legal implications first, and right now, I really resent that."

This time, his mom sighed. "I know, sweetheart. It sucks. My suggestion is to get it over with and then get blindly drunk."

Samuel laughed. "I already did that last night."

"By yourself?" his mom asked, clearly surprised. She should be, as drinking that much was not a habit for Samuel.

"No, with a friend." And then, because he'd always been a mama's boy and because no one could listen like his mom, he said, "He's the guy who told me about Evan's cheating. He stayed when I broke up with Evan, and when Evan got physical, Tris escorted me out. We went out for dinner, then drinks."

"Something tells me you didn't make it home last night," his mom said, her smile audible.

"No, and that was a good thing, because Evan tried to get into the apartment to pick up his stuff and do god knows what else. I got lucky, because I had sent a locksmith to change the locks, and he called the cops on Evan."

"Oh my god. That was quick thinking on your part, to change the locks."

"Not my idea. Tris brought it up during dinner and I had a friend of his do it."

"Samuel," his mother said slowly. "I hate to go all protective on you again, but are you sure that was wise? If he changed your locks, that means he now has access to your apartment. If he and this new friend of yours are in cahoots, they could rob you blind."

Samuel hated to admit it, but she was right. In theory, that was, because he did trust Tris, though he couldn't even explain why. But his mother had a point that he had been a little naive in given him that much trust.

"I'm pretty sure my instincts with him are spot-on, but you have a good point."

"Maybe have your lawyer run a background check on him and that locksmith as well, just to be sure."

"You know what else sucks about being rich?" Samuel said, his voice gloomy.

"I know, distrusting people on principle doesn't come naturally to you. I was the same way, but your father taught me that it's a necessary skill in our circumstances. So let's talk about something far more pleasant. How was the sex?"

Samuel burst out laughing. "Mom! Not discussing my sex life with you."

"No?" she said, laughing as well. "Bummer, because I just read about your brother's latest exploits in the tabloids, and I figured you would be competitive enough to best him."

Samuel shot up straight on the couch. "Who? Daniel?" he asked, referring to his younger brother. It had to be him, since he was the one who usually made the tabloids with his latest girlfriend of the day.

"No, because if it had been him, you wouldn't have bothered. No, it's Adam."

"Adam has a girlfriend and it made the tabloids?"

"Wrong again. Adam has a *boyfriend* and it made the tabloids."

How well his mother knew him. Adam and he had always been competitive, probably because they were only a year apart in age. They got along great, but there was definitely a sibling rivalry. The one thing they hadn't really competed in was dating, because as far as Samuel had known, Adam had been straight. That theory now went out the window, and wouldn't you know it, Samuel did feel a little rivalry brewing inside him.

"We had sex on the kitchen table. Really great sex."

He could still hear his mother dying of laughter when he ended the call, feeling much better already.

12

After Samuel left, Tris spent two hours going through his bills and updating all the numbers for his company. It was a necessary evil that he tried to do every weekend, so he knew exactly where he stood as the new week began. The first few minutes, his thoughts had kept going back to Samuel, but then he had forced himself to focus on what he needed to do and got the job done.

But after that, it was hard to keep himself busy enough not to think about Samuel. He tried to relax with a movie, but his mind kept wandering off. That night, he dreamed of him and he woke up with an impressive erection he gladly took care of in the shower.

He had just finished doing laundry—his usual thing on Sunday mornings—when his phone rang. One look at the caller ID and he wondered what had taken her so long. "Hey, what's up?" he said, pretending to not know why she was calling.

"You know that's not going to fly with me. What the hell

was going on yesterday? Who did you have in your bedroom?" Cara said, her voice low, probably so the boys wouldn't hear her.

"Going straight for the good stuff, huh?" he said with a little sigh.

"Don't tell me you expected anything else. Come on, Tris, I want details. Was it good sex? Bad sex? Worth repeating?"

He loved that she never identified gender. You could say what you want about his ex-wife, but she had fully embraced his identity and really had zero problems with it. Still, he wasn't sure how much he was willing to spill just yet. Even though his heart was bubbling over with excitement, it still felt so fragile, as if the wrong word could permanently damage it.

"It was spectacular sex," he said, knowing that he had to give her something. "And definitely worth a repeat."

"That's amazing," Cara said, and her tone had changed from morbidly curious to warm and affectionate. "What can you tell me about them?"

"I can't say too much yet, because it's all very new and fast. But he's sweet and wonderful and we really connected. It's just complicated, since he just got out of a bad relationship," Tris said.

Of course, there was also the added complication of Samuel's family and his money, but he wasn't mentioning that to Cara just yet. He would protect Samuel's identity as long as he could, especially after he'd seen some stories about both of his brothers. He had zero desire to end up in the tabloids, and he assumed Samuel felt the same.

"I'm so happy for you, and I'm rooting that it will work out. Let me know if you need me to take the boys for a few weekends so you have some extra time together," Cara offered.

"Thank you. I may take you up on that, but I'll let you know. And thank you for covering for me yesterday. As you may have guessed, you guys came at a rather unfortunate time."

Cara's laugh was instant. "I'm so sorry. I promise I will text before I stop by, okay? It's just never been an issue before, so I didn't even think about it."

"I know, no worries. And I'm happy to report that the kitchen table is quite sturdy," he said.

Cara was still laughing when he ended the call. He finished putting away the clean laundry, then took a quick cleaning tour through the house, vacuuming the living room and the kitchen, cleaning the guest bathroom downstairs as well as the master bathroom that was connected to his room. He even changed the sheets on his own bed, nodding with contentment as he inspected the results.

And then it hit him. Unconsciously, he'd been preparing his house to have Samuel over again. And that was ridiculous, of course, because first of all, they had decided to take it slow and second, the guy had a multi-million-dollar apartment on Manhattan. Why the hell would he want to hang out in some small house in Jersey?

He slowly made his way downstairs, sitting down with a cup of coffee at the very kitchen table where he and Samuel had made such passionate love the day before. Was it possible to miss someone you had met not even two full days before? Because that's what it felt like. His house had never felt empty to him, not even when the kids were with Cara. After three years, he'd gotten used to not having them around all the time. But for the first time, he felt alone, wanting someone with him. Not just someone—Samuel.

He had his phone in his hands before he could think better of it, and the call went through instantly. He was relieved when Samuel picked up quickly, almost as if he'd been hoping for a call and keeping an eye on his phone.

"Hi," he said, and even that simple word made Tris feel better.

"Hi," he said back. "I missed you," he added on impulse.

"I thought you wanted to take it slow?" Samuel said, but it wasn't harsh or critical.

"That was the theory," Tris admitted. "It turns out it's quite hard to execute that in reality. But chatting on the phone doesn't hurt, right?"

He heard some rustling on the phone that sounded as if Samuel was settling down in bed or on the couch. "Chatting on the phone is nice," he said.

"Did you talk to your lawyer yet?" Tris asked.

"Yeah," Samuel said with a little sigh. "I did the whole nine yards yesterday. My lawyer, my investment banker, and my accountant, just to cover all bases. And my mom, because my day wasn't fun enough."

"Was she upset you guys broke up?"

"Hell no. Turns out, my parents never liked Evan, but they didn't want to say anything. They did that once to my younger brother, offering some critical comments on the woman he was dating, and he didn't speak to them for a few months. They've learned their lesson, I guess."

"If they had said something, would you have listened?" Tris wondered.

"I've asked myself the same thing, and the truth is that I don't know. I'd like to think I would've taken them seriously, especially since me and my mom are close, but that's hindsight. But really, the call with her was good. She asked for details on the sex."

Tris's coffee almost went down the wrong way and he coughed a few times to recover. "Please tell me you didn't share anything with her."

Samuel laughed, and the sound made Tris happy. "She pitched me against my older brother, who I have a bit of sibling rivalry with. Apparently, he made the tabloids yesterday with his new boyfriend, and considering we thought he was straight, that was quite the news. So I had to tell her something to best him."

Tris groaned, though why he would be embarrassed at the idea that a woman he'd never met had heard anything about his sex life, he didn't know. "Let me guess, you told her about the kitchen table."

Samuel's giggle was melodious, and it made Tris miss him even more. "Of course I did. That was one hell of a sturdy table you built."

"As long as you focused on the table and not on other details, I think we're still good."

"What other details are we talking about? Did you really think I would mention the size of your dick to my mom?"

"The thought crossed my mind," Tris said with a laugh.

"Dude, at some point, I'd want you to meet her. No way am I telling her that."

Tris let that casual remark sink in. "You want me to meet your mother?"

"Yeah. So far for going slow, huh?"

There was something apologetic in Samuel's tone, something that made Tris need to reassure him. "I feel the same way. I know we said we should go slow, because rationally, that makes total sense, but my heart is saying something else entirely."

The silence hung heavy between them, and Tris

wondered if he had said too much. Then Samuel said, "Tris, I want to ask you something, and I really hope you won't get offended. It's just that after my experience with Evan, my mother suggested I do a little more due diligence before I got serious with someone."

It took Tris a second or two to put it together. "You want to run a background check on me," he said.

"I want to ask your permission to run a background check on you," Samuel said, sounding apologetic. "I know it's awful and sounds like I don't trust you, but—"

"It's fine," Tris interrupted him. "I completely understand. You have my permission, and thank you so much for asking me. I have nothing to hide from you. All you're going to find are some speeding and parking tickets, since I am from Jersey after all. Oh, and I got arrested once for public indecency, the results of a stupid drunk bet in high school."

"Thank you," Samuel said, his voice soft and somewhat emotional. "And thank you for understanding. I hate doing this. I hate having to be so distrustful, but after Evan, I can't help it."

"Samuel, baby, don't worry about it. I really do understand," Tris said, the term of endearment flying off his lips all by itself. "But tell me, did your lawyer or your other people find anything suspicious?"

"My accountant and my investment banker were positive there was nothing suspicious, but my lawyer is just getting started. She asked me if I had ever signed stuff for Evan, like paperwork he'd put in front of me. I haven't, because while I may have been naive, I'm not quite that stupid. That doesn't mean he couldn't have falsified my signature on something, though, as he's certainly seen it plenty of times. So that's what my lawyer will look into, with the help of an investigator that's on her firm's payroll. He's also the one who will be doing the background check on you."

"I'm glad they're doing a thorough investigation to make sure he didn't get to you in any way, but I'm so sorry this is necessary. And if that guy has any questions for me, he can contact me directly. I promise I will fully cooperate, because I want you to be able to trust me."

Samuel was quiet for a few beats. "I do trust you, but this time, my brain is telling my heart to double check."

"Stop worrying about it," Tris said, dropping a little more force in his tone.

That got a little chuckle out of Samuel. "We really should try daddy kink some time," he said. "You've got that stern voice all down."

"I was thinking along the lines of a principal with a naughty student," Tris said.

He smiled when he could hear Samuel swallow. "That sounds really good," he said, his voice having dropped a little lower.

And suddenly, Tris had a wonderful idea. "I'm pretty sure you went to private school, right?"

"Yeah, why?"

"Do you still have your uniform?"

The sound Samuel made was pure sex, a low little growl that made Tris instantly hard. "I do."

"Your place or mine?" Tris asked, giving Samuel the choice.

It took about three seconds for him to answer. "I'll be there as soon as I can."

~

SAMUEL WAS SHAKING with nerves during the whole ride. He'd called Neil, his chauffeur, to pick him up—something he didn't do often, since it screamed privilege, but in this case, he really didn't want the hassle of taking an Uber and having to make conversation. Or worse, taking the subway and train and having to navigate the Sunday-morning traffic, including the ever-clueless tourists. No, at least now he had some time to compose and prepare himself.

He was wearing his school uniform, which mercifully still fit, though it was indecently tight around his groin and ass. It was strange to once again see himself in the charcoal gray pants and blazer, with the burgundy red pullover and the striped tie he'd once hated so much. If Neil had opinions on Samuel wearing a school uniform, he hadn't shown them —not that Samuel had expected anything else. His family paid well for discretion like that.

He'd also packed a small bag with some essentials, just in case... Just in case he decided to spend the night. Like he hadn't already decided that. Well, it still depended on Tris, obviously, but Samuel couldn't imagine he'd send him home after what he hoped would be an amazing night. He sighed again as the possible scenarios played through his head. He'd been hard as a rock since he'd gotten changed, so pumped up about this encounter that it was difficult to even think. It was everything he'd hoped to find with some-one, this kinky, adventurous sex.

And Tris had suggested this scenario, not Samuel, which made it even better. It meant he was into this as much as Samuel was, and that thought alone made him even harder. Oh, the scenarios they could play together... They'd defi-nitely have to play daddy and son sometime...or a dirty uncle, that could be fun. Or maybe a mean boss who forced his employee to suck him off under the desk. Samuel shifted in his seat, rearranging his leaking cock.

Principal and student were a great one to begin with, though. Would Tris be in character right away? Or would he want a discussion first? The latter made more sense, but god, the first one would be so hot. Would he spank him? That kind of went with the scenario, right? But they hadn't discussed it, and now Samuel regretted that. It would suck to have to get all formal first. He'd leave it to Tris, he decided, and follow his lead.

All the way to Jersey, he kept playing scenarios in his head and by the time he arrived, he was tense as a coiled wire, ready to be sprung.

"Do I need to pick you up, sir?" Neil asked as he parked the car in front of Tris's house, stubbornly sticking to the formal *sir* even after Samuel had told him otherwise at least a dozen times.

"I don't think so, but I'll let you know. Thank you."

"My pleasure, sir, as always."

Samuel zipped up his coat, as much to keep the cold wind out as to prevent Tris's neighbors from getting a look at his uniform, because *that* wouldn't be awkward at all. Then he grabbed his bag and got out of the car. The front door opened before he was even halfway up the driveway, and Samuel stopped in his tracks.

Tris was dressed in a pair of formal pants, a tight-fitting dress shirt, and a tie. He tapped his watch with an impatient gesture, and Samuel's heart soared. He was in character already. They were really doing this. He hurried to the door. "I'm sorry for being late, sir," he said.

"I'm sick and tired of your excuses, Mr. Norris. I've warned you time and again. I'm done giving you second chances. Get your ass into my office," Tris barked at him, and Samuel shivered with excitement. God, that *tone* of his, that deep, strict voice.

"Yes, sir," he said, stepping through the door, not meeting Tris's eyes.

Tris closed the door behind him, then pointed at a coat rack. "Hang your jacket up. Shoes on the rack. Bag in the cubby."

He waited with his arms crossed as Samuel carried out his instructions, his hands trembling. When he was done, he stood in front of him, not daring to look him in the eyes. "What's next, sir?"

"What's next is your punishment. Your tardiness and attitude have gone unnoticed for too long. You need a lesson, young man, one you won't forget anytime soon."

When Tris was quiet for a few seconds, Samuel realized that this was his implicit way of asking for consent without breaking the scene. "Yes, sir," he said. "I know I've been bad. Whatever punishment you see fit, sir."

"Good. Follow me."

He stayed behind Tris as he walked into the living room, where he had a desk set up in a corner. It made Samuel wonder for a second why he'd been using the kitchen table as an office then, but he pushed that thought down as it didn't matter right now. His sat down on the desk chair, an ancient-looking dark wood monstrosity that didn't even have wheels.

"Take off your blazer, Mr. Norris. You can drape it over that chair there."

Samuel did as he was told, then resumed his position in front of Tris, his hands folded behind his back and his eyes trained on the floor.

"I've received complaints about you, Mr. Norris," Tris

said, still in that deep voice that reached deep inside Samuel. "Complaints from teachers about your behavior."

"Complaints about what, sir?" Samuel asked, gladly playing along.

"They've reported to me that you're promiscuous. That you're soliciting the older boys and several teachers for sexual favors. Is that true?"

Samuel's cheeks flushed with how *wrong* this was and how right it felt at the same time. "Yes, sir."

"I will not tolerate that kind of wanton behavior in my school, Mr. Norris, do you understand me?"

"Yes, sir."

"I will have to punish you for this. Tell me what punishment you think you deserve?"

He'd done it, allowed Samuel to communicate his boundaries without breaking the scene. He was so good at this, and Samuel could've wept with relief. Instead, he took a deep breath. Tris was offering him a chance to live out a fantasy and hell yeah, he was gonna grab it with both hands.

"I think you should spank me, sir. I deserve that."

His voice sounded remarkably calm considering the fact that his heart was racing, his palms were sweating, and his cock was only a few touches away from exploding in his pants.

"I agree. Look at me, Mr. Norris, because I'm gonna give you a choice."

Samuel looked up to meet Tris's eyes first, which showed the same heat he was feeling inside, but then his gaze dropped to what Tris picked up from the desk. Oh god. Samuel's body jerked as if shocked, simply because he had so much excitement that he could barely hold it anymore. His underwear was soaked, and he feared it would start seeping through his pants any moment now.

"The choice is yours. I can spank you with my hand on your bare ass, or you can keep your pants on but I will use this paddle. What will it be?"

It was such an easy choice. Samuel would love to experiment with the paddle someday, but not right now. He wanted to feel Tris's hand on him, on his bare skin. Without saying anything, he unbuttoned his pants and dragged his zipper down.

"I see you choose to bare your bottom for me. I should not be surprised after all of the rumors. I guess you really are a little boy slut, aren't you?" Tris said with such a sneer that Samuel shivered again.

It was *perfect*, the derision in his voice. So fucking perfect. He felt so dirty and so good at the same time. "Yes, sir," he managed, his voice croaking.

"Take them off, then. Show me what you've been baring for god knows who."

He kicked off his pants and underwear because he wanted to be naked for him, needed so much more of what Tris was doling out. He kept his shirt and pullover on, daring to steal a glance at Tris from between his lashes.

"Turn around. Show me your bottom," came the command.

Samuel didn't even hesitate but did as he was told, lifting his shirt so Tris could have a good look. That, of course, didn't go unnoticed. "Look at you, parading your body around. You like it when people see you naked, don't you?"

"Yes, sir," he said, his voice barely above a whisper.

"Bend over. I want to see what all the fuss is about."

Tears sprang to Samuel's eyes, but they were good tears. Tears that came because finally, someone understood what he wanted, what he needed, and gave it to him. Tears because every single word out of Tris's mouth was perfection. Tears because he was seconds away from blowing his load without ever touching his dick, which would only result in more humiliation, which would make him even happier.

He bent over, spreading his legs a little and showing his hole to Tris. It was dirty and filthy and so fucking wrong, but he needed it at the same time.

"It's shameful, is what it is, you displaying yourself like that. We'll need to find a way to make sure you never show your bare ass to anyone else ever again. Now, come here and we'll see if we can spank it out of you."

Samuel shuffled over to him, his dick slapping against his stomach with every step, spreading precum everywhere. Tris chose to ignore that, he noted, and instead pointed at his knee. Samuel lowered himself, shifting a little until he'd found a good position. His cheeks had grown warm with the humiliation of this position. Why was that so hot?

"I find it quite frankly shameful," Tris began, and his hand came down on Samuel's right cheek twice, jolting him. "That a boy like you..."

Two more slaps, now to his left cheek.

"Would beg for sexual favors from everyone. Such a filthy boy..."

Samuel had been shocked into silence at first, trying to process the sensation of Tris's strong hand on his ass. It hurt, but it also felt good, and he was still trying to determine if he liked it or not when his cock made the decision for him. It sought friction against Tris's leg, and that little boost was enough. He short-circuited, his body jerking wildly as his balls clenched, squeezing the cum out of his cock and sending ropes of cum all over Tris's legs. The combination of pain, arousal, friction, and humiliation made him come so hard he saw stars.

He went slack on Tris's lap, too overcome with sensations and emotions to be able to hold himself up. Tris caught him effortlessly, then hauled him to a sitting position and parked him on his lap. His head fell against Tris's broad shoulder and he had to close his eyes, because it was all too much. Too perfect.

13

Tris was content to hold Samuel in his arms until he felt his heart rate calm down and his breathing even out. My god, that had been the single hottest thing ever. At first, he had been aware of the role he was playing, but as they had progressed, it was like he had slipped into this different persona. Even then, he'd been aware of the need to keep a close eye on Samuel and make sure he wasn't crossing any boundaries, but every little reaction had shown Samuel had been as caught up in it as Tris.

The way he had reacted to that little bit of humiliation, that had been insanely hot. Definitely something they should experiment with a bit more. Next time, because he felt they'd gone deep enough for the first time, and Samuel had clearly reacted emotionally to it.

"How are you feeling, baby?" he asked, softly caressing his back, his hand under his shirt.

"I've never come so hard in my life," Samuel whispered against his chest, and a surge of pride rushed through Tris.

It was ridiculous, of course, to be proud of *that*, but he was. Especially knowing that Samuel had struggled in his relationship with Evan on the sexual level, it felt so good to be able to give him this.

"You were so hot," he said. "The way you bent over for me, I had to restrain myself from taking you right then and there."

Samuel slowly lifted his head and looked at him, his eyes dark, the arousal still visible. "We're not done yet."

Tris frowned. Had he misjudged it? Had Samuel wanted to continue the role play?

"Not the principal scene. Us. Sex." When Tris still looked puzzled, Samuel added, "You didn't think I would leave you hanging, did you?"

"You're under no obligation to get me off," Tris said. "I'm sorry if that sounds crude, but this scene was for you. Don't feel pressured into doing something you're not in the mood for anymore."

Samuel studied him for a few seconds, his face unreadable. "You know, I really appreciate you saying that, if only because I've never heard a guy say that so explicitly before. Usually, there's like a mutual unspoken agreement that both partners need to get off."

Tris shrugged. "I'm not denying I'm hard as rock, but my right hand works just fine. As I said, this was for you, though damn, that was so fucking hot. I'd love to do that again."

Samuel's face broke open in a wide smile. "Same here."

"You seemed to really like the little bit of humiliation," Tris said carefully. He wasn't sure how much Samuel was willing to talk about this. He didn't know that much about it, but it seemed like a kink a lot of guys would feel ashamed about.

But Samuel's smile widened even more, if that was possible. "I did. I never knew I was into that until you went that route."

Tris breathed out with relief. "I hadn't planned it, but when I saw how you reacted to my impulsive comment about being promiscuous, I decided to push it a little further."

Samuel's smile grew cheeky. "You can push me anytime."

Tris chuckled.

"I have a few suggestions where you can push..." Samuel said, winking at him.

"Damn, that's cheesy. Hot, but definitely cheesy."

Samuel slid off for a second, then straddled Tris. With his eyes trained on Tris's, he reached for his belt. "I wasn't joking."

Tris didn't catch on until Samuel had unzipped his pants and taken out his cock, which was wet with fluids. "Where's your lube and a condom, principal, because this naughty boy wants to ride your cock."

Tris swallowed, then slowly pulled open the drawer of the desk, taking out the lube and condoms he'd stashed there earlier. He wanted to ask if Samuel was sure, but one look at his burning eyes made him close his mouth again. Samuel took the lube from him, then pointed at Tris's pants.

"This might be easier if you took those off."

"That would be easier if you weren't on my lap," Tris said with a laugh.

Samuel rolled his eyes at him. "You always have to have the last word, don't you?"

But he was smiling as he slid off Tris, leaving a trail of dried cum in his wake. Tris quickly got rid of his pants, then decided he really didn't want to fuck with a shirt and tie on either and took those off as well. Samuel pointed at the chair, and so Tris sat down again. With quick moves, Samuel rolled a condom on Tris's dick, slathering it with lube, then kneeled on the floor and with his ass toward Tris, efficiently worked himself open. It was incredibly erotic to see, and Tris made a mental note he should incorporate that in play sometime. They would both love that.

When he'd gotten three fingers in, Samuel rose again and walked up to Tris with a look in his eyes that left little to the imagination. Wordlessly, he stepped over Tris's legs, then grabbed his dick from behind and positioned it before carefully lowering himself. The little sounds that flew from his lips as Tris's dick breached him were intoxicating, and Tris couldn't look away from his face. His brows scrunched, his nose all crumpled up in concentration, and then those full lips went tight with the effort of taking him in.

He slid in slowly, allowing Samuel to set the pace. What a sight it was to see, the way Samuel took him in, still wearing his dress shirt, pullover, and tie. He didn't look young enough to be a schoolboy anymore, what with his beard and all, and yet it added a sense of wrongness that Tris found incredibly hot.

God, he felt so snug and warm around his cock that Tris had to resist the urge to push in hard. But Samuel seemed in a hurry as well, steadily lowering himself, letting out little puffs of breath, until he was completely seated on Tris's dick. When he was, he did a little circular motion, as if he wanted to screw it in all the way.

Samuel closed his eyes for a second, letting his head fall back a little, and Tris was struck all over again by how gorgeous he was. The way he looked now, completely over-taken by the sensations, so lost in lust and the enjoyment of Tris's dick inside him, he was breathtaking. It was a heady feeling that he caused that in him, that the two of them made a connection so strong it affected him this deeply.

Then Samuel's eyes opened, finding Tris's, and he slowly raised his hips, then sank down again. Tris's hands found a spot on Samuel's hips, and he let out a moan. "You feel so good," he said, his voice deep.

"So do you. Your cock really is a thing of beauty," Samuel said, letting out another one of those intoxicating little gasps as he sank down again. "I don't know if I want to ride you all day or take you in hard and deep."

Tris was with him on that, because he didn't know either. On one hand, he was impatient to chase his orgasm, his balls full and heavy. But on the other hand, he never wanted this feeling to end.

"We'll just have to keep doing this until we've tried every option there is," he said, and he wasn't even joking.

Samuel's eyes found his again. "That sounds really good."

They smiled at each other, and then Samuel increased his tempo. Tris loved the slick, dirty sounds of Samuel bouncing on his cock. And bounce he did, finding a rhythm that made him slam down hard, forcing the breath out of his lungs with an audible sound every time he came down. Tris intensified the grip on his hips, helping him raise and lower himself, pushing him down hard on the downward move.

Then that wasn't good enough anymore. He needed to be even closer, to feel him, sense his every breath and heart-beat. So he let go of his hips and gently wrapped his hands around Samuel's neck, collaring him. He tightened his grip just a little, not because he wanted to choke him or even pretend to, but because he wanted to feel that pulse against his hands, sense his breaths that grew labored as he bounced harder.

"Tris..." Samuel moaned, and Tris could feel that against his hands, too. "Need to come again."

"Then ride me till you do. No hands," Tris told him, this

hot, tight need inside him unfurling to see Samuel pleasure himself on his cock.

Samuel made a sound, deep at the back of his throat, that came out like a mix of a moan and a grunt. So fucking arousing. And his body kept moving up and down, rougher and harder, the sounds increasing in intensity. He bit his lip, then let go as his ragged breaths forced his lips apart again. And Tris still held on to his neck, sucking it all in. Inside him, his need intensified, rose, grew until it was so big he felt like he would burst. His skin felt tight, flushed, his balls throbbing and heavy.

"Tris!" Samuel shouted out, desperate now, his voice raw with the effort of his vigorous moves.

"Come on, baby... Ride me. Ride me hard. Make me come..." Tris egged him on, his own voice filled with need and desire. "Let my fat cock split you wide open. Feel how deep I am inside you? Someday, I'm gonna own your ass bareback, because I want to see my cum dripping out of you. Then I just might humiliate you for it a little, tell you how incredibly dirty and filthy you look with a man's cum trailing down your legs."

It didn't make sense that he could be this turned on by his own words, by the visual he painted, but it was the truth. All he needed to do was to imagine what Samuel would look like, and that was enough. His vision went black for a second as he came, his balls unloading with a force that made him gasp for air.

Samuel followed suit, giving a few last, uncoordinated bounces before his cock once again released its load, spraying all over himself and Tris. Tris finally let go of his neck, then opened his arms and allowed Samuel to collapse against him.

"Best sex ever," Tris managed after at least a minute of

heavy breathing for both of them, surprising himself he could even talk after that.

It shouldn't be this easy, being together with someone he'd met only two days ago. And yet Samuel loved being with Tris, experiencing none of the stress he'd had in the first weeks with Evan or with previous dates and boyfriends. He and Tris somehow just *fit*, despite the fact that at first glance, they didn't have that much in common. They came from different worlds, almost literally, and yet the conversation flowed easily between them.

Tris wanted to see some of Samuel's work, so he looked up some clients and campaigns online and showed them to him, getting high praise in return. They talked about architecture, art in general, movies, politics, and more—and discovered they had much more in common than they'd realized. Most importantly, there was an easy familiarity. Samuel felt like he could be himself, not pressured into keeping up appearances.

They had sandwiches for lunch, ordered takeout for dinner, Tris singing the praises of a local pizza restaurant. After eating three slices of the best pepperoni pizza he'd ever had, Samuel had to agree with him. They settled on the couch after dinner, Samuel curling up against Tris, who pulled him close, then draped a throw over them both.

"I'm stuffed," Tris said.

Samuel debated making a joke, then decided it was too easy and raunchy.

"You totally wanted to go there, didn't you?" Tris said with a laugh.

Samuel tilted his head back to look at him. "It was too easy. No fun in that."

Tris kissed his forehead, a gesture so simple, and yet it made Samuel's heart do a little dance. "I appreciate your restraint."

Samuel sank back against Tris's chest, mulling the last forty-eight hours over in his head. His life had been upended, and yet where he'd expected to feel pain and grief, he felt lighter, happier. Shouldn't he at least miss Evan? Was he fooling himself by rushing into this, using it as an escape from reality?

Tris pushed against his forehead with his index finger. "You have a worry frown."

Should he be honest with him? Samuel's first instinct was to pretend he was fine. No man wanted to hear about an ex-boyfriend, right? But then he reconsidered. Part of his issues with Evan had been caused by the fact that he hadn't been honest with himself but also not with Evan. And clearly, his asshole ex hadn't been honest with him. Maybe a little more openness wasn't such a bad idea.

"I was thinking about the last two days," he said.

"If that makes you look so worried, that's not a good sign," Tris said, and Samuel could hear he tried to make light of it but was concerned as well.

"No, not like that," he said quickly. "My time with you has been amazing. But tomorrow is Monday and it's just..."

He stopped, not knowing how to put it into words. It was still so fragile, what they had, and he was scared to break it with the wrong words.

"Tomorrow, we're back to real life," Tris said, his voice warm. "And it makes you wonder if what we have is real and if it can survive that dose of reality."

"Yes," Samuel whispered. "This weekend has been crazy, but also a bubble of just you and me."

"Tomorrow, we go back to our jobs and our lives, and the question is if our bubble is strong enough to add my kids, your ex, both of our jobs, and the distance between us to the mix," Tris said.

It hung between them, the question, before Samuel dared to ask it. "Do you think it is?"

In response, Tris shifted positions and Samuel went with it, so they ended up on their sides on the couch, their faces almost pressed against each other. Tris caressed Samuel's cheek. "I have so much I want to say to you, but I'm scared it'll scare you away."

Samuel swallowed, butterflies exploding in his stomach. "Good scare or bad scare?"

"Good scare. Very good scare."

"I think I can handle it."

"Are you sure? I don't want you to start running because it's too much too fast."

Tris's brown eyes stared straight into his, and Samuel's heart surrendered to the inevitable. He'd never felt like this. *Ever.* With Evan, it had been high stress, anxiety, always worrying he'd do the wrong thing. And yet it had felt so infinitesimally small and limited, their relationship, compared to the two days with Tris. It was like comparing a cocoon to a butterfly, the unfulfilled with the splendor and freedom of how it should be.

He took a deep breath. "I'm sure," he said, his voice soft. "Because I think I could love you sometime soon."

He didn't even have time to worry if he'd given away too much, because Tris's reply was instant. "I think I'm already in love with you."

Samuel's heart felt like it would burst and his whole

belly was doing somersaults. "We suck at this whole *taking it slow* thing."

"We really do."

He only had to lean in an inch and so he did, their mouths melting in the sweetest of kisses, all unhurried and perfect. Samuel was floating—no, soaring, more like it.

"I want you to meet my boys," Tris said.

"I want you to meet my parents," Samuel said, smiling.

"No more moving slow."

"No. I've been stuck long enough. I want to jump in."

"I've never felt this way," Tris said with such an adorable, goofy smile that Samuel's insides went all soft again.

"Me neither. There's so much I want to do with you, explore with you."

"We'll make a list. A really long one. And we'll work on it diligently."

"You were so fucking hot as a principal," Samuel said with a sigh, excitement coursing through him as he went over the endless possibilities.

"Wait till you see me as a cop," Tris said, his voice dropping to that seductive low that made Samuel shiver. "Or as a prison cellmate."

Samuel had to swallow again, as his mouth had gotten dry over that visual. "Or you could play my brother who catches me jacking off…"

"Mmm, sounds dirty. I could rant at you for being such a dirty boy," Tris said, his breath dancing over Samuel's skin. "You'd like that, wouldn't you?"

Samuel could only nod, unable to find words.

"Baby, you'll have to tell me how far to take it. Promise me you'll signal me when I go too far."

"We're not even close to being too far," Samuel said.

"So let's make sure we never get there. How about we agree on a safeword you can use to stop the scene?"

Samuel nodded, since the thought had crossed his mind as well. He just hadn't wanted to bring it up out of fear of taking things too far too soon. Well, that ship had left the harbor for sure now. "How about indigo? It's my favorite color."

"Sounds good."

"I'm gonna cancel the background check on you," Samuel decided. "It feels so distrustful and that makes no sense after what we've shared already."

Tris put a quick finger on his lips. "No. I'm fine with it. More than fine, in fact. I want you to have no doubt whatsoever about me, about us. I have nothing to hide, so please, I want you to do it."

Samuel kissed him again for that perfect answer, and this time, the kiss lasted minutes, the two of them tangled up in each other.

"One more thing," Tris whispered against Samuel's lips. "I want you to set up an ironclad contract of some kind that makes sure I can't touch your money in any way. I don't ever want to be accused of being after your money."

"I know you're not," Samuel said, surprised at the depth of emotion in Tris's voice. "You didn't even know who I was at first."

"Others may think differently, and I want something legal in place that dispels them of any notion. I understand that dating you comes with some public attention and scrutiny, and I'm okay with that, but that needs to be clear. I'm not some gold digger."

It was official. He'd found the anti-Evan, and wasn't that a comforting thing to know? Still, he couldn't resist lightening their heavy conversation a little, because this time, he wouldn't resist the easy joke. "You can dig me anytime," he said, his smile widening as Tris laughed.

"Dude, that's the cheesiest joke ever," Tris said.

Samuel wiggled his eyebrows. "But I thought you loved digging me."

Tris caught his bottom lip in a little nip that sent a thrill through Samuel's body. "Digging, drilling, pounding, I wanna do all the dirty things to you...and the sweet ones too."

"Can I spend the night?" Samuel asked.

Tris frowned. "I was kinda counting on that, but what kind of non-sequitur is that?"

"I just thought that if I didn't have to leave anytime soon, we could do more of that drilling and pounding you promised me..."

Tris was still laughing when he claimed Samuel's mouth in a kiss that left him panting, and then they were too busy getting undressed to laugh anymore.

EPILOGUE

S amuel rushed through the streets of Manhattan, eager to get home from work. Snow was tumbling down from the sky—big, white snow crystals twirling in their unhurried path. Tomorrow, that pristine, white snow would become a gray, slushy mess, but right now, Samuel loved it. Plus, with the sturdy boots he was wearing and his jeans, he wasn't that worried about getting wet or dirty.

His coworkers had been teasing him a little about his change in style, going from suits to far more casual wear, but the teasing had been good-natured. Hell, more than one of them had voiced their astonishment at the change they'd seen in him overall. Happier, many people had said. Glowing. So clearly in love it would be nauseating if he wasn't so adorable about it, his secretary had commented, which had made him blush.

But tonight, he wanted to wear something more formal. A suit, definitely. Maybe the dark blue one with the lavender shirt that made his eyes pop, as Tris had pointed out. He could wear it with the tie Tris had once used to tie him to the bed when they'd played the boss who'd caught his employee jerking himself off in the office and pleasuring himself with a fat dildo. God, that one had been fun, Tris tying him to the bed and then edging him for two hours before he'd finally allowed him to come.

It was a little worse for the wear, that tie, but Samuel cherished the memories. And he wanted to wear something special for their one-year anniversary. Plus, it was Valentine's Day and Tris was taking him out to dinner, so that deserved a bit of dressing up.

God, he was happy. He'd never thought he could be this happy, that he even had the capacity. Every memory of the trauma around Evan had been wiped from his brain. Oh, he thought of him occasionally, when he was reminded of something they'd done together. But it was more with a distant sense of how he could've ever been so blind, a bafflement at how he had thought that had been happiness. He'd been so stuck, and he'd never noticed until that day.

His parents and brothers loved Tris as well. Tris had been worried about meeting them, he'd confessed to Samuel, fearing that he would be judged not good enough, but Samuel had assured him his family wasn't like that. They wouldn't judge Tris on his money or lack thereof, only on his character. And he'd been right. They'd welcomed him with open arms, and Dean and Paul as well.

Hell, they'd even invited Cara and Colin over so she could meet them and feel safe leaving her sons with them at times, because Dean and Paul had found a soulmate in Samuel's younger brother, Daniel, who loved gaming as much as they did. When Paul and Dean had seen Daniel's gaming room, they'd flat out screamed with excitement and had promptly spent the night because they didn't want to leave. They now tried to organize a game night at least once a month, but usually more often.

And Tris's sons had accepted Samuel as well. It helped that Cara had been nothing but supportive from day one, encouraging Samuel with little tips to help grow closer to the boys. It turned out Paul loved drawing comics, and as soon as Samuel found out, he'd sat down with him to create a comic together. He might've ended up in graphic design, but he still loved to draw, and he'd spent hours drawing comics as a teen. Dean had been a little harder to crack, but they'd bonded over a love for movies.

No, Samuel's life was perfect. Well, almost perfect. All that was missing was that technically, he was still living in his apartment, while Tris was in Jersey. Samuel understood that he didn't want to move, what with his kids being in school and all. Plus, at first, he'd wondered if a move to Jersey would really make him happy. It was a bit of a commute to work on the days he stayed over—which lately was more often than not. But he missed Tris so much when they were apart.

He spotted him as soon as he turned the corner of his block. Tris was leaning against the door, taking shelter under the apartment's canopy. Samuel's face lit up, like it always did when he saw him, and he hurried toward him. Tris's kiss was possessive, longer and deeper than most people would consider appropriate in a public place, and Samuel loved it. It felt like being claimed all over again, and he let out a little sigh against Tris's lips.

"Hey baby," Tris said in that warm tone he only used on Samuel. "How was your day?"

"Long. Good, but too long. Am I running late, that you're already here?"

He raised his arm to check his watch, but Tris held him back. "Nope, perfectly on time. Let's go."

"Go? I still need to get changed," Samuel protested.

Tris looked him up and down. "No need. You're perfect the way you are."

"I still have my bag," Samuel said, pointing toward his messenger bag with his laptop.

"Do you have your wallet and phone on you?" Tris asked and Samuel nodded. "Then hand this off to Ben and he'll keep it safe till we get back."

The doorman was already hurrying toward the door at Tris's friendly wave, and Samuel held out his bag to him. "Thank you, Ben."

"Anytime, Mr. Norris. Have a wonderful evening."

Tris slung his arm around his shoulders and Samuel nestled against him as they walked, much slower than he had before. "Where are we going?" Samuel asked. It was clear Tris had a destination in mind, but he couldn't figure out what.

"We're gonna go back to where it all began," Tris said cryptically, and when Samuel opened his mouth to ask another question, Tris shot him a look that made him shut his mouth again.

It took him another two blocks to realize it, and by that time they were already at the entrance. Evan's former building, the one where they had met exactly a year ago. "What are we doing here?" Samuel asked, a little puzzled.

"You'll see, baby. Trust me."

Samuel allowed himself to be pulled inside, surprised when the receptionist only sent them a friendly smile and didn't ask for ID, even though he'd never seen her before. Tris didn't stop, but gently led them toward the elevators, where he pressed the button to go up. Questions were burning on the tip of Samuel's tongue, but he held them back. They couldn't be here for Evan, because he'd been fired a few months ago when the cops had arrested him for falsifying paperwork and taking bribes. That had just been the initial charge, but many more had been added after his arrest.

It had been Samuel's lawyer who'd tipped the district attorney off, after discovering some of the shady deals Evan had been involved in. She'd also made sure Evan wouldn't go after Tris in that revenge that he'd threatened with, and the end result had been glorious. Evan had not only been barred from ever practicing law again, but was currently serving a two-year prison sentence. Karma was such a bitch.

The elevator dinged and they stepped inside. Samuel's eyes widened as Tris pressed the button for the twelfth floor. But as soon as the doors closed and the elevator started moving, Tris sank to one knee, and then it hit Samuel, even before Tris reached in his pocket and flipped open a little velvet box that contained a simple golden ring. No diamonds, no fuss, but the real thing.

"Marry me?" Tris said, his voice constricted. "Marry me and move in with me, because I don't ever want to spend another night without you. God, I love you, so, so much."

"Yes." The word rolled off Samuel's lips without a second's pause. "Hell yes."

Tris slipped the ring on his finger, then rose and captured his mouth in a kiss that lasted till the doors opened with a little bling. Then loud applause erupted, and Samuel saw the faces of his parents, his brothers, Paul and Dean, and even Cara and Colin were there.

Tris held their joined hands high. "He said yes!" he announced, as if anyone had any doubt after seeing them.

What followed was a whirlwind of hugs and slaps on his back, kisses and sweet words, until Samuel's head was dizzy with the excitement. Last year's Valentine's Day had turned out pretty well in hindsight, but this one? *Best. Valentine's Day. Ever.*

ASSEMBLY REQUIRED

NOTE FROM NORA

This story was originally part of Heart2Heart 2, where it was called *Helping Hand*. To avoid confusing with my Perfect Hands series (those titles all have "Hand" in them), I have retitled it *Assembly Required*.

PROLOGUE

H elp Wanted

NEEDED: Someone with serious furniture assembly skills and a buttload of patience who speaks IKEA.

I have an Ektorp, various Malms, an impressive number of boxes labeled Bestå, and a whole lot more. What I don't have is the skill to build these. Nor the patience, as it turns out. My apologies to my new neighbors for the curses I let fly, unaware my windows were open. Anyway, if you're fluent in IKEA, I will pay you handsomely to build this stuff for me. Marriage and/or my firstborn are negotiable as well.

Help me, Obi-Wan, you're my only hope...

Text me for details. 555-867-5309.

1

A J Wilson snickered as he read the ad on Heart2Heart. It never failed to amuse him that the very thing that brought him relaxation was such a source of stress for others. Then again, he'd built so many cabinets and beds and dressers by now that he rarely needed the instructions anymore unless it was a new product.

He might as well help this guy out before the dude gave himself a heart attack out of frustration and make a few bucks in the process. His bank account could use it, he'd ascertained that morning. Until he heard back from the dozens of emails he'd sent out with pitches for shoots, this would have to pay the bills. As cute as they were, Mike and Melissa didn't bring in money either—his million Instagram followers who had fallen in love with the little mice notwithstanding.

He shot off a quick text.

AJ: Hej! (That's Swedish for hi.) I'm AJ, and I speak IKEA fluently. I'm also available on a short-term basis, have tons of patience, and ask for a reasonable payment. No need for marriage or babies, Princess Leia. ;)

He put his phone down to grab his camera and take his daily picture of Mike and Melissa and hopefully Mini when his phone pinged with an incoming message. IKEA guy was that desperate, huh? Instead, it was his oldest brother on their group app.

Donovan: Call Mom. She complained to me AGAIN.

Before he could even reply, one of his other brothers, Nicolas, chimed in as well. Oh lord, now it was only a matter of minutes before all four of his brothers jumped on it.

Nicolas: To me too. Call her bro, no joking. I don't need her riding my ass to get you to call her.

AJ: I freaking called her TWO WEEKS AGO!

AJ: Like, I can't go a week without checking in?

Donovan: lol

Nicolas: Sweet summer child

Stephen: He still hasn't figured it out, has he?

Donovan: Nope.

Nicolas: You gotta call every week at least, man.

Dandy: You're the baby. You know she worries.

Ugh, Dandy had to go there, didn't he? He was exactly six months older than AJ, and he couldn't stop rubbing it in every chance he got.

AJ: Oh shut up, you.

AJ: You call her every other day, you little brownnoser.

Dandy: Yeah, and I ain't getting any messages from my brothers that I need to call her, now do I?

AJ: All right, whatever, I'll call her. Sheesh.

Donovan: Good boy.

Dandy: Good *baby*, lol.

God, his brothers sucked. He loved them more than anything, but they still sucked donkey balls.

With a deep sigh, AJ hit the speed dial for his mother, walking out to his deck. If he was gonna spend half an hour on the phone, he might as well grab some vitamin S, as his mom always called it. She always said sunshine made you feel better, and well, she wasn't entirely wrong.

"AJ!" The joy in his mother's voice was unmistakable, and for a second, guilt barreled through him. "I was about to sic your brothers on you out of fear you were lying dead in your bathroom."

And...guilt evaporated.

"How are you, other than overly dramatic, Mom?"

He settled into one of the Adirondack chairs he'd built himself and had painted bright red.

His mom huffed. "I haven't heard from you in weeks."

"Two weeks, Mom. I called you thirteen days ago...and I told you it would be a while since I was traveling."

He'd traveled for exactly four days, a quick out-and-back to a London suburb to shoot a gorgeous classic English rose garden, but his mom didn't need to know the details.

"Right, right. What magazine was that for again?"

"A British garden magazine. They're sending me a copy when it's published, so I'll show you when I have it."

"And they flew you in all the way from Maryland?"

"They loved a spread with my pictures in their American sister magazine. That was that wild garden I shot in Connecticut."

He caught movement from the corners of his eyes and turned his head. Ah, his new neighbor was out of the house. He'd seen the guy move in two weeks ago, noting with interest that he was not only single—at least, he was moving in by himself and AJ hadn't spotted a significant other—but made his gaydar go off. And he was exactly AJ's type. The chances of them being a good fit sexually were low, as always, but he could damn well hope.

So far, he hadn't actually spotted the man outside after his move. That was a shame because with that house, he had bought himself a gorgeous garden that had been meticulously maintained by the previous owners. Granted, Mrs. Harrison's fondness for birdhouses had been a bit over the top even for AJ's tastes, but she'd had a great eye for color. In months like this, the middle of July, that garden was an explosion of purples and pinks.

"I worry about you, baby," his mom said, rounding up what seemed to be another mini-sermon he'd tuned out.

"You should worry about my brothers." He had no qualms throwing them under the bus. They'd do the same to him. "Did you know Donovan broke up with his girlfriend?"

"He did? You boys will be the death of me. How can I raise five boys and not have a single wedding to plan, huh? Not even one grandchild..."

He grinned. "Don't look at me for the latter, Mom. I miss the necessary equipment to get pregnant, and you know girls are not my thing."

"You need to find yourself a nice boy and settle down."

AJ let out a mental sigh. He had zero interest in *boys*. He wanted a *man*. But at the same time, he didn't want to *be* a boy either, which was the role most men he met wanted to push him into. The cute twink who bottomed for them. The boy to their Daddy, the submissive to their dominant, the one on his knees. Oh, he didn't mind being on his knees, but on *his* terms. When he *chose* to, not because some guy got off on wielding his physical strength over someone half his size.

No, he wanted a man who was big and strong and yet willing to let AJ be himself. A fucking unicorn, that's what he was looking for. Something that didn't exist. But right now, he'd settle for a hookup, because he could use it, that was for sure.

Maybe with a man like...well, like his new neighbor, for example, who had taken off his shirt and was now performing a series of yoga poses in ways that showed off his body. His big, furry body, which was strong yet soft in all the right places. He had dark hair that looked like he needed a haircut and a little scruff on his chin. AJ couldn't make out the color of his eyes from that distance, but the whole package was hella attractive. Now, *that* was what his ideal man looked like. *Yummy.*

"All my gray hairs are because of you boys." His mom was still going strong.

"You love us, Mom, and you know it. You chose us, hand-picked us."

"And you guys remind me of that every single chance," she shot back.

He'd been the last addition, the last boy Brody and Elaine Wilson had adopted from foster care. At four years old, he'd lost his mom and dad in a car accident when they were on their way to pick him up from pre-K. With no other relatives to take care of him, he'd ended up in foster care until the Wilsons had taken him in. He was their fifth lost boy, as they called it, and they'd loved him as one of their own, just like his four older brothers.

His mom was the most overprotective mom that ever mommed, but she loved them fiercely, and god help whoever tried to hurt them. She'd been notorious among their friends and teachers, many of whom would ten times rather deal with his laid-back dad than with his mom, who could incinerate you with one look.

"I love you, Mom." The familiar mix of love and gratitude welled up inside him. He could bitch all he wanted, but at the end of the day, he knew beyond a shadow of a doubt that she loved him. And so did his brothers.

"I know you do. Now work on that wedding, would you?"

AJ thought of the ad he'd replied to with the marriage option thrown in and grinned. He'd better not tell his mom. She'd start planning the wedding right away.

His eye fell on his neighbor, who had bent over in a downward dog, his ass toward AJ. Mmm, such a damn perfect ass it was…a gorgeous, firm butt that begged to be kneaded and would jiggle perfectly when fucked. Marriage was still a long ways off, but maybe he could introduce himself to his neighbor first?

"How are the little mice?" his mom asked, and AJ launched into a tale of the latest adventures of Mike, Melissa, and baby Mini.

2

One more try, Las promised himself. He'd give this motherfucking piece of shit IKEA crap one more shot at cooperating before he threw money at that crazy guy who'd answered his ad. Why anyone would volunteer to build this was beyond him, but there were all kinds of crazy people. This AJ definitely belonged in that category, though his Star Wars reference had been cute.

Las flipped through the manual—and there was a charitable description for something that didn't even include words, for fuck's sake—back to the first page. The picture clearly showed he had to put what would become the bottom of the dresser with the two little holes to the front, right? Then why wouldn't it fit when he tried to screw the thingamajiggies in?

Oh, wait, maybe he needed to flip it upside down. Did he have it the wrong way up? He tried again, his muscles cramping as he held the two slabs of wood at a ninety-degree angle with one hand, while twisting the screws—those were the right screws, weren't they? Just when he thought he had it, the doorbell rang, startling him enough to let go, which made the whole thing collapse yet again.

"Motherfucking son of a gun!"

Oops. His windows were open. Again. He shook his head as he pushed himself to his feet, almost tripping over the IKEA box on his way to the front door.

"Oh, for fuck's sake, you piece of shit!"

Oops. He cringed as he opened the door, expecting another eighty-something neighbor with freshly baked cookies. His neighborhood might have been overwhelmingly comprised of senior citizens, but holy hell, these women could bake.

"I'm sorry for the cussing..." he started as he opened the door, but instead of a gray-haired lady, there was a slim guy with messy dark curls and a pair of brown eyes that sparkled. "Oh....hi," Las said lamely.

"Hi." The guy didn't even bother to hide his amusement. "I'm your neighbor. I take it things are not going well today?"

Las dragged a hand through his hair, which had to be sticking up in every direction by now. It was a hundred degrees out, and the AC guy wasn't coming in till tomorrow to fix the AC that had worked fine when he'd bought the house. He was sweaty, hot, and not at all looking his best, which sucked because he'd hoped to make a better impression on what seemed to be his very gay, very cute neighbor.

"I'm having a difference of opinion with my newly bought IKEA furniture." He extended his hand after quickly wiping it on his cargo shorts. "But it's nice to meet you. I'm Las."

"The struggle with IKEA seems to be going around. I'm AJ."

Las frowned. "AJ?" Why did that name sound so familiar? Then it hit. "You wouldn't happen to be the AJ who texted me about being available to build IKEA stuff, would you?"

It seemed unlikely, if only because AJ didn't seem like the type. He looked like a ballet dancer with his slim, graceful body. Then again, a lot of men looked slim and graceful next to Las.

AJ's eyes grew big for a second. "I am. So that's you? That's a funny coincidence, but it does explain the stream of colorful curses I heard through your open windows."

Las cringed. "Yeah, sorry about that. I'm not used to having the windows open...or anybody able to hear me."

"No worries. It's nothing I haven't heard or said before. Wanna show me what you're building?"

Relief bubbled up inside Las. "For real? I don't even have AC, man. It's a fucking oven in here."

AJ frowned. "Your AC broke down?"

"It never worked. I mean, it did when I bought the damn house, but when I actually moved in and wanted to turn it on, it never kicked in."

"It turns on and doesn't cool, or it doesn't even turn on?"

"It's completely dead."

"Mind if I take a look? I'm good with stuff like that." AJ probably added the latter because Las hadn't been able to hide his surprise at that offer.

"Dude, if you can fix my AC and build my IKEA stuff, I will marry you and have your babies," he said, and he wasn't even sure he was joking.

AJ's face lost the slightly sour expression he'd gotten when Las had shown surprise at his skills. "I'll keep that in mind. Let me look at the outside unit first to see if anything looks weird."

Las followed him as he confidently walked around his

house, then crouched down in front of the AC fan. "Hmm, nothing strange here. Let me look at your breaker panel. Maybe it tripped a breaker. Or the Harrisons turned it off because they did that every time they went on a trip. Mr. Harrison was terrified of things turning on by themselves and running up a huge electric or water bill, so he always shut everything off when they left for vacation."

With a sinking feeling in his stomach, Las realized he'd never even considered that. Hell, he wasn't even sure where his breaker panel was, but AJ seemed to know, since he marched straight for the garage where he pushed Las's bike aside and opened the gray metal door to the panel.

"Yup, they switched it off. I guess you hadn't tried to do laundry yet because the washer and dryer are switched off as well." He flipped the three switches on. A hum sounded, and then the AC kicked in, the unit making a rattling sound before settling into a faint rhythm.

"Oh god," Las said. "You should really consider my marriage proposal."

AJ chuckled as they walked back into the house, where a cool breeze danced over Las's overheated skin.

"Now show me your stuff."

Las couldn't help lifting an eyebrow at that remark because hello, double entendre much?

AJ smirked. "Not *that* stuff, neighbor. Let's start with an IKEA date before we move on to the naughty bits, hmm?"

3

AJ felt Las's eyes on him as he worked on the second Malm dresser. They really weren't hard to put together when you'd done it a few times. He'd built at least twenty by now, so he didn't even look at the manual.

"You do this for a living?" Las asked.

"No. More like a side hustle." He checked if the metal rails for the drawers were aligned before tightening the screws. "I'm a nature photographer, but I don't make enough with that yet to support myself."

"A photographer? That's cool. So you travel a lot?"

"When I have assignments, yes. I do a lot of work for garden magazines, and that does bring me to some exotic places. How about you?"

Las smiled. "I'm the opposite because I rarely leave my house. I'm a writer—a science fiction author, actually."

AJ looked up from the screwdriver he was wielding. "An author? I read sci-fi, so have I read your books?"

Las's cheeks grew red, and AJ's heart did a funny little

jump at how adorable that bear of a man looked with a blush. "Maybe? I don't know. I write under I.H. Legos."

The name sounded familiar, but where had he heard it before? "The Trouble on Katoom series. I have it on my Kindle, but I haven't gotten to it yet."

Las's blush deepened. "Thank you? I mean, I hope you'll like them." He waved with his hands, clearly uncomfortable. "It's always so weird to meet people who read my books. I never know what to say."

AJ grinned. "I have the same with fans of Mike and Melissa who gush over their pics."

Las's eyes grew big. "That's you? You take those pics?"

Las knew about Mike and Melissa? Oh god, that was unexpected. AJ nodded. "Right in my backyard, man. You can see their little house from your deck, I bet."

"You're kidding me. I want to see!"

Gone was the slightly embarrassed, blushing guy from before. Instead, his eyes gleamed as he got to his feet and headed out to the deck. AJ made sure the half-built dresser would hold on its own, then followed him out.

"It's right in that corner." He pointed to the mossy area where he'd built the little Hobbit-like structure for the mouse he'd found in his yard one day.

Much to his surprise, Mike—as he'd named him—had loved AJ's construction and had moved in instantly, bringing his wife Melissa with him. AJ had taken pictures from day one, opening an Instagram account for it on a whim, and before he knew it, people from all over the world were following the adventures of Mike, Melissa, and the latest addition, baby Mini.

He'd kept adding to their abode, beautifying it with patches of moss and flowers until it looked like a little piece of heaven. By now, the mice were used to him and happily posed for pictures in exchange for some nuts or peanut butter.

"I can't believe that's you. I love those pics. That baby is the cutest little mouse I've ever seen."

It was endearing to hear this big guy gushing over mice. "Thank you. You're more than welcome to stop by some time and see them up close."

A big smile spread across Las's face. "Really? I would love that."

"Sure thing. Early morning or dusk is best to catch them. Now, let's head back in and work on your *stuff*."

"You're not gonna let that go, are you?"

AJ grinned. "Not unless something better comes along. If you wanna marry me, you'd better get used to my teasing. I have four brothers, so it's what I do."

"Four brothers?" Las held the patio door open for him, then slid it back closed behind them. "I can't even imagine."

"No siblings?"

Las shrugged. "Nope. I was the last-chance baby of an academic couple. My parents are both professors in English Literature."

AJ cringed in empathy. "And you became a sci-fi author. How did that go over?"

Las jammed his hands into the pockets of his jean shorts. "Let's just say the word *disappointment* wasn't mentioned, but it was clearly implied."

AJ plopped back down on the floor next to the half-finished dresser. "That sucks, man. My brothers tease me mercilessly since I'm the youngest, but we have each others' backs. If someone were to hurt me, I swear they'd come down on them like the Avengers."

"My relationship with my parents is...complicated. They mean well, but they're a little much."

"You do you, man. You gotta do what makes you happy, not your parents."

The smile was back on Las's face as he leaned back against the couch, having found a spot right next to AJ on the floor. "I love writing. My office is my happy place."

"Good for you. I love photography. I don't mind this, honestly, but I can spend hours with my camera and never get tired."

"I can't believe you do this sort of thing for fun." Las shuddered. "I got so frustrated I was ready to return all of it and buy something else. Which reminds me—make sure to keep track of your hours so I can pay you."

AJ looked up. "You're not paying me. We're neighbors."

Las shook his head, his mouth setting in a determined look. "You can't do this for free. This will take you the whole day to finish."

AJ looked at the packages that still had to be built. "Probably, but that's fine. I had nothing else to do today."

"Nope, that does not work for me. I can't let you do this for free."

AJ had to smile at the earnestness in his tone. "Feed me throughout the day, and we're all good."

Las scrambled to his feet. "Oh god, I forgot to offer you something to drink. I'm the worst host ever. Sorry. What can I get you?" He checked his watch. "And are you ready for lunch yet? I can have some delivered. Just tell me what you want."

"If you have a Coke, I'd love one. And I could eat something, but you can make a sandwich. No need to order something on my account."

"Oh hell no, I'm not making you a sandwich."

It sounded so resolute and abrupt that AJ frowned. Had he said something wrong?

"No, not because I don't want to! Well, I don't want to, but not because... Let me start over. I'm the clumsiest guy on the planet. See this?" He pointed at a nasty scar that ran across his kneecap. "I needed surgery on my knee after tripping over Legos. That's how clumsy I am. There's no way I'm doing anything involving knives when someone else is around. God knows I'll cut off a finger or something."

AJ blinked at the barrage of words. He'd tripped over Legos and needed surgery? How did one...? *Legos.* That was his pen name. I.H. Legos.

"I hate Legos," he said slowly. His face broke open in a wide smile. "I.H. Legos. I hate Legos—that's your pen name. Oh my god, that's insanely funny!"

He burst out laughing, doubling over when Las rolled his eyes at him, before joining in with a slightly embarrassed grin. "It's not very subtle, but it's heartfelt."

"I love it! It's so freaking hilarious. I guess you didn't want to use your real name, since it's rather unusual. At least, I've never heard Las before."

Las's smile tightened. "It is unusual. Something else to thank my parents for."

His tone alerted AJ something more was going on. Should he ask? "Does it have a meaning to them? Is it something from literature?"

He tried to think of a classic book with that name but came up short.

"It's not my full name. They named me Legolas," Las said between clenched teeth after a pause of several seconds.

AJ's eyes widened. "Oh god. I take it they were Lord of the Rings fans?"

"They worship Tolkien at a level that worries me sometimes."

"So you shortened it to Las?"

AJ's hands rested now. He was too invested in this story to keep working on the dresser, which was almost done anyway.

"As a kid, everyone called me Legos. And they thought it was funny to keep buying me Legos, so every birthday, all I got were Legos. I had a whole room full of Legos that I was forced to play with. To this day, I hate them. I hate them with the fire of a thousand suns."

AJ fought hard to keep his face in neutral and not show the huge grin that threatened to erupt on his face. "Gotcha. No Legos for you."

Las's face relaxed, and a soft smile played on his lips. "Now that I've shared about my embarrassing childhood, what would you like for lunch?"

4
———

They shared Chinese, AJ wolfing down an impressive amount of orange chicken before he finished off the rest of the General Tso's chicken Las had left.

"I'm a growing boy," AJ said with a quick grin.

Las held up his hands. "Go for it. I need to be careful. I'm sitting all day, so it starts adding, you know?" He patted his stomach, which had been flat once upon a time, but could now charitably be described as soft.

AJ's eyes flashed with something wild. "I like a little padding on a guy."

Las swallowed, something stirring inside him. "Yeah?"

AJ put down his fork, then slowly wiped his mouth off with a napkin. He gave Las a thorough once-over, and a tingle meandered down Las's spine.

"Mmm." AJ's voice dropped low. "Very much so."

There was a way to segue into more, Las knew it, but his brain wouldn't come up with anything. How was it possible that at thirty-four, his flirting game was still a disaster? Because AJ *was* flirting, he was sure of it. He stared at him.

AJ's brown eyes were dark and heavy, completely focused on him. "D-do you want anything more to drink? Another Coke?"

AJ's mouth pulled up in a slow smile that made his belly go weak. "Do I make you nervous?"

Oh god. Las had to swallow again before he could answer. "I suck at flirting."

That smile widened, AJ's eyes sparkling now. "At least we've established that you recognized I was flirting. That's progress."

"For someone who makes a living using words, I'm horribly inept at using them in actual conversations," Las admitted.

"Well, we know you can curse up a storm."

"Not very effective for flirting, I've discovered."

"And you have verbal diarrhea at times, like the whole explanation of why you wanted to order lunch and not make it."

Las groaned. "Really? You needed to remind me of that?"

AJ leaned back in his chair, folding his arms behind his head. "You also have online flirting cred because that whole marriage thing in the ad? Total flirting."

"I was desperate! Plus, I never thought anyone would actually answer."

"So what you're saying is that you're not desperate enough yet to flirt with me. Got it."

Las's eyes widened in shock, until he saw the laughter in AJ's eyes. "Considering it's been a while since I...you know... I should be desperate enough."

Oh god. Where had his brain-to-mouth filter gone?

AJ's hands came forward as he leaned on the table, slightly cocking his head. "Define *a while*."

"You first," Las shot back, hoping AJ would be embarrassed as well and that would be it.

AJ shrugged. "Not that long. A few weeks, maybe?" He seemed to think. "Yeah, last time was in some club in Phoenix when I traveled there for a shoot. It was one of those random bathroom hookups, but man, it was satisfying."

Las could never understand how people could talk so casually about sex. His best friend, Cory, was the same. They never batted an eye, not even when describing some sexual encounter in graphic detail—which they only did to rile up Las. It must have been his rather prudish upbringing that still made him blush every time the word *sex* was even mentioned.

AJ cocked his head. "Your turn."

Las swallowed, avoiding the brown eyes that were focused on him. "It's, erm...it's been a while longer than you. Like, a few months."

When AJ didn't say anything, Las looked up, meeting a pair of raised eyebrows, a silent request for more info. God, there was no way out of this, was there?

"Ten months. It's been ten months."

"You haven't had sex in ten months," AJ said slowly.

"That depends on your definition of sex. I mean, my right hand still works."

Way to dig that hole deeper and deeper. At this rate, he'd end up in Australia.

AJ grinned. "Glad to hear it. But dude, what the actual fuck? Ten months? Why?"

Las blew out a slow breath. He could have said it was too personal because in a way it was, but despite the embarrassment, he liked that AJ asked. It had been a long time since a guy had been interested in him enough to even ask. That was all him, of course. It was hard to meet people when you rarely left the house.

"I find it hard to navigate," he finally said.

"Sex?"

"Dating, sex, all of it."

"Isn't that why they invented Grindr? What's hard to navigate there?"

He should've known AJ wouldn't let go.

"You know what? I'm gonna continue building your Malm, and you're gonna sit with me and explain," AJ said, and Las found it easy to do as he was told.

"You're quite bossy." If he hadn't been watching AJ, who had already picked up a screwdriver again, he'd have missed the flash of hurt on the man's face.

"So I've been told."

He didn't like it, being called bossy, but why? There was something there, Las thought, something far deeper than he could ask. "I like it." AJ looked up to meet his eyes. "I like that you're bossy and in charge."

"You do?"

"Yeah." He thought of their earlier conversation about AJ liking a little padding on a guy. "Very much so."

The left corner of AJ's mouth pulled up. "Glad to hear it. Now, talk to me about what's so hard about scoring a hookup."

A chuckle escaped from Las's lips at the lame double entendre, but then he sobered. How could he put into words what he hadn't even fully grasped himself? It had taken him a long time to realize what the issue was. No, not an *issue*. There was nothing wrong with him. It was how he was wired, he thought, repeating what Cory had told him a thousand times. They were the only one he'd been able to discuss this with. Then again, Cory knew a thing or two about being different.

"It's okay if you don't want to talk about it," AJ said, his voice warm and understanding. It was the last little push Las needed.

"I'm not what men expect considering my body type and age. In sex, I mean. Sexual roles or whatever you want to call it."

AJ looked up from the dresser, his eyes narrowing as they scanned Las's body again. Las waited, knowing AJ was smart enough to figure it out. And there it was, the flash of recognition in his eyes. But instead of saying the platitude Las had expected, AJ said something else entirely.

"Neither am I."

either am I.

AJ hadn't even hesitated in baring himself. How could he not, after what Las had shared? It had been the easiest thing in the world to admit what was usually a struggle for him, no matter how open he was about sex.

"Then you know navigating a hookup isn't that easy," Las said. "How do you do it?"

AJ shrugged. "Oral sex and hand jobs. That's where it doesn't matter much."

Las breathed out audibly. "Yeah." There was a lot of emotion in that one word.

"That doesn't do it for you?"

It didn't come easy to Las, talking about sex; that much was clear by now. But AJ didn't think Las wanted to stop talking. It was more that he struggled with it, with the embarrassment, his cheeks flushed and his eyes frequently avoiding AJ's.

"I l-like bottoming," Las said, followed by a soft sigh of relief, as if he was proud he'd said it.

AJ kept his focus on the dresser as he put in the last two screws. "It's much more intimate."

Las hummed in agreement. "I like that intimacy aspect. And I suck at oral."

AJ bit his tongue to prevent himself from making any of the jokes that jumped into his mind, but luckily, Las let out a laugh himself. "God, that was horribly worded."

"I deserve recognition for not making any jokes," AJ pointed out, which made Las laugh even more. It was a wonderful sound, this happy, carefree laugh, which rumbled through the room. He didn't laugh enough, AJ decided. A constant sadness hung around Las, like a thin veil that surrounded him, clouded him.

"There are certain tricks and techniques to it," AJ said.

There, all done with the dresser. He tested each drawer again to make sure it opened and closed smoothly, then nodded in satisfaction. He moved over a few inches to start on the next project, which Las had already removed from its box. Ah, the Besta storage system. That one was easy.

"I'm sure there are, but it's not like I can go anywhere to take lessons, you know?"

AJ opened his mouth, then closed it again. He'd better not.

"You were gonna offer I could practice on you, weren't you?"

AJ looked up, grinning. "The thought crossed my mind."

"How selfless and noble of you."

"Always happy to take one for the team."

"Such a hardship too, having someone suck you off."

"Well, you said you sucked at it, so I mean, I'm sure there's some suffering involved."

There was that happy laugh again that did funny things

to AJ's insides. God, he was a sucker for wounded souls, and there was no doubt Las belonged squarely in that category.

"What's next? You're gonna offer to fuck me?"

All the oxygen left the room as AJ's head came up with a jerk.

The images flooding his mind right now. Las underneath him, that full, round ass of his open wide for him...his soft, furry body writhing on his cock...the sounds he would make. AJ's cock grew hard in seconds, and he put the screwdriver he was holding on the floor before it dropped out of his hands, which felt clammy and weak.

Las's cheeks flushed crimson red, his eyes darting from left to right. "Oh god..." he groaned. "I... Forget I said that. My filter clearly is malfunctioning today."

"Do you want me to?" Las kept looking everywhere but at AJ. "Las, look at me."

It took a few seconds before Las lifted his eyes, and AJ had no trouble spotting the mortification there. Still, Las raised his chin ever so slightly. "I don't need your pity."

AJ scoffed. "You think it would be a pity fuck?" His eyes held Las's, demanding he keep eye contact.

"What else could it be?"

Las's voice, soft as it was, cut deep. This man had been wounded badly. AJ crawled over to him, still holding his eyes. "Las," he said softly. "Didn't I tell you you're exactly my type?" When Las's eyes went down, AJ put a gentle finger under his chin. "No, don't look away. You're hot as fuck in my book. Why would fucking you be a pity thing for me?"

Oh, that sigh Las let out. It drifted out but crawled inside AJ, penetrating his heart, which got all mushy and soft as a result.

"Because...because look at you. You're gorgeous and flirty and clearly experienced, and I'm...me. I flat out admitted I suck at this, so why the hell would you voluntarily pick me?"

Words tumbled through AJ's head. Words that explained his attraction to Las, both physical and emotional. Words that could maybe convince him how serious AJ was. But maybe he needed something other than words.

He leaned in and brushed his lips across Las's. The man's eyes went wide, but he didn't pull back. AJ cupped his cheek before moving in again. He covered Las's lips with his own, gentle and careful, wanting to give Las every opportunity to retreat. Instead, he opened for AJ with a sweet sound, a little hum of surprise and pleasure that had AJ fired up.

He crawled closer, not letting go of Las's mouth or his cheek, then wrapped his other hand around Las's neck to pull him in deeper. He tasted like sunshine, warm and happy, the taste humming through AJ's veins. Another soft gasp had him push Las's body backward, and the man went willingly, lying down on the floor. AJ rolled on top of him, covering that big body with his much smaller one.

"AJ..." Las groaned, and AJ pulled back to meet his eyes.

"This okay?"

Las nodded, his lips still wet and swollen from kissing. "Yes. Very okay."

AJ's heart did a funny tripping thing, and he swiped those soft lips with his thumb. "Wanna kiss some more?"

Las nodded again. "Please."

When asked so nicely, how could he refuse? Not that he wanted to. He fused their mouths together again, catching the happy sigh Las let out. He lazily explored Las's mouth, sinking into him until he didn't know where he ended and Las began. The kiss had him hard as iron in his shorts, but butter soft on the inside, where his stomach was going all fluttery.

His eyes had slipped closed long ago, caused by a need to focus on that taste, that feeling of those lips against his, that tongue that wanted to be chased, to be captured. Las was so pliant in his arms, so willing and sweet in his surrender, allowing AJ to set the pace, to lead. There was no fight for dominance here, no alpha posturing. Las was apparently happy to submit to a twink half his size, and that knowledge buzzed through AJ's veins.

"AJ…" Las whispered, and AJ pushed himself up. Las's green eyes met his, something burning there, fierce and more confident than before. "Did you mean it?"

AJ's mind scrambled to figure out what *it* referred to. "Wanting to fuck you?"

He willed Las to keep eye contact. "Yes." His voice was a hoarse whisper, but he held AJ's gaze.

"God, yes."

Las blinked a few times. "And no pity?"

AJ shifted slightly so his throbbing cock met Las's, which was equally hard. "Does that feel like pity?"

Las slowly shook his head. "No. That feels like heaven."

AJ held back a moan. The man had no idea of the effect his words had. He rolled his hips in an agonizingly slow move, which had Las create a delicious sound far in the back of his throat. "Do you want it, baby?"

The endearment had left his mouth before he realized it, but Las didn't seem to mind. He closed his eyes for a few seconds, then opened them again, his Adam's apple bobbing as he swallowed. "Yes."

It thundered through AJ, this sweet surrender, this fierce need that radiated from Las's eyes. The man's willingness was a precious gift, and AJ felt a deep desire to take care of him. "I'll make you feel good, baby, I promise."

Had he ever felt this protective before? He couldn't

remember, but definitely not with someone he'd just met. But Las made him feel so soft inside, so gooey and tender, with feelings he'd never experienced before.

Las looked up at him with complete surrender in his eyes. "I know. I trust you."

Oh god. He was in so much trouble with this man. This wasn't going to be a one-time hookup, was it?

6

L ook, Las was no virgin. He might not have been the most experienced man in the gay scene—far from it—but he'd had sex. Multiple times. Enough times that he knew what to expect. Except AJ didn't follow those expectations at all.

Las had thought he'd go straight for it—no pun intended—but instead, AJ had resumed kissing him. Granted, his kisses made Las weak in his knees, and he caused Las to create sounds he'd never heard from himself before. His skin was on fire, his body feeling like it was too big to be contained, too restless. He twitched, shifted, seeking...something.

Writhing.

That's what he was doing. He'd never writhed before, but he was now, his body shifting and twitching underneath AJ's as it craved more.

"Hush, baby, I've got you," AJ whispered against his lips, his breath dancing over Las's mouth, then his cheek. AJ wrapped his lips around his ear, his teeth gently scraping the delicate line of his ear shell. Las shivered, his hips reaching upward instinctively.

AJ's tongue followed his teeth, and Las had to clench his jaw to keep himself from crying out when AJ licked a hot trail down from his ear to his throat, finding a spot so sensitive it made Las squirm. Then AJ closed his mouth around that same spot and sucked hard. The blood rushed from Las's head for a second before storming back in, making his head spin.

"Did...did you just give me a hickey?" he asked, his voice hoarse.

AJ lifted his head, studying Las's throat before meeting his eyes. "It seems I did."

It was a wildly territorial thing to do, something primitive that Las had always thought was either for teenagers or for men who needed to show their dominance. He'd never thought it sexy. Until now. The idea of AJ marking him made his cock grow even harder, which he would've said was impossible if asked beforehand.

"Should I apologize?" AJ asked.

Las touched the mark on his throat. He couldn't see it, but he felt the tenderness of it, the slight throb that indicated he'd see the result in the mirror that evening. He pictured himself, standing in front of the large mirror in his bathroom with AJ's marks all over his body. His heart skipped a beat. "No." He dropped his hand and turned his head sideways, exposing his throat to AJ. "I like it."

The growl coming from from AJ's mouth was almost feral, and it made Las's blood pump even faster, his heart rate speeding up more. "The things you say," AJ said. "It's making it fucking impossible to go slow."

"Why would you need to go slow? I'm not a virgin."

The look AJ gave him made him melt on the inside.

There was fire there, want, but also something more. Tenderness. Protectiveness. "You deserve slow, baby." The protest that had been on Las's lips died when AJ found a new spot on his shoulder to lick and suck.

Las's shirt was pushed up to facilitate AJ's unhurried exploration of his body, then pulled over his head. AJ's mouth was everywhere, and he had to be ambidextrous, his hands kneading and stroking, touching and pinching, playing with Las until every nerve he had was alive and tingling. The front of his pants was wet, his cock leaking copiously, but Las had stopped caring.

He'd been worried about AJ's reaction to seeing him naked. Well, his upper body anyway. He wasn't anywhere close to being ripped or even toned, but AJ didn't seem to mind. In fact, he let out these approving hums and murmurs as he mapped every inch of Las's body, running his hands through his chest hair, the thick happy trail downward that he'd considered manscaping but had never gotten around to.

He hadn't 'scaped *down there* in ages either, seeing no need as he had zero plans to score. Until now. But every thought of embarrassment or worry over that was gone when AJ slipped a hand under his waistband and reached inside. "Mmm, you're so hard for me..."

Las groaned, the sound impossible to hold back when AJ's hand wrapped around him. Then his thumb rubbed Las's slit, and he moaned even harder.

"So wet already..."

"AJ..."

Las bucked, his hips moving up to pump his cock into AJ's hand. AJ let out a chuckle. "A little more patience, sweetheart. We're not there yet."

Oh god. How slow was he planning to go? Las would spontaneously combust if AJ kept this up. "AJ... Please."

"Mmm, I like it when you say my name like that."

"I'll say it as many times as you want me to, just please..."

AJ pressed his thumb down on Las's slit, hard enough to make his balls quiver for a second. Oh god, he shouldn't *like* that, should he? His mind might have been confused, but his body wasn't, a wave of heat pulsing through him so strong, it felt like he was seconds away from coming.

"Do whatever you want," Las said breathlessly, closing his eyes.

The pressure on his crown decreased.

"God, you're stunning." AJ's voice was low and throaty.

That made Las open his eyes again, and he found AJ staring at him with fire in his eyes. No one had ever looked at him like that, with so much want and need. His heart stumbled, and he was enraptured by the look in those brown eyes. This was really happening. AJ was going to fuck him.

Then it hit him, and the wave of embarrassment was so big, it made it hard to breathe. His cheeks grew hot as his mind raced with how to bring this up with AJ. He had to say *something*. But before he could, AJ's hand stilled.

"What's wrong?"

"Nothing," Las said quickly. It was a bold lie because something *was* wrong, but how could he say this without bringing the whole thing to a grinding halt?

"Baby, I can see on your face something happened, so tell me. Do you want me to stop?"

"No. Yes. No. I mean, I need five minutes."

AJ rolled off him instantly. "Okay."

It made Las's eyes water, this easy acceptance. AJ didn't

even ask questions but simply honored Las's statement
without needing an explanation. It made him want to
provide one all the more, no matter how humiliating and
mortifying this would be.

"I... I haven't had sex in a long time," he said softly.

AJ cocked his head. "You told me."

"I wasn't expecting a hookup." Maybe AJ could read
between the lines?

AJ frowned. "Me neither, but hurray for spontaneity?"

Oh god. He'd have to spell it out, wouldn't he? He sat up,
forcing himself to meet AJ's eyes. "I haven't prepped."

There, he'd said it. He held his breath, waiting for AJ to
reply. He saw it register with AJ, and the man's eyes softened.
"Gotcha. Go take care of it, sweetheart. I'll wait for you in
your bedroom, okay?"

7

AJ waited until he heard the shower run in the master bathroom before he entered Las's bedroom. He smiled at the sparse decorations, his smile widening when he spotted the mattress on the floor. Right, the bed still had to be put together. He'd make sure to get that done today.

After, though. After he'd taken his time with Las. If there had ever been a man who deserved to be treated like a prince, every inch of his body lavished with adoration, it was this gentle giant of a man. He towered over AJ, but his heart was just as big...and so fragile.

AJ had spotted it in his eyes, the mortification when he'd admitted he hadn't prepped. It had been on the tip of AJ's tongue to say he didn't care. Hell, he could've easily wiped him clean a bit beforehand, but he'd felt this was something Las needed to do, something that would cause him embarrassment if he didn't. And since sex was already something slightly stressful for him, AJ had understood.

In a way, it was sweet, him wanting to make sure he was fresh and clean for AJ. He just hoped that the time apart wouldn't make Las reconsider. Then again, he didn't want it to be a heat-of-the-moment decision either. It had to be something Las really wanted, and if a few minutes on his own made him doubt that, it wasn't the right step. Yet.

After grabbing a few packets of lube and a condom from his wallet and taking off his clothes, he installed himself on Las's bed. The temperature had finally come down to a reasonable seventy-four degrees now that the AC had been on for a while. He smiled as he thought about poor clueless Las, suffering in the heat.

It endeared Las to him, Las's sweet clumsiness. It triggered deep protective instincts in AJ that had lain dormant for a long time. He loved how Las made him feel, like he was so much more *man* than he'd ever been before, as caveman-like as that might sound.

The door from the master bathroom opened, and AJ turned his head. Las stood in the doorway, a dark blue towel wrapped around his waist. His chest hair was still damp, water meandering down his torso in rivulets. His hair was a spiky mess, which showed he hadn't checked himself in the mirror. It all spoke of eagerness, a haste to get back to AJ.

"Hi, sweetheart," AJ said, letting his eyes roam Las's body.

"I'm ready," Las said, the words barely audible, then cleared his throat. "I'm ready."

AJ let out a hum of approval, then slowly fisted his cock. Las's eyes widened as he caught the movement, then fixated on AJ's deliberate strokes. A low sound flew from his lips, one that had AJ smiling. "See something you like?"

"God, yes," Las said, surprising AJ.

"Show me." He pointed at the towel. "Show me yourself, baby."

A flash of insecurity clouded Las's eyes before he steeled

himself and unflipped the towel's loose knot, letting the towel glide to the floor. God, he was beautiful, a furry tower of a man, sheer male perfection from his broad, hairy chest to his round stomach, his meaty thighs, and his rather impressive cock jutting out from a nest of dark hair. His balls hung low and heavy, and AJ regretted he wouldn't be able to smell their unique musk since Las had just showered.

AJ had the perfect viewpoint from the mattress on the floor, able to appreciate every detail of the man's body. "Mmm, you're perfect," he purred, letting his eyes feast on Las's body. "I wanna shoot you sometime to capture how beautiful you are in a picture. I'd blow up that picture, hang it on my bedroom wall, and jerk off to it every night."

Las blinked a few times, then laughed. "That's got to be the strangest compliment I've ever received. Thank you, I guess? For being deemed worthy of becoming your wanking fodder?"

AJ grinned, then motioned with a single finger for Las to climb onto the bed. A small shudder went through his body and then he obeyed, sinking to his knees on the mattress. He scooted over to lie down next to AJ, facing him. His knees bumped into AJ's, and their cocks brushed up against each other before he stilled, his eyes carefully meeting AJ's.

"Hi," he said.

AJ suppressed a smile. God, he was cute. "Hi."

Las kissed the tip of his nose, an oddly intimate gesture that made his heart do a little jump. God, he was in so much trouble with this man. Las made him feel all the things, so much more than he was supposed to with a hookup. Then again, this had stopped being uncomplicated sex, hadn't it?

"Do you still want to continue?"

Las's face tightened slightly. "Do you?"

So insecure. So vulnerable. AJ wanted to bubble wrap him. "God, yes. But I want to make sure this is what you want."

Las's face relaxed, those green eyes radiating trust. "Please."

AJ was on him before he'd even finished sounding out the last letter, capturing the sound with his mouth as he rolled on top of him. Las let out a surprised groan that AJ swallowed as he invaded his mouth. How sweet Las tasted, how eagerly he followed AJ's lead. He kissed Las until they were both panting, then started his descent. His hands roamed that perfect body, the smooth planes of skin, the soft curves. Strokes and caresses were followed by nibbles and licks, and he quickly discovered Las loved it when he used his teeth a little.

Las's cock was a thing of beauty, so hard and leaking for him. AJ breathed him in, nuzzling his balls, happy when he could still detect a little of Las's own smell. A big drop of fluid pearled at the tip of Las's cock, and AJ swiped it with his thumb, then held it out to Las to taste before he could even think about it. Las didn't hesitate but opened his mouth and sucked in AJ's thumb. The sucking sound he made, the eager look in his eyes as he swallowed AJ's thumb, shot straight to AJ's cock.

"And you said you were bad at oral?" he groaned, pushing his thumb in deeper. "Look at you, baby..."

Las moaned around his thumb, his eyes meeting AJ's. It was almost like a porn scene, except it was real, and AJ was so fucking hard.

With regret, he pulled his thumb back. How he wanted to feast on Las's body, but it would have to wait until next time. Because there *would* be a next time. One time would not be enough with this man. He'd already snuck under AJ's skin, into his blood, his heart.

He kissed Las softly, then ripped open a packet of lube and spread some onto his fingers. Las's cheeks flushed, and AJ's insides went mushy again. He didn't dally, sensing that would only make Las more nervous, but instead found his entrance and gently pressed with his index finger. Las tensed up, then audibly breathed out and bore down as AJ pushed inside.

"That's it, baby. Relax and breathe for me."

Las's eyes lit up, and AJ felt the tension in his muscles release. Words. Las needed words, which made sense, since he was an author. And so AJ kept talking to him, encouraging him and praising him as he worked him open.

"Are you ready for me?" he asked as he had three fingers deep inside Las.

Las nodded, his cheeks flushed and his eyes glazed over. "Please."

Was there a more beautiful word in the English language?

8

All his nerves were gone. Las felt nothing but eager anticipation as AJ rolled a condom onto his cock, then tore open a second packet of lube and spread it evenly. He'd taken such care preparing him, helping him relax with those sexy words that set Las's body on fire. Whereas before, he'd had trouble sometimes with tensing up, AJ had helped him breathe and feel good. AJ's fingers had brushed his prostate a few times, and sparks had shot through his ass, a promise of what was to come.

He pulled up his legs, grateful for the yoga he did daily, which made him surprisingly limber for a man his size.

"Oh, that's sexy as fuck." AJ kneeled between Las's legs. "Look at you all spread out for me."

Las held his eyes, determined to be brave enough to face him. "Please."

He kept saying it, the only word his frazzled brain could come up with right now. But AJ seemed to like it because his eyes darkened a little every time Las said it, and he got this look on his face like Las was some exquisite meal, and he was starving.

AJ positioned himself, spreading Las's legs wide as he pushed against his hole. Las blew out a breath and bore down. An involuntary moan slipped from his lips as AJ sunk inside him, a testament to the care AJ had taken in prepping him. He halted when he was halfway in, his eyes wordlessly checking in with Las, who nodded. He was fine. Hell, he was more than fine.

Magnificent.   Fantastic. Supercalifragilisticexpialidocious.

That's how he was, closing his eyes as the sensation of AJ slowly burying himself deep inside him became over-whelming. It was fullness, the slight stretch with this amazing tingling of his nerves inside, this sensation of being taken and claimed. It was too much and not enough, and he wanted it to never end.

When he was in completely, AJ waited a few beats, stretched out on top of Las. Their height difference was too big to kiss, but AJ found Las's nipples instead and sucked. Hard. Las's eyes flew open as he shivered. AJ blew a hot breath over his hard, wet nipple, which made another shiver tear through him.

Then AJ started moving, raising himself up on his arms and sliding out all the way before surging back in. It was slow and precise, and Las felt every inch fill him up to that perfect fullness, before AJ pulled back, leaving him feeling bereft.

It was torture, sweet torture. Torture that lit a fire in him that built higher and higher, making sweat pearl all over his body as his breathing grew faster and his heart rate sped up.

"Please," he said again, and AJ had this crooked grin on his face, this slow, sexy smile that made Las's stomach dance, even as the fire inside him roared into an inferno.

"I like hearing you beg," AJ said.

Something hard flashed over his face, as if he was worried he'd said the wrong thing. Somewhere in the back of his mind, Las knew things were going off the rails, that they were saying and doing stuff that didn't fit into a casual hookup, but hell if he cared. AJ made him want all the things, made him believe he could have them. And so Las jumped in, opening up as well.

"You make me want to beg…"

"God, Las…" AJ breathed. He shoved inside Las, hitting his prostate dead on, and Las felt himself hurtling toward his orgasm. His hand sneaked in between them, wrapping around his cock. His dick was throbbing in his hand, almost painful to the touch with how hard it was. A few good strokes, and he would…

Then AJ slammed inside him again, and he lost it. The slight pressure of his hand folded around his cock was enough, and his vision went white as his balls clenched, then released, shooting thick ropes of cum out of his cock. His orgasm was endless, his body shaking with the blinding force of it. AJ didn't move, staying buried deep inside him, as if he didn't want to miss a single tremor that wracked Las's body.

It took a long time for his body to stop trembling and shaking, and when it finally did and he was able to open his eyes again, he found AJ staring down at him with a soft expression on his face. "You needed that," he said, more a conclusion than a question.

Las lifted his head to examine himself and AJ. God, he'd shot his load everywhere. His hand had caught some of it, but he'd done a piss-poor job at aiming, clearly, as spurts had landed on his pecs, on AJ's smooth chest, and even some in his hair. He winced, raising a slightly unsteady hand and wiping a thick drop of cum from one of AJ's curls.

"Sorry," he whispered.

AJ grabbed his hand before he could wipe it off on the sheets, then brought it to his mouth. Las's cheeks heated up all over again as AJ opened his mouth and licked off the cum, sucking on Las's fingers until they were clean. Fuck, that was hot and filthy.

"Mmm," AJ hummed, "delicious."

He carefully pulled out of Las. Wait, he wasn't gonna finish? Had Las done something wrong? His brows furrowed as he did a quick mental check. AJ hadn't come yet, that he was certain of. Didn't he want to? Or had Las fucked up somehow? He couldn't think of anything.

His worries intensified when AJ rolled off the condom and tossed it aside, until Las saw the heated look in his eyes. "You look thoroughly debauched," AJ said.

Debauched. He liked that word, especially if it made AJ look at him like Las was his favorite candy. And it was fitting, he guessed, considering what he must look like, all covered in his own cum, his body still sweaty and flushed from the thorough fucking.

Then AJ wrapped his hand around his own cock and stroked himself, and any self-doubt fled from Las's mind. He could only watch, completely entranced, as AJ devoured Las with his eyes while he jacked himself off. Slick noises danced through the room, interspersed with low grunts from AJ. Las swallowed, growing hard again from watching AJ losing himself to his pleasure.

He was doing what he had told Las he'd do with a picture of him: jacking off. The thought that the view of his body alone was enough filled Las with wonder. Oh, he'd met plenty of men who liked his body, but they'd all wanted him to be the dominant one, to lead, to be their strong man. No one had ever wanted to take care of him like AJ did. No one had ever said his body was their idea of perfection. No one had ever gotten him, until now.

When AJ's breathing sped up and his moves became jerky, irregular, Las did what came naturally. "Please," he whispered, then opened his mouth.

Seconds later, cum hit him on his chin, then in his mouth and on his cheeks. "God, sweetheart, you're perfect," AJ groaned, shivering as he ejected the last bit of cum. "I need to photograph you looking like this, all covered in my cum. I've never seen anything more beautiful in my life."

Las swallowed, then beamed at him. "I've never *felt* more beautiful in my life."

9

They spent the rest of the day together in an easy companionship. They showered, and then AJ built some more furniture before Las decided to take him up on his offer to practice giving oral. It was a solid A-plus for effort, AJ told him, then painted Las's face with cum all over again because swallowing might have been a bit much to ask. Turned out that was a good call.

AJ made sandwiches for them for dinner, which spent chatting over anything and everything, then built Las's bed afterward. When Las haltingly invited him to spend the night, AJ didn't even have to think before saying yes. He fell asleep with Las holding him, knowing that he could easily get used to this.

The next morning, he took Las into his garden to meet Mike and Melissa. It was still early, the garden damp with morning dew. AJ took some sunflower seeds from his little garden shed and led Las to their dwelling in the back of his yard.

"Come sit with me," he whispered and pulled Las down onto the wet grass.

Las immediately sat down, folding those long legs. AJ let out a soft whistle between his teeth, and only seconds later, Mike's head popped up. The little gasp from Las made AJ smile.

"Good morning, Mike." AJ held out his hand and dropped some seeds on the grass. "Where's your family?"

The little mouse cocked his head as if he was listening, then disappeared again. AJ took Las's hand and squeezed it in reaction to a soft sound of disappointment from him. "He'll be back."

He was right. A few seconds later, the mouse scurried out of his little house, followed by his wife Melissa. She took a good, long look at Las as if she realized he was new.

"This is Las." AJ was unapologetic about his need to explain this to two mice. "You'll be seeing much more of him." Las made another sound, and AJ lifted the hand he was still holding and pressed a kiss on it. "At least, I hope so."

He shot a look sideways. Las shifted his attention from Mike and Melissa to AJ, his eyes growing big for a second before they softened. "I hope so, too," he said, and AJ kissed him until they were rolling around in the grass, giving Mike and Melissa something to watch as they made quick work of the sunflower seeds.

By the time AJ had his fill of Las, the mice had long since disappeared again, and the two of them were covered in grass stains and other evidence from their romp. That, of course, led to another shower together—this time in AJ's house, where Las laughed at all the IKEA furniture AJ had, including the exact same bed he'd put together for Las.

The shower resulted in AJ giving a lesson in blowjobs, which, of course, Las had to reciprocate to demonstrate he'd paid attention. Breakfast was easy and relaxed, and since they both wanted to get some work done, AJ carried his laptop over to Las's house and found a spot at the second desk in his office while Las wrote.

Two weeks later, they realized they hadn't spent more than a few hours apart...and celebrated that with another round of sex, with Las bent over the bed and AJ letting loose on him from behind. It was perfect.

Until his brothers started texting. Again.

Nicolas: Call Mom.

Stephen: I can't believe we're having to do this again, bro.

Dandy: How long has it been this time?

Donovan: Two weeks again. That little shit never learns.

AJ: Excuse me for being a little preoccupied...with my boyfriend.

Nicolas: What?

Dandy: Come again?

Stephen: We're gonna need details, little bro. Or we're siccing mom on you.

AJ grinned as he pressed speed dial.

"AJ!" his mom said as soon as she picked up. "What on earth is more important than your mother?"

He could tease her for a bit, but he really didn't want to, not when he was dying to share his news with her. He laced his fingers through Las's and sent him a look that he was sure said everything he hadn't put into words yet. Oh, it was there, this feeling that was so big and all-encompassing. He recognized it for what it was. And it would've scared him probably, if not for the fact that he saw his own emotions mirrored in Las's eyes. No, he hadn't said the words yet, but he would. Soon.

"Mom, I want you to meet someone. His name is Las."

He had to hold his phone at arm's length to protect his

ears from the scream of joy she let out. "Arnold Jedidiah, what have you been keeping from me?"

AJ winced as Las's mouth dropped open before he slammed a hand in front of his mouth and burst into silent giggles. "Arnold Jedidiah?" he mouthed at AJ.

AJ rolled his eyes. "Don't ask," he whispered back.

"Don't ask?" his mom said. "Of course I'm gonna ask. I want to know everything."

Las was finally done laughing and pressed a kiss on AJ's hand. If he was still staying after hearing AJ's name was just as horrific as his own, if not worse, it had to be true love. The soft smile Las gave him, those green eyes so sweet and loving, confirmed it. He'd found his unicorn.

AJ smiled. "It all started with an ad for someone to build IKEA furniture..."

HOT FOR HIS ASSISTANT

This one is for my own humble PA, Vicki. This Boss Lady couldn't function without you anymore. Thanks for your fun idea for this story.

1

*J*ordan's stomach fluttered as he pulled up to the mansion he'd only ever seen pictures of. Finally, he'd find out for certain if Bryan felt the same for him. He parked his car on the...

MATTHEW FROWNED. What was that called again, that area in front of big-ass houses where cars could pull up? It had a name.

He closed his eyes and rubbed his temples as the words flew through his mind. Not the driveway. A square? No, that wasn't it. And the portico was what you entered the house through, like a porch but more classical in style. Dammit, it had a name, but what was it? He hated shit like this, those moments when his brain just wouldn't cooperate.

He didn't have time for this. Two more chapters to go and this book would finally be finished. About damn time. It had taken him a full week longer than planned, and as a result, he was behind on schedule. That didn't make him happy—very little did these days if he were honest.

Somewhere along the way, he'd become a hermit, one of those grumbling men who snarled at the TV and had the social skills of a raccoon. The two grumpy old men from the Muppet Show had nothing on him.

Being an author was a solitary profession, and the fact that he lived in a town so small it didn't even have its own post office didn't help. After he'd become distinctly unhappy living in New York City, he'd thought buying a house out in the boonies, as his brother had called it, would be the right move. It would certainly prevent a repeat of the biggest mistake of his life, aka Geoff. What an idiot he had been. He'd gotten off lucky there, saved only by his instincts. If not for those, he might've ended up in jail.

No, moving in itself had been the right call, but he still wasn't sure if he'd chosen the right spot. Maybe the little town he'd picked was a bit too far off the grid. He loved the peace and quiet, but he'd grossly overestimated his ability to make new friends here. Hell, he barely knew his neighbors. And they hopefully hadn't found out his pen name, which he guarded like Fort Knox. On the plus side, crime was nonexistent here, and he rarely bothered to lock his doors or his car. That had been a big change after New York City.

He was used to the dichotomy by now, being Matthew for most of the day while only switching to Avery when he had to. Funny how Matthew felt much more like his true self now than Avery ever had. Maybe because Avery had fucked up with Geoff? The name felt a bit tainted now, strange as that might sound.

He cracked his knuckles. Right. Back to Jordan and Bryan, the two main characters in his latest book. He still had those last chapters to finish. The grand finale where they'd declare their love and then one last sex scene and a schmoopy epilogue, and he'd be done. A bad boy billionaire with a twist was how he would market it, and the cover his designer had come up with was brilliant.

So, okay, Jordan was pulling up to Bryan's mansion, the one he'd inherited from the English ancestors he'd never known he had. A house that came with a title, just to make it even more over the top. His readers would gobble that up. If he could only figure out what that damn spot was called.

With a sigh, he clicked open the iMessage app. He'd have to ask for help, as much as he hated this.

Bossman: what's that area called in front of a grand mansion? Like, where they used to pull the carriages up?

HumblePA: I don't know... A square?

Bossman: No, not square. It has a word.

HumblePA: Can I point out that square is a word as well?

Bossman: [rolling eyes emoji]

HumblePA: Well, am I wrong? Isn't square a word as well?

Bossman: Of course it's a word, but it's the wrong word. I'm looking for a different word.

HumblePA: Right. I've got lots of words for you, but not the one you're looking for, I'm afraid.

Bossman: You're as helpful as ever. Remind me why I pay you again?

HumblePA: Because you get to dump everything you hate to do in my lap and tell me to do it? [grin emoji]

Bossman: Good point.

HumblePA: I have my moments. Now, may I kindly suggest you get back to writing? That book isn't gonna write itself.

Bossman: You're getting way too cheeky. Someone needs to teach you a lesson.

HumblePA: Leave the spanking for your books, boss. It don't impress me much.

MATTHEW FOUND himself grinning as he went back to work. Those rapid-fire text exchanges with Jace were far more fun than he'd ever admit to anyone. Especially to Jace himself, who'd been his personal assistant for two years now. He'd made himself indispensable, no matter how much Matthew hated it.

He'd call it a square for now and highlight it so he could find the exact word later. Otherwise, he'd get sucked into Googling shit, which would inevitably lead to Googling more shit, and before he knew it, he'd have wasted two hours learning obscure facts that had exactly zero relevance for the book. Hashtag been there, done that.

An hour later, he had everything done except the last sex scene. God, why did he always keep those for last? Few things were less sexy than having to write what was supposed to be a hot scene under extreme time pressure. Being creative there was *hard* enough as it was—har, har.

After all, there were only so many ways to describe tab A being put into slot B, even for an author like him who was known for his steamy scenes. They didn't write themselves, and many of them had required *solid* research, like hours of watching the Ballsy Boys. Being an author really was a hardship. Even more when you could deduct said porn from your taxes as business expenditure, but that was beside the point.

Even after pleasurable and extensive study, one still had to write the damn scenes, and in this case, he had one more tender scene left. Fine, he'd do it the next day. He'd managed almost five thousand words, so surely he deserved a reward, right?

Like curling up on the couch with Campbell's tomato bisque soup and garlic bread while watching The Great British Bake Off. He had no idea why he was so fascinated with it when he couldn't even bake banana bread without burning it, but it was oddly relaxing. And he was wiped, a faint headache brewing from his sinuses, so he needed to chill.

BOSSMAN: Signing off for today. One more scene tomorrow and I'm done.

HumblePA: Let me guess. Gonna watch Daddy Paul Hollywood give someone a handshake for baking a pie without a soggy bottom?

Bossman: You'd kill for a Daddy like Paul, and you know it.

HumblePA: Nah, not my type. Anyway, have you let Eileen know you're sending her the book for editing in a few days?

Bossman: No, but I'll do that before I log off.

HumblePA: I'll check with the designer for the final cover files to make sure you have those on time. Are we doing audio for this one?

Bossman: I love how you say "we" when you mean me.

HumblePA: You say it all the time when you mean me, so I figure this is only fair. We'll call it the royal we.

Bossman: The royal we?

HumblePA: Yes, like royals refer to themselves as "we, the King of The Netherlands" or whatever.

Bossman: Never knew that. But yes, "we" are doing audio, so I'll need the audio cover as well.

HumblePA: Okay, I'll add it to the launch checklist.

Bossman: Thanks. I wouldn't know what to do without you.

THE THREE LITTLE dots popped up, then disappeared again. Matthew frowned. Had he said something wrong? He checked his last few texts. Nope, he'd been nice even. Nothing Jace could complain about. Not that he ever did. In jest, yes, but never for real. The kid—Jace was almost fifteen years younger than Matthew, so he was pretty sure that qualified him as a kid, even though he was twenty-four— worked hard and rarely messed up.

And Matthew hadn't lied. He really wouldn't know what to do without him. In more ways than just for practical stuff. His interactions with Jace were the highlights of his day, and how sad was that? He'd never tell him that. Way too much information. Jace probably had a life—unlike Matthew.

His social media pics certainly suggested he got more action than Matthew did. Well, that was zero, so the bar was low, but still. He'd posted a Halloween pic a few weeks before of him in a super tight Spider-Man costume that had definitely inspired some superhero fantasies in Matthew. He wouldn't mind playing those out with Jace...

But that would never happen. Jace was too young, probably not interested—the kinds of pics he posted of men he found hot certainly suggested Matthew wasn't even close to being his type—and role-play was a thing of the past for Matthew. Too risky.

Finally, Jace responded.

HUMBLEPA: Thank you. That means a lot.

. . .

MATTHEW HAD MEANT it more as a joke, but too late now. If he retracted his statement now, he'd come off as a jerk. And Matthew was pretty sure Jace already thought him an asshat half the time, so no need to add fuel to that particular fire. Jace had a stellar reputation, and plenty of authors would be all too happy to steal him from Matthew given half the chance. Nope, not happening. He'd keep Jace, even if he had to suck up a little to keep him happy.

He grinned. It might have been a while, but he'd always been good at *sucking*. His smile disappeared when he sneezed hard. Ew. He wasn't coming down with a cold, was he? He washed his hands, then sent off a last text to Jace.

BOSSMAN: You're welcome. Now go do whatever it is you do so I can focus on my priorities. It's bread week, so I'm excited.

2

Jace ran down his checklist one last time to make sure he hadn't forgotten anything. Matthew had finished his book—finally, as it had taken him two days to write that last scene—and sent it off to the editor, so that meant Jace's work of preparing the launch started. He'd gotten the two graphics from the designer for the social media posts, he'd found some fun games for the takeover Matthew had later that day, and he'd contacted the winners from the last giveaway. Yup, that was it.

Now if only Matthew would answer his message about the launch plan Jace had sent him, he could set that in motion and cross that off as well. He'd texted him two hours before, but still no response. It sometimes happened when Matthew was in his writing cave, as he called it, though he usually checked in for five minutes every hour. He wrote in sprints, and he made sure to contact Jace between sprints, if necessary.

Vague unrest tickled the back of Jace's mind. It wasn't like Matthew to take this long in responding. Was his power down again? He lived so off the grid that that was a regular occurrence, though he had bought a generator, so that wouldn't keep him offline for long. And even if the cable was out, he had good signal there, and he'd be able to use his cell phone as a hotspot. So why wasn't he responding?

Had Matthew messaged him earlier about being offline? Jace double-checked to make sure, even though he already knew the answer. He wouldn't have forgotten something as important as that. If Matthew knew in advance he'd be offline, he always let Jace know. He'd become diligent at that, and in return, Jace always informed him about appointments as well so Matthew was aware if he was unavailable for a few hours.

Not that it happened often. Jace took his work seriously, and Matthew was his first priority. He'd given him a chance at becoming his PA when Jace had been completely new at it, and Jace had never forgotten it.

Matthew was his only author client, but Jace did work for three other people as their PA. He liked the variety of what he did, and working from home was the biggest plus ever. Hello, pajamas and sweat pants. And in the summer, the sweet relief of AC all day, as Maryland could get brutally hot and humid.

He quickly handled a request from one of his clients, a woman who ran a successful Etsy shop selling handmade signs, then checked in with his other clients. An hour later, Matthew still hadn't replied, and the vague unrest grew into full-blown concern. Matthew had seemed *off* the day before. Distracted and forgetting things they'd already talked about. Was something going on with him? The previous message still showed as unread, but Jace messaged him again anyway.

. . .

HUMBLEPA: Everything okay? Haven't heard from you in a few hours.

TOO DISTRACTED TO WORK NOW, he made another cup of tea, his phone in hand. Nothing. This was so unlike Matthew. He called him, but it went straight to voicemail. That meant Matthew had his phone on Do Not Disturb. Had he forgotten to turn that off that morning? He hadn't sent a good-morning message either. Matthew tended to work late and then sleep in, but he usually messaged Jace when he was up and at 'em. Not today.

Jace checked the time. Past two already. Matthew would be up for at least four hours now. Why wasn't he responding? Maybe others had heard from him? He fired off some quick messages to Matthew's author friends. Half an hour later, they'd all replied...and no one had heard from him.

What should he do? His rational mind told him he was overly worried. Matthew was a grown-ass man at thirty-nine, more than capable to take care of himself. Except for the fact that he could be incredibly absentminded at times... forgetting important events unless Jace reminded him. Matthew called it hyper focus. He'd explained he could get so focused on writing that he literally forgot about everything else. Was that what was happening? Had he simply gotten sucked into writing?

That didn't make sense. He'd just finished a book the day before. He always took off at least two days before starting a new one. Cleansing his head, Matthew called it— he'd do some much-needed chores, tidy and clean his office, and prepare himself mentally for the next book. Jace had learned a lot about Matthew and his work process in the last two years. Apparently, Matthew didn't do much household work between those cleaning sprees. Jace shivered thinking about it.

If only he had a way to have someone check in on him. But Matthew had broken with his family, save his brother, and Jace only knew his nonauthor friends by name. He didn't have contact information for them. Matthew was fiercely private, guarding his real identity with fervor to readers and his pen name to his neighbors. Few people knew both, but Jace was one of them.

Not that he'd ever share that information with anyone. He never even called him Avery, his real name. Always Matthew, just to prevent him from accidentally saying the wrong name. After all, their relationship was purely digital as they'd never met in person. Hell, Jace didn't even know what Matthew looked like. Matthew never posted pics of himself online.

Oh, Jace had conjured up a picture in his mind of a tall man with burning blue eyes and blond hair, long enough that it would curl in his neck. Long, muscled legs and a smooth chest. Like a cowboy. His voice certainly sounded like it, all gravelly and sexy.

Jace had told Matthew he needed to start narrating his own audiobooks, but Matthew had instantly rejected that idea. Too bad. Jace was pretty sure that hearing Matthew read one of his own sex scenes would make him come handsfree. That man's voice just did something to him…and his books were hella hot.

Jace kept halfheartedly trying to get work done, but when Matthew still hadn't responded by dinner time, his worry increased tenfold. Maybe his phone had died? But then he still would've been able to email Jace. Maybe he'd lost power again? Jace bit his lip as he heated up leftover pizza he'd ordered the day before. Nothing about it made sense. Matthew was absentminded, but not careless. He would've made an effort to contact Jace if something had happened.

While eating his pizza, he Googled what Matthew's nearest police station was. They had a sheriff where he lived. Should Jace call them to do a welfare check? It seemed so over the top. If they even took Jace seriously in the first place. Besides, he was risking Matthew's privacy, and that wasn't something Jace would ever jeopardize. No, he couldn't contact outsiders. Not yet.

When bedtime came and Matthew still hadn't answered, Jace's stomach was all in knots. What should he do? He'd have to sleep on it. Wait till the morning. If Matthew was incommunicado for twenty-four hours, Jace would have a reason to act. Until then, he'd have to try his hardest to get some sleep.

It took long before he finally fell asleep, and when he did, he dreamed of blue eyes that pleaded with him for help. And when he woke up at six in the morning and his phone still didn't show a text from Matthew, he straightened his shoulders. He'd have to do something. He wasn't sure what, but somehow he knew Matthew needed him. And Jace wouldn't let him down.

3

H ow had he gotten here?

Matthew groaned as he woke up on the floor, the plush carpet pressing against his cheek. His muscles protested as he tried to push himself up but failed miserably.

He'd been in bed, hadn't he? Then why was he here on the floor in the middle of the living room?

Oh, wait. He'd tried to get to the bathroom to get ibuprofen. He'd actually made it there, but then he'd had to pee, and after that, he'd been too damn tired and disoriented to remember the Advil.

He wasn't sure what was wrong with him, but his body was hurting all over, and no matter what he did, he couldn't get warm. A fever, that had to be causing the shivers running through him, but he didn't have a thermometer. He was never sick. He didn't do sick. Rarely anyway other than the occasional cold. But this felt like something much more serious.

He lifted his head and looked to his left, judging the distance to the bathroom. If only he hadn't been so stupid to buy a house without a master bathroom. Otherwise, he wouldn't have had to cross the living room to get to the good bathroom. The big one rather than the sad excuse for a half bath he still needed to get redone.

Right. Priorities. If he had a fever, he needed fluids. Considering he was already halfway to the bathroom, it would probably be smart to pee again—if he could even pee. He hadn't had much to drink in the last...

He frowned. How long had he been asleep on the floor? It was dark outside, so most likely a good few hours. He'd gone to bed by nine, too tired to stay up, but with a killer headache.

When had he undertaken his trek to the bathroom? It was all incredibly fuzzy. The drum band practicing in his head didn't help matters either. How much time had passed? It couldn't be more than a couple of hours. In all likelihood, it wasn't even morning yet. Maybe six or so? It was winter, so dawn wouldn't break for a while.

But if he was sick, he'd better message Jace and let him know what was going on. Where was his phone? In the bedroom. On the nightstand, where he'd left it. Okay, so... phone or bathroom? He wouldn't have the energy for both.

Bathroom first. Peeing, fluids, and Advil took priority. And who knew, maybe he'd feel better after getting some meds in him and drinking water. He all but crawled to the bathroom, his legs too weak to hold him.

Once there, he pulled himself up by the sink. His hand was shaking as he opened the medicine cabinet and took out the Advil. Thank fuck he had a glass he used when brushing his teeth. He took two tablets, then greedily drunk four glasses of nasty tap water.

He couldn't pee, no matter how hard he tried. That wasn't a good sign, was it? He needed sleep. He'd feel better after napping a little more. He managed a few shaky steps into the hallway, then had to hold on to the wall to support himself. God, he felt like crap. And so fucking cold that his teeth were chattering. Shit, he'd forgotten to put his pajama pants back on. They were still on the bathroom floor. Hell no, was he going back for it. But he did need something warmer.

He had that stupidly warm fleece blanket he'd gotten two years ago when he'd bought the house and had imagined himself sitting in front of the fireplace on cold winter nights, huddled comfortably under that blanket. It had turned out fireplaces were a lot of work, especially dragging all the wood in, not to mention splitting it into manageable pieces, so that had never materialized. And that blanket was way too fucking warm to ever use with central heating. But it would be heaven now. Where had he put it?

By his reading chair. He'd put it in that woven basket, thinking it looked stylish. Well, as stylish as he could pull off anyway. He wavered several times as he made his way over there. Kneeling to get the blanket out of the basket proved to be too much for his muscles, and he sagged onto the floor, muttering something he couldn't even decipher himself.

He needed the damn blanket. He'd never get warm without. With his last strength, he dragged it out of the basket and wrapped it around himself...then closed his eyes and promptly fell asleep again.

He woke up, then dozed off again. Stirred but couldn't keep his eyes open. Why was it so hard to stay awake? He drifted in and out of sleep as time ceased to exist.

Jace. He had to message Jace. The kid would be worried about him. He was a worrier, sweet Jace. Sweet, sexy Jace, who was way too young for Matthew, way too pure and innocent. Who could never know that Matthew had jacked off hard at some pics Jace had posted, showing his body in just a pair of tight shorts. All that creamy skin on display, those smooth muscles, not a hair in sight.

The things Matthew wanted to do to him. Lick him everywhere. Eat him. Defile him. Dress him up as a schoolboy and discipline him. Play Daddy and boy with him. Doctor and patient. Oh, the options were endless, but they all ended with him balls deep inside that peachy ass, spilling his load. Mmm, yes. Jace. He needed Jace.

Not now. When he was better. When his teeth would stop chattering, and he'd stop shaking and shivering. Later.

No, he couldn't ever pursue Jace. Not after what had happened with Geoff. His kink was too risky. What if history repeated itself? Jace seemed sweet, but so had Geoff. But he could dream about Jace... Mmm, such perfect dreams.

His head hurt almost as much as his muscles. And how could he still be cold with that blanket around him?

God, his back hurt. He had to get off that damn floor.

Jace. Jace had to be so worried.

Where was his phone? He crawled to the hallway, dragging the thick blanket with him, then collapsed again, his muscles giving in. And as his eyes sunk close, all he could think of was sweet Jace, who'd become Matthew's best friend and probably didn't even know it.

4

H e was crazy. Certifiably out of his damn mind. And yet Jace didn't slow down as he drove as fast as he dared. He'd left Maryland when the day had just started, and now he was racing through Pennsylvania in his battered but trusted Impreza, beyond grateful for the all-wheel drive that would allow him to keep driving even when he'd hit bad weather. He hadn't even checked the forecast like he usually did, so all he could do was hope and pray he wasn't about to hit snow, now or on the way back.

If he'd be able to return quickly, that was. He had no idea what was going on, and maybe this whole trip was a colossal waste of his time, going beyond his responsibilities and maybe even the boundaries of the complicated relationship he and Matthew had. Maybe Matthew would get so upset with him he'd lose his job, but even that horrible prospect couldn't deter Jace. He needed to know Matthew was okay.

He kept trying to call Matthew, but it went straight to voicemail every single time. He stopped for gas and a pit stop, then drove another three hours. Lunch was a McDonald's Drive Thru where he loaded up on nuggets—easy to eat in the car—and a large coffee.

He made it to Matthew's house in eight hours and forty-three minutes. He pulled straight into his driveway, which was empty. Well, the man had a garage, so that would make sense. No one sane this far north would voluntarily park their car outside, knowing they might very well have to dig it out of the snow.

Jace shivered as he put on his winter coat, then rushed to the front door, where he rang the doorbell. No reaction. Not even a faint sound. He peered through the front door, then through the windows of what he assumed was the living room. But the curtains were pulled, and he couldn't look inside. Everything was dark, not a single light peeping through. It almost looked like no one was home, but how could that be?

His heart skipped a beat as cold fear clenched his stomach. What if Matthew had been in an accident and the hospital hadn't informed anyone? Jace probably wasn't on the list of Matthew's emergency contacts. His brother was the first contact, presumably, and Jace assumed Matthew had friends who were much closer than him. And they wouldn't know to contact Jace.

Should he check with the local hospital? Chances were it wouldn't get him anywhere. He wasn't a relative, so they'd never give him information. No, he needed to make sure first that Matthew wasn't home. For all Jace knew, Matthew could've slipped in the bathtub and knocked himself out. A shiver ran down his spine.

He grasped the front door handle, but it didn't turn. Then he walked around the house, looking for a way in. A stone path led to the back yard, where he found a back door. He tried it. Unlocked! He pumped his fist in victory.

He knocked first, just to be safe, but of course, no one answered. He opened the door, which led into a mudroom where Matthew's shoes lay haphazardly in front of the shoe rack that was right against the wall. Jace smiled. Classic Matthew. He always had great intentions but was usually too distracted to follow through on them.

The mudroom led into a dark kitchen. Jace frowned. The heating was on, which would suggest someone was home, but why were all the lights off, then? He checked his watch. Almost four thirty.

A sound drifted in, and Jace froze. Someone was there. Why hadn't they come to the door? All his alarming thoughts about Matthew getting hurt rushed to the forefront, and he swallowed. "Matthew? It's Jace."

Another muffled sound. He tiptoed into what he assumed was the living room, his eyes needing a second to adjust to the dark. No one there. The sound had come from farther in the house, and he walked into the hallway to the front door, his eyes straining to make out shapes, then stopping on a motionless form on the floor. His heart seemed to stop for a second, then galloped like crazy. "Matthew!"

He rushed over and knelt beside the body wrapped tightly in a blanket. This had to be Matthew, right? He looked nothing like Jace had imagined. Instead of the blond head of Jace's imaginary cowboy, this man had dark hair peppered with silver strands and a strong face lined with stubble. Jace would bet his eyes were brown.

Matthew's eyes were closed as he moaned softly. Jace put his hand on Matthew's forehead. Good god, he was burning up. The man had a high fever. What was wrong with him?

He'd have to wait to find out. First he needed to bring that fever down. Fluids and Tylenol, maybe with some ibuprofen on top to give his body some extra help. And he'd have to get him into his bedroom. How the hell was he going to manage that? He couldn't judge the man's weight accurately, since the blanket covered most of his body, but he was tall and didn't look like he had Jace's slim build. Jace guessed him to be at least two hundred pounds, so how the fuck would he be able to drag him to wherever his bedroom was?

Matthew's eyes fluttered open. "Jace..." he croaked. Then he frowned. "I'm hallucinating. I must be sicker than I realize."

He wriggled his arm out of the blanket. His bare arm. Was he wearing anything? Jace took the hand that reached for him. "It really is me, Matthew. You're not dreaming."

Matthew's frown turned into a smile. "Best dream ever. Pretty Jace. Sweet, pretty Jace."

His eyes fell close again as Jace sat motionless, his heart beating fast. Sweet, pretty Jace? Where the hell had that come from? That Matthew had recognized him didn't surprise Jace. Unlike Matthew, he had posted pictures of himself on his social media, so Matthew must've seen those. But sweet, pretty Jace? What the hell was that?

It didn't matter. Well, it did, but not right now. He needed to get him into bed and help him get better. "Matthew, you need to be in bed."

"Can't. Too tired," Matthew mumbled without opening his eyes.

"I'll help you."

"You're not real. Hallucinations can't help me."

"I promise you I'm very real, but find out for yourself. Come on, dude, let's go."

"Where are we going?"

"Bedroom."

"Nah. I'm not feeling like sex right now. Wait. Who are you?"

God, he sounded all but delirious with fever. "I'm Jace. Your PA."

"Jace lives in Maryland."

"Yes, I do, but I drove here because I was worried about you."

"Why?"

"You weren't answering your phone."

One eye blinked, then the other. "You came because I didn't answer my phone for a few hours?"

God, he was really out of it, wasn't he? "You've been offline for well over a day now. More like thirty-six hours."

"That can't be right."

"It is. You have a high fever, Matthew. Let's get you to bed."

"None of this makes sense," Matthew muttered. "Jace is in Maryland. He can't be here. And I just closed my eyes and took a nap. I haven't slept that long."

"How about we argue later and for now, you just cooperate?"

"You're a bossy Jace. It's hot."

Jace suppressed a smile. Matthew would be beyond embarrassed when he found out what he'd been saying while feverish. "Thank you. You're hot too, but not in the good way. Let's go."

Matthew protested weakly but allowed Jace to help him to his feet. He almost tripped over the blanket he still had wrapped around him, and for a moment, his full weight rested on Jake's shoulders. Jace grunted. Damn, the man was heavy.

"Ditch the blanket," he said.

"I'm cold."

"I'll bring it once you're in bed. If you trip over it again, you'll fall."

"But I—"

"Just do what I ask you. Please?"

Matthew mumbled something that sounded an awful lot like bossy Jace again, but Jace didn't care. Matthew did let go of the blanket, which pooled at his feet.

Oh, good lord in heaven. The man was naked. Completely, utterly naked. Jace swallowed. Perving on a man who was delirious with fever wasn't his finest moment, but hot damn, that body. Not the smooth, sculpted cowboy he'd pictured but a furry bear with a strong chest, a pair of biceps Jace wanted to worship, and softness in all the right places. No six-pack but a round belly and thighs that looked like they would squeeze the fuck out of Jace when they'd...

No. Oh, no. No way. He couldn't go there. He worked for him, and besides, the man was sick. Jace cleared his throat. "Okay, let's do this."

Matthew leaned heavily on him as he stumbled to his bedroom, his big, soft cock dangling between his legs. Mmm, Jace wanted to suck that baby, swallow it deep, it all the way into his throat. Give it the proper respect and attention it deserved. And then he'd take it in. Ride that fat dick until he sprayed his cum all over them both.

His cheeks heated as he caught himself. Again. God, this had to stop. He had to stop. This was...insane. Immoral. And so fucking hot, even if the man's body was all flushed with fever.

He helped him to his bed, a four-poster queen that looked hella inviting. He was fucking exhausted after driving for so long, barely taking time to rest. Matthew all but collapsed onto his bed, and Jace tried to look away as he swung his legs onto the sheets. Okay, he didn't try very hard

—the man's cock was right there—but he'd given it a good two seconds' effort.

He covered him with the comforter. "Don't fall asleep yet. You need fluids and meds."

"I've had Advil."

"How much and when?"

Jace flipped on the lamp on the night table. Matthew's eyes were glassy. "Two. And I don't know, a few hours ago?"

Judging by his state, that could be anywhere between twelve hours and twelve minutes. He'd have to take the risk. An overdose of Advil was damn near impossible, so he'd be fine. "Where can I find it?"

"Bathroom."

"Okay. I'll be right back."

He easily found the bathroom. The pair of dark blue pajama pants lying on the tile floor explained why Matthew was naked. Advil and Tylenol were in the medicine cabinet, and he checked the expiration date. Both still good. Awesome. Now he needed water and something else to drink. If Matthew had been this sick for thirty-six hours, he had to be dehydrated by now, which meant he needed to replenish what he'd lost. And quickly.

Jace rummaged around in the kitchen without much success, then opened a door and discovered a small pantry. Bingo. Storage racks held cans of food and bottles, including a row of Gatorade blue. Perfect. He had to search a little longer before he found a travel mug, the kind that came with a small opening to sip. He cleaned it for good measure —one never could be too careful—then poured in the Gatorade.

Matthew was dozing when he walked back in, and he put a gentle hand on his shoulder. "I'm back."

Matthew's eyes flew open. "Jace."

Was he getting more lucent? "Yeah, it's me. I've got your meds. Sit up for a moment."

He had to help him sit up far enough so he could take the pills with the water Jace had brought. "I'm so fucking tired..." Matthew muttered.

"I know, baby, but stay awake a little longer. You need to drink."

Baby? Where the flying fuck had that come from? Was he getting feverish himself? Or was it the exhaustion speaking?

But Matthew didn't react other than to dutifully drank from the travel mug. He kept sipping until his hand started shaking. Jace took the mug from him. "Good. Now you can sleep."

Matthew crawled back under the covers, his teeth chattering. "I-I'm so f-fucking c-cold."

"I know. The meds will help break the fever."

"Thank you. I know you're not real, but thank you anyway..." Matthew's eyes fluttered shut, and a soft smile played on his lips. "Sweet, pretty Jace. Bossy Jace."

Jace stood motionless, his heart beating fast. He wasn't serious, was he? His words had to be induced by the fever.

Just when he thought Matthew was asleep, he mumbled, "Sexy Jace. Wanna fuck you so bad."

5

Matthew woke up slowly, his head pounding and his mouth so dry every breath hurt. And that wasn't the only place he was sore. His whole body ached, including in places where he didn't even know he could hurt. He licked his lips, but it offered little relief.

The only good thing was that he wasn't cold anymore. In fact, he was sweating like a mother, and sometime in his sleep, he'd kicked off most of the covers, only a sheet remaining. His fever must have broken. The meds must've done their job, then.

The meds. Jace. Had he been dreaming Jace was here? But if it had been a dream, then how had he gotten back to bed? He turned his head, and his eyes found the travel mug on the night table. Not a dream. Jace was really here. How on earth was that even possible?

He pushed himself into a half-sitting position, the best he could manage with his non-cooperating muscles. "Jace?" he called out, his voice barely more than a croaky rasp.

But Jace must've heard it anyway because only seconds later, he hurried in. "You're awake."

"You're real."

Jace's lips curled at the corners. "I am. Not a hallucination."

Had he thought that? What had he said to him? Matthew couldn't remember. "I can't believe you're here." The broad smile on his face made Matthew's insides all warm. Jace had been so worried about him he'd come all the way to... "How did you even get here?"

"I drove."

"You drove from Maryland to here?"

Jace shrugged. "Took me under nine hours. It was fine."

Matthew reached for the travel mug, but his arm felt like lead. Jace immediately stepped in. "I've got it."

He took the mug and handed it to Matthew, who greedily drank until it was empty. "Gatorade?"

"Mmm. My mom always gave us that when we were dehydrated. It has essential minerals and a shit ton of sugar, so that helps too."

"Huh. Smart."

"My mom is pretty damn smart. She's a doctor. A hematologist."

"Wow."

Not very eloquent, but his brain was definitely not firing on all cylinders yet. He opened his mouth to say something else, but a coughing spell had him all but hacking up his lungs until his eyes were watering.

Jace waited patiently until he'd caught his breath, then held out the glass of water. Matthew drank it, the cool liquid wonderfully soothing to his throat. "I think I have the flu."

Jace looked serious as he nodded. "I think so, too. I called my mom, and she said the same thing. You have all the symptoms."

"You should be careful you don't get it."

"I had a flu shot. I'll take my chances."

He should protest more, he really should, but at the same time, he loved that Jace was here. It was awkward as fuck, and three days from now, he'd curse himself to hell and back for giving in to this strange need to be taken care of, but he just couldn't muster the energy to protest.

"Everything hurts," he whispered.

Jace nodded in sympathy, his eyes soft. "I know. You can take your next round of meds. Give me a minute."

Matthew could barely stay awake until Jace came back, but he dutifully swallowed the pills, then fell right back asleep again. He dreamed of Jace, who for some reason was his slave, sitting at Matthew's feet, naked and catering to his every whim. All he had to do was snap his fingers, and there was pretty Jace, wrapping those soft lips around his cock. Mmm, yes, so good.

One more command and Jace bent over, spreading his legs wide and pushing back his peachy bottom, revealing a pink hole that was just begging to be touched. Kissed, licked, tongue-fucked. Eaten out until it was all soft and pliant and ready for Matthew's cock. Fuck, he'd look even prettier with his hole stretched wide open, stuffed to the max with his cock.

He could dress up as a cop and make Jace the guy who got pulled over and offered a blow job to get out of a ticket... Or he'd be the emperor and Jace a slave who wasn't allowed to say no as he was told to please his master. A Daddy, disciplining his boy with a good spanking. Mmm, Jace's bubble butt would look luscious, all red and hot.

Hot. So hot. He kicked off the covers. Why was he in bed? Hadn't he been fucking Jace? Pretty Jace with his slim, smooth body, begging for his touch. Begging for his cock. Jace, who was so willing and eager, so deliciously needy. His hand curled around his cock, which was like iron in his fist. It hurt, touching himself, his body fighting the effort, but he had to come.

"Matthew."

Jace didn't sound happy. Why not? Wasn't he enjoying what they were doing?

"Matthew!"

His eyes flew open. He was on his back in his bed, his hand fisting his cock, which was throbbing and leaking precum. And he was naked, uncovered, the comforter kicked down. Oh shit. Oh shittidy shit.

He yanked his hand back. "Sorry, sorry. I was... I was dreaming."

He scrambled for the covers, but he couldn't reach them. He was so slow, so sluggish. Jace took mercy on him and covered him up, the boy's cheeks fiery red. "You were saying my name," he said, avoiding Matthew's eyes. "Otherwise, I wouldn't have walked in."

"I was..." *I was dreaming about fucking you and getting all horny and jacking myself off.* Yeah, that really didn't sound good, did it? "Never mind," he said lamely. "I apologize."

God, how could he ever face him again after this? Maybe the gods would look down on him with favor and grant him acute amnesia when he woke up again so he wouldn't have to remember any of this. So he could pretend he hadn't been jacking off to super sexy dreams of his assistant. Again.

And if that didn't happen, he could always pretend, right? Just flat out act like he couldn't remember a damn thing. Couldn't remember the dream he'd had, how eager and needy Jace had been, how much he'd wanted to...

Stop. For fuck's sake, stop already.

This whole fever thing sucked. If he kept losing control

of himself, Jace would slap him with a sexual harassment lawsuit.

"I would never do that," Jace said, sounding positively indignant.

Had Matthew said that out loud, about the lawsuit? Oh fuck, what else had he been thinking out loud rather than in his head? He'd better start praying to his ancestors and whatever gods would listen right fucking now if he wanted to salvage this situation. Until then, he'd just pretend he was asleep. That had to work, right?

6

J ace slept fitfully that night. He'd installed himself on the couch, which proved to be far more comfortable than he had expected, and yet he couldn't relax. His mind kept buzzing. Matthew's room was close enough, and he'd left the doors open, but he was too worried about him to sleep. He'd set alarms every three hours to check on him, and Matthew was still restless and mostly out of it throughout the night.

When dawn broke and a ray of sunlight peeped between the curtains, Matthew had finally fallen into a deep sleep. Jace, of course, was wide awake.

He took the liberty of using Matthew's shower. The hot water did him good, and once he'd gotten dressed again, he felt a little more human. A quick check in the fridge told him that Matthew needed groceries, and he made a list of things he'd have to get for the next few days. He wasn't going anywhere until he was convinced Matthew could take care of himself. And judging by how sick he still was, that could take a while.

Matthew had his Wi-Fi password taped to the router, so

that made things easier, and a short Google search later, Jace had located the closest grocery store. No Instacart options here—not that he had expected them. The town was way too small to warrant such a service.

When he walked into Matthew's bedroom, the man was awake, staring at Jace with glassy eyes. "You're really here."

Oh boy, how often were they going to do this? "I am. How are you feeling?"

"Like I got hit by a truck."

"The flu will do that to you. Do you have a thermometer? I couldn't find one in your bathroom."

"I don't need a thermometer. I'm never sick."

"You are now, and I'd love to keep an eye on your fever. But it's fine. I'll get one when I buy groceries."

"You're buying groceries?"

"Dude, your fridge is all but empty, and you're almost out of coffee. I don't know which of those two is worse."

Matthew rubbed his temples. "I meant to go shopping, but I wasn't feeling well."

"You don't say. But no worries, I can manage. Is there anything specific you need?"

Matthew merely blinked. "It's really hard to think right now."

Jace smiled. "I bet, big guy. I'll do my best not to forget anything. But before I go, you need your next dose."

When Jace held out the Tylenol, Matthew didn't protest and dutifully took them with the water Jace handed him. After that, Jace made him drink more of the Gatorade, then allowed him to settle back under the covers. Still naked, but he forced himself not to think of that.

"Get some more sleep," he told him as he walked out. "Sleep is the best medicine, my mom always says."

He was almost in the hallway when Matthew said, "Jace."

He turned around. "Yeah?"

"Thank you. I don't know if I said it already, but I didn't want to forget. Thank you."

Jace sent him a wide smile. "You're welcome. I'll be back as soon as I can."

The benefit of small towns was that navigating was easy, and Jace had no issue finding his way. He stopped by the pharmacy—which was an old-fashioned drug store that sold everything under the sun—to get a thermometer, then headed to the grocery store. Their selection was limited, but they had everything he needed.

"Are you visiting?" the cashier—a woman in her fifties—asked him as she rang him up. "I've never seen you here before."

"Yes. I'm from Maryland."

"Oh, how nice. Where are you staying?"

"With a friend."

She looked at him for a moment as if trying to assess if she could get any more information from him, then went back to scanning his items. "Make sure to keep an eye on the weather, honey. That storm will hit us hard, it looks like."

Storm? What was she talking about? He'd better find out and fast, but he wasn't showing her he was clueless. "Yes, I'm tracking it. Thank you, though. I appreciate it."

"We look after each other here, honey."

Jace thanked her again, then hurried out with his groceries. As soon as he'd put the bags in his trunk, he slid behind the wheel and opened the weather app on his phone. He hadn't even checked it before he'd left Maryland, which, in hindsight, hadn't been smart.

He pulled up the forecast, and a gasp flew from his lips.

Between sixteen and twenty-four inches? Were they insane? That was two feet of snow. And it would hit in two days. If he wanted to make it back before that storm arrived, he'd have to leave the next day. Would Mathew be recovered enough to fend for himself?

He pondered it as he drove back. The man still had a fever, though Jace wouldn't know how high until he could put his newly acquired thermometer to use. But he guessed it was still substantial, and it would linger longer without someone to help remind him to take his meds. Would it go down in a day?

As he let himself in through the front door—he'd found a key in a kitchen drawer—he still hadn't made up his mind. Matthew was still asleep, and so he unpacked the groceries and went to work. As the soup simmered, he put his laptop on the kitchen table and messaged his clients to see if they needed anything from him.

Good thing he had Matthew's passwords so he could post a quick update on his Facebook and Instagram. "Caught a bad case of the flu. Will be offline for a few days to recover. Stay healthy everyone!" he wrote, then double-checked for spelling errors and posted it.

Two hours later, he'd crossed off everything on his to-do list and was doing some research on Facebook ads for Emmy, his Etsy client, when Matthew called from the bedroom. "Jace!"

He hurried in and found Matthew sitting on the edge of the bed, only a sheet draped around him. He was swaying a little, and his forehead was sweaty.

"What are you doing out of bed?" Jace asked, and it came out much sharper than he'd intended.

"Bossy Jace is back," Matthew said slowly, sounding like he was drunk. "I like bossy Jace."

"So we've established. Now answer the question, boss."

"If you call me boss and I call you bossy, it's gonna get confusing."

Jace rolled his eyes. "What's far more confusing is why you are trying to get out of bed when you're sick as a dog."

"I need to pee."

Right. He could hardly tell him he couldn't. Besides, it was a sign he was hydrating again. "Okay. I'll get you something you can pee in."

Matthew frowned. "I'm not peeing in a bottle or some shit. I'll drag my sorry ass to the bathroom like a man."

"I'm not sure what peeing has to do with masculinity, but are you sure that's a good idea? You're not too steady, and you're not even standing yet."

"I was hoping you'd help me."

Oh dear heavens, how was he supposed to say no to that? Matthew looked at him with sad brown eyes, like a puppy that wanted a treat for being a good boy. "Oh, for fuck's sake," Jace muttered. "All right, I'll help. Let's get you some pants first."

"Why would I need pants if I'm going to have to take them off again?"

"I'm not escorting you naked to the bathroom."

"You don't have to be naked."

Jace let out a growl of frustration. "You're deliberately misunderstanding me."

"Of course I am. I'll take my fun where I can get it, especially when I feel like utter crap."

"That's mean."

"No, that's entertainment. Now set aside your delicate sensibilities, please, and help me get to the bathroom. I promise seeing me naked won't scar you for life."

He was infuriating. How could the man be foggy from

fever and yet so sharp? It was the same wit that had become a trademark of his books. "I don't have delicate sensibilities, I assure you. It's not like I'm some blushing virgin who's never seen a cock."

"No? I want to hear all about that while you accompany me."

"I'm not talking to you about my sex life," Jace said as he took position next to him, then helped Matthew off the bed. The sheet slid down, revealing his semi-erect cock.

Matthew looked down, then shrugged. "All that talk about virgins and naked cocks..."

"Just don't get any ideas. This whole thing is all kinds of inappropriate as it is."

They shuffled through the bedroom, Matthew leaning heavily on Jace's shoulder. "Oh, I know I don't stand a chance. I'm not your type," Matthew said, panting slightly.

Jace frowned. "What do you mean? How would you know what my type is?"

Matthew huffed. "Have you seen the pics you post on Facebook? They're all the same kind of guys. Pretty guys. Flawless. Fitness models and personal trainers and guys who chop wood for a living or some shit."

Wow, where did all that bitterness come from? All thoughts of Matthew's nakedness were forgotten as the emotion in his words hit Jace much harder than anything else. "That doesn't mean anything. I mean, of course I post them because I think they're gorgeous, but that doesn't mean they're my type."

"That makes zero sense."

Jace led Matthew into the bathroom, where the man slapped his hand against the tiles and stood still for a moment, his chest heaving with heavy breaths.

"Why wouldn't that make sense? Just because I think

someone is gorgeous doesn't mean I want to date only guys who look like that...or just have sex with pretty guys. Those are two completely different things."

This had to be the weirdest conversation ever. Under Matthew's confusing remarks, Jace sensed a layer he didn't understand, something that sounded far more important and sensitive than the man let on.

"So who's your type for sex, then?" Matthew asked.

Yeah, he could've seen that one coming. Jace's cheeks heated up, but dammit, he refused to feel ashamed for this. He raised his chin. "I'm not that discriminatory. I like sex. If I can find a guy who's single, practices personal hygiene, is not too much of an ass, and knows how to use his dick, I'm game."

7

How the fuck was Matthew supposed to keep breathing after a statement like that? As he inhaled a little too deep, his lungs rattled ominously, the next coughing fit only one wrong exhale away.

"You need to leave," he said.

Jace flinched. "Why?"

The poor kid must think it was because Matthew judged him for his sex remarks. Little did he know. Matthew sighed and pointed at his cock, which was showing his enthusiasm for the whole conversation. "Because I need to pee, and this conversation makes that impossible."

Jace's cheeks grew even redder, which was so adorable Matthew cursed his sick body. "O-okay. I'll be outside." Then he recovered. "And once you're done, we'll put on your pajama pants. No more walking around naked."

"You afraid you're gonna jump me? Too hot to resist?" Matthew couldn't help teasing, even though he knew it couldn't be further from the truth. No matter what Jace said, he clearly wasn't interested in Matthew. Not that Matthew wanted him to be despite the dreams and fantasies he'd had of him and Jace. It would be awkward. Inappropriate even.

"You wish," Jace said, but the words held little force.

"You have no idea," Matthew muttered as Jace walked out.

It took him a few minutes to be able to pee, his treacherous cock preferring to reminisce over visions of Jace on his knees, naked, catering to Matthew's every whim. The fantasy was fueled by the still slightly delirious state of his brain, and he embraced it with all he had. He could be mortified later.

He washed his hands, sweat pearling on his forehead from the exertion. When he opened the door, Jace stood waiting for him, concern painted all over his face. "You okay?"

"Yeah. But about to collapse, so let's get moving."

"You need to put on your..." Jace pointed at the floor, where Matthew's pajama pants still lay.

"I'm pretty sure that if I even try to stand on one leg right now, I'd keel over, so the risk is on you."

Jace sighed. "Whatever. Let's go."

"What's that heavenly smell?" Matthew asked, desperate for a change of subject.

Jace's hands were cool on his skin as the boy steadied him. He leaned on him just a little more than he had to. "I'm making chicken soup."

"You mean heating up chicken soup."

Jace chuckled. "No, making it from scratch."

"You can make soup from scratch? Marry me?"

It slipped right out, and for a second, he feared he'd gone too far, that Jace would be offended. But instead, Jace giggled. "You're that easy, huh? All you need is someone to cook for you."

Matthew grunted as his body protested against the slow trek back to his bedroom. "I basically need a handler, but yes."

"I thought I already was your handler."

It sounded like a joke, and yet the simple remark hit deep with Matthew. Jace wasn't lying. He quickly had become indispensable to Matthew, making his life so much easier in every way. Ever since Jace had become his PA, Matthew had never forgotten an important deadline, had never had to stress because he'd lost overview of what he had to do. His social media accounts were updated regularly, which made his fans happy, and his sales had even increased because his marketing was so much better.

But Jace showing up here because he'd been worried about Matthew topped it all. Matthew might not have told Jace he'd become his best friend—and Matthew had no intention of telling him because how pathetic would that be?—but he clearly meant something to Jace as well. Otherwise, the kid wouldn't have driven nine hours just to make sure he was okay. That went far beyond dedication.

"Remind me to give you a raise after this is over," Matthew said.

Jace made a sound of protest. "I'm not doing this for money."

"I know. That's not what I meant. I just... It was my poor attempt at acknowledging what you've done for me."

"You already said thank you. That's enough for me."

"Oh."

Matthew let that sink in as his lungs hurt with every breath he took. Had he unintentionally offended Jace? It had been an offhand remark on his side, something he'd said to... Why had he said it? Jace was right. Matthew had already thanked him, so why had he felt the need to offer him money? Was he that uncomfortable with accepting help? The thought was sobering.

By the time he was back in bed, he was shivering again, his teeth chattering. "Fever's back," he said.

"Hold on one sec. I've got a thermometer."

Jace rushed out and came back a short while later, still removing the thermometer from its packaging. He made it beep, put a plastic cap on the tip, then put it in Matthew's right ear. "Hold still."

Warmth spread through Matthew's insides. Not the kind of warmth that made the chills stop, but the kind that soothed his heart and made the aches in his body a little easier to bear. How long had it been since someone had taken care of him like that? Years. Many, many years.

"A hundred and two. Yeah, you still have a fever. Let's load you up with more Tylenol."

Matthew nodded weakly. "When can I have some of the soup?"

"After you've slept. This was quite the exertion, so rest for a bit while I finish the soup. It'll be waiting for you when you wake up."

Matthew's eyes drifted shut as Jace walked around in his bedroom, doing god knew what. A cool washcloth was placed on his forehead, and he sighed in relief. "I'm just gonna wash your face," Jace said softly. "You've been sweating quite a bit, and I don't want it to irritate your skin."

He must stink by now, having spent at least two days without washing or showering. Maybe more? He was still fuzzy on the timeline. "I'm sorry I smell."

"You don't smell."

"You're a bad liar."

His voice was weak as sleep was pulling at him. The cool cloth was wonderful, but even that couldn't keep his eyes open. He'd all but drifted asleep when soft lips touched his forehead. "Sleep well, baby. Get better."

8

Matthew was beautiful in his sleep. Jace told himself that he'd set up shop in Matthew's bedroom to keep an eye on him, but the truth was that he couldn't keep his eyes off him as he slept. Creepy for sure, and yet here he was.

He'd fantasized about Matthew in many different ways, but never like this. In his imagination, Matthew had been sexy and suave, a man of the world who could seduce men with a simple look—a player for sure. Maybe because his books were so fucking hot and sexy?

Jace was well aware he had a little crush on him, which was stupid. They'd never even met in person or even seen each other. They mostly texted and messaged with the occasional phone call, but never through FaceTime, Zoom, Skype, or any video conferencing platform. Matthew had stated he disliked those, and Jace had never pushed. He'd been content to dream from afar, picturing Matthew in his mind.

The truth was far more complicated...and yet surprisingly captivating. God, yes, the man was sexy, but not in a slick way. He was rugged, with slightly untamed edges, a little grumpiness, and a lot more hair than Jace had thought. A bear. The man was a certified bear, and while that had never been Jace's preference, he found himself incredibly fascinated by the fur on Matthew's broad chest, the thick happy trail leading straight down to his groin, and his heavy cock, nestling in dark public hair, framed by a set of big balls.

Even thinking about it made Jace lick his lips, and for probably the seventh or eighth time that day, his cock stirred. He'd stopped telling himself to cut it off because it hadn't worked. How could it when he was constantly feeding his weird obsession by studying the man in his sleep?

After the soup was done, he'd poured it into a container and placed it into the fridge to cool off. Then he'd brought his laptop to the bedroom and had set himself up in a comfy reading chair—after he'd removed about a week's worth of clothes. He'd thrown them in the washing machine, along with a bunch of laundry he'd found strewn throughout the house: towels, dishcloths, socks, even a pair of boxershorts on the living room floor.

Matthew was a slob, and what should have turned Jace off instantly instead made the man even more endearing. Every time he'd finished a book, Matthew would sweep through his house like a madman, cleaning left and right, but after that, he'd forget all about it again and focus on his writing. He'd explained that more than once to Jace, who found the concept equally fascinating and worrisome.

Matthew clearly needed someone to run his life so he could focus on writing. And Jace found himself wanting to be that person, now even more than before he'd met him. How silly of him and most likely utterly futile, and yet as he sat there and tried to get some work done, his mind kept wandering off to how good he could take care of Matthew.

He'd always been a caretaker. He'd gotten that from his mom. She'd hoped he'd become a doctor as well, but he'd never had the grades for it. He wasn't stupid, not by any standard, but he wasn't the kind of driven, A+ student who would get into med school. He liked serving behind the scenes, out of sight, just helping people. Tending to whatever they needed.

"Hey," Matthew croaked, startling Jace.

"Hi." He put his laptop down and got up. "How are you feeling?"

"Like I could eat a bowl of that delicious-smelling chicken soup."

Jace smiled, his insides strangely warm at that praise. "You haven't even tasted it yet. For all you know, it tastes like wallpaper glue."

Matthew chuckled, but his laugh transformed into a nasty cough. Jace handed him water, then patiently waited until Matthew had regrouped. "Nothing that smells that good can taste nasty," Matthew said, his voice hoarse.

"Can I take your temperature?"

"Sure."

Jace sighed with relief when he saw the result. "A hundred point three. Much better."

"I feel better."

"It's not gonna last."

Matthew rolled his eyes at Jace. "Spoilsport."

"Just managing expectations here. I checked with my mom, and she said it could take a week until you're recovered enough to be up all day again and another week to feel like before."

"Ugh, great. Just what I needed."

Jace bit his lip. Should he bring up the snowstorm? He had no intention of leaving Matthew on his own to face that, but it didn't seem fair to keep it from him either. "If it's okay with you, I'll stay for a few more days. Just to make sure you're all right."

Matthew pushed himself up, the sheet sliding lower and revealing his chest. Jace swallowed. "I appreciate the offer, but I'm sure I'll be fine on my own again tomorrow. I mean, you have a life to get back to...a job."

"I can do my job from anywhere. That's the beauty of working from home anyway. It doesn't have to be my home."

"Right. But I'm sure you'd rather be home. With your family. Friends. It was super sweet of you to drive all the way here, but I'll be fine, I promise. I'd be happy to reimburse you for your gas—"

"There a snowstorm coming," Jace said. "A big one."

Matthew grunted. "When? And how big are we talking?"

"Day after tomorrow. Up to two feet of snow."

"Holy shit. God, I never should've fucking moved to this town. In the city, I had an apartment where someone else shoveled the sidewalk. Here, I have to do everything myself. My driveway, the path to my front door, everything."

"You won't be shoveling snow in two days. You'd kill yourself with the exertion."

Okay, so maybe he was exaggerating a little, but it was for a good cause, right?

Matthew raised an eyebrow. "Kill myself? Feeling dramatic, are we?"

"Dude, you cough up a lung every time you breathe in too deeply. Imagine how that would go over outside at freezing temperatures when you try to shovel two feet of snow."

"I have a snow blower, actually."

"Same difference."

Matthew's shoulders dropped. "Dammit. I hate it, but you're right. Maybe I could call a neighbor and ask them for help. I think there's a high schooler a couple of doors down who would maybe do it for twenty bucks or so."

Jace crossed his arms. "Or you could stop being so damn stubborn and accept my offer to stay."

Mathew looked away. "I don't like the idea of taking advantage of you."

"You're not. I'm offering."

"It feels that way. You're my PA. This falls far outside your purview."

Jace waited for Matthew to raise his eyes again and meet his gaze. "You know I'm not here because I'm your PA," Jace said softly. Maybe he was giving away too much, but all this talk about what sounded like duty made him crazy. He wasn't here because he'd thought it was his job or his duty. "I care about you."

Matthew licked his lips. "You do?"

"Come on, why else would I drive for nine hours? It's not like it's part of my job description to take care of you when you're sick."

"I really like that you're here..."

Matthew's tone was hoarse, but it held something else as well. A layer of affection that rung deeper than more gratitude. It made Jace open up a little more. "I wouldn't want to be anywhere else right now."

"If that's really true..."

"It is."

"I'd love for you to stay until after the storm."

"It will be my pleasure."

"Really?" Matthew's smile was hopeful as his warm brown eyes met Jace's.

"Yes." Jace took a deep breath. "I really like taking care of you."

"I really like it too," was Matthew's soft reply, and suddenly the air between them crackled. Could this really be happening? Or was he imagining things? And he shouldn't forget that Matthew was sick, still had a low fever. He shouldn't get his hopes up too much.

"I'll heat up some soup for you," he said.

"Will you come sit with me when I eat it?"

Jace's heart was a little lighter again. "I'd love to."

9

When he woke up the next day, Matthew's head had stopped hurting. He felt like he still might have a bit of a fever, but nowhere near as high as it had been. Jace had made sure he kept taking his meds throughout the night, and clearly, they had helped. That or the combination of the delicious chicken soup and the sweet care Jace had given.

Matthew had known his PA was very efficient and detail-oriented. What he hadn't known was that he was a caretaker at heart, who clearly took great pleasure in making sure Matthew had all he needed. He'd brought water, more Gatorade, soup and crackers. He'd wiped down his face again with a cool cloth and had changed his bed linens while Matthew had hung like a sack of potatoes in his reading chair with a sheet wrapped around him. The fresh sheets had been heaven after the sweaty, stinky ones.

Jace had done laundry, had gotten groceries, and he'd asked Matthew for a list of things he needed to do to prepare for the snowstorm. After that, he'd tested the emergency generator, had filled up the oil, and had gotten two five-gallon canisters of gas.

And in between, he'd checked in, made sure Matthew was okay, and had sat by his bed, quietly typing away on his laptop. The kid was about as perfect a companion as Matthew could've wished for...and it made things only harder. It made *him* only harder, especially now that he was recovering from his bout with the flu.

He wanted him. He'd wanted him before he'd met him in person, purely based on the pictures Jace had posted of himself. But god, now that he'd seen him with his own eyes and had experienced his intoxicating mix of sexy and sweet, he couldn't stop thinking about him.

At first, he'd blamed it on the fever. That had certainly triggered his erotic dreams of Jace serving him in every single way. But even now that the fever had mostly subsided, the dreams were still there. They'd become daydreams now, highly sexual fantasies, but they hadn't lessened in intensity. The kink he had buried so deep after what had happened with Geoff had come back with a vengeance, his mind conjuring up countless scenarios he could play out with Jace. He wouldn't, not only to protect Jace but also himself, but how he wanted to.

"Good morning," Jace said as he walked in, that shy, sweet smile on his face.

Matthew pulled up his legs to hide his morning wood. He still wasn't wearing pants, though by now, he had no real excuse anymore other than that he liked the idea of Jace seeing him naked. Not that the boy was even protesting anymore. "Morning."

"Did you sleep well?"

He would have made an excellent nurse. It was another fantasy Matthew had thought of: playing a patient and Jace giving him a sponge bath. He pushed it down. He could flirt with him a little, maybe, and if Jace seemed open to it, have some fun between the sheets once he was recovered, but that was as far as it could go. "I did. How about you?"

"Not bad. Your couch is pretty comfortable."

Matthew winced. "I'm sorry I don't have a guest room for you."

Jace shrugged, his smile not dimming even a little. "It's fine. Like I said, your couch is surprisingly comfortable to sleep on."

The idea popped into Matthew's head so fast he'd opened his mouth before he even realized it. "You should sleep in my bed tonight."

Jace's mouth dropped open. "Excuse me?"

Matthew gestured at his bed. "It's king size. Surely that's big enough for the two of us to share it."

Jace in his bed... Now there was an idea he could get behind, pun intended.

"Don't be... I couldn't... It wouldn't be appropriate," Jace stammered.

"Sweetie, you've seen me naked more than once by now. I'm pretty sure the line of appropriate is far behind us by now."

"Doesn't mean we should continue to push it."

Mathew crossed his arms, suppressing a smile. Jace could be proper in a way that made Matthew want to do very improper things with him. "In my experience, most fun things come from pushing boundaries...hard."

Jace gaped at him, stunned, but then he giggled. "That was the single worst double entendre you've made so far."

Matthew grinned. "Yeah? I thought it was pretty damn funny."

"But seriously, I can't share a bed with you."

"Of course you can. You don't want to, and that's fine, but you can."

"Nothing good could come from that. In fact, I suspect a lot of bad things could happen."

"Like what?"

"Like you pushing those boundaries you're so fond of mentioning."

"I won't push any further than you'd want me to."

Ah, there it was again, that sizzling electricity in the air between them. Did Jace feel it too? He had to, judging by the pretty blush on his cheeks and the way he bit his lips. "You need to stop flirting with me."

"Why?"

"So you admit you're flirting?"

Matthew chuckled. "Of course I'm flirting with you. It's not like I'm shy about it or try to hide it."

"But you can't."

"You know, you keep saying 'can't' when you mean 'shouldn't.' Those are two different things. Why shouldn't I flirt?" Matthew's face grew serious. "Because if you truly object, I'll stop. You know I'll respect your no."

He held his breath, waiting for Jace's reaction. The boy finally let out a sigh. "It's not that, but... I work for you. You're my boss."

"I'm well aware, but it's not like you and I have a traditional boss-employee relationship."

"You could still fire me if things went south."

Matthew frowned. "Do you really think I would do that?"

Jace sighed as he sat down on the bed right next to Matthew. "No. You wouldn't, and I know that."

"Then what's the issue? You already told me you like sex and that you're not demanding a declaration of love. I'll admit I've had a bit of a dry spell, so why not see if we could create some magic in bed?"

He was surprising himself with how much he meant it. No, he could never find more than temporary fun with Jace. The kid was too young for him and Matthew still too fucked up about how his fantasies had landed him in trouble. But they could have some fun together. Some very sexy fun.

Jace studied him. "You're awfully chipper for someone who was delirious with fever yesterday."

"I feel much better. Besides, I wasn't that delirious..."

"You were jacking yourself off, saying my name...and you told me I was sweet and sexy and bossy and that you wanted to fuck me."

He had? Damn. "None of it was a lie."

"You think I'm sexy?"

"I think you're cute and sexy and utterly fuckable." He might as well come clean now, right?

"I can see where you get those catchy oneliners in your dialogue from. This whole spiel is pretty seductive."

"Yeah? Does that mean you're saying yes?"

"What would I be saying yes to, exactly? Like, what's your endgame? Moving in? Getting married? Kids?"

All the blood withdrew from Matthew's face at the sight of Jace's serious expression. Marriage? Kids? Oh god. Had he misjudged Jace? How the fuck did he fix this? Because no way in hell would he ever make promises like that when he had zero intent to keep them. His stomach protested as his mind frantically searched for words. But what words could possibly salvage this?

The corner of Jace's mouth trembled, and then he burst out laughing so hard that the tears streamed down his face. "Your face!" he said between laughing fits. "Oh god, your face... You looked as if you were facing a firing squad."

He'd played him. The realization brought sweet relief as well as a healthy amount of respect. Not many people could pull that off. "You little shit..."

"Oh, admit it. That was comedy gold... I wish I'd been able to capture your expression. Best thing ever."

Matthew laughed along now, the last tension in his body dissipating. "You really had me fooled... Marriage and kids... I should've known you were fucking with me."

Jace's face sobered. "Some day, I'd love that, don't get me wrong. But I know that's not what you're after, and that's fine. I heard you loud and clear, and I'm okay with that."

Somehow, hearing Jace voice the very conclusions Matthew had come to himself made them sound harsh and cold. And disappointing, which didn't make sense at all. "Does that mean you're saying yes?"

"That means I'm telling you to get better ASAP so you can deliver on your promises of fun in bed."

Matthew swallowed, heat flashing through him. "Yeah? Think we'll have fun?"

Jace's eyes were pure fire, and Matthew was hard in seconds, his cock filling so fast it took his breath away. "Oh, I know we will. I've seen your cock, and I've got just the place where you can put that..."

10

Had he capitulated too soon, too easily? Jace still wasn't sure as he watched Matthew sleep again. They'd shared breakfast, and Matthew had napped afterward. Then Jace had served more chicken soup, and Matthew had still been fever-free, so that was progress. Jace had told him to nap anyway, and Matthew had obeyed without protest.

He was healing well. Jace had checked in with his mom, and she'd confirmed he was on track for a speedy recovery. The fact that he was beating it this quickly was proof of a strong immune system.

Jace had gone over all the reasons why he'd been an idiot to agree to Matthew's proposal. Yes, Matthew was his boss, and even though he didn't fear getting fired, it still wasn't smart to sleep with him. It would make their work relationship much more complicated potentially, and Jace would hate to see that change. They'd always been perfectly in tune, and this could mess with that.

But that wasn't even his biggest worry. Hell no. The fact that he'd never met a guy he'd wanted to sleep with for more than, say, a few weeks would be much more of a challenge. He loved sex. He absolutely did. Loved it all. Blow jobs, rimming, getting fucked, and everything else. But never for long with the same person.

Oh, he'd tried. In fact, he must hold some kind of record for the most relationships a guy his age could have...none of them lasting longer than three, four weeks. Something always happened to make him walk away. Or, in all fairness, make the other guy break things off.

They thought he was too needy. He thought they were too boring. They wanted him to stop mothering them. He wanted them to accept that was how he was wired. They asked him to top. He said no, thank you. They claimed he asked for too much sex. He thought sex was part of the deal. They felt he should change his hair, his style, his job, his everything...and he refused.

Yes, he was a walking contradiction. A guy who was a little shy but also quite bossy at times. Someone who was happy to be in the background but still wanted to be seen and put first. He loved sex and lots of it, but he got bored if it was the same thing every single time, like a paint-by-numbers. And why should he feel ashamed he wanted sex? It was what he needed, so what? Also, yes, he was a planner who loved to-do lists and spreadsheets, but he still abhorred routines, especially when it came to dating and sex.

So he probably was too demanding, asking too much. He'd gotten that message over the years. For that very reason, he'd given up on the hope of finding someone he could build a future with because honestly, if he couldn't even keep a guy for longer than month, a lifetime seemed pushing it.

But could he manage to keep Matthew happy long enough to at least walk away as friends? What if Matthew felt the same way about him as the other guys, like he was too...something? Too much of whatever. Or what if he got bored with him before Matthew wanted to end things? Things could get beyond awkward.

But could a man who wrote amazing books like Matthew really be boring in bed? Matthew wasn't just known for his inventive sex scenes but also for incorporating all kinds of kink. He'd written about every kink under the sun, and even though a lot of them didn't appeal to Jace in real life, he loved reading about them. Could someone who wrote so openly and accepting about kink and who focused on people expressing themselves authentically really be close-minded in real life? It was hard to imagine.

A strange sound made him look up, and Matthew was stretching, his face distorted in a wide yawn. "Did you have a good nap?" Jace asked, almost automatically by now.

Matthew turned on his side and faced him. "You should know. Something tells me you were watching me the whole time."

"I was working," Jace protested, embarrassment coloring his cheeks. Had he called it or what? Matthew was already noticing his weird behavior.

"Hey," Matthew said softly, and Jace met his eyes. "I was messing with you."

"Oh. I thought you were... Never mind."

"It's not like I mind you watching me..."

"No?"

"Why would I?" Matthew looked puzzled as he propped himself up on his arms.

"Because it's mothering you or even smothering you, maybe?"

Mathew studied him. "I'm gonna take a wild guess and

conclude that someone accused you of doing that...an ex-boyfriend, maybe?"

Jace hesitated but then nodded. "More than one, actually."

"No chance of that with me."

Matthew's tone had grown serious, much more serious than Jace had expected. "Why?" he dared to ask.

Matthew sighed as he reached for the water on his nightstand and greedily emptied the glass. He wiped his mouth, then put the glass back. "My mother was a prostitute who got addicted to crack when my brother and I were just kids, and I have no idea who my father is. Let's just say that I didn't grow up with anyone taking care of me, so when someone does that for me...it means a lot."

Jace's heart filled with warmth. "Okay."

"Does that make you feel better?"

"Yeah. I'm... I'm not good at holding that part of myself back. It comes so naturally to me."

"So let it out. I don't mind."

"Not even if all we're meant to have is fun between the sheets?"

Matthew's smile was sweet. "We're also friends, aren't we? Pretty sure that taking care of a friend is perfectly acceptable behavior, even without the sex."

"Okay."

"That being said, I do look forward to the sex part."

Jace grinned. "You'll have to be able to breathe without coughing first, big guy."

Matthew sighed dramatically. "I hate it when you get all reasonable."

Jace genuinely felt sorry for him. Being sick was never easy and especially not when you had things you wanted to do. Good things. Sexy things. "How about a shower?" he suggested. "Or a bath?"

Matthew's eyes lit up. "I'd love a bath. Will you scrub my back, then?"

Jace laughed. "Deal. And if you behave, I may even scrub more than that…"

He pushed down his remaining doubts as he walked over to the bathroom and started a bath, throwing in some bath salts he found in the cabinet. He'd have to take the jump and see what would happen. He tested the temperature with his hand, then headed back to the bedroom.

Matthew had worked himself into a sitting position on the edge of the bed. He still had the comforter draped across his waist, but Jace already knew what he'd see once the man would get up. That beautiful cock, begging for his touch. His lips. And if things continued the way they had, he might just get his wish.

Matthew got up without his help, and all Jace could do was stare at the man as he carefully made his way to the bathroom. His ass was almost as impressive as his front, and Jace licked his lips. "Like the view?" Matthew asked over his shoulder, his voice raspy.

How freeing that Jace didn't need to hide anymore. "Very much."

Matthew leaned on him as he stepped into the bathtub, then carefully lowered himself until he'd sunk deep into the water. "God, this feels amazing."

"Want me to wash your hair?"

"Hell, yes."

Jace found shampoo, but before he could squeeze some out onto his hand, Matthew grabbed his wrist. "You'll get all wet."

"I don't mind."

Matthew rolled his eyes at him. "Not the point. Wouldn't it be better to prevent your clothes from getting wet by, I don't know, taking some off?"

Jace chuckled. "Smooth."

"I thought so too. I may be too damn weak to do much, but I'd sure as fuck would love to look..."

The man had a point, and Jace quickly stripped down to his underwear. The low, appreciative noise off Matthew's lips made his belly tickle inside. He put a hand on his hip as he posed. "Like the view?"

"God, yes. You're sexy as fuck."

His first instinct was to offer him a blow job as a reward, but then he caught himself. He had to be careful.

"What's wrong?" Matthew asked.

"Nothing."

"Please don't lie," Matthew said, his voice holding a sharp edge. "You can tell me to fuck off, but please don't lie. I saw something passing over your face, something that made you sad."

Jace's cheeks heated. His shoulders slumped. "Sorry. I didn't mean to, but... I was worried about something."

"Wanna talk about it? My hair can wait."

Matthew's tone was so warm and welcoming that Jace sat down on the bath mat right next to him. "All the kink you include in your books, is that from your own experience?"

"Some of it, but other things I've researched. Why?"

"Do you mean what you write about people expressing their true self? That they should act out how they're wired?"

Matthew nodded slowly as something painful flashed over his face. "Yeah. It's not easy, especially when people judge you for it, but I believe that we can't change what makes us tick, what turns us on or off. So if someone isn't understanding of that, it's time to move on and find someone who is."

"What if you can't find someone willing to accept you for who you are?"

"Then I'd say you have to keep trying..."

Jace smiled, even though sadness lingered in his heart. "You're a true romantic, despite pretending to be all tough and casual."

Matthew froze, and the pain on his face took Jace's breath away. Oh no. What had he done?

11

M atthew felt naked. Well, he *was* naked, but that was his body. Jace's words had bared his soul, and it had made it hard to breathe for a moment. How could Matthew tell him that he had to express his truest self while at the same time admonishing himself to keep that part of his life hidden and closed off? He was a hypocrite, and what was worse, he was wrong in pretending he could wish away his needs and desires.

That, of course, led to a whole different problem. Jace. He had to be honest with him, even if this was mere sex. He deserved that much after showing the depth of his friendship by driving all the way here to take care of Matthew. Maybe Jace would run away after Matthew told him, but if so, at least he'd been honest.

"Did I say something wrong?" Jace asked in a small voice.

"No. No, you said something very right. Or rather, you asked the right questions and forced me to face an uncomfortable truth..."

He reached out a wet hand and cupped Jace's neck. That

simple contact sent a shock through him, but not nearly as intense when Jace leaned into his touch with a sweet surrender that made Matthew feel all the things he never thought he'd feel again.

"I had a boyfriend back in New York," he started. The words surprised him as much as they did Jace.. But once that first sentence was out, it became easier. "His name was Geoff. We met in a club, and at first, we had fun. Great chemistry, hot sex, all casual. I'd discovered I really liked role-play, and I introduced him to it."

"Role-play," Jace said slowly. "Like you described in your book 'He's the One.' I loved that one... So hot."

Matthew nodded, pleased with that reaction. "We tried different scenarios for the next few months, and it went well. He seemed into it. But he wanted more than I was ready for...or maybe more than I was willing to give. He knew I was a writer and he'd realized that I was doing well financially, though I never told him my pen name, and he wanted to make things more official...and more permanent."

"But you didn't," Jace said.

"No. In hindsight, I'm still not sure why, but maybe I had picked up on his intentions unconsciously. I don't know. We had a huge fight over it, and he was furious. We made up, but things weren't the same. And then..."

Matthew swallowed. How could it still hurt so much two years later? He let out a sad sigh. "He suggested we'd try consensual noncon play..."

"Oh god..." Jace whispered.

"Yeah. I'd never done it before, and I should've never agreed, but the idea was arousing, and so we set things up..."

"He set you up."

Matthew nodded. "He did. He filmed the whole thing

without my knowledge, and if I hadn't sensed something was off and had aborted, he might've pressed charges against me... I could've ended up in jail because I had no proof whatsoever it was play and not real."

"Matthew... I'm so sorry. He betrayed you in the worst way."

"He did. I still don't know why he did it. I safe worded out before things got real because it felt *wrong*, and I've never been more grateful for listening to my gut...but it left its marks."

Jace sought his touch, and matthew let out a breath of relief. "Have you ever played again since? Role-play, I mean?"

Matthew shook his head. "I was too scared. But that's why it hit me so hard when you asked me about it because it's how I'm wired. I love playing out these fantasies. In fact... I've had quite a few about you and me."

Jace jerked his head up. "Yeah?"

"Do you want to know?"

"I think I do...very much so."

"I've had one where I was an emperor and you were part of my harem and you had to do everything I told you..."

Jace's eyes darkened. "That sounds...hot."

"Mmm, yes. Or where I was a doctor and I had to give you a very thorough exam."

"I'm all for that."

"You're a nurse giving this poor patient a sponge bath..."

"Not sure that's a fantasy anymore, considering what we're doing right now."

"It ended with you giving some special attention to my cock...washing it with your mouth, your lips, your tongue."

"I think that could be arranged..."

Matthew's cock was rock hard as it poked out of the

water. "I have so many things I want to do with you...once I'm better. So many fantasies I'm dying to try."

"I'm game," Jace whispered. "I'm game for each and every one. But promise me one thing..."

"What, baby?"

Oh, how easily that word flew off his lips.

"Promise me you'll tell me if I become too much."

"Too much what?"

"Too needy. Too mothering. Too demanding. Too anything."

"I promise, but I don't think you have anything to worry about."

"Then promise me one more thing..."

"Anything."

"Promise me you'll hurry the fuck up in getting better."

That was a promise Matthew could easily make. "Don't kiss me yet, not until I'm better...but could you touch me, please?" he begged.

"Touch you where?" Jace said in a teasing tone.

"Anywhere. Everywhere."

His body was on fire, but Matthew wasn't sure if it was because his fever was back, because he was hot from the bath, or because the anticipation was killing him.

"Let's get you out of this bath and back in bed."

Matthew opened his mouth to protest, then snapped it shut. Oh, he loved the gleam in Jace's eyes. He'd better see what his assistant had planned. Jace's hands were soft as he toweled Matthew off, paying special attention to Matthew's cock, which showed its enthusiasm for that treatment. Leaning on Jace just a little, Matthew made his way back to the bedroom, where he dropped back in bed. Jace helped him get comfortable, and then he stared at him with hungry eyes.

"Can I?"

"I don't know what you want, but the answer is yes. Hell yes."

Still dressed in his underwear only, Jace climbed onto the bed and stretched out on his stomach, his face inches away from Matthew's cock. "You said I couldn't kiss you...not your mouth, at least. But I could kiss you here?"

Matthew almost strained his neck with how fast he nodded. "Yes. Please, yes."

Jace didn't make him wait long. His first touch was soft, his warm lips pressing light kisses on Matthew's cock. Even that seemingly innocent touch made him moan. Jace's tongue peeped out, and he licked, kissed some more, sucked as he explored Matthew's cock and balls. So damn good.

Jace repositioned himself, grabbed Matthew's base with his right hand, and looked him in his eyes. "You may wanna hang on."

Matthew didn't even have time to respond. Jace sucked him in hungrily, first the tip, but then his whole cock, swallowing him like it was nothing. The groaning sound Matthew let out was loud and almost embarrassing, but how could he hold it back when it felt this amazing?

Jace's cheeks hollowed as he sucked hard, pulling Matthew's dick all the way into his throat, humming happily. He was greedy, eager. No forced pleasure here, no reluctance, but genuine excitement, a desire to please.

Matthew laced his hands through Jace's hair. "Tell me if I get too rough."

He thrust up into his mouth, carefully at first, but when Jace took it with ease, harder. His muscles protested, but he ignored the pain. It wouldn't take long anyway, not when his cock was being sucked so expertly.

Jace's left hand cradled his balls, rolling them between

his fingers and gently squeezing with perfect pressure. Oh, he was good at this. So damn good. Matthew couldn't wait to see what other talents the kid had.

He shivered, his body tensing as his orgasm approached. His balls tingled and drew up tight against his body, firing up all the nerves in his body. His thrusts were irregular now, almost frantic. "Baby," he groaned. "Oh god. I'm... I'm coming."

He let go of Jace's head, giving him the option to pull back, but he didn't. Matthew's vision went black as he came, pouring his release down Jace's throat. "Oh fuck, baby... fuck.... So good. God, your mouth..."

Jace's movements slowed down and became gentle as he cleaned Matthew's cock, suckling until it was completely soft in his mouth. The smile he gave Matthew as he let go was blinding. "Yummy."

"You're gonna be the death of me, aren't you?"

"You're about to find out."

12

I t took a week for Matthew to be up to his old energy levels again, but Jace loved the time they spent together. They hung out, talked, and Matthew shared ideas for future books with him. They watched TV and movies, discovering they had similar tastes. Jace introduced Matthew to Stranger Things and The Mandalorian, and Matthew showed him the wonders of Buffy. It had been a good trade-off.

The snowstorm buried them in almost two feet of snow, but Jace managed to keep the driveway clear with the snowblower. Matthew was upset he couldn't do anything, but Jace waved his protests away. He didn't mind, even though his muscles hurt from the exertion the next day.

He demonstrated his blow job skills again and managed to make Matthew beg, an accomplishment he was damn proud of. Once again, Matthew lamented his inability to return the favor. Jace dryly pointed out that getting a massive coughing fit from a blow job was not exactly sexy, and that was that.

Matthew entertained him by sharing his fantasies, all

kinds of different scenarios they could act out together. His imagination knew no limits—the Viking and the thou-protesteth-too-much Englishman. Two Scottish clan chiefs secretly meeting, bare asses under their kilts. A neighbor, catching the kid next door spying on him, and teaching him a lesson. Jace had been so aroused he'd jacked himself off in front of Matthew—a first for him. Matthew's eyes had eaten it all up.

On day eight of his stay, Jace woke up where he'd awoken the six nights before: in Matthew's bed. Jace was a massive snuggler, but Matthew didn't seem to mind. He hadn't commented on anything Jace had done so far—not in a negative way, at least. He'd praised Jace into high heavens for what he'd done in terms of cooking and cleaning and doing laundry, and Jace had loved it. He'd never felt so appreciated in his life.

"Morning," Matthew mumbled in his ear, his voice deliciously low and sexy.

"Morning. Did you sleep well?"

Matthew kissed his ear. "Never slept better. Love having you in my bed, baby."

That, too, had changed. What had started as purely sexual, a mutual agreement to keep it light and casual, had grown into much more. Hell, they hadn't even reached the sexual stage yet aside from those blow jobs, but Jace hadn't minded at all. Neither of them had said it out loud, but somehow he knew things had changed.

"Love waking up in your arms," he said with a happy sigh.

"What's on today's schedule, my esteemed PA?"

Jace giggled. "I don't have anything planned, Bossman. It's Sunday, and I've got your social media posts scheduled already, so we're off from work for the rest of the day…"

Matthew nibbled on his ear lobe, sending shivers down Jace's spine. "Oh my goodness, whatever will we do with ourselves?"

Jace let out a hum of pleasure as he cuddled closer to Matthew. "Can your lowly PA make a suggestion?"

"Anything, baby. Anything."

Two hours later, Jace knocked on the bedroom door. "Your Majesty?"

"Enter," Matthew called out, sounding positively arrogant.

Jace's stomach fluttered as he opened the door, completely naked. "Your humble servant, Your Majesty."

He peeked from underneath his eyelashes. Matthew lay spread out on the bed, as naked as Jace was, pillows supporting him on every side. His face was harsh, like the cruel emperor he was playing, but warmth shone from his eyes.

"Finally," Matthew snapped. "I've been waiting forever. On your knees, slave. I want to see you crawl."

Jace instantly dropped to his knees. He'd never thought himself submissive, not in the traditional way anyway, but the humiliation of what he was doing made him hard as a rock. His cock bobbed as he crawled toward the bed. "Yes, Your Majesty."

"Silent, slave. Your mouth isn't for talking. It's just to shove my cock in."

Oh god, that was hot as fuck. Who would've thought he was into humiliation? Well, a little anyway and maybe only because he knew this wasn't real. But still, the pretending thrilled him, and he had never felt so alive.

He kneeled next to the bed, then waited. "Ride me, slave," Matthew ordered casually. "I'm too lazy to do the work, so you'll have to do it for me."

He forced himself to stay silent as he climbed onto the bed. Matthew's eyes probed him, giving him the gentlest of nods as Jace sent him a half smile to signal he was okay. Hell, he was way more than okay. If he had known how hot this shit was, he would've tried it years ago.

He'd prepped himself well, at Matthew's urging, and so Matthew's command didn't surprise him. He'd known Matthew might not be up to a whole lot of physical exercise yet. Matthew looked at him impassively as Jace lifted his leg.

"Don't face me. I want to see your ass, not your face. You were selected for your bubble butt, slave. Show me how it swallows my fat cock, how you get split wide open..."

The man knew how to use words, that was for sure. Jace's cheeks heated as he turned around and straddled him. Matthew's hard cock bumped against his ass, already slipping between his slick crack. He reached behind him and positioned himself, taking a deep breath.

It should feel impersonal, getting fucked like this, and yet it didn't. Matthew had asked three times if Jace was sure he was okay with it, but he truly was. It felt right, that they'd start this way, that they'd carry out what they had fantasized about together. They'd shared their latest test results, allowing them to go bare, and Jace was *so* ready for this.

Matthew's cock pressed against Jace's hole, and he bore down, letting him in. He lowered himself steadily, his body welcoming the intrusion like an old friend. He bit his lip, but a moan slipped out anyway.

Matthew immediately picked up on it, of course. "You're a slut for my cock, aren't you, slave?"

Should he answer? No, he wasn't allowed to speak. But oh, he wanted to. He wanted to answer that hell yes, he was. He'd been looking forward to this for a week, and he wasn't ashamed of it.

"Mmm, yes. Such an innocent face, but we know better, don't we, slave? We know you're a needy one, so desperate for my cock that you'll do anything for it..."

Jace's body trembled as he rose and sank back down, the tip of Matthew's cock dragging along his prostate, sending tingles all through his ass. He did it again, then again, and then he fucked himself on that cock, abandoning any pretense that he wasn't chasing his own release.

Matthew snapped his hips, driving deep inside him, and Jace's eyes crossed. Glory hallelujah, the man really did know how to use that amazing cock. They worked in tandem now, Matthew meeting his downward moves with hard upward thrusts, flesh slapping against flesh. They were both panting, and for a fleeting second Jace worried about it being too much for Matthew, but then his own pleasure took over again.

His cock leaked, slapping against his stomach every time he sank down. He grabbed it with his right hand, but Matthew's hand shot out, circling his wrist. "Nuh-uh, slaves don't get to pleasure themselves. Hands off."

Was he fucking serious? The question burned on his lips, but he held it back. He wouldn't break character, not the first time they did this. He gritted his teeth as he pulled his hand back. He was so damn close, just three, four tugs away from coming...

Matthew drove inside him again, his body trembling underneath Jace's. Then his hands dug into Jace's hips, locking him into place as Matthew thrust fast and deep. "Ungh... Oh, fuck, oh fuck, oh fuck..." he called out, and then he came, spurting his warm load deep inside Jace.

It almost sent him over the edge. How had he never known how hot going bare was? He sneaked his hand toward his cock again, but Matthew was faster. "I said no!"

Goddammit, was Matthew not gonna let him come? In what universe was that fair? He was nowhere near submissive enough to accept that, and he opened his mouth to protest, but then Matthew said, "You brought me pleasure, slave. You deserve a reward. Turn around."

He'd never moved faster. A smile crossed Matthew's face. Matthew totally broke character, but it didn't matter to Jace. By now, he was ready to beg or do whatever it took to be able to fucking come.

Matthew chuckled. "Come here, slave." He patted his mouth. "Feed me your cock."

Hell to the fucking absolutely yes. Jace scooted forward and, when Mathew opened his mouth, sank his cock inside the man's mouth. He wouldn't go too deep, but oh god, that felt amazing. He slowly rocked his hips, sliding his cock in and out of Matthew's mouth.

"You have a talented mouth, Your Majesty," he teased.

Matthew slapped his ass in what Jace assumed was a "you're not allowed to talk" signal, but fuck if he cared. That warm, hot mouth was heaven, and he wanted to stay there forever, but after not even a minute, he spilled his load, half in Matthew's throat and the rest over his lips and chin. Damn if that didn't look good on him.

Matthew licked his lips, and the smile that spread across his face told Jace they were done playing. He climbed off him, then stretched out next to him. Before he could say a word, Matthew grabbed his neck and pulled him against him. His lips were firm and hot, skipping the tentative foreplay and going straight for their target. Jace moaned as he opened up and let him in, tingles exploding in his belly when their tongues met. He tasted himself on Matthew's tongue and eagerly lapped up his cum, sucking on his tongue and chasing him until every last drop was gone.

Matthew pulled him on top of him, and Jace spread his legs, content to slowly rock his pelvis against Matthew's belly, smearing his sticky cock all over him. Whatever. They'd take a bath afterward.

The kiss slowed down and became lazy, two people exploring each other's mouth. Matthew's firm hands kneaded Jace's ass, teasing his still wet crack, even sinking two fingers deep inside him and dragging cum out when he pulled them out again.

"That was so hot," Matthew finally whispered, both their mouths swollen from kissing. "You were so hot."

"You liked me as your slave, huh?"

Matthew's eyes softened, and instead of the heat and passion from before, they glowed with something infinitely more tender. "I can't think of a role I wouldn't like you in." .

13

*S*mack!

The snowball splatted against the back of Matthew's head, then slid down into the collar of his winter jacket. God, that was cold. He shivered. That little shit.

He spun around. "Who did that?"

Across the yard, Jace stood, looking shocked as if he hadn't expected to hit him. Well, neither had Matthew, so that made two of them.

"What do you think you're doing?" he bellowed. Good thing he didn't have any close neighbors because they would no doubt have had an opinion on what they were doing.

"I'm sorry, Mr. Wilson," Jace shouted back, managing to look almost contrite.

"I've warned you what would happen if you bothered me again, didn't I?" Matthew said as he stalked toward him, closing the distance between them fast.

"Yes, Mr. Wilson."

Jace's eyes burned hot, and Matthew was sure his own

face reflected that same arousal. "Then you know what's gonna happen."

"You're gonna punish me?"

Matthew suppressed a smile, loving that Jace hadn't quite succeeded in keeping the eagerness out of his voice. Jace was into this as much as he was.

"Yes, young man. Now follow me."

He grabbed Jace by the arm and pulled him inside. Once they were in the mudroom, he kicked off his winter boots and shrugged of his winter jacket, shivering when the snow Jace had slung at him dripped underneath his sweater. Dammit, that was cold. He yanked Jace toward him and stripped him off his winter jacket as well. He'd already removed his boots. Good boy.

With a firm hand wrapped around Jace's wrist, he dragged him toward his study, where he had the perfect chair for doling out his punishment. He plopped down in the chair, letting go of Jace's wrist. "Drop your pants, young man. You're about to feel the results of your pranks on your bare ass."

"But, Mr. Wilson, I didn't mean to hit you..."

"Drop. Your. Pants."

Jace trembled as his hands went to his jeans, and he unbuttoned them slowly. He shimmied out of them, the pants pooling at his feet. The look he gave Matthew was the perfect mix of innocent and seductive.

"Underwear too."

"That's inappropriate, Mr. Wilson."

"Do I look like I care? I've warned you enough. Bare that ass. You'll feel the force of my displeasure, kid."

Oh, the *look* Jace shot him as he pushed his ass back and slowly, oh-so fucking slowly, pulled down his underwear, revealing that peachy ass. Matthew had fucked it, licked it, bitten it, rimmed it until Jace had begged for relief, and still he hadn't had enough of it.

Matthew patted his thighs, his cock like iron in his pants. "Over my knee, kid."

Jace obeyed, but his eyes sparkled. "You're being mean, Mr. Wilson."

Matthew waited until Jace had settled. They'd done one spanking before—a principal and schoolboy scenario—but he'd kept it light then, unsure what Jace could take. He longed to push him a bit further.

He forced Jace's neck down with one hand, bringing his other immediately down with a firm slap. Oh, how pretty his handprint looked on that creamy skin. He'd never been a sadist, not even close, but he understood where the desire to mark someone came from. Seeing his handprint on Jace's ass got him so fucking hard.

"Ow! That hurts, Mr. Wilson!"

"That's the whole point," he growled and slapped him again. One, two, three, four strikes and then he waited, giving Jace the chance to recover. He trembled on his lap, his skin hot as Matthew rubbed his ass cheeks.

"Mr. Wilson..." he half wailed. "It really hurts. What do I need to do to make it stop?"

Ah, his smart, sexy Jace, ready to bargain his way out of this. "I don't know, boy. What do you think you could offer me?"

Jace raised his head, his eyes suspiciously moist. Had they teared up from the spanking? It was all kinds of wrong, but Matthew really liked that idea. Jace bit his lip, pretending to be innocent. "I don't know, Mr. Wilson. Can't you think of anything else you'd want to do to my poor bottom?"

To underscore he knew exactly what he was doing,

Jace's hand traveled to Matthew's straining cock, trapped behind his underwear and jeans. Matthew fought with himself for one, two seconds, then surrendered to the inevitable.

"You devious little shit," he said with a sigh as he hoisted Jace off his lap. Within seconds, he'd unzipped his jeans, dragged them down along with his underwear, and had kicked them off. He spread his legs. "On my cock, you dirty boy."

Jace grinned deviously as he climbed back onto his lap, and Matthew sank inside him in one easy thrust. Of course Jace had prepped. Smart ass. But how could Matthew get upset with him when the result was what they both craved? Matthew balls deep inside him and the two of them bringing each other to a roaring climax.

He kissed him as he fucked him, first fast and furious, but then slowing down. He wasn't in a hurry, not anymore. He had been initially, feeling like he had to get out of their affair what he needed before it was over. But Jace had been here for four weeks now, and neither of them had mentioned him leaving. The thought alone made Matthew cold inside.

He nibbled on Jace's bottom lip as he pulled him down onto his cock until he was buried inside him. And suddenly the words came, words he'd never thought he'd ever utter again. "I love you. Stay. Stay forever."

Jace's smile was blinding. "I'd love to...because I love you too."

Matthew kissed him, his heart so full it felt like it would burst. "I think I've found the role I want you to play more than anything else."

"Yeah?"

"Mmm. The role of my boyfriend."

Jace leaned his forehead against Matthew's. "Does it come with good benefits?"

"The very best there are."

"Okay. In that case, I accept."

And what had begun as sexy play became sensual love-making, Jace riding him until they came at the same time, their gasps mingling in a passionate kiss that lasted forever.

ONE YEAR LATER

"Honey, I'm home!" Matthew called out as he walked through the front door.

Fast feet came running, and then Jace launched himself at him. Matthew dropped his backpack on the floor and held him tight as Jace wrapped his legs around him. "I missed you," Jace said with a deep sigh. "I missed you so fucking much."

"The next time I have a conference, you're coming with me. I don't care what everyone thinks."

Jace leaned back, his eyes sparkling. "You could always introduce me as your cousin..."

Matthew grinned. Who could have thought that Jace had a dirty mind that rivaled his own? Between the two of them, they'd come up with all kinds of scenarios they wanted to play out, and their latest one had been a guy who caught his cousin masturbating and decided to teach him how to do it properly.

"That'd sure as fuck shock the hell out of everyone."

He kissed Jace firmly, then put him back on his feet. He

hadn't been kidding. A week without Jace was too long. They'd become inseparable since Jace had driven up to take care of him. Fun fact: he'd never left. One week had become two and then a whole month, and two months later, they'd made the trip to Maryland together to pack up Jace's apartment and move all his stuff into Matthew's house.

"I have a new role I'd love for you to play," he told Jace, who cocked his head and looked at him expectantly.

"You know I'm always game for whatever dirty scenario your mind comes up with. What is it this time, and more importantly, do I get to wear a costume again?"

They'd discovered Jace got a kick out of the dressing up part of their role-play, and so they now had a wide variety of outfits he could put on. "Yup, a very fancy one. Super stylish."

Jace frowned. "Fancy and stylish? Are we doing a regency ball or something?"

"Nope, though there will be dancing."

"I have no clue, so hit me with it."

Matthew felt for the little box in his pocket, then sank to one knee and flipped it open. "The role of my husband…"

"Matthew…"

He'd never become Avery to Jace. In fact, he'd begun to introduce himself as Matthew, even when he met new people. Avery was the past. Matthew was the future. Jace's husband. "What do you say, baby? Ready to play that role for the rest of your life?"

Jace's eyes filled with tears. "Yes. A thousand times yes."

He slipped the simple ring onto Jace's finger, his own eyes growing moist, then kissed his hand and rose to his feet. He cupped Jace's face in his hands. "I love you so much. Please don't ever stop taking care of me…"

"That's an easy one," Jace said. "I promise. Forever."

IN THE MOOD for more winter romance? Check out *Coming Out on Top*, where a top Twink gets snowed in with a gentle giant and discovers that they have more in common than he'd ever thought possible...

LAYOVER

1

M unich Airport reminded Micah of an ant colony. It was busy, but efficient and organized. Despite not speaking German, he had no trouble finding his way, slaloming through the hordes of people to the check-in desk. When he got there, the expected line was absent, and in its place was utter chaos. What the hell was going on?

People were angry, that much was clear by the raised voices, sharp gestures, and the excessive pointing at the screens above the check-in desks. He looked up to see what they were pointing at, and his stomach sank. Behind their flight number and destination—JFK airport— a big, red-letter word flashed. Delayed.

His eyes dropped lower to the new expected departure time, and that's when he broke out in a sweat. Their flight was supposed to leave at noon, and instead, it now showed noon again. Twenty-four hours later, that was. It was delayed by twenty-four hours? Holy crap.

What the hell was he supposed to do now? He ran a mental check of his calendar for the next day, and to his relief, he didn't come up with anything urgent he would need to reschedule. He had already counted on having jet lag with the six-hour time difference, so he had scheduled a day working from home. That, at least, was covered then. The question was, what would he do in the meantime? He had twenty-four hours to bridge, but where?

All around him, fellow travelers were asking the same question, though a little less polite and a lot louder than he had. They were the usual bunch of business travelers like him, some who had raised the art of looking bored and unimpressed to a level he would never achieve. Then there were the groups of friends and couples of various ages, probably on their way to a trip to New York City. The rest were the unidentifieds, as he called them, people that made him wonder why they were traveling to New York.

All of them were asking that same question: *now what?*

"They'll put us up in a hotel," a young, male voice to his right said.

Micah turned his head, curious to see who was talking and if it was directed at him. His eyes met those of a guy his age, casually dressed with a backpack flung over his shoulder. He was cute, Micah noticed, with messy hair, a short scruff, and a pair of crystal blue eyes.

"I'm sorry?" Micah said, not sure if that had been the guy who spoke.

The man shrugged. "Everyone's getting so worked up, but there's no need. They'll put us up in a hotel. It's what they always do."

Something about his calm confidence spoke to Micah. The man clearly had a lot more experience traveling than Micah did. "Do you know why the flight is delayed?"

"Did you see the news about the plane with the faulty

landing gear in L.A.? The one that had to execute an emergency landing?"

Micah nodded. He'd caught it on CNN the night before in his hotel, grateful to spot an American news channel in his hotel's channel lineup.

"Well, that's why. The FAA has issued a directive for all airlines to perform a check of the landing gear. Apparently, something turns loose after so many hours of flight, I don't know. I'm not an engineer, but I do know that I prefer my planes to be thoroughly checked before going up in the air, so you won't hear me complain about this one. This airline flies a lot of that type of plane, so they can't offer us an alternative either, and from what I've heard, all other flights to major cities on the East Coast are already overbooked, since many airlines are struggling with this same issue."

"I am an engineer," Micah said. "And I wholeheartedly concur that I'd rather be delayed than take my chances with a faulty airplane."

Knowing there was a valid reason for the delay did bring his frustration down somewhat. As a quality control engineer, he could appreciate the checkups the FAA ordered in cases like this. It was what his whole job was about, developing fail-proof procedures and then making sure everyone stuck to them.

"What kind of engineer are you?" the guy asked, his face open with curiosity.

"I'm a quality control engineer," Micah said with the familiar rush of pride at his job. He would never forget how far he had come, and conversations like this brought that home to him all over again.

"How cool," the guy said. "Then I'm sure you can appreciate measures like this."

"You said they will put us up in a hotel tonight? How does that work?" Micah asked.

"Well, you can either wait for them to arrange a hotel for you, which they will do in cases like this where a whole plane gets stuck, or you can book your own hotel and get reimbursed. Either way, the airline will pay for your stay, and they will also have to offer you a hefty compensation of around six hundred euros, I think."

The guy sounded like he knew what he was talking about, and Micah was impressed. He hadn't traveled much so far, and this was his first trip to Europe. He'd prepared extensively, but he had never expected to encounter a delay this long.

"Which one do you recommend, waiting for their hotel or booking one yourself?" he asked.

"Oh, I'm not gonna wait for them to arrange something. By the time they're getting into motion, all the best hotels are booked. The ones close to the airport, I mean. They're going to shuttle you to the other side of Munich, which will be a major hassle tomorrow when we have to get back to the airport. So no, I'll book my own hotel, thank you very much."

Micah swallowed, his pride battling with his need to make sure he had accommodations for tonight. If what the guy said was true, he would be in ten kinds of trouble. Waiting for hours for the airline to find him something and not knowing where he was going to end up, that would send him into a major panic. On the other hand, acknowledging to a complete stranger he had no experience with this kind of thing wasn't attractive either.

In the end, his need for control won over his need to pretend he was cool. As usual.

"Is there any chance you could maybe do the same for

me? I don't speak German, and my company booked my hotel for me here, so I have no idea what I'm doing."

The guy sent him a smile that lit up his face. "I figured as much, but that's okay. I'd be happy to help. What kind of hotel are you looking for?"

"The same one where you're staying?" Micah said. He didn't realize how flirty it would come across until he saw the guy's grin broaden, and his cheeks flushed with embarrassment.

"In that case, I think it's custom we introduce ourselves first." The guy extended his hand. "Hi, I'm Forest, outdoors fanatic. I test outdoors gear and I write for an outdoors magazine."

Micah took it, certain that his whole face was red as a beet. "Micah. And I really didn't mean it like that. I'm just a little uncomfortable traveling in a strange country, so I figured if you knew where you were going, I could, like, tag along?"

Forest squeezed his hand before he let it go, still showing that gorgeous smile that made Micah's stomach do funny flips. "Oh, sweetie, you can tag along as long as you want."

MAKING a hotel reservation took Forest all of two minutes, aided by the fact that he contacted the hotel he'd been staying at the night before. He usually stayed at an airport hotel the night before flying out, because of the free airport shuttles that made getting to the gate on time so much easier. The hotel receptionist even remembered him from checking out earlier that morning, courtesy of some innocent flirting he had done, and immediately procured a room for Forest. He'd added a second room for Micah, putting it in his name until he could check in himself.

Micah was still flustered from his little goof, which Forest had found insanely adorable. He had to resist the urge to tease Micah with it, guessing that he was genuinely embarrassed by it, even though Forest thought it was cute. The whole package was cute, he mused, from Micah's carefully styled dark hair, his brown puppy eyes, to his neatly groomed beard. The guy must have some Mediterranean blood, he guessed, judging by his gorgeous skin. He was ten kinds of yummy. Too bad Forest didn't do hookups anymore.

"What are your plans for the rest of the day?" he asked once they were seated in the small van to the hotel. He'd gently ushered Micah out of the chaos to the curb, where they caught a hotel shuttle almost immediately.

Micah carefully straightened his suit and tie before answering. "Work, I guess."

Forest raised his eyebrows. "Work? Don't you want to see something of Munich? I assume you haven't had time for that since you were traveling for business."

Micah avoided his eyes, straightening his tie again. "I don't think I would feel comfortable exploring an unknown city by myself. I don't know anything about Munich, and I don't speak the language. Plus, I don't have any other clothes, so I would be pretty uncomfortable."

With anyone else, Forest would've accepted it for the truth: a long list of reasons why they preferred to stay inside. But something about Micah tickled him. He couldn't be much older than Forest, and yet he chose to stay inside on this glorious, sunny May day, rather than venturing out into this fascinating city. Micah had spent two days in Munich after a backpacking trip in the Bavarian Alps, and he would gladly add one more day to his stay.

"They're used to tourists," he said gently. "Most people understand enough English to communicate. It's a beautiful city, you know, and pretty safe, especially in the center this time of day."

Micah looked out the window of the van as he spoke. "I'm sure you're right, but I just don't see myself going out on my own."

"Do you want to come with me?" Forest asked before he could squash down this weird urge to spend a little more time with this cute guy who looked like he would rather attend an execution than go on a little adventure in a new city.

Micah's head whipped around. "With you? To do what?"

Forest shrugged, pleased that there had been an excitement in Micah's voice that hadn't been there before. "I could show you around a little. I speak enough German to get by, and after spending two days exploring the city, I'm well familiar with the city center, the *Altstadt*."

"What does that mean?" Micah asked.

"Altstadt? It literally means old city, or more loosely translated, the old city center. Munich dates back to the twelfth century, you know, and there are still a lot of gorgeous churches, houses, and even residential buildings from centuries ago. The city center is dripping with history."

"I hadn't realized it was that old," Micah said. "The factory I went to was north of Munich and looked very modern, as did the buildings around it."

"Sure, the city has a lot of modern buildings as well, particularly in industrial areas like the one you were in. Are those shoes comfortable?"

He eyed Micah's build. They had to be pretty close in size, with Micah probably being an inch shorter than he was. Still, he would probably fit into a pair of jeans and a shirt from him to replace the stuffy, if dashing, suit he was wearing.

Micah looked down at his feet, then up again, his brows frowning in confusion. "Not particularly, no. Why?"

Forest put his own foot flush against Micah's. It wrapped their legs together, sending a spark of electricity through him. "You wear what, a size nine? So do I."

The van stopped in front of their hotel, and Forest unbuckled his seatbelt and got up. He looked down at Micah, who was still seated but staring at him with a mix of terror and excitement. "Take a risk, Micah. Hang out with me today and explore Munich with me. I promise you it will be fun."

For a few breathless seconds they stared at each other, and Forest saw the battle inside Micah. He wasn't sure why the man had such a hard time with something as simple as this, but he figured he'd done enough pushing for now. In the end, it had to be Micah's choice to take the next step. Or not. But god, Forest was hoping he would take the jump. He wasn't ready to say goodbye to him just yet.

"You'll stay with me, the whole day?" Micah asked, then let out a soft gasp at his own words. "I didn't mean to—"

Forest cut him off by extending his hand and pulling him out of his seat. "Yes, I'll stay with you until we are back at the hotel. I promise. I won't let anything happen to you."

"Ve are ghere," the driver said in heavily accented English, but Forest ignored him, holding his breath until Micah answered.

Micah took a deep breath, then straightened his shoulders. "Okay," he said. "Okay, I will go to Munich with you."

Impulsively, Forest leaned in for a quick peck on his cheek. "You won't regret it. I promise."

2

M icah couldn't believe he had agreed to spend a whole day with a complete stranger in a city he'd never been to before, wasn't familiar with, and didn't speak the language. After checking into the hotel, where they had been given adjoining rooms, Forest had handed him a pair of jeans and a T-shirt, as well as a pair of Converse. Micah had protested, but not enough to deter Forest, who had been like a little bulldozer in asserting his will.

A happy, bubbly bulldozer, Micah had to admit, which made following the man's lead not so bad. His stomach was still all pretzeled in nerves, but he couldn't deny he was a tad excited as well about the prospect of spending more time in Forest's company. The man would undoubtedly get frustrated with him within hours, but hope sprung eternal, he guessed.

Forest had led them back to the hotel shuttle, which had dropped them off at the airport's subway station. It was called the U-bahn, Forest had explained, and he had expertly procured subway tickets for them, then guided them to the right line.

"So, Micah, tell me what you like to do when you're not working," Forest said as they seated themselves in the subway.

Micah wiped his clammy hands off on the jeans, remembering too late they weren't his. Traveling always made him a tad nervous, and in this case even more, because he literally had no idea where they were going.

"Cooking," he managed, then swallowed and told himself to get a grip. "I love cooking."

It calmed him, cooking the by-now familiar recipes he always made for his mom and him. The routine of it soothed him.

"Cool. You cook for yourself or is there someone else you cook for as well?" Forest asked, and Micah couldn't help but smile at the cheeky way Forest had just checked if he was single. Still, he was about to lose major cool points with his next bit of info.

"Mostly for my mom and myself." He waited for Forest to say something, but when he merely nodded with a smile on his face, Micah continued. "I do enjoy cooking for my friends once a month when we get together."

He smiled as he thought of his bunch of ragtag friends, an eclectic group of nerds, dorks, and people who could charitably be called plain weird. Still, they were his people and they had been for a long time. Plus, they put up with all *his* quirks as well, and they were extensive.

"If you love cooking, I know exactly where to start our little exploration of Munich," Forest said, his smile broadening.

"And you? What do you like to do besides traveling and outdoors stuff, I guess?" Micah asked. They were seated next to each other, and he loved how their legs touched every now and then, shooting little sparks of excitement through him.

"I love learning new things," Forest said. "I am incurably curious, according to my mom, and I think that's a pretty accurate description. I don't have one specific hobby, I tend to get immersed in whatever holds my attention at that particular moment."

Micah frowned, not sure what Forest meant. "Can you give me an example?"

"Sure. Last year, I was determined to learn paragliding, so I took a few courses and now I can paraglide. Right now, I'm thinking I want to learn how to surf. Which reminds me, I totally have to show you this giant park in the center of Munich, which is a lot like Central Park, actually. It's called the *Englisher Garten*, which is, as you might've guessed, German for English Garden. It's super cool, and there's this one spot that you really have to see. But we'll start with the food thing first."

Micah smiled at Forest's obvious enthusiasm. "Paragliding? Isn't that, like, super risky?"

Forest nodded. "Yeah, it kinda is. I mean, if you asked the people who do it all the time, they'd deny that it's any more dangerous than a lot of other sports, but there are formidable risks, obviously. It's one of the reasons why I couldn't see myself doing it long term, but then again, I've not been known to do anything long term, really."

He laughed at himself, and Micah chuckled as well. "Sounds like you are the exact opposite of me," he said.

He frowned as his own words registered. That made him sound boring again, didn't it? His shoulders dropped a little. This was why he struggled with finding a boyfriend, or even with dating. He had no issues with the initial contact, but once they got into the getting-to-know-you phase, he always came across as boring.

"This is our stop," Forest said, and when Micah didn't respond fast enough, Forest took his hand and pulled him up. Micah followed him out of the subway, strangely excited Forest was holding on to his hand.

Once they stepped outside, he had to shield his eyes from the sun until they got used to the intensity of the light. There were a lot more people than he had expected, the streets filled with people of all ages and nationalities, judging by the languages he picked up. He looked up at the old buildings around him, his heart squeezing in excitement as much as fear. He was so far out of his comfort zone, his friends wouldn't even believe them if he told them. God, he had to take pictures. Lots and lots of pictures.

That was when he discovered Forest was still holding his hand, looking at him with a sweet smile. "Is this okay? I just want to make sure I don't lose you."

Butterflies danced in his stomach. "Are you sure that's okay here? We're not gonna get in trouble?"

Forest shook his head. "No, no worries. First of all, Germany is pretty liberal, and secondly, the big cities are even more liberal, though Munich is more conservative than, say, Berlin. If you ever want to see a wonderful collection of the weirdest but most wonderful people on the planet, you have to go to Berlin. I love that city."

He started walking and Micah followed, forcing his breathing to slow down. He could only hope his hand wouldn't get too sweaty with Forest's fingers laced through his.

They rounded a corner and entered a large square that was filled with dozens of stands, all neatly lined up in rows. A huge blue-and-white striped pole rose above it all, wooden signs attached to either side depicting people dancing, drinking, and having fun. At the top was a flowery wreath with ribbons.

"What's this all?" he asked.

"This is the *Viktualienmarkt*, a farmer's market held six days a week. It's a food gourmet's dream come true, I'm telling you. They have dozens of cheeses I've never seen before, all kinds of local products, game, too much to take in."

Micah's mouth dropped open a little as he looked around, trying to take in what all the stands offered. To his right stood a row of actual shops, all fairly small, and by the looks of it all offering specialty products. One featured all kinds of tea, another looked like a specialized wine store, and one said *Metzgerei*, which he took to mean butcher, considering the meats displayed in the window.

"Come on, let's walk around," Forest said.

They started with a stand that offered more kinds of olives than Micah had ever seen in his life. The woman manning it was dressed in a rather unpractical-looking white blouse with puffy sleeves and a pink dress that highlighted her ample bosom. She looked beautiful, but Micah couldn't help but wonder if it was the most suitable outfit to sell olives in.

She said something, and Forest quickly replied. "She asked if we wanted to try one," Forest explained.

Micah nodded instantly. They all looked delicious, shiny olives filled with garlic, cream cheese by the looks of it, and red peppers, he figured. He pointed toward the cream-cheese-filled one, and the saleswoman stuck one on what looked like a toothpick and handed it to him. The flavor exploded in his mouth, the salty, slightly bitter taste of the olive mixing perfectly with the rich, round cream cheese, which was mixed with some herbs, he figured.

"That's delicious," he said to the woman, hoping she could at least understand that.

Her face broke open with a big smile. "Yes, *sehr gut, nah*?"

Gut, that was a word he could translate, and from the context, he gathered that *sehr* had to mean very. "Very, very good."

The next stall held specialty cheeses, a display of mostly French, Italian, and German cheeses, most of which were completely foreign to Micah. They all looked equally delicious, but then again, he had a weakness for cheese.

"American?" the sales guy asked, and Micah nodded, surprised the man had guessed correctly. "Bavarian cheese," the man said, pointing toward the front row of his display, pride ringing in his voice.

Bavaria, that was the state Munich was in, Micah remembered. That meant these were all local and regional cheeses the man was pointing to. His mouth watered at the sight. "Which one is the best?" he asked. "Which one do you recommend?"

He wasn't sure if the man had understood him, until he pointed at one particular cheese and said, "The best."

It wasn't eloquent, but Micah understood him perfectly. He turned toward Forest. "Can you buy me a little? I'd love to try it."

Forest smiled at him, then turned toward the man, and within a minute had purchased a little piece of the cheese. As soon as he had paid, Micah unwrapped the cheese and took a little bite. He moaned with pleasure as the taste hit him, perfectly creamy, rich, thick cheese that filled his mouth and stuck to the roof of his mouth in the best way possible. All it needed to be even more perfect was a drop of sweetness, for instance a little raspberry jam.

"I take it it tastes good?" Forest said, and Micah spun around to face him, embarrassed that he completely forgotten about him.

He held out the cheese. "Want to try some?"

Forest sent him a cheeky smile. "I'd love to, especially after the way you moaned. That has to be some orgasmic cheese."

The fact that Forest was eating the cheese prevented Micah from having to answer, but he felt his cheeks flush once again. Had he really moaned that loud? Maybe he had.

Forest let out a little sigh of pleasure himself. "That is damn good cheese," he said, and Micah was strangely pleased.

They wrapped up the rest of it, and Forest stuck it in the messenger bag he was wearing over his shoulder. They walked around the square for over an hour, trying various things. Micah was amazed at the products they saw, almost everything fresh, artisan made. There was a whole corner of stalls that sold fish, something he hadn't expected to find this deep inland. But there were also all kinds of meat, including homemade sausages.

"You have to try the *Weißwurst*," Forest said, pointing at a rather unappetizing looking sausage. It was white, the skin strange looking, almost see-through but not quite.

"What's so special about that one?" Micah asked. He could spot at least ten sausages that looked a hell of a lot more appetizing than the alien-looking one.

"It's a regional delicacy. It's what Bayern—Bavaria—is known for. It's a kind of sausage that you don't grill, but you slowly heat it in warm water, making sure it doesn't actually boil. And when it's warm, you eat it with sweet mustard. It's actually a sin to eat it right now according to locals, considering it's afternoon and it's a breakfast food, but as foreigners, we'll get away with it. It's absolutely freaking delicious, and you have to try it."

After a passionate plea like that, how could Micah refuse? He watched as Forest chatted in German with the girl behind the stall and she got them two of the white sausages that she lifted from a large pan. There were a few bar tables you could use to eat, and he and Forest put their paper plates down on one to eat their sausage, which came with a huge pretzel—a *Breze*, Forest told him.

Micah wasn't too sure about the combination of that strange, white sausage with the mustard, but he figured he might as well try it. He watched how Forest cut the sausage lengthwise and then sort of scraped the meat out of the skin and copied him. After the first bite, his eyes widened.

"Oh my god, you were right. That is insanely good."

The sweet mustard mixed perfectly with the hearty sausage. Micah would've never thought it went well together, but it was a match made in heaven. They both devoured their sausages, eating about half of the pretzel before they called it quits.

"If you want to go all traditional, you'd drink a *Weißbier* with this, but it's a little too early for me," Forest said, gesturing at the Biergarten behind them, which was packed with people drinking tall glasses of beer.

"Yeah, I'll pass as well, thanks," he said.

Micah's heart skipped a little when Forest took his hand again, like he'd done ever since they walked out of the subway. He would've never admitted it to the other man, but it did give him a strange sense of security to literally hold on to Forest. That, of course, didn't make sense at all considering they barely knew each other.

Forest took him on a walk through the old city center, the Altstadt, and Micah tried to take it all in, the old buildings, the churches, the gorgeous rooftops, everything. Forest pointed out things left and right, explaining a little background or history of what they walked past.

"You learned all this in two days?" Micah asked.

Forest laughed. "No, I did my research beforehand. I always do when I'm traveling to a new place. My main focus is writing about outdoors stuff, but I sell the occasional travel article as well. Some travel writers argue that you should come in as a blank slate, so you're not affected by what other writers have written about a place already, but that doesn't work for me. I love discovering new things, but the first few days, I always start with the most touristy places. There's a reason they're so popular, you know? And to me, reading up about the history of a place is important, especially when you travel to areas like this."

He pointed out another gorgeous church, and Micah took a picture with his phone, then checked to make sure the picture had turned out okay.

"What's so special about the history of Munich?" he asked as they walked further, and this time he reached for Forest's hand before even realizing it.

"Good heavens, where do I start? You know how Americans joke that New York City is not like the rest of the US? It's the same with Bavaria. It's part of Germany, but it has its own distinct culture and a rich history. It used to be a kingdom, not even that long ago, and you can still see many remnants of that era, including some stunning castles. More recently, this was where Hitler started his rise to power. His first attempt at a coup took place right here in Munich."

As they walked along, Forest shared some of the history of the city and the state, and Micah was amazed at how much he knew about it. He'd never been a big fan of history, but hearing about it as you saw the remnants with your own eyes, that was different.

"This is one of the most famous landmarks in Munich," Forest said, pointing at a richly decorated building that had a big sign that said *Hofbräuhaus*. "It's the main brewery in Munich, or it used to be, and now it's a massive *Bierkeller*, literally beer cellar or beer basement, or what the English would call a pub. But it has its own distinct traditions and culture, like a reserved table for some long-time patrons called a *Stammtisch*."

They continued their stroll, and Micah was amazed at how much he was enjoying himself. His previous stress had vanished, replaced by a deep contentment at how beautiful the city was...and how beautiful his company was. If Forest was already growing bored by Micah, he wasn't showing it, and sparks of hope fired in his heart. Maybe, just maybe, he could pull it off to appear interesting. For once.

3

Forest was relieved to see Micah's stress levels lessen. It had been easy to spot that a trip like this was a huge step out of his comfort zone, and Forest had been a little surprised that Micah had taken him up on his offer in the first place. Once he had, he'd clearly been freaked out about his own choice, as evidenced by some nervous tics he had displayed.

Forest had debated offering him to cancel, not wanting to force him to do anything he didn't want, but in the end, he decided to just take him to the Viktualienmarkt first, because he figured Micah would love that. That turned out to be an excellent choice, because his love for food had made Micah forget about his worries of being in a new city, it seemed.

They never ran out of topics to talk about, Forest noticed with joy. Sure, he was playing a bit of tour guide with his explanations of what they encountered on their stroll through the Altstadt, but Micah asked plenty of questions of his own, both about the city and about some other things.

"You have seven siblings?" Micah asked with the amazement Forest had grown accustomed to over the years when talking about his family.

"Yup, five brothers and two sisters. Three of my brothers and my sister Rain are older, the rest are younger than me. But that's not all. I also have a mom and two dads, as my parents are in an honest-to-god threesome."

They came to a sudden stop when Micah yanked on his hand, forcing him to turn toward him. "You're kidding me."

He laughed. "I swear. They're what you would call free spirits, but they're wonderful, loving parents, and they have raised us with nothing but respect for them, for each other, and for the world we live in. As evidenced by not just my name but those of my siblings. Forest, Rain, Ocean, Sky, all super new age. They're very in touch with nature."

"That's amazing. It sounds...chaotic, but also wonderful."

"What about you?" Forest asked as they started walking again. "Any siblings?"

It took so long for Micah to answer that Forest shot a concerned look sideways. Had he inadvertently touched on a subject Micah didn't want to talk about? He was just about to say something when Micah finally spoke up.

"My mom raised me and my brother by herself, since my dad was sentenced to a long prison term and she divorced him after a couple of years. But my brother, I guess you could say he got lost along the way and started hanging out with the wrong crowd. He started using heroin, and it affected all of us. My mom tried, she tried really hard, but in the end, she had to kick him out because he kept stealing our stuff to sell it. He died of an overdose a couple of years ago."

The sheer heartbreak in that simple statement was so staggering, it took Forest back a bit. How could he respond to that? What was there to say that wouldn't sound trite? In the end, he decided to go for honesty.

"I'm so sorry, Micah. It sounds like you were handed a rough deal from early on. I have no idea what that must've been like."

Micah's voice was soft when he spoke. "Few people do, thankfully."

"But you're close with your mom?" Micah asked.

"Yes, very close. It's why I still live in her basement. I didn't want to leave her, not after what we've been through. Someday, I'll move out, but not yet."

That made sense to Forest, and he thought it showed Micah's character, that he wanted to make sure his mom was okay.

They walked in silence for a few minutes, but it didn't feel loaded or tense to Forest. He was glad when they reached their destination, because it would allow him to distract Micah from his sad memories.

"We're at the entrance of the park now, the *Englisher Garten*. It's about the same size as Central Park, but there is a river that runs through it, the *Eisbach*."

They walked into the park, which was busy, even on a weekday. But the weather was gorgeous, so a lot of people had sought out the shade of the big trees in the park or to dip their feet in the cold water.

"There's this one spot I want to show you," Forest said, and he took Micah by the hand to the place he'd discovered a few days before. "Look."

He watched Micah's face as what he was seeing sank in. "They're surfing? Holy crap, they're surfing!"

The man's face showed the same excitement and wonder as Forest had felt when he'd seen it a few days before. On a small stretch of the river called the *Eisbachwelle*—he'd looked it up afterward—surfers in wetsuits were jumping on a surfboard, one at a time, to surf the current, going from left to right between two concrete, low walls. Forest wondered if someone had ever smashed into those walls, but it clearly didn't deter any of the surfers. There were eight of them right now, each patiently awaiting their turn to surf until they either got wiped out or got out of the water.

"That is definitely something I wasn't expecting," Micah said, gasping as one of the surfers went down, getting swept under only to pop up again about twenty feet downstream.

"I know, right? I couldn't believe my eyes when I saw it. It's some kind of freak wave effect, caused by the water coming in from the *Isar* river. Apparently, in the summer, there is a long line, even though you have to be pretty good to be able to ride this current."

They walked further into the park, where moms with children were playing in the grass, couples were lounging on big towels near the water, and a few were even splashing around in the shallow ends of the river. It felt like an oasis away from the busyness, like a place to breathe and relax.

It was dinner time by now, and Forest convinced Micah to have dinner in the restaurant in the garden. It wasn't the most exclusive cuisine possible, but they served local specialties, and the location was hard to beat. He talked Micah into ordering a *Wiener Schnitzel*, a giant portion of tender, flattened veal with a crunchy batter, deep-fried to perfection. They served it with a berry sauce that was the perfect accompaniment, as well as with classic German *Kartoffelsalat*—potato salad—and a small portion of thin, crispy fries.

"My god, this is delicious," Micah said, and he did that moaning thing again that made Forest's cock hard in an instant. "I was under the impression that the Germans didn't exactly excel in the kitchen, but I have to admit I was wrong. This may not be haute cuisine, as you said, but damn, it's good."

He smiled, happy that he'd steered Micah in the right direction. "See? It pays off to try something new."

Micah shot him a sheepish look. "You picked up on my aversion to the unknown, huh?"

Forest wanted to make a joke about it, until he saw the underlying vulnerability. "Yeah, I did," he said. "And I don't want to make you uncomfortable, but why are you reluctant to explore new things? It's not a judgment, but I'm trying to understand."

Micah sighed. "In college, I started developing some serious tics, and my resident advisor picked up on them and advised me to see a psychologist. Long story short, she concluded that the years of upheaval and chaos with my brother have resulted in a strong tendency for order and predictability."

As rationally as Micah explained it, Forest picked up on the emotion underneath. There was sadness there, a dash of anger when he mentioned his brother, but also embarrassment and a feeling of hopelessness. Almost as if he expected Forest to judge him for it after all.

"That makes total sense, that you would resort to strategies like that to keep your sanity," he said. "Is it something that bothers you? Or are you okay with it?"

Another deep sigh, this one filled with frustration. "I want to be more spontaneous, but it's hard for me. One of my goals for this year, and New Year's resolution if you want, was to step out of my comfort zone."

Forest leaned forward, resting his arms on the table. "And? How has that been going for you?"

Micah shook his head softly. "It's been a struggle. The most adventurous thing I've done is wear colored socks instead of black ones." He lifted his jeans up to show a pair of baby blue socks that peeped out from the Converse. "That's pretty sad, right?"

"That's not sad," Forest said, making sure his voice was warm. "It's a small step, but every big change consists of a ton of small steps. As I said, you were handed a rough deal in life, Micah. Don't judge yourself or condemn yourself for how you survived."

"It's not just me who is judging," Micah said. "Why do you think I'm single?"

Forest understood what he wasn't saying. He must've had some difficult moments with past boyfriends or even dates who wanted to do things he couldn't make himself commit to.

"Well, I think we'd both agree that I'm pretty open to new experiences, but I'm single as well. So I'm not sure if that's the reason. Maybe you just haven't found the right person yet, the guy who not only tolerates who you are, but embraces you."

Micah cocked his head as if he didn't believe him. "Is that why you're single? Because you haven't found someone to accept you? I can't imagine you're hard to live with."

He cringed a little again, something Forest noticed he did a lot whenever he felt like he was giving away too much. Something or someone had taught him to be cautious of his words, and Forest hated seeing that insecurity, as if Micah feared Forest would either blow up or be somehow upset the moment Micah showed even the slightest attraction to him.

"Because of my job, I travel quite a bit, and I'm often gone to test gear, or do outdoorsy stuff, like hiking or rock climbing," Forest said. "I haven't found anyone yet willing to put up with a boyfriend who's absent that much. They either complain, they want to come with me, or they try to guilt me to quit my job and stay home."

Micah's eyes softened. "Maybe you just haven't found the right person yet, that guy who either doesn't mind you following your passion, or who is worth staying home for."

ALL DURING DINNER, Micah was amazed at how easily the conversation flowed. And it wasn't like they only talked about casual things either. He'd shown Forest more of himself than he had shown to anyone else in years, aside from his friends who were all too familiar with his sad story.

They'd been his friends all through high school and had stuck with him through the lows of his brother's addiction, the constant drama in his house, his mother's breakdown, and ultimately, his brother's death. They'd come to his brother's funeral, not so much because they'd had a shred of sympathy left for his brother, Gabe, but because they wanted to be there for Micah and his mom. And they had been, every step of the way.

They were the only ones who accepted his resistance against change and who accommodated it as much as they could. They would be so proud of him now, taking this huge leap out of his comfort zone with Forest. The funny thing was that what had felt like a jump out of an airplane this morning, now felt so much less intimidating. Maybe it was because he'd come to know Forest a little, he wasn't sure.

The guy sure inspired a strange confidence in Micah that he'd never felt before. As if with him, he could slay all the dragons that were in his way. Of course, that was ridiculous to feel about a man he'd only just met.

"Where did you go in your head?" Forest asked, sending him a soft smile. "You looked a million miles away."

He smiled back. It was hard not to, with Forest being so open and kind. He drew you in, or at least, he did Micah. It wasn't like he was flirting, more like he was so genuine and himself that it was hard to resist.

"Not quite a million miles, but a couple of thousand at least. I was thinking of my friends back in New York. We have quite the tight-knit group, still together after high school. They're the best friends a guy could have."

"If I may ask, are you out with them? In general?"

It took a second or two for the implications of that question to sink in. "Why would you deduce I'm in the closet?" he asked, genuinely baffled.

He didn't advertise his sexuality, but he never made a secret of it either. He'd never outright told his coworkers, for instance, but if the topic had come up, he hadn't denied anything. What had made Forest think he was ashamed of his sexuality or hiding it?

"I hope I don't upset you, but a few times today, you looked embarrassed or ashamed when you said something that indicated you might be attracted to me. I was just wondering if you were upset with yourself about that because you didn't like showing you were gay."

Wow, he had picked up on that, Micah thought. That was quite perceptive, or maybe he hadn't been as subtle as he'd hoped. Fuck knew that wouldn't be the first time. He'd never been exactly suave when it came to flirting or navigating anything from hookups to relationships.

"I don't have a lot of experience with this." He gestured from himself to Forest and back. "As you can probably imagine, hookups don't really work for me because they knock me off my routine too much. I've dated, but I've rarely made it past the first date. Guys seem to like me until they get to know me. At a certain point, I learned to not even bother anymore and sort of hide if I was attracted to someone else, knowing it would probably lead to nothing anyway."

That was quite the personal stuff he was sharing here, but somehow, it felt safe with Forest. The guy hadn't shown any frustration so far with him, so even if he didn't reciprocate the attraction Micah fell toward him—which Micah was still considering the most likely scenario— he would probably react with kindness, which was all Micah could ask for.

Forest studied him for a bit, his crystal blue eyes assessing yet warm. It didn't feel like judging, more like Forest was trying to figure out how to respond.

"I used to do hookups all the time. After discovering that relationships were not an option with my chosen career, I figured I might as well enjoy the sex part of it, you know? But after a year or so of that, I got so bored with it. I like sex as much as the next guy, I would assume, but I came to hate how empty it was. I would start asking questions, wanting to get the know the guy I was hooking up with, and some of them got quite upset for making it personal when it was just supposed to be about sex. That kinda made me feel like I was being used or was using them, and I stopped doing it."

That was not what Micah had expected Forest to say, and yet somehow it sounded not only true, but true to him. "That makes us a couple of rather sad cases," he said.

Forest's eyes twinkled. "Did you just call me sad?"

"If the shoe fits," Micah fired back. "You did just admit to not having had sex in a while."

He almost held his breath, waiting for Forest to respond.

He couldn't believe he had jumped to flirting with him. It felt scary as hell, and yet wonderfully safe because he somehow knew Forest wouldn't hurt him, not even if he wasn't interested in him.

Forest leaned forward over the table, gesturing for Micah to do the same. "The question is which one of us is the saddest. Which one of us hasn't had sex longer? Care to do a little bet?"

A giggle of excitement escaped from Micah's lips, and his hand flew to his mouth when he heard the sound. Was that him, this carefree laugh? He hardly recognized himself.

Forest reached out for his hand and grabbed it, lacing their fingers again as they'd done all day. "I love hearing you laugh," he said softly. "It's a beautiful sound, and your whole face lights up when you do it."

The butterflies in Micah's stomach returned in full force, and suddenly, he started doubting his conviction the attraction wasn't mutual. Would Forest say something like that if he didn't feel it as well?

"I love that you make me laugh," he whispered.

They stared at each other, the air between them humming with excitement.

"Take the bet," Forest said, still keeping his voice low. "I promise there will be no losers."

Micah swallowed back the instinctual fear inside him at the idea of engaging in something he didn't know the rules of. "Okay," he said. "May the odds be ever in your favor."

Forest's face broke open in a big smile. "I'm so proud of you. If I win, you'll spend the rest of the evening with me here in Munich. We won't go back to the hotel till midnight."

Suddenly, losing didn't sound so bad, Micah thought. "And if I win?"

Forest squeezed his hand that he was still holding. "If you win, we'll go back to the hotel and we'll spend the rest of the evening there together."

Electricity crackled between them, and Micah's hands got clammy. "That sounds like a win-win to me."

"Time for the truth," Forest said. "How long has it been for you?"

Somewhere, in the back of Micah's mind, a flash of fear went through his brain, accompanied by blips of movies he'd seen. Scenes where someone had been asked to the prom only to be dumped or where they had dressed up for a date only to be rejected. Was the same about to happen to him here? Was he about to get massively humiliated? Again? He pushed it down.

"Nine months," he whispered.

"Twelve months," Forest countered. "The last time I hooked up was a year ago when I was traveling the Canary Islands. It'll be exactly a year tomorrow, actually."

Micah's head swarmed with conflicting emotions. A strange satisfaction that it had been that long for Forest, even longer than for him. That meant he wasn't as much of a loser as he'd come to believe. Excitement and fear that he'd lost the bet and would have to spend more time in the city with Forest. Disappointment that he'd lost the bet that they would go back to the hotel where maybe things could've...

"Do you want to go back to the hotel? With me? To prevent it from becoming an anniversary tomorrow?"

As soon as the words had left his mouth, his adrenaline spiked. What the hell was he thinking, blurting out a proposal like that?

4
___

For a second, Forest thought Micah was joking, because surely he hadn't just suggested they go back to the hotel and hook up? But then he caught the look of sheer panic on Micah's face and realized that's exactly what he had suggested, even if he was regretting it now. He squeezed his hand again.

"It's okay, Micah. We don't have to do anything you don't want."

He held Micah's eyes, watching emotions flash over his face. "It would never work, you and me," Micah said. "You'd grow frustrated with me just like all the others."

"Sweetie, we're not talking about a long-term commitment here. Let's take it one step at a time. But like I said, you don't have to do anything you don't want to."

Micah shook his head. "But you didn't want hookups anymore, so where does that leave us?"

The joke that he wasn't ready to pick out rings just yet was on Forest's tongue, until he realized that Micah was genuine in his concern. Micah needed more certainty, a definition maybe, before he could commit himself to this.

"I said I wasn't happy with doing anonymous hookups anymore, but I feel we've gotten to know each other quite a bit today, haven't we? I think we've connected on a far deeper level than just sexual chemistry, don't you?"

Micah nodded. "Yeah, we have. And I'm sorry for nagging and making this far more complicated than it should be."

Micah's hints at failed hookups and attempted relationships made a lot more sense now. His need for clarity and managing expectations had clashed with romance and sexual lust, if Forest had to take a guess. Most guys weren't willing to engage in a conversation like this with a guy they had just met.

"I'm starting to appreciate complicated," he said, sending a warm smile in Micah's direction.

The look on Micah's face made his stomach do a happy little dance. "Yeah?" the guy asked, his face lit up with the sweetest smile.

"Yeah, I'm starting to appreciate complicated a lot. But the choice is yours. We'll do whatever you're comfortable with."

He saw Micah take a deep breath and felt the tension in the hand he was still holding. "In that case, I would love to go back to the hotel."

They didn't speak much as they walked to the closest U-bahn station. Instead of holding his hand, Forest pulled Micah close to his side with his arm around his shoulder, and after a little gasp of surprise, Micah returned the gesture and held his waist. Their bodies were rubbing against each other, sending tingles of excitement through Forest's body. No matter what happened tonight, he was already happy with this perfect day, with this man who he connected with so much deeper than purely physically.

When they got back to the hotel, he felt Micah's body tremble next to his. "We do this at your pace," he told him in the elevator up to their rooms.

Micah bit his lip. "I want this. I'm not scared of doing this with you. But I am scared of embarrassing myself because... It's been so long, you know?"

If that was supposed to deter Forest, it wasn't working. On the contrary, it affirmed his own fears. Ever since Micah had uttered those crazy words about going back to the hotel, Forest's cock had been unrelenting, and he feared he was gonna come the second he took his clothes off. Or when Micah took his clothes off.

He cupped Micah's cheek and gave him a quick kiss on his lips that left his own lips sizzling. "If that happens, I'll probably be less than a second behind you. We're in this together."

They didn't speak until they got to their rooms and since Micah was already holding his key card, they went into his. For a second, Forest wondered how they were going to do this, but then he spotted the insecurity on Micah's face and knew he'd have to take the lead.

He let the door fall closed behind him and reached out for Micah's hand. "I would really like to kiss you if that's okay. I've been wanting to do that since the moment I saw you."

"Really?"

The disbelief in his voice warmed Forest's heart almost as much as his cute smile. "Really," he confirmed before slowly backing Micah into the wall. He waited for another second to see if he'd protest, but when Micah closed his eyes in anticipation, Forest moved in.

Micah's lips were soft under his, moving hesitantly at first, until Forest coaxed him into deepening the kiss. Then

Micah's hands came around his neck, dragging him closer, as they both sank into the kiss. Sparks fired all over his body as he tasted Micah, so sweet and perfect for him. He stepped in a little closer, wanting to feel their bodies flush against each other. He loved that they were so close in height that he could gently rub their cocks together, both hard as iron.

Micah let out a little moan into his mouth, and the sound shot straight to Forest's balls. His hands found Micah's T-shirt and he pulled it out of his waistband, teasing the soft skin of his back. He could feel the man break out in goosebumps at his touch, and that fired him on. He wanted nothing more than for Micah to feel good about himself. Really, really good.

He kept kissing him as his hands explored his back, creating soft, caressing trails, then finding their way to his stomach, between their bodies.

Micah suddenly pulled back. "Stop."

Forest took a step back, releasing him instantly. Had he done something wrong? Was Micah regretting this already? The man's face was tight with tension, so clearly something was the matter.

"I'm sorry," Micah said, and Forest's stomach sank. "I'm too close. If you keep touching me, I'll come."

Forest blinked. That was not what he had expected Micah to say. "Then we'd better take off our clothes so they don't get dirty," he said. "Because a minute more of that and I would've jizzed my pants as well."

Micah looked at him in disbelief, but when Forest pointed to his dick to confirm the veracity of his statement, Micah's face broke open in a sexy smile. "I'm down with that."

In terms of elegance and grace, it wasn't an award-winning show as they both got rid of their clothes as fast as possible, but Forest couldn't care less. He watched with a warm feeling as Micah neatly put his clothes on a chair, whereas he dropped his carelessly on the floor.

He whistled as he took in Micah's toned body. He wasn't overly bulky, but he clearly worked out, his muscles defined and strong in all the right places. He had a nice dusting of dark chest hair, and the sexiest happy trail ever that lead downward to his perfect, hard cock.

"Holy moly, man, you were hiding something under that suit."

Micah looked down at his own body, rubbing his right hand over his abs. "I work out when I get stressed. I guess it's been quite a stressful year," he said with the self-deprecating humor that Forest loved so much.

He stepped in closer, then put his index finger on Micah's chest and let it slide down slowly. "You should teach me how to release my stress like that. I eat when I'm stressed. It's not pretty."

Micah blinked, then sent him a cheeky smile. "You must've had a relaxed year, then."

Forest laughed and so did Micah, until Forest's index finger found his happy trail and followed it down. Micah's laugh transformed into a gasp as Forest's finger caressed the velvety soft skin of his cock, all the way from the base to the very tip. Micah shivered under his touch, and it made Forest's own dick harden even more in response.

He couldn't wait to feel that gorgeous cock inside him. He halted in his own thoughts. He was vers, so it really didn't matter much to him, but maybe Micah had strong preferences. Considering how Micah struggled with the unexpected, maybe with him this was a conversation they needed to have beforehand, even if it did take away some of the spontaneity.

"Do we need to talk about expectations and logistics?" he asked softly.

The look of sheer gratitude that filled Micah's eyes let him know he'd pegged him correctly.

"That would really help me," Micah said. "I know it's not spontaneous, but—"

"How about you stop apologizing for something I suggested myself?" Forest interrupted him, then to soften the impact of his words, he stepped in and kissed him again until they were both panting.

He had to refrain from rutting against him, because that would end their sexual adventures all too soon. Then again, maybe that was exactly what they needed to take the edge off, considering they were both so excited.

"I could start by rubbing us off together?" he suggested, his voice low and soft.

He wrapped his hand around both their cocks and gently rubbed them together. To make it even better, he would need some kind of lubricant, but this would give Micah an idea of what he meant.

"I have lotion," Micah said, thrusting slightly into Forest's hand. *Bingo*.

"Get it, please?"

He let go of him and Micah shook his head as if to clear it, then hurried over to the suitcase on the luggage rack, opened it, and took out a small bottle of lotion that he handed to Forest. It only took seconds for Forest to squeeze something into his hand and get back to the delicious task of rubbing their cocks together, made so much easier by the slick lotion.

The sensation was incredible, those two, hard, now slick cocks sliding together. Shivers of desire danced down his spine, and his ass cheeks clenched in anticipation. Oh, they wanted that cock as much as he did. Micah's dick had that perfect curve that would hit his prostate spot on and damn, it was thick. Forest swallowed, biting down on his body's urge to speed things up.

"God, that feels good," Micah moaned, thrusting into Forest's hand.

Forest clenched his teeth, already dangerously close to coming. "I can't hold out much longer," he said. "You're so fucking hard in my hand. You feel so good."

Micah moaned again, then thrusted faster. "I can't... Forest, I'm... Oh, fuck!"

Forest felt it coming, Micah's cock twitching in his hand a millisecond before it erupted, and he let go of his own orgasm, jerking in his hand. They were both thrusting as much against each other as against his hand, cum flying everywhere, hitting him on the chest, the stomach, and even some on his cheek. He moaned loudly, his vision going white for a second with the sheer intensity of his release.

Before he'd even let go of their cocks, Micah had pulled his head in for a deep, sloppy kiss. It was anything but coordinated, the way their frantic mouths found each other, their tongues everywhere, but it was hot as fuck. He let go of their cocks, allowing them to rub wet and spent against each other between them, smearing their cum everywhere.

They kissed until their pace slowed down, and their kisses became more sensual, teasing and seducing and coaxing each other in a delicious game. God, this man could kiss. They kissed for minutes, unhurried now, their most desperate need staved off. Still, Forest wanted more.

"Do we need to clean up?" he asked softly, his forehead leaning against Micah's.

"I'd love to do more," Micah said to his delight.

He had to kiss him for that answer, and he plunged his

tongue in all over again, unable to get enough of the man's sweet taste, and the perfect way his mouth fit against Forest's own.

"I would love for you to top me," he said after at least another three, four minutes of kissing. "But if you prefer to bottom, that's all fine with me."

"I'm vers as well," Micah said. "And I would love to fuck you. I have condoms."

There were advantages to being a control freak, Forest thought. He had condoms in his wallet as well, but he couldn't vouch for them not being way past the expiration date.

"See? You and me, we're a match made in heaven, baby."

His heart jumped up as he felt those words in his soul, then clenched painfully at the thought that tomorrow, this would all be over.

MICAH HAD NEVER FELT like this. Every date he'd ever had, every hookup he'd ever attempted, he'd always been completely stressed out. His fear of being rejected had grown so deep that he'd tried to be someone else. Anything and anyone but the tight-ass who couldn't be spontaneous and fun, as one date had described him. He never dared to be himself. Until now.

For some reason, Forest didn't seem to have an issue with Micah's need for control at all. He had accommodated him throughout the day and that hadn't changed now that they were here, doing *this*. And oh my god, *this* was epic, wonderful, defying every description Micah could come up with.

Forest was right. They were a match made in heaven.

Too bad it would only be for one night. But he wouldn't let that ruin it. He refused to let his anxiety and sadness over their impending departure take over this glorious experience of being with this man.

He allowed Forest to slowly move them toward the bed as they kissed, and they tumbled down, scooting up until they were plastered together, the remnants of their previous releases still smeared between them. He loved it. He loved this sensation of being utterly taken over by lust, of feeling debauched and filthy. He might have control issues, but he didn't have a problem with being dirty like this. On the contrary, he loved it.

Forest's body fit perfectly against his own, lean muscles with soft skin, a round ass that begged to be used, lines and curves and dips that needed to be explored. He let go of Forest's mouth and rolled on top of him, then started a slow exploration downward.

He nuzzled his neck, licking a single drop of sweat that tasted perfectly salty on his tongue. He gently bit Forest's earlobe, then teased that sensitive spot behind his ear with the tip of his tongue, eliciting a delicious sound from Forest's lips. His hands touched, wandered, followed by his lips and his tongue. If this was his one lucky chance at the perfect hookup, he would enjoy every second of it.

Forest's nipples were hard, pleading to be licked and sucked, so he did, loving how Forest's whole body responded to that simple touch. He found some remnants of cum here and there, his or Forest's, he didn't know and he didn't care. He cleaned them up with his tongue, creating a wet trail all over Forest's body. His stomach was perfect, not as hard and defined as Micah's own was but so responsive to his touch.

Forest's fingers laced through his hair as he continued

his journey farther south. He kneeled between his legs, and Forest pulled them up and opened for him without any shame. He was so beautiful, so perfect. There was none of the awkwardness he always had in encounters like this, none of the nerves or stress. It just felt right, more right than he'd ever felt before.

He used the lotion to create a slick trail behind Forest's balls, rubbing him and teasing him until he reached his hole, tapping and caressing until it softened under his fingers.

"Please, sweetie. I'm so ready for more," Forest begged, rolling his head from left to right and back.

"Do you need a lot of prep?" Micah asked. He didn't want to ruin the moment, but he wanted to make sure he did it the way Forest would get the most pleasure out of it.

"I love a little burn," Forest moaned as Micah slipped his middle finger in. "So don't take too much time prepping, please. I'd love to be stretched by your cock."

After just a few moves, Micah added a second finger, hoping for another one of those low, sexy sounds from Forest. He wasn't disappointed, and he smiled. He stretched him a little further, and then Forest's hand found his wrist.

"I'm ready," he said.

Micah pulled his fingers out and quickly got up to get a condom. He fumbled a little with rolling it on, clearly out of practice, but it didn't seem to bother Forest who was watching him with heavy eyes.

"You're gonna feel so good inside me," he said.

Micah hesitated for a second about their positions, but he figured that if Forest had wanted to be fucked in a different position, he would've moved while Micah got the condom. Instead, Forest pulled his legs wide and up, opening for him, and he lowered himself on top of him, his cock almost immediately finding the right spot. He pressed in slowly, his eyes completely focused on Forest's.

"Oh my god," Forest said, then again, "oh my god. Oh, you feel so good. Keep going, please. It burns in the best way."

And so Micah kept going, pressing inside him until he was balls deep. A shiver tore through him at the sensation of his body so flush against Forest's, completely joined, and he lowered his upper body on top of Forest's, wrapped his arms around his neck, and started moving.

It felt like an out-of-body experience, like he was rising above himself, watching himself taking this wonderful, gorgeous man, both with an expression of complete bliss on their face. How was this him? How had he gotten so lucky to meet this man?

He thrust in deep and steady, snapping only his hips while keeping his upper body mostly still, flush against Forest's. Their heartbeats thumped through him, one even faster than the other, and he felt one with him.

"I wish I could keep doing this for hours," he said wistfully, nuzzling Forest's neck.

Forest scraped his ear with his teeth, and Micah shivered. "Do you hear me objecting?"

Micah smiled as a strange excitement rushed through him. He wanted more time with him. More time to explore him, more time to get to know him, more time to be together. He'd have to make every hour they had last.

And no, Forest didn't object when Micah made them both come hard, Forest coming all over him. He also didn't object when Micah told him he wanted to bottom for him. They took a shower together afterward, still not able to let each other go. When they woke up after a few restless hours of sleep, they did it all over again.

The objections didn't come until they had to go back to the airport, first sitting hand-in-hand in the hotel shuttle to their gate, neither one of them speaking. Then when they checked in, begging the ground crew for two seats together, which they magically managed. They were inseparable for the entire flight to New York, never once letting go of each other.

Cold, hard reality hit after landing, when Micah picked up his luggage and had to walk outside to go home...and Forest had to catch his connecting flight to Portland. They stood staring at each other. Micah didn't want to accept this was the end, and he saw his own emotions mirrored on Forest's face.

But what could they do? They had jobs to get back to, lives to get back to, and they lived on opposite sides of the country.

And so they left after one last kiss, Micah fighting to keep his tears at bay until he'd caught a cab home. Only then did he let go, and his heart broke into a million pieces.

5

A s soon as he was outside the Portland airport, waiting on the curb, Forest pulled out his phone. Three messages had come in from Micah.

Micah: How was your flight?

Micah: I know you're still in the air, so you can reply when you land

Micah: Or whenever you have time

FOREST SMILED as he read them. It was the first time he smiled since he'd said goodbye to Micah in New York. How had this man managed to invade his heart in such a short time? It felt like he'd been with him for weeks instead of just one day. No, he needed to stop thinking about that, because he would get sad all over again. It had taken all his willpower not to bawl his eyes out the entire flight to Portland.

He quickly tapped out a reply to Micah.

Forest: I just landed. Happy to see your messages. The flight was sad if that makes sense.

· · ·

HE WANTED to add *"I miss you already,"* but he wasn't sure if he should. Sure, they had exchanged phone numbers, but they'd been pretty clear this wasn't a relationship. It couldn't be, not with them on opposite sides of the country and them being so different. It could never work, his head said, but his heart squeezed painfully at the thought of never seeing Micah again.

A car honked, and he looked up, spotting his sister Rain a few cars down, waving at him frantically. He made his way over, throwing his backpack in the back seat of her car.

"What's with the sad face?" Rain asked after he'd hugged her.

He'd always appreciated his older sister's mad skills as a psychologist, but not today. "Can we not talk about it?" he asked. "I need to settle a bit first."

She sent him a smile, then drove off. "Of course. Just know that I'm here to listen."

It was about an hour's drive from the airport in Portland to where he lived, in a small log cabin on his parents' property. It was far enough away from their house to have independence and privacy, but he loved living close to his parents and siblings.

His mom and dads had bought a gorgeous piece of land out in the forest and had transformed it into a little piece of paradise, if you asked Forest. He'd debated moving to Portland multiple times, but he couldn't make himself leave behind the sound of the birds singing that he woke up to, or the deer that came to his yard in the early morning, or the calming sound of the little brook that passed by his cabin.

It was another strike against even the possibility of the relationship between him and Micah, because they came from different worlds. Forest couldn't see himself living in the city, and it was a safe bet Micah would never want to leave his job in New York. And never the twain shall meet, he thought, and let out a deep sigh.

"How was Munich?" Rain asked.

The simple question stabbed Forest in the heart, and he felt his eyes well up. "I can't, okay? I can't talk about it."

Rain shot him a concerned look sideways, then took his hand for a second to squeeze it. "Okay."

They drove in silence until his phone beeped with an incoming message.

Micah: I know all about sad.

On some level, knowing that Micah shared his sadness comforted Forest, but only a little bit. It also stressed the impossibility of their situation, and as they got closer and closer to his cabin, he had to ball his fists to keep himself from crying.

They talked and texted and video-called every day, as much as they could both squeeze in. For the first time in his life, Micah was slacking a bit on the job, his head more with Forest than with the processes and procedures that had always been his passion.

"What's going on with you, baby?" his mom asked that night. "Ever since you came back from that trip to Munich last month, you've been different."

He put the mashed potatoes on the table and checked to make sure he had everything, then took a seat across from her. It had been a miracle he'd been able to keep this from her this long, especially considering they lived in the same house.

It was a sad reality that at twenty-eight, he still lived with his mother, but what else could he do? After his brother died, he couldn't move out. He couldn't leave her by herself, even though she was in good health and worked a full-time job. It just didn't feel right, as if he was abandoning her.

"I know, mama. Something happened on that trip, and I've had a hard time bouncing back from it."

His mother's eyes narrowed in concern. "Something bad? Why didn't you tell me?"

He added some green beans to his plate. "No, mama, something good. I met someone, but...it's complicated. We really connected, but our lives are miles apart, literally and figuratively."

"Complicated can be good," his mother commented, and he couldn't resist a smile. It reminded him of what Forest had said, that he was starting to appreciate complicated.

"I know. But sometimes, the complications are too big to overcome."

Thankfully, she let it go. "Thank you for cooking, darling. I'll be out of your hair in a few minutes, because I know your friends are coming over."

His mom never failed to give him privacy during his monthly hang out with his friends, and he loved her for it. He had everything cleaned up and some snacks ready when his friends started coming in. He hadn't seen them since he'd gotten back from Munich, and it didn't take long for them to see something was different about him as well. He wasn't sure what they saw, until Lex, one of his friends, put it into words.

"Micah, honey, what's with the aura of sadness hanging around you? What happened?" they asked.

And looking at his friends, Micah knew he owed them the truth. "I met someone in Munich."

Lex put their hand on Micah's arm. "Judging by that sadness, I assume it didn't go well?"

"It was wonderful. We really connected on every level, but it was just for one night, you know? He lives in Oregon, and I have my life here, and he's an outdoors and travel writer who never stays in one place, and I am...me. How the hell would that ever work?"

He appreciated that none of them came with quick fixes and easy answers, but took their time asking questions about Forest and about their time together, and so he shared everything with them. Well, not everything. He kind of summarized their *other activities* in a single sentence, but they got the drift.

"If anything were possible, if nothing held you back, what would you do?" Kennedy asked.

Micah let out a deep sigh. "Well, we all know there's a lot holding me back, but in a different world, a different time, and a different me, I guess I would quit my job, find another job near Portland, and move there to be with him."

"You never liked living near the city," Kennedy said. "You've talked for years about wanting to be in a less populated area, closer to nature."

Micah scoffed. "I've talked about a lot of things, but I've never actually done them, have I? We all know it's not gonna happen."

He looked around the room to his friends' faces. Kennedy gave a reluctant nod, and he saw the resignation on the faces of the others as well. The only one who looked like he didn't agree was Thomas, who studied him, his head cocked.

"There's an interesting dynamic at work here," Thomas said.

The others started groaning, used to Thomas's somewhat lengthy explorations in philosophy and psychology, but Micah leaned forward. "What do you mean?"

"The concept of a self-fulfilling prophecy is well documented, and many psychological experiments show that it is legit. Now, we know that you struggle with change and that you have a hard time letting go of the need to know what's going to happen. Right? It's not exactly a control issue, because you're not super dominant in nature, but you can't let go and follow until you have clear expectations. Does that sound right?"

Micah nodded, curious where Thomas was going with this.

"We know where this tendency stems from. We've all seen the complete chaos your asshole brother brought into your life and that of your mom. But ever since you were labeled, for lack of a better word, with this struggle, ever since that shrink helped you define it and explained where it was coming from, you've kept stressing it to yourself and also to us. I'm starting to wonder if you're not reinforcing it by doing that. In other words, how much of your struggle is real and how much is caused by self-fulfilling prophecies? If you tell yourself you're going to have an issue with something, isn't that exactly what's going to happen?"

An almost revered silence hung in the room when Thomas was done, and Micah merely blinked, trying to process what his friend had said. Thomas had never finished his master's degree, but he'd sure had fun experimenting with five different majors, and in moments like this, his knowledge showed.

"You're saying that if he starts telling himself he's no longer afraid of change, he won't be?" Kennedy asked.

"I don't think it will be suddenly gone," Thomas said. "But I do think he's reinforcing it with his attitude. And I realize it's kind of a vicious circle, but if we can find a way to help him gain more confidence that he *can* change, he may be able to reduce it to a level where it won't affect him so much."

Micah swallowed. It wasn't easy to be confronted with your weaknesses like this, but he couldn't deny Thomas had a point. He'd almost used his diagnosis as a shield, as an excuse. "How come you never said anything before?"

"Because you never had something worth fighting for, but now you do. The way you talk about Forest, that sounds like someone worth changing for. Tell me I'm wrong."

Micah's eyes grew misty. "I think he is. I don't know if he feels the same way about me, but I think he might. Our texts have grown more personal and intimate, and I know he keeps telling me he misses me."

Lex took his hand and squeezed it gently. "Micah, babe, do you want to change for him? Because if you do, we will help you. We're here."

Nerves tore through his body, his hands clammy and his heart racing, but the truth had never been clearer to Micah. "Yes. Yes, I want to change."

6

Two months after his unexpected encounter with Micah in Munich, Forest was surprised to find himself in a long-term relationship. No matter how much Micah and he had both stressed it would never work, neither of them were willing to actually end it. Whatever *it* was. They texted throughout the day and did a long video call at night.

Forest had been lucky that he'd been traveling mainly in the US itself as well as one short trip to Costa Rica, only small time differences with Micah. The three-hour time difference between him on the West Coast and Micah on the East Coast was an issue sometimes, but Micah usually started calling him as soon as he got in the car after work, and switched to video call when he got home.

They had talked about everything and anything by now, and the more Forest got to know Micah, the more the distance between them hurt. How long could they keep this up? It was the question they never brought up, probably because neither of them had an answer.

Forest would leave for a ten-day backpacking trip to

Peru tomorrow, and for the first time in his life, he was dreading leaving. He wouldn't have cell reception for most of his trip, meaning he wouldn't be able to talk to Micah for at least a week.

"At some point, you're gonna talk to us, right?" Rain said, quietly leaning against the wall of his kitchen while he packed his gear.

Forest sent her a tense smile and shrugged. "Not sure what good talking is going to do in this case."

He'd told his parents and siblings about Micah, but not more than the basics. Somehow, it felt too fragile and intimate to share more with them. All they knew was that the two of them had met in Munich and that Micah lived in New York.

"We're worried about you," Rain said.

"I'm fine."

"You're not fine," Rain insisted. "The only time you're fine is when you're on the phone with Micah, and even then, there's this lingering sadness in your eyes."

His jaw tightened. They didn't understand. "Look, I know that you're a big fan of the 'love will conquer everything' club, just like mom and dads, but in reality, it isn't quite that simple. I want to be with Micah, but I can't, so this is all we have."

Rain walked up and gently pulled his hands off his backpack, forcing him to face her. "Tell me why, please, because I don't understand. I can see how much he means to you, so what could possibly be so important that it's keeping the two of you apart? Doesn't he feel the same?"

Exhaustion filled Forest, and he let his head rest on his sister's shoulder, stepping into her embrace. She hugged him, kissing his head.

"He has a job in New York City, a job that means every-

thing to him. I have a job here, so there's our first problem.
Aside from that, Micah went through some shit in his past,
and as a result, he has a hard time dealing with change. I
can't ask him to quit his job and move across the country for
me. It would totally freak him out. So where does that leave
us? I have all these trips that I do for the magazine, and you
know I've always said I would not give them up for anyone,
but right now, if somebody were to call me and tell me our
trip to Peru got canceled, I would pop open a bottle of
champagne. I don't want to leave, I don't want to not be able
to talk to Micah for a week. This was supposed to be a one-
night stand, but I'm in over my head and I don't know what
to do."

His heart did feel a little lighter now that he had shared
this with his sister, but when she remained quiet, he figured
she'd helped him the best she could by listening. And she
was right, it wasn't like anybody could do anything.

"Do you want me to just listen to you or can I offer some
advice?"

He stepped out of her embrace, looking at her with
curiosity. "You have advice?"

She nodded. "Really good advice. Want to hear it?"

He nodded, a sliver of hope unfolding in his heart.

"You always told us you wouldn't stop traveling until you
were done with it yourself, that you wouldn't give it up for
anyone. You're not giving it up if you choose to travel less
because you want to be with Micah. That's not giving it up
for him. That's realizing that spending time with him means
more to you than spending time by yourself, even if you're
traveling. He's not asking you to, Forest. You're *choosing* to.
The fact that you're so reluctant to spend ten days in beautiful Peru should tell you all you need to know."

She was right. Forest stared at her, his brain considering

her words from every angle and not finding any fault in her reasoning. He'd always blamed previous boyfriends for either wanting to come with him on his travels or asking him to stay home. Micah had done neither. He had never so much as protested against Forest's chosen profession, not even when it separated them even further.

And it *was* true. He didn't want to go to Peru, because he didn't want to lose out on that time with Micah. Every day, he looked forward to their calls so much that he'd started to clear his entire schedule to make sure he would have time.

"There's more," Rain said, and Forest blinked.

"I understand why it might be too hard for him to uproot his whole life and move here. So what is keeping you from moving to the East Coast? What is holding you back from moving to New York? And don't tell me it's giving up nature, because if you are in love with him as much as I think you are, that is a sacrifice you should be willing to make. Besides, who says that after spending some time together, you couldn't pick a place where you would both be happy, just not under the incredible pressure that you are in right now."

Forest blinked again, his mind completely blank. He was sure he'd had reasons why he couldn't move east, but right now, none of them seemed to make as much sense as his sister's simple words. Then it hit him, the even deeper truth in her words.

"I'm in love with him," he said slowly as tears filled his eyes. "Oh my God, Rain, I'm totally in love with him. I don't want to be without him anymore."

Rain's face broke open in a blinding smile. "Do you need a lift to the airport?"

Hours later, he was on a plane to New York, his heart still racing from the craziness of his endeavor. He'd texted Micah that he had an urgent appointment and wouldn't be able to video call with him before he left on his trip. Micah had reacted with disappointment but had said he understood. Of course, Forest hadn't told him that he canceled the Peru trip. That had been easier than he'd expected, as a friend of one of the other guys had been happy to take his place.

He didn't get to Micah's house till almost midnight, surprised to see all the lights still on inside. Micah usually went to bed pretty early, but maybe he'd changed his plans because it was a Friday night and Forest had canceled their call?

He rang the doorbell, a little nervous about how Micah would react to him showing up out of the blue. Maybe he shouldn't have sprung this on him, considering the guy's aversion to the unexpected.

When the door opened, Forest almost took a step back in surprise. That was not Micah but a gorgeous man... woman?...person wearing a flowery skirt, a tight top, and the prettiest purple mascara he'd ever seen.

"Can I help you?" they asked, apprehension coloring their face, until their eyes narrowed as they took in Forest. "Wait. You're Forest. Oh my god, he's gonna flip."

Forest smiled nervously. "Yep, that's me. Flip in a good way or bad way? Should I leave?"

A strong hand dragged him inside, closing the door behind them. "Oh no honey, you're not going anywhere. You're going to be as surprised as he is," they said, then giggled melodiously.

Forest was pulled into the living room, where his eyes immediately found Micah, who sat on a chair next to three other men, all with their bare feet in small, blue basins with water. The room smelled of lavender, and Forest wondered what the hell they were doing.

"Micah," the person who had opened the door sing-songed.

Micah looked up and his mouth dropped open, before he jumped up and yanked his feet out of the basin, sending the water sloshing over the edges on every side. With soaking wet feet, he closed the distance between them, and all Forest could do was open his arms and catch him.

He closed his eyes, holding him so tight he felt it in his muscles, inhaling the scent that was uniquely Micah.

"Oh god, I've missed you," he breathed into his ear. "I've missed you so fucking much."

He gently pulled him back by his neck, needing to see his expression. The shock had been replaced by an emotion so deep that Forest had no doubt Micah loved him.

"I love you," he said, unable to keep it in any longer. "I love you more than I had ever thought possible."

"Forest..." Micah sighed against his lips, and in that one word, Forest heard everything he needed to know.

He kissed him, first tender and sweet, then deep and with the urgency of the two months he hadn't seen him. And Micah kissed him back just as hard and deep and frantic, until wolf whistles around them brought them back to reality.

The others had abandoned their basins as well, and a few towels had been thrown on the floor to soak up the water that was everywhere.

"These are my friends, Kennedy, Lex, Thomas, and BJ," Micah said, his voice thick with emotion. "Everyone, this is Forest. In case that wasn't clear."

Forest waved at the people in the room, refusing to let Micah go just yet. "What were you all doing?" he asked.

"It was supposed to be a surprise for you," Micah said sheepishly. "We all agreed that I needed a little push to help me overcome my fear of change, so for the last month, they've all given me challenges with new things I had to try."

"He went rollerblading with me," Kennedy said. "And he had to cook a new recipe twice a week."

BJ nodded. "I took him to my yoga studio every week for a session, and I made him buy new underwear." He giggled his eyebrows suggestively, and Forest grinned.

"We did a sushi workshop together and an introductory course to meditation." That was Thomas, who looked very bohemian, Forest decided.

"My contribution to the new Micah was to make him get a haircut and introduce him to the wonderful world of a mani-pedi. Tonight, we were just gonna soak our feet in some lovely lavender cleansing salts," Lex said.

Forest looked at Micah, whose eyes showed insecurity. "Those are some pretty big changes," he said softly. "How did that feel for you, to try so many new things?"

Micah put his head against Forest's shoulder, and a rush of warmth went through Forest at the memory of how perfect that body had felt against his. He couldn't believe they were together again.

"The first few ones were scary, but my friends were super supportive and understanding. Thomas helped me see change in a different light and formulated a process, a procedure that had steps I could identify, and that resistance was a natural part of that process. We talked about how I could push through it, and that really helped."

Forest smiled, recognizing the description from his sister's approach. "A little cognitive therapy, huh? I'm so proud of you, baby, and so happy to see that it worked for you."

Micah looked up at him. "It's not all gone. I mean, this is all still hard for me."

Forest put both his hands on Micah's shoulders and made eye contact. "You made progress, that's what matters. You're growing, that's all anyone can ask of you."

Micah's face broke open in a smile, and then Forest saw him take a deep breath. "I want to move west with you. I would love to move away from the busyness of the city, and what you've told me about where you live and the pictures you showed me, it looks amazing. But I'm not ready yet. That's too big of a step right now."

Forest's heart felt so big it could burst. "Baby, I would love that. But in the meantime, I'm moving here."

"You're what?" Micah asked, furiously blinking.

Forest cupped his face with both his hands, kissing him tenderly. "I want to move here. I want to be with you. We'll figure out the where of it all, but these two months without you were hell."

"But... But your job? How are you going to do that?"

"I've told the magazine I am going part-time, only doing those assignments I want to, the ones that don't take me away from you for too long. Maybe in the future we can travel together more, but for now, you are my priority. I have some money saved, and there are enough freelance writing jobs available around here, so I'm sure I will find something."

"Move in with me," Micah said. "My mom has been on my ass to move out, and she's right. But I want to do it with you."

"Babe, that's a pretty big commitment and a huge change. Are you sure you're ready for that?"

Micah looked up at him with big eyes that radiated love. "With you, changes don't seem so big and scary anymore. Besides, I love you too."

With tears in his eyes, Forest kissed him again, and then

he couldn't let him go again. Apparently, Micah felt the same, because he started tugging him toward the stairs to the basement where his room was.

"You guys go," BJ waved. "We promise we won't listen in."

Someone laughed, but Forest was too preoccupied with Micah to see who it was. "You mean we won't listen in and you'll have your ear on the floor."

"Come on, let's clean this up so his mom doesn't come home to a mess. We'll leave her a note," someone else said, and then Forest closed the door to the basement behind them and focused on the beautiful man in front of him.

His man.

EPILOGUE: A YEAR LATER

Micah looked around the living room, finally happy with the way it looked after rearranging it four times.

"We good now?" Forest asked with the patience that characterized him.

Micah nodded sheepishly. "Sorry, I wanted—"

He stopped talking when he realized he'd uttered the forbidden word.

"Uh oh," Forest said, putting down the box of books he'd just picked up from the hallway. "I heard that."

"It was an accident," Micah said, knowing it was useless to argue with Forest. The man had installed a rule a few months ago that Micah couldn't apologize for himself anymore, not for things he couldn't help.

"Nope, not buying it. Choose a punishment from the jar. I unpacked it first thing, and it's on the kitchen counter."

Micah pouted, but Forest merely laughed until he relented and got the jar from the kitchen. It held dozens of little notes, all written by Forest, containing all kinds of creative punishments for Micah. They usually involved him doing something weird, new, or daring. It was another fun way in which Forest constantly challenged Micah to push the boundaries of his comfort zone.

He'd grown more than he thought possible, his move to Colorado the biggest proof of that. They'd met each other kind of halfway after Forest had been approached about a job at an outdoors activity center that organized events like hiking tours in the Rockies and rafting. Micah had gathered all his courage and had asked his company for a transfer to Boulder, and they'd been delighted to have him. They'd bought a cute house on two acres of land, both excited to live close to nature.

Micah held the jar and with a dramatic gesture, took out a note. "I cannot wait to see what torture you've devised for me now," he muttered, then folded open the note and read it.

Marry me.

His breath caught in his lungs and his head jerked up. Forest was sinking to his knee, holding out a small velvet box, and Micah's eyes filled.

"Please, say yes?" Forest asked, and Micah didn't even think.

"Yes! Oh god, yes. No one else but you," he said, then caught Forest in the most awkward hug ever, which they quickly corrected into a passionate kiss.

"I love you so much," Forest said with his lips against Micah's. "And I don't want to spend another day without you."

He knew him so well, Micah realized, not making a grand thing out of this proposal, but doing it as low key as possible so it wouldn't freak him out. "I love you," he whispered. "And I can't wait to spend the rest of my life with you."

THE END

WAITING FOR ALEXANDER

NOTE FROM NORA

This is a brand new, never before published story. If you've read Coming Out on Top (previously titled Snow Way Out), you may remember that Quentin did research into small town dynamics. When he visited the gas station in Northern Lake, he caught an argument between two men, Alexander and Langley.

This is their story.

PROLOGUE

Five Years Before

NORTHERN LAKE in the winter was a miserable, cold-as-fuck hell, tucked away in the New York Adirondack Mountains. Common wisdom said hell was hot, but to Langley, being frozen was ten times worse than sweating your ass off, so hell being cold made way more sense to him. Why the fuck had his father decided this was the perfect place to move to? They could've moved to Arizona, for fuck's sake. Texas. Even Florida. Granted, the people there were nuts, but at least it was warm.

The skies were blue, the sun was bright, and a biting wind clawed through his winter jacket, nipping at his bones as he hurried across the parking lot into the main entrance of Lakelands High School. He was late. Again. And since he already had three tardies and last time, Principal Riggings hadn't seemed inclined to let him off with a warning until

Langley had finally persuaded him, he'd better not run into the man.

He dashed through the hallway, the empty state of which told him he'd already missed the buzzer. Crap. The only hope he had was that he had gym first period and that Coach Meyer really liked Langley as his star quarterback, so hopefully that would get him off.

But when he stormed into the locker room, it wasn't Coach Meyer who stood there waiting for him. Nope, it was Alexander Wingard, owner of Northern Lake Gas and Convenience and Lakelands High School's pride and glory and single claim to fame, as he was the only alumni who had ever made it to a professional sports team. Or to anything famous and of importance, really. Unfortunately, a devastating knee injury in his rookie year on the Red Sox had ended it all for him.

"Oh," Langley said as he skittered to a full stop. He was eloquent like that, especially when confronted with the sight of Alexander's magnificent body packed in a pair of shorts and a tight T-shirt. *Hello, Daddy.* Cue drool.

"You're late, Mr. Malcolm."

"You know my name?"

The other boys in the locker room snickered. "Your class has ten students, Mr. Malcolm. Even this dumb jock can check off nine names and deduce you must be the tenth one."

Right. Fuck. "Okay. Just making sure, since I'm new in town."

Brilliant dialogue. Absolutely dazzling. No wonder Alexander—Mr. Wingard—looked at him as if he was spouting nonsense. He kinda was.

"Not that new. You've been here, what, six months now? I've seen you at the gas station at least ten times."

Did that mean Alexander—oh, for fuck's sake, he had to think of him as Mr. Wingard—had been looking for him? Paid attention to him? "Erm, yes, sir. Coach. Mr. Wingard. Six months and ten days."

The man's mouth pulled up in one corner. "I see we're keeping track."

Busted. "I guess?"

"Let's get back to the previous topic. You're late."

All the excuses that always came so easily stayed quiet, nothing popping into his brain. "Yes, sir. I apologize, sir."

"No need to call me sir. As I was telling the others before you interrupted me with your late arrival, Coach Meyer had a car accident yesterday evening. He's in stable condition, but he won't be returning to the classroom anytime soon, so Principal Riggins has asked me to fill in as PE teacher, probably until the end of the school year. You guys can call me Coach Wingard."

Oh god, he would be *teaching* them? Holy shit, that was... A problem. A *big* problem. About seven inches, to be exact. Alexander Wingard was many things to many people, ranging from one hell of a baseball player to a businessman, a neighbor, a friend, and more. But to Langley, only one thing mattered. Alexander was gay. Out and proud gay, though he didn't flaunt it.

And while Langley had been suspecting for a while he himself wasn't straight, he hadn't known for sure until the first time he'd met Alexander. Lightning had struck, angelic choirs had sung, and Langley had barely caught himself before he'd literally drooled. The man was...hot. Seriously hot. The stuff of highly erotic dreams in which he'd worn even fewer clothes than he did right now and had been a hell of a lot nicer to Langley.

Having him as his substitute PE teacher meant a few

things. One, he'd never be late again for gym. Two, he'd better wear double layers of damn tight underwear because no fucking way would he not get a hard-on from watching him. And three... He'd had a third point. What was it again?

Right. Three, he would use this opportunity to subtly signal to Alexander that he, too, was gay. He was two months away from graduating, and he was already eighteen. Surely he'd be able to convince Alexander to *coach* him in a different way, no?

Oh, who the fuck was he kidding? Fuck subtle. He knew what he wanted, and he wasn't gonna stop until he had him. Alexander Wingard was *his*.

1

No matter how often Alexander ran the numbers, it always came down to the same thing. Funny how that worked with math. The bottom line was that he was fucked. Utterly, completely fucked. Bankruptcy-and-sell-his-house-and-business fucked. He pushed back the keyboard of his computer and got up, taking off his Red Sox cap for a moment to scratch his hair. He needed a haircut, he noted absentmindedly. If he could even still afford one.

Bitterness burned sharply in his stomach. What did he do now? He couldn't sell. This was his dad's legacy, the one thing he'd left Alexander. Besides, he'd already failed at his baseball career. He couldn't fail at this as well. But what could he do? His father might've left him the gas station and the little house behind it, but it had come with a shitload of debt that Alexander had not known about. Some kind of investment his father had made that had been a scam. He'd borrowed money for it, and he'd been trying to pay it off since. Was that what had caused his heart attack?

He'd never breathed a word of it to Alexander, always

keeping up a good front. Apparently, that ran in the family, as did pride. Unfortunately, pride didn't pay the bills. Was Northern Lake simply too small to sustain a gas station slash convenience store? In the summer, things were better, and the weekends and breaks in the winter, when the slopes brought in skiers, were good as well. But that left a lot of days where no one would come in for hours.

He looked at the clock. Case in point. It had been over an hour since his last customer, and that had been Tim Capes who'd filled half the tank of his old truck, netting the shocking amount of not even twenty dollars. Yeah, he'd better learn how to cut his own hair. And maybe start baking his own bread and learn how to grow a veggie garden or some shit. Lord knew he had the time between customers.

Should he try to get some substitute teacher jobs again? At least he'd have a bit of extra money to keep him afloat... As long as he didn't run into another Langley, he'd be fine. That boy had been stubborn as fuck...and too cocky for his own good. Pretty damn sexy too—not that Alexander would ever tell him that. He'd done his very best to stay away from him, knowing damn well that boy was trouble with a capital T.

Langley had left town right after graduation, for which Alexander would be eternally grateful, even if it had taken months before he stopped looking for him every time a black pickup truck pulled up. Temptation had removed itself—although he'd certainly helped that happen with a few harsh words—and Alexander had been relieved. Kind of. He hadn't seen him in five years, and he probably never would again, which was for the best. Langley had been too young for him, too innocent, despite his attitude.

Speaking of Langley, maybe he should try to set up a

meeting with Langley's father, Nick Malcolm. The man was one of the richest businessmen in the area, and from the grapevine, Alexander knew that he regularly helped neighbors with loans on friendly terms. Maybe if he could get a loan, he'd be able to make it. If he could just pay off the debtors and start from zero...

The motion sensor buzzed, and he looked on the security monitor that showed him the camera feeds outside. He didn't recognize the sparkling red pickup truck, but for the thing to be this pristine in this weather, it had to be either brand new or just washed. Snow and salt did horrible things to cars.

He walked into the shop in case the customer needed to pay inside. The driver was getting gas now, and he could only see him from the back, bundled up in a winter jacket with a beanie pulled low over his ears. Alexander only guessed the customer was a man based on his height, which had to be well above six feet. But he still didn't look familiar. Probably a tourist. The ski resort nearby drew a lot of visitors each season.

For some reason, he kept watching through the window, waiting until the man was done filling up. Damn, that was one hell of a nice truck. Brand spanking new, if Alexander had to take a guess. The man closed the gas tank, straightened, and turned around. Alexander gasped, and his heart skipped a beat. It couldn't be. He'd literally been thinking about him minutes before. It couldn't be Langley. He was imagining things.

But when the man walked into the store, the bell above the door chiming happily, Alexander's stomach flipped. It was him. "What the fuck are you doing here?"

Langley unzipped his jacket, then stalked toward

Alexander, clearly unfazed by Alexander's rude remark. "Is that how you greet me after five years?"

"What, you expected a red carpet? I told you to leave."

"I did. I haven't been back since that day."

"Then why are you here now?"

Fuck, his eyes were as ice blue as they'd always been, always drawing Alexander in. Ridiculous. He should've gotten over this weird magnetism thing years ago.

"I came back for you."

Alexander's eyes widened. "The fuck you did."

Langley slowly shook his head. "Tsk, accusing me of lying, Xander?"

"My name is Alexander, and yes, I am. Besides, I told you to leave and never come back."

Langley stepped close to him. So close, Alexander could smell his subtle cologne, could feel the warmth of Langley's breath on his skin. "Now, who's lying?"

"What do you mean?" Oh, he knew, but he'd hoped Langley had forgotten. He should've known better.

"You didn't tell me to leave and never come back. You told me to leave and come back when I was a man rather than a boy. Well, here I am, Xander."

Alexander swallowed as he took a step back. Fuck, fuck, fuck. Of course he remembered. Langley had an elephant's memory. "It's been five years. Are you seriously telling me you think you're a man at twenty-three?"

"Mmm, someone has been keeping track again... Did you miss me, Xander?"

"Like a pain in my ass. And stop calling me Xander."

"A pain in your ass, you say? Interesting. I'd thought you were a strict top."

"I'm... You're... That's highly inappropriate!" Alexander sputtered. Fuck, if Langley only knew.

"Inappropriate?" Langley laughed, and Alexander's belly did a flipflop. Had he stepped forward again? They were close once again. "We're not in high school anymore where I had to call you Coach, and you stubbornly kept calling me Mr. Malcolm."

He'd had to. If Alexander had allowed himself even an inch of liberty, he wouldn't have been able to resist Langley. He'd been cocky, all six foot four of him, and fuck, his body had been...perfection. Smooth muscles, all athletic and graceful, and Alexander had never so much as *looked* at Langley in the locker rooms, too scared he'd catch him naked and pop a boner.

"I'm still seventeen years older than you," he said, jamming his hands into his pockets as he increased the distance between them again.

"Yes, and you always will be. I get it. But I'm no longer in high school, and you're no longer a substitute, so what reason do you have now to keep me at arms' length?"

Alexander avoided his eyes. "How about the fact that I just don't like you?"

Langley grinned, winking at him. "You may not like me, but you sure as hell want to fuck me. You did five years ago, and you still do. But I'll give you some time to get used to the idea." He pulled a fifty out of his pocket and held it out to Alexander, who accepted it automatically, then mentally cursed himself. "That's for the gas. Keep the change. I'll be back, Xander."

2

"I still don't understand why you're back," Langley's father muttered as he sipped his coffee and stared at Langley from across the breakfast table. "Thank you, Di," he said to their housekeeper, who came to collect their plates. "Delicious as always."

"Don't you like having me here?" Langley asked.

"Of course I do, but you were crystal clear on how much you hated Northern Lake. I have vivid memories of detailed rants about the weather, how isolated you were here, and that no decent college recruiter would ever come here to watch you play."

Langley grinned. "It is still cold as fuck here, I do object to the fact that there's not a Starbucks in a fifty-mile radius, but I did get a football scholarship..."

"And now you're back."

"For now."

"You're not staying?"

Langley sighed, avoiding his father's scrutinizing look. "I haven't decided yet what my next step will be."

"Langley, you have your MBA...and with phenomenal

grades, I might add. What the fuck are you doing here rather than accepting one of the dozen job offers you received?"

Langley couldn't look away anymore, not when his father's concern for him was so genuine. "I need a little break, Dad. Just a few weeks, maybe a month or two, three. I've worked my ass off the last five years. I just need a breather."

His father's eyes softened. "Okay, I can understand that. You have worked hard to graduate this quickly, and you know how proud I am of you. It's not that I don't love having you here because I do."

Langley and his father had always been close. His dad had raised him after his mom had walked out on her marriage and her son when Langley had been four. "I know, Dad. And I'm happy to spend some time with you as well. Maybe look over your shoulder in some of your business dealings here. I'm sure I could learn a lot from you."

His father laughed. "Smart move, young man, buttering me up."

Langley winked at him. "I learned from the best."

"You sure did. Speaking of business dealings..." His father checked his watch. "I have a meeting coming up, so I'm heading to my office. A businessman in town who's asked for my advice."

"Who?" Langley asked, more out of habit than anything else.

"Alexander Wingard, the owner of the gas station." Langley's quiet gasp went unnoticed when his father frowned. "Didn't you have him as a substitute coach in high school?"

"Yeah." Langley cleared his throat. "Coach Meyer had

that accident, remember? And Alexander...Mr. Wingard... played for the Red Sox for a season as a shortstop."

His father snapped his fingers, his face lighting up. "Of course, now I remember."

"What does he need your help with?"

"I don't know yet, but I'll be able to tell you more after."

"Maybe that could be a good case for me to have a look at..." Langley tried to keep his voice as casual as possible, and it seemed to work because his father nodded.

"Sure, but let me find out what he needs first, okay?"

Langley didn't leave the living room, passing the time by playing games on his phone and checking the news while keeping an eye on the front door. As soon as his father walked in, he jumped up and greeted him in the hallway. "Hey, Dad. How did the meeting go?"

His father looked taken aback for a moment. Oops, he'd been a little too eager, maybe? "Erm, good, but why the interest?"

Shit. His father couldn't know why Langley was so involved in this. The man was absolutely no homophobe, and he'd barely blinked when Langley had come out, but if he found out about Langley's crush, he'd never allow him to consult with him on whatever Alexander had asked for help with. "Oh, just curious... You know, not much else to do here, so..."

"Right." His father shot him a last probing look, then seemed to accept Langley's explanation and hung up his coat. "He's in deep financial trouble. It's a sad situation, since most of it isn't even his fault but the result of a crushing debt his father left behind when he died seven years ago."

Financial trouble? That didn't sound good at all. "How serious is it?"

"Serious enough that he swallowed his pride and asked me for help. He's asked for a loan."

"Are you gonna give it to him?"

His father sighed and walked into his office, Langley on his heels. "I don't know, to be honest. I'll need to study his numbers in more detail, but I'm not sure he'll ever be able to pay it back, not with what little profit he's making."

"So what he really needs is to increase his sales."

"Yes, but that's not an easy feat in a town this small. The market is limited."

"Dad, can I take this case from you? As, like, something to help me get real-world experience?"

His father put his briefcase on the floor next to his desk, then slowly turned around. "Why this case? I can think of at least three projects I'm working on that would be far more interesting to you, including the expansion of the ski resort."

Langley waved his hand dismissively. "Yeah, but with those, I'd be working under you. This is a small enough scale I could do it on my own. Get my feet wet."

"Mmm, true. Good point." He seemed to think for a moment, his brow furrowing, and Langley waited with bated breath. "Sure, why not. I already informed Mr. Wingard one of my associates would most likely contact him, since this project is below my scale, so I don't see why that couldn't be you. You're on the payroll anyway, so all you need to do is sign an NDA, and we're good."

For tax reasons, Langley had been an employee in his father's firm since he was old enough to work. It had been a tax-friendly way to pay for his college, and now it came in handy even more.

"Thanks, Dad. I'm excited."

His father reached for his briefcase again and pulled out a file. "Here are my notes from this morning. Mr. Wingard's contact info is in there as well, so make sure to give him a call to inform him you're taking over from me."

"Will do." He took the file, barely able to hide his glee. Working with Alexander on this project was divine intervention, if nothing else. He'd be able to keep him from going bankrupt while at the same time spending time with him and convincing him they'd both waited long enough. Fuck knew Langley was done waiting. Five years was enough.

3

I t had been stupid to meet with Nick Malcolm. The man was Langley's father, for fuck's sake. And yet Alexander had forced himself to go through with the meeting, even after Langley had unexpectedly shown up at the gas station. What other choice did he have? None. Nothing. Nada.

But still, shame had sat heavy in his stomach, even though Nick Malcolm had been nothing but friendly and professional. He'd listened to Alexander, had asked him a ton of questions, and had made notes. That was a good sign, right? At least he took it seriously. He'd given Alexander a warm handshake, assuring him someone from his firm would be in touch. That had been yesterday, so surely, he wouldn't hear anything yet today. Those things took time, and it wasn't like he was in a position to make demands.

A shiny red truck pulled up and parked in front of the store. Alexander's heart skipped a beat, and he forced himself to stay calm as Langley got out and bleeped his car locked. Why the fuck did he still do that? This was Northern Lake. Nothing ever got stolen here. In the seven years he'd run the gas station, he'd had one case of shoplifting, and that had been some tourist kid from the city.

Langley sauntered into the store. Alexander frowned. Langley was dressed...differently. Gone were the tight jeans that sculpted his ass and made his legs look a mile long. Instead, he was wearing dress pants...with dress shoes...and a dress shirt with a tie.

"Good morning, Mr. Wingard," Langley said, beaming Alexander a smile so broad it had to make his jaw ache.

Mr. Wingard? What the fuck was that about? And what was with the outfit? He opened his mouth to snarl a response, but then it hit. Langley was dressed like a businessman...like his father. He'd come back to town...and he had an MBA. Oh please, no. Please don't let him be the—

"My father sends his regards. He's asked me to take on your case."

Fuck. Fuck. Fuckity Fuck.

He wanted to slap him. Pull back his fist and knock the cocky little shit out cold. And then kiss him and fuck his brains out, but he shoved that thought down. "I wasn't aware you worked for your father. Otherwise I would've made it clear I didn't want to work with you."

"You're hurting my feelings, Xander."

Well, at least he'd switched back from Mr. Wingard to Xander, and Alexander wasn't sure which one he hated more. "I didn't think that was even possible, considering how thick your skull is."

"My skull and my skin are two different parts of me, Xander. But I'll overlook it for now. I'm excited to work with you on this. All I need for now is access to your books and a time and place we can meet to discuss everything in detail. Dinner at your place at eight, when the store closes? I'll bring the food."

Alexander opened his mouth, then closed it again when a car pulled up at the pump. Mrs. Mosely. She'd need his help. Maybe Langley had a point that they needed to have this conversation in private. "Fine. I'll email you access info to my online accounting." Fuck knew he had to change his password first. No way in hell was he sending him his current password—QB26, after Langley's jersey number in high school. Talk about embarrassing. He wasn't even sure why he'd picked it...and then had never changed it.

Langley handed him a business card. "Perfect. That's my personal cell." He tapped the number with his index finger. "Call me any time, day or night."

Alexander ground his teeth. "Leave, would you? Before I shock Mrs. Mosely into a heart attack by slapping that grin off your face."

Langley merely winked. "See you tonight."

How the hell he managed to make that sound sexy and husky, Alexander didn't know, but he totally did. Cocky little fucker. Someone ought to teach him a lesson, but it wouldn't be Alexander. He'd stay as far away from him as he possibly could.

He put on his gas jacket, as he called it—his old winter jacket, which always smelled of gasoline. No sense in ruining all his clothes when he helped customers. Mrs. Mosely was still in her car, lowering her window. "Thank you, Alexander. I wouldn't know what to do without you," she said in her soft, creaky voice.

"My pleasure, Mrs. Mosely. Fill her up?"

Please let her say yes. That massive Lincoln town car she drove had a gas tank big enough it would buy him groceries, especially since she tipped royally. "Yes, dear. Thank you."

Halle-fucking-lujah. How sad was it that he was happy to have a customer who filled up their entire tank? Didn't that perfectly sum up the whole problem? He shook his head at himself as he took the cap off her gas tank. No need to let himself get sad all over again. Nope, given the choice between being depressed and being angry as fuck at Langley, he'd take the latter any day.

4

Bringing dinner had been a challenge. Langley's first thought had been that it couldn't be anything ostentatious, but then he'd laughed at himself. This was Northern fucking Lake. These folks wouldn't know ostentatious if it hit them over the head. But once he'd gotten past that, he'd frowned, trying to come up with a solid option. The local pizza joint was meh, Mary's Convenience and Café closed at five, the burgers Todd's Burgers served were so greasy you could squeeze them, and the two bars in town only served appetizers and snacks. What else was there?

To his shame, it took him an hour to come up with the solution, and by then, he wanted to slap himself that he hadn't thought of it. And so he drove to Xander's with steaming hot lasagna on the passenger seat, the smell of which filled his whole car and made his stomach rumble. Luckily, Xander opened the door as soon as Langley walked up. He wouldn't have been able to ring the bell with his hands full.

"Thanks," he said, walking right past Xander. No need to give him an opportunity to protest, right? "Kitchen?"

Xander frowned, then closed the door. "Second door on the left."

"Perfect."

Ah, great. The man had an oven. A remarkably clean one too. Langley turned it on, setting it to 425, and put the lasagna inside. He'd add the garlic bread once the oven was fully preheated. "Dinner will be ready in about fifteen minutes."

When he closed the oven door and looked up, Xander was standing in the doorway, looking at him funny. "We're eating lasagna," Langley said.

"I like lasagna."

They were making progress. Good. "I know."

Xander frowned. "How would you know?"

"Remember that Italian restaurant we went to after we beat Woodrow Wilson High?" Woodrow Wilson High had been their arch enemy, or so Langley had been told. He didn't care one way or the other, since he hated losing on principle, but after beating them 38 to 6, they'd been treated to an Italian dinner, sponsored by the PTA.

"Yeah, what about it?"

Langley grinned. "You ate your weight in lasagna."

"You remember that?"

He hadn't intended to go there, not this quickly, but he wouldn't lie either. He took a few steps toward him, Xander watching him with hooded eyes. "You'll find that I remember a lot about you. Everything, in fact. Including the fact that you love Italian food."

The air between them sizzled, and Xander licked his lips. Fuck, Langley wanted to kiss him. He wanted to do a hell of a lot more than that to him, but kissing would be a great start.

Xander took a step back, averting his eyes. "Where'd you even get lasagna? The nearest Italian restaurant is an hour's drive one way."

Langley smiled. "Rosaria made it. She's our cook, and she makes the most incredible lasagna."

"Your cook." Xander's face tightened. "Must be nice to have someone who cooks for you."

"It is, and I appreciate her just as much as I appreciate all the other staff my father has. I don't take it for granted, Xander. I'm rich, yes, but I'm not spoiled. I'm well aware of how lucky I am."

He kept his tone light. No sense in showing Xander how much he hated remarks like that. Of course things were easy for him when it came to anything material. His father had the money to pay for anything Langley had needed or wanted. He hadn't even needed scholarships or loans. Didn't mean he wasn't aware of his privilege and appreciated it.

Xander cleared his throat. "I don't understand why you invited yourself to dinner. This is not exactly a business setting."

"Because you've been on your feet from before six this morning until a few minutes ago, so the last thing I wanted was for you to have to leave the house. Just sit down, eat, and we can talk at the same time."

Something passed over Xander's face. "That's... I appreciate that. I am tired."

"I can imagine. Fourteen-hour workdays without breaks aren't healthy, and even less when you do this six times a week and then pull another eight-hour shift on Sunday."

"Do you think I don't know that? I have no choice. I can't afford to hire someone else."

Xander's voice broke a little near the end, and Langley's whole heart went out to him. "I know. That's why I'm here. To help."

"I need your father's money. That's all I need."

Langley took a deep breath. He shouldn't take this personally. Xander was exhausted, and he was taking it out on Langley. Understandable, even more considering how much Langley had riled him up. "Unfortunately, my father's money comes with strings attached. In this case, me and my help."

"Are you saying that if I refuse to work with you, I won't get the money?"

"What do you have against my help?"

Xander scoffed. "You don't know the first thing about running a gas station."

"And my father does?"

"No, but he's an experienced businessman."

Another deep breath. "I have an MBA. I literally studied this."

Xander blinked. "Right. Of course. I forgot for a second."

Forgot for a second? He said that as if he'd known what Langley had done the last five years. "Did you keep track of me?"

Much to his surprise, Xander looked away, shuffling his right foot over the scratched hardwood floor. "I was curious. You're a former student and one of the few who I thought would go far."

Langley's heart skipped a beat, and butterflies gathered in his stomach. "And? Did I make you proud?"

Xander looked up, and for the first time, he let his guard down, his blue eyes open and honest. "Yeah. Very proud. You have the whole world to explore, Langley, so why the fuck did you come back?"

Langley didn't think. "I came back for you." Xander's eyes widened as the rest of his body froze, but Langley wasn't deterred. "We had unfinished business, Xander."

"I don't know what you're talking about."

Oh, but he did. His reddening cheeks told Langley a whole different story than Xander's words did. Langley smiled. "You can deny it all you want, but we both know better. And I'm not going anywhere until we've worked this out...or fucked it out. Now, dinner's ready, so let's eat."

et's eat? Langley had to be kidding, right? He couldn't just say things like that and then expected Alexander to sit down and have a normal conversation over a steaming dish of lasagna...which smelled absolutely heavenly, by the way. And so did the garlic bread that had browned deliciously in the oven. Fuck, Alexander was hungry. All right, so he would sit down and eat. But only because it would be a shame to let the food go cold.

He watched with a combination of amusement and amazement as Langley moved around his kitchen as if he'd been there a million times before, opening drawers and cupboards until he'd found plates, glasses, and silverware. And if it was the most normal thing in the world, he cut out a quarter of the lasagna and put it on Alexander's dish. "There's your appetizer," he said with a wink, and fuck, that was funny. He'd always had a sense of humor.

For the first few minutes, neither of them spoke, both too busy wolfing down the garlic bread while waiting for the lasagna to cool off enough to eat. Once Alexander dug into the rich, creamy pasta, Langley spoke up. "I looked at your numbers over the last few years, and it's easy to see where the problem is."

"Yeah?" Alexander mumbled with his mouth full. "Please enlighten me."

"Don't be a dick. You know what the problem is as well. Your accounting system might be rudimentary, but it's meticulous. You know exactly what your issue is."

Alexander swallowed, then sighed. "Even without the debts I'm still paying off, I barely break even. This town isn't big enough to sustain a gas station."

Langley nodded. "Exactly. I've done some calculations, and for the last five years, you would've made less than a thousand dollars profit per month if I take out the payments you did toward your father's debt."

Your father's debt. Alexander couldn't explain it, but it meant a lot to him that Langley had reported it like that, as if stressing these debts were not Alexander's fault. He had inherited them, not caused them himself. "You made those calculations already? That's quick."

Langley shrugged. "Like I said, your books are meticulous. Once I had access, it wasn't that hard. I've become pretty handy with Excel sheets. I'll show you after dinner, but the bottom line is that your business model is not sustainable in the long run."

"That's a fancy way of saying I'm fucked."

Langley leaned forward, his eyes seeking Alexander's, and he didn't speak until Alexander met his intense gaze. "No. It's a fancy way of saying you need to make some changes."

"Like what? Sell?"

"Fuck no. Why would you sell? Unless that's what you want? My father told me you wanted to keep it, both the gas station and the house."

"I do, but I don't see any way I can make that happen, not in the long run. I know I shouldn't be telling you this, but it's not like you or your father wouldn't be smart enough to figure it out yourself. A loan from you would tide me over for maybe a year, but after that, I would be in the exact same situation."

"Exactly. That's what I'm telling you. You do need to make some changes, but that change is not selling. It's diversifying your offerings. You need to change your business model and become far less dependent on the sales of gas alone."

Despite himself, Alexander was intrigued now. He had to admit that he hadn't expected much from Langley and especially not for him to have an analysis already. "I don't know what else I could sell. Not without getting into trouble with Mary, who is already a competitor since she added a convenience store to her café."

"Your busiest day of the week is Sunday, correct?"

Alexander nodded.

"Do you know why?"

Huh. Good question. He'd never actually thought about it beyond some assumptions. "My idea was it had to do with tourists and especially people heading for the slopes."

"That's certainly part of it, but quick analysis shows that local sales are up on Sunday as well."

"They are? How would you explain that?" Despite himself, he was now intrigued by what Langley was hinting at.

"Is Mary's still closed on Sundays?"

"Yeah, but..."

"Unless something has changed, your gas station is the only store that's open on Sunday in the area. It was like that when I lived here, and I doubt that much has changed in between."

"It is, and everyone knows that, so I'm not sure how that would get me more sales. I mean, I know Sundays are my busiest days, but it's still a small town, so there are only so many customers, even on a busy day."

"That's why the goal isn't to draw in more customers in the first place but to make them spend more. If they already come here for the quick groceries they forgot to buy during the week, we need to give them a reason to buy more than what they came for. Impulse buys. Things they don't need but that they want when they see them. Or things they never knew they wanted until they saw them."

Impulse buys. In theory, Alexander knew what those were, but what on earth could he offer in a gas station? "What are you thinking of?"

Langley shook his head. "That, I haven't figured out yet. I'm fast, but not that fast. I'll have to do some market research."

Much to his surprise, Alexander had finished not only his first plate but was halfway through his second portion of lasagna, which Langley had sneakily put on his plate. "You're good at this," he admitted reluctantly.

Langley chuckled. "Don't sound so surprised. It's not good for my ego."

Alexander couldn't help but smile. "Your ego can take it to be pegged down a rung or two."

"You think I'm arrogant?"

"Arrogant? No. Cocky. Incredibly self-confident. In the most annoying way."

"Ah, you flatter me."

"Calling you annoying flatters you?"

Langley waved his hand dismissively. "That's just you in

the throes of denial. We both know how closely related hate and lust are. No, the self-confident part. The fact that you don't think I'm arrogant. That's a compliment."

Alexander slowly shook his head. "I certainly didn't mean it as such."

"Oh, I know, but that's all part of that confidence you find so irresistible."

"Pretty sure I called it annoying, not irresistible."

"Semantics."

"Not really. Annoying and irresistible are opposites, wouldn't you say?"

"Nah. Like I said, it's like hate and lust. They're much closer than people think."

"Are you saying I'm lusting after you?"

Langley's smile bloomed slowly, his whole face lighting up as he leaned forward, put his elbows on the table, and said, "Oh, we both know you are. You've wanted to fuck me since I was eighteen years old. It's the reason why you told me to leave and why you didn't want me to come back... But it's also the exact reason why I'm back. We're not done, you and me. In fact, we've only gotten started."

6

L angley had wanted nothing more than to drag Alexander across the table and kiss the living daylights out of him until the man would finally admit the sexual tension between them. But he had enough professionality to keep his hands to himself, considering he was technically on a business dinner. Mixing the two was already mucky. No need to add more complications to the mix.

So he'd left after giving Alexander his first quick analysis of the numbers so the man could read it over and give it some thought. He'd told him he'd be back in a couple of days, after he'd done some market research. That, of course, was way too fancy a word for this town and its potential, but he would take this more seriously than his final project for his MBA. This was Alexander's livelihood, his inheritance, and despite everything else that was happening between them, Langley was well aware of the emotional ties Alexander had to the place.

So he'd made himself useful and had questioned his father first, then several of his former high school buddies who had stayed or come back to the area. He'd hung out in Mary's café for an hour or two, devouring her homemade apple pie and totally writing it off as a business expense. He driven around time ten times, had Googled until his eyes had crossed, and then he'd come up with a plan. A pretty spectacular one if he said so himself.

When he showed up at the gas station—dressed in a pair of faded jeans and a black leather jacket, since he wasn't feeling the business outfits today—a car was parked at one of the two pumps. No one was in it, so the customer must be inside to pay. Langley parked in one of the parking spaces, doing a quick look around to confirm what he had come up with. Yeah, Alexander had a prime lot here that he could utilize to increase his revenue. Langley all but rubbed his hands as he walked inside.

He passed what had to be the owner of the car, an incredibly pretty twink with a pair of gorgeous green eyes. Langley sent him a friendly smile, then strode toward the register.

"Langley," Alexander greeted him, as always hiding his pleasure at seeing Langley. But even with his eyes shooting daggers, the man was hot as fuck.

"Xander," he said back, allowing a little sharpness in his own tone.

"I told you a thousand times my name is Alexander, not Xander."

Oh, for fuck's sake. How long would Alexander deny the truth? "Yep, I told you I'll keep ignoring that as long as you ignore the truth."

Fuck, he was getting tired of this. Even if Alexander didn't want to act on the sparks between them, would it kill him to just acknowledge them? This was getting beyond childish.

Alexander stepped from behind the counter and stood opposite Langley, crossing his arms. "And what truth are you referring to today? That I've been somehow secretly pining for you for the last five years?"

"Not so secretly, considering you admitted to keeping track of where I was and what I was doing."

"I told you I was—"

"Stop. Fucking. Lying. Seriously, don't you get tired of ignoring and denying the obvious? Why the hell is it so hard for you to just admit you're attracted to me?"

"I'm not—"

Fuck this shit. With a lightning-fast move, Langley closed the distance between them, then curled his hand around Alexander's neck and pulled him in. From the second their lips touched, a battle ensued. The kiss was fierce, raw, but the bottom line was that Alexander was kissing him back. Their tongues were dueling, fighting for control, and they surged into each other's mouths before pushing each other out again.

Back and forth it went until Langley had pushed Alexander with his back against the wall and was rubbing himself against Alexander. Fuck, Alexander's body was exactly like he had imagined it. Hard, tough, rough. His hands were bruising as they clamped down on Langley's ass, kneading it, pulling him close against his own body.

Hard cocks met, as eager for contact as the rest of their bodies. Langley's hands slipped under Alexander's waistband, boldly grabbing his bare ass. The moan Alexander let out into Langley's mouth made his cock jump. Not attracted to him, his ass. Literally.

The sound of a car pulling up at the pump had Langley jump back. Not that he gave two shits about being seen kissing another man, but he wouldn't do that to Alexander, especially not in his place of business. Alexander looked at him, his lips swollen, his cheeks reddened, and his expression dazed. His chest was still moving quickly with his breaths, which were almost synchronized with Langley's panting.

Langley swiped his thumb over Alexander's mouth to wipe off the wetness, then noticed the man's impressive erection and smiled. Since Alexander seemed to be stupefied to do anything, Langley pulled the man's T-shirt down so it covered his groin.

"There. You look presentable again. We'll talk later. I'll be back."

Fuck if he was presenting him the plan now. Not when he'd just kissed him into a stupor. Business would have to wait a little longer.

7

L angley hadn't stopped by for a whole week, which had pissed Alexander off, though why, he couldn't explain. Maybe because after that scorching hot kiss, he'd expected him to drop by the day after? Or even that same night? But nope. Alexander had to make do with his right hand and some very detailed fantasies of Langley to get rid of the crazy tension in his body.

What Langley *had* done was sent him a thorough analysis of Alexander's business, showing exactly what his busiest hours were each week and each day and which products sold well. Despite everything, Alexander had been impressed. Some of it he'd known, other facts matched his gut instincts, but Langley had also pointed out some things he hadn't expected. He'd emailed him back—that was only professional after all—with some questions, and Langley had responded, all business.

His last email had contained a business plan, and Alexander had gasped when he'd read it. Doing a remodel of the shop and adding square footage to create more floor space, a section with fresh take-home meals, and a café?

Was Langley crazy? But when Alexander looked at the market research Langley had done and the numbers, it had been damn hard to argue with them.

Still, when Langley finally walked into the gas station again, Alexander tore into him. "What the hell are you thinking, proposing I spend even more money?"

"And a good day to you too."

"Whatever. Langley, I can't afford this!"

"You can't afford not to. You need to diversify your business model and be less dependent on gas sales alone. Northern Lake doesn't have enough takeout places where people can get a fresh, tasty meal for a decent price. Mary's isn't open for dinner nor on Sundays, and the other places don't offer quality or only have a limited menu."

"I get that, but spending twenty thousand dollars when I'm already in the red?"

"That's where the loan comes in."

"How would I ever pay that back?"

"With the extra sales you'll generate from the expansion."

"I don't know, Langley. It feels so counterintuitive to me to invest this much in a dying business. It seems to me I would only get deeper into debt. You've seen my numbers… I'm drowning."

Langley put his hands on his hips, his eyes shooting fire. "If you hadn't been so goddamn proud and stubborn and had asked for help sooner, it wouldn't have gotten this bad."

"Langley…"

"No, don't you 'Langley' me. I've given you another week to get used to the idea of executing this plan and accepting the damn loan, but we are doing this. I will not allow you to go bankrupt just because of your pride."

Alexander hadn't even noticed someone had walked in

until Langley stopped talking, and then he recognized the pretty twink who'd been in the week before as well. He pasted a smile on his face and stepped away from Langley. "Hi, can I help you?"

"Just here to buy milk."

"We'll talk tonight. I'll be at your place at eight. With dinner." Langley's tone left no room for debate.

Alexander watched him stalk out, and his heart ached. If only Langley wasn't so much younger. After that kiss they had shared the week before—where Alexander had enthusiastically kissed Langley back, to say the least—denying he was into Langley seemed indeed childish. But fuck, it chafed to admit Langley had been right. If only he didn't have so much potential, way too much to waste in a small town like this. Whatever ran so hot between them had no future. Alexander couldn't give in to it because he'd only end up failing all over again, this time at the cost of a broken heart.

When Langley showed up, he seriously debated not opening the door, but even Alexander wasn't enough of a dick to do that. "Langley," he greeted him, then stepped aside to let the man pass. He was carrying two oven dishes this time, both covered with tinfoil.

"Did you preheat the oven like I asked?"

Langley had texted him fifteen minutes prior, and Alexander had dutifully turned on the oven on the setting Langley had asked. "Yes."

"Good. We're having grilled salmon with Hasselback potatoes and roasted asparagus."

Alexander swallowed, his stomach rumbling so loudly it was embarrassing. "Hasselback?"

"It's when you slice a big potato into super thin slices but not all the way through. It looks pretty, and Rosaria adds some kind of creamy cheese topping that's just to die for."

"Fancy."

Langley removed the tinfoil off one of the dishes and put it in the oven. "It is. Rosaria is a great cook. She could easily have her own restaurant. That's why I proposed she and her daughter come work for you as cooks to prepare those takeout meals. I swear, they'll sell like hotcakes. I've already found an affordable supplier of environment-friendly containers, and I've contacted the New York State Health Department to ask about permits and laws."

He turned toward Alexander, who felt strangely nervous, his stomach all fluttering like he was a teenager again. Not that surprising, considering the kiss they'd shared and the fact that Alexander had no idea what came next. They'd kissed the week before, then had fought earlier that day, and the whole situation had him on edge. Langley was talking business, but Alexander wasn't there yet. He needed to know where they stood.

He cleared his throat. "I just wanted to make sure that... Not that I think you'd be unprofessional, but seeing as there's a lot on the line for me, I..."

"That kiss we shared last week has and will have nothing to do with me consulting you about your business or with you getting the loan." Langley sounded so goddamn adult the way he said that. Much unlike Alexander's impersonation of a stumbling idiot.

"I didn't mean to imply that you would... You know."

Langley's eyes softened. "I'm well aware of what's at stake for you. I promise you I can keep the two separate. When we fuck, it will have no bearing on my consulting or the decision whether you'll get a loan."

Alexander swallowed. "*When* we fuck...?"

"Still not ready to admit the truth?"

Langley sounded disappointed, and for some reason,

that got to Alexander. Langley had a point. Alexander was being childish and ridiculous in denying his attraction to him. Even if nothing could come from it long term—and they both knew that was the case—there was no reason not to be honest.

And maybe no reason not to give in to this crazy attraction, if only for a while. Maybe Langley had been right, and they could fuck it out of their system. Langley was no longer a student, they were both of age, and nothing about this was illegal or even improper. The least Alexander could and should do was be man enough to tell the truth.

"Will those dishes hold if you turn the oven off?"

Langley's eyes widened, but then he smiled. "I'll eat them stone-cold if I have to. What did you have in mind?"

Alexander walked over to the stove and turned the oven off. "I haven't given you a proper tour of my house. Wanna start with the bedroom?"

Funny, now that he'd made his decision, his nerves were gone. Langley had been right about that as well. Alexander had called it annoyance, but what it had been was attraction. Lust. Wanting to peel Langley out of those faded jeans and do all kinds of unspeakable acts to him. Preferably ones that involved Langley's cock and Alexander's ass, though that was a discussion he hadn't had with him yet.

"Fuck, yeah."

Langley's grin was contagious, and Alexander found himself grinning as well. "What are you waiting for, then?"

"For you to lead the way."

He didn't know why, but he reached out, and Langley took his hand, and that was how they walked into his bedroom, where the bed was neatly made, like it was every day. He'd already pulled the curtains shut when he'd taken a quick shower after closing the gas station, and the smell of his body wash still hung in the air.

And for all their fire and the heated kiss they'd shared earlier, they were both much calmer as they stood across from each other in the bedroom. "I've waited five years for this," Langley said softly.

What else could Alexander say but the truth? "So have I."

They smiled at each other. "Fuck, I feel like a virgin again." Langley laughed.

"But you're not, right?" Alexander checked.

"No. I did my fair share of experimenting. Figured I'd get some practice in so that when we finally got to it, I'd know what I was doing."

Here went nothing. "When you...experimented, what position did you usually have?"

Langley frowned. "Sex position? As in missionary or reverse or whatever?"

Fuck, why was this still so fucking awkward? Stupid expectations. "No. I mean..."

Langley's eyes lit up. "I'm vers, so I'm okay with bottoming, since I assume..." Alexander's face must've given something away, and Langley's expression changed. "I assumed wrong, didn't I, when I called you an exclusive top?"

Alexander inhaled deeply, then nodded. "Yeah. I much prefer to...not top."

"Okay."

"Yeah?"

"Why would that not be okay? I told you I'm vers. I'm happy either way, baby."

Alexander cringed. "Please don't call me baby."

"Why?"

"Reminds me too much of the anonymous Grindr

hookups where you call each other baby because nine out of ten times, you never even introduced yourself...or don't remember the other's name."

Langley stepped so close Alexander could feel the warmth radiating off his body. "Are you saying I mean more to you than a nameless hookup?"

Fuck pretending. "If you didn't, do you really think I would've resisted this long?"

Oh, that wicked smile on Langley's face. It made Alexander's heart beat ten times faster. "That honesty deserves a reward...Coach."

Alexander laughed. "Is that what you're gonna call me now? Although I have to admit, you do make it sound sexy..."

"You have no idea how much I was hoping back then you'd *coach me* in some other rigorous activities."

Damn, that look on Langley's face, the way he wiggled his eyebrows, how he licked his lips... It shot straight to Alexander's cock, and he was done waiting, done talking. "Strip naked, Mr. Malcolm. Time for some one-on-one coaching."

8

Fuck, yes. Finally. Langley wasn't sure why Xander had changed his mind about the two of them or why he'd decided to stop pretending, but he wasn't gonna ask. Enough with the talking. He stripped naked in ten seconds flat, and Xander laughed as Langley all but stumbled onto the bed as he pulled off his last sock. Because leaving your socks on during sex? Fuck no. About the most unsexy thing ever.

Since he was on the bed anyway, he stretched himself out, offering Xander a good view. He studied Langley in great detail, his gaze slowly traveling from his feet upward. "You're so goddamn perfect…"

Langley was stupidly pleased. "Thank you."

"Your body is…perfect. Everything about you is just… Fuck, I should've majored in English Lit rather than physical therapy so I'd have better words."

That stopped Langley's hand, which had been fisting his cock. "You majored in physical therapy?"

"Yeah. Gave up my job when my dad got ill, and after he

died, I never went back to it. Mmm, want me to give you a massage?"

"Fuck, yes... Though not now. I had other plans for now."

"What kind of plans?"

"The kind that involves you being naked as well."

Xander looked away for a moment. "Langley, I'm not... I'm turning forty in a few weeks. I'm not... I don't look like that anymore. My prime days are well in the past..."

Langley's heart grew all soft and warm. "Strip, Coach. You look damn fine to me the way you are."

Xander met his eyes again, and then he took off his clothes, revealing a slightly soft but still fucking gorgeous body. Gray hairs sprinkled his chest between darker ones, and Langley loved it. His heart softened even more when he saw the messy scars on his left knee, the one that had ended his short career. Xander was all male, every inch of him sexy as fuck, and Langley held out his hands. "Get your ass in here, Coach. Time to get this party started."

Much to his relief, Xander didn't hesitate anymore but crawled on the bed, and Langley pulled him toward him, drawing Xander on top of him as he instantly fused their mouths together. Mmm, the man tasted so good. The kiss started lazily with Langley just roaming Xander's mouth, getting to know him, soaking up his flavor, but it quickly grew urgent.

Langley flipped them, pinning Xander down underneath him, and a laugh rumbled up from Xander's chest. "You manhandling me?"

"You complaining?" Their eyes met, and lightning struck all over again, setting Langley on fire.

"No," Xander whispered hoarsely. "Not complaining at all."

Langley kissed him until his lips ached, throbbing and stinging. "Ready for the next item on the itinerary?"

Xander shot him a lazy grin, looking delicious with his hair all messed up, his cheeks red, and his eyes a little glaze. "That depends on where the itinerary will lead."

Langley flipped them again, then sank his hand between Xander's ass cheeks, rubbing his hole. "That's the final destination, Coach. You good with that?"

"Fuck, yeah."

More kissing, and then Langley maneuvered Xander on his belly, nudging his legs until he spread them wide. He was so beautiful. He ran his hand down Xander's back, then palmed his ass cheeks and squeezed. Still tight as could be. Heaven.

"Are you gonna keep staring at me, or can I expect some actual action?"

"Just admiring the view."

"Yeah?" Xander sounded ridiculously pleased, and Langley grinned.

"Your ass is the stuff of wet dreams, man. Your whole body, in fact."

He trailed his index finger down Xander's spine, then followed his crack all the way to his hole. The man shivered from that simple touch, so he did it again. He dipped his head and blew a hot breath over Xander's skin, which broke out in goose bumps instantly. Wasn't it crazy how he'd always been in a hurry to fuck and yet now, he wanted to take his time?

He kissed those tight globes, reveling in the salty taste of Xander's skin when he licked them. Sucked them. Nibbled around while his fingers explored, and Xander's body jerked under his hands and mouths. "Langley..."

Nope, not a protest. Not even close. That was the sound of a man who was being driven insane, and that was exactly how Langley wanted him. He spread those ass cheeks wide and breathed on Xander's hole, which twitched under his stare. Fuck, yes. Without a second of hesitation, he bent over deeper and laved that pretty little star with his tongue.

Breath rushed from his lungs as a current of electricity shot up from his balls down the length of his cock. One would think it couldn't possibly feel that good to touch someone else, but oh god, did it ever. He dragged his tongue over Xander's hole again, and the needy growl the man let out was like an aphrodisiac. Xander's hips jerked as if he couldn't keep still, and Langley pinned him down with one hand as he licked again, swirling his tongue around that entrance that beckoned him.

"Fuck, that's..." Xander moaned, arching his back and pushing his ass upward.

Langley didn't respond. Talking was not a priority when he could taste Xander. He hitched that ass closer to his mouth and went to work. The pink hole softened quickly under his ministrations, opening up for his tongue. He'd never thought he'd be into rimming, and yet here he was, his tongue inside another man, and he fucking loved it. Absolutely craved more, like he was addicted already.

He dropped a thick string of saliva onto Xander's hole, then another one. His thumb spread it around as he nibbled on his ass cheeks, just rubbing ever smaller circles until he pushed a little harder and slipped inside. His thumb went in all the way, sank in until he could go no deeper, and even better than the way Xander's velvety hot channel was clenching around it were the sounds he was making. The hitchy breaths and little moans as he pinched his eyes shut and restlessly moved his hands as if searching for something to hold on to.

"Langley..." Xander sounded exasperated and more than a little impatient.

"You in a hurry?"

Xander pushed himself up a little and met Langley's eyes. "Honestly? Yeah. I've bottled up this insane need for you for years, and now that I've let it out, it's impossible to wait any longer."

Good point. He'd simply have to rim him again another day. And suck him off. And sixty-nine him. Fuck his mouth. Come all over him. So many things he wanted to do to this man, with this man. "Fuck that English Lit degree. That was perfect. Please tell me you have lube somewhere." His voice was raspy.

"Drawer." Xander vaguely gestured.

Langley found lube and condoms in the drawer of Xander's nightstand. Bingo. He rolled the condom on first. That way, he could focus completely on getting Xander ready and not have to interrupt himself again. He squirted some lube, coated himself, then got some more on his fingers.

"How do you want this, Coach?"

"Don't go slow. Wanna feel you."

The words sank their claws inside Langley, firing him up even more. Oh, he'd make damn sure Xander would feel him. Every inch of him and then some. The man would be walking bow-legged when he was done with him. But he understood what Xander was saying. He wanted it fast, not endless foreplay. They were on the same page, then.

Two fingers pushed, and Xander let him in, muttering a groaned curse as Langley sank deeper. So freaking hot and silky. He'd waited so long for this. A few careful pumps had Xander making more noises. "Fuck... That feels..."

That was all he managed, but Langley got the idea and slid his fingers in and out until Xander's body relaxed around him. "Three?" he asked.

"Nah. Gimme the main show."

"On your back."

Xander hesitated. "Isn't it easier if...?"

"I don't care about easy. I've waited five years for this, so I damn well wanna see your face when I'm inside you."

"Holy Christ, you're a bossy little fucker," Xander grumbled, but he did turn onto his back and pulled his legs up, opening himself wide.

"Yeah, and you don't mind half as much as you're pretending. Don't think that I can't see through you."

Something flashed over Xander's face. It would have to wait, but they would talk about this. Later. After he was done claiming him.

Langley positioned himself, his muscles trembling as he lined up. Finally. He barely had to push, Xander letting him in at the first touch. He was evidently a man who liked to play with himself. Langley approved. In fact, he wanted to see it someday—Xander bringing himself to a shattering climax while Langley watched and jerked off to it. His own private peep show. Hell yes.

Xander moaned as Langley thrust carefully. "Fuuuck..."

"Good?"

Langley asked more out of reflex than because he was even the slightest bit worried. Xander's expression made clear how the man felt.

"Don't you fucking dare stop."

See? All systems green. He sank in deep, rocking his pelvis until he was flush against Xander's flesh, buried all the way. "You feel so goddamn good, Coach. So fucking tight and hot."

Snapping his hips, he pulled out and plunged back in, drawing a sharp gasp from Xander. Someone liked that. He did it again, shifting his angle of penetration ever so slightly. Xander bucked underneath him as if electrocuted. Jackpot. "Hang on, Coach. We're about to hit a home run."

9

Xander was still laughing when Langley sank inside him again, and his laugh transformed in a low, rumbling moan that drifted up from his chest. Fuck, that cock felt perfect. Thick, stretching him, hitting all the right spots. And that face... Langley had crazy long lashes for a man, and they fluttered now as he pumped Xander's ass, his eyes going dreamy.

How ridiculous of him to think he'd ever stand a chance against him, against the sheer stubbornness of this man. Langley had decided he wanted him, and what Langley wanted...he got. Though Xander had to admit he'd never experienced a more satisfying loss.

"Kiss me?" He'd meant it as a command of sorts, but it came out as a needy question.

Langley didn't seem to mind. His eyes heated up even more, and he all but dive-bombed Xander's mouth. His thrusts became shallower as he fucked Xander with his tongue as well, the combined sensation setting Xander's body on fire. His balls fucking *ached*, and his cock was craving friction. The pressure of Langley's body against it wasn't enough, although at this point, he really didn't need that much more.

"Such a sweet ass," Langley growled against his throbbing lips. "And such a sweet mouth."

"No one's ever called me sweet before."

"That's because you don't show that side of you to everyone, now do you?"

Fuck that cocky shit and his self-confidence. Why could he spot so easily what others never have? "Overconfident much?"

Langley pushed himself up on one arm, his other hand curling around Xander's throat, not so tight he couldn't breathe but definitely enough to get his attention. "You're not pushing me away again, Coach."

His blue eyes were more intense than Xander had ever seen them, and he resisted the urge to squirm under that scrutinizing stare. "Can we save the psychological analyzing shit for later? I'd really like to focus more on *carnal* pleasures right now."

It took a few beats for Langley's expression to change, but then his mouth pulled up in a grin as he let go of Xander's throat. "Carnal, huh? It literally means meat."

"I know."

"As in, my meat in your ass."

Xander rolled his eyes. "Yes, I got the reference, thank you."

"So you're saying you want to focus on the pleasure of my meat in your ass."

"Will you just fuck me already?" Xander snapped, and Langley was laughing as he slammed into him.

"Like that?"

"Ungh!"

"Or more like this?" Another hard thrust. Jesus, any

more force and Langley's dick would touch his tonsils. But apparently, Langley didn't really need an answer, which was just as well because with the brutal pace he was setting now, words were impossible for Xander. He fisted the sheets as Langley fucked him, every shove perfectly rough and electrifying.

He closed his eyes, his hand slipping between their bodies to curl around his cock. Fuck, he was close. The way Langley fucked him was perfection, and if he kept his eyes closed, he didn't have to think of—

"Look at me."

His eyes flew open again at that command. The fuck? "You're not pretending to be with anyone else but me, Coach."

Despite everything, Xander had to admire the sheer balls of that statement. Langley was fearless, and damn if Xander didn't value that. "Yes, sir," he said jokingly. Only it didn't quite come out that way.

Langley's eyes widened, and a slow grin spread across his mouth. "Oh, I like that."

"I bet you do. It was a joke, asshole."

Langley just winked at him. "Keep telling yourself that."

Fuck that little shit. Arrogant cocky bastard. Xander should....

Oh, fuck, that felt good. Langley had changed his angle again and was now hammering Xander's prostate dead on, every thrust sending lightning bolts up his ass and radiating outward. His balls tingled, and his grip on his cock tightened as he fisted himself.

"Finish yourself," Langley instructed, his voice raw. "Wanna see you come."

How could he say no to that? He fought to keep his eyes open, consumed by this strange desire to please Langley, as he mercilessly jacked himself off, bringing that little sharpness, that sting of pain that always got him off so hard. His muscles clenched tight, his balls pulled up, and his cock all but vibrated in his hand. Just one more...

"Ah...!" The last jerk did it. "Fuck!"

The breath whooshed from his lungs, and his mouth hung open in some frozen suspension as his balls emptied, shooting his load up his shaft, then all over his hand and his belly. Fuck, he unloaded as if he hadn't come in days, pumping his cock until he winced with how sensitive it was.

"Jesus fuck, that was hot," Langley growled. "I could almost come from that alone."

Xander didn't want to look at him anymore, didn't want to see Langley's eyes, which showed so much more than mere lust, but he couldn't look away. And so he kept his eyes trained on Langley, who never even blinked as he thrust inside Xander, the air between them so charged, it almost hurt to breathe.

"Oh damn..." Langley grunted. "Fuuuuck...."

One last ruthless shove and he came, his body shaking as he filled the condom inside Xander. How would that feel bare? He'd never considered it, had never even wanted it, and yet here he was, with a man seventeen years his junior, and all he could think about was how good it would feel to have his cum dripping out of his ass. And how amazing it would be to wake up with Langley in his bed. In his arms.

Fuck, he was in so much trouble.

Also, when the fuck had he started to think of himself as Xander rather than Alexander? That little shit had gotten to him...

10

The sex had been phenomenal, but something had changed afterward. Langley couldn't put his finger on it, but Xander had been different. More subdued, a little aloof. They'd talked over a late dinner, and Langley had run all the numbers by him. He knew his proposal was sound. Hell, he'd even discussed it with his father, who had been impressed. "That's a highly creative solution," he'd said. "I'm not sure I would've even come up with that. Great work. I'll happily extend the loan under favorable conditions."

Xander, of course, was still not on board. Stubborn asshole. Monday morning—which was about as dead in the gas station as it could get, Langley knew—he drove over again. As soon as Xander saw him, the wall came down, the mask over his face that guarded his real emotions. Why?

"Have you given the proposal any more thought?"

Xander shook his head. "I can't do it. It's too risky. Too much money. I'll end up like my father, with a debt I'll never get rid of."

"If you don't do this, you'll go bankrupt. You have maybe

six months left at this rate, and that's it." Maybe confronting him with the cold, harsh truth would help.

Xander looked away. "Then maybe that's what needs to happen. I can't accept your help."

His help? Wait, was Xander mixing two things? "Why not? Because the proposal is too risky or because being with me is too risky?"

"I thought you said the two weren't connected."

"They're not, but I think you mixed them up anyway. This loan has nothing to do with you and me. You know that."

"You're seventeen years younger, Langley. I don't see a future for us."

A future? What the... Oh. Oh, wow. He'd expected Xander to need more time to get to that point, but apparently, he was already there. "So you're finally admitting that what we have is more than just attraction."

"I don't know what it is, but it can't last. Not with the age gap between us."

"Coach, I've been in love with you since I was eighteen years old. I've waited five goddamn years for you, and if you seriously think I'm gonna let you reject me just because of my age, you're dead wrong."

Xander cleared his throat, subtly gesturing, and Langley turned around. A guy had walked in, and judging by the way he was leaning against the wall, he'd been listening in for a while. "Rude much?" Langley snapped.

The guy walked toward them, and holy shit, that guy was *built*. Tall, with a chest twice as big as Langley's and legs the size of tree trunks. He had tattoos peeping from under his hoodie and several visible piercings. Not the kind of guy he wanted to get into a fight with, not even with Xander on his side. Hopefully. "Sorry, I didn't mean to..."

The man gestured. "Is o-o-okay. I w-w-was being r-rude."

Wow, he had a severe stutter. Langley felt even worse for being so snappy with him.

"Can I help you?" Xander asked, his voice a hell of a lot more friendly than Langley's had been.

"I o-o-verheard some of your c-c-c-onv-versation. It's n-none of my b-business, b-b-but I just w-wanna s-s-say that you sh-should stop being so st-st-stubborn. I'm ab-bout to drive c-c-cross-country to b-b-be with my b-boyfriend. He m-moved to C-c-california and I need to b-be w-with him. I s-sold everything to f-f-follow him. If s-s-someone l-loves you and you l-love that p-p-person as w-well, you n-need to hold on t-t-to h-him and not b-be a stubborn assh-h-hole."

Langley's mouth had dropped open, and a quick look at Xander showed him equally flabbergasted. First of all, that guy was about the last man Langley would've expected that speech from. Second, that dude was *gay*? Damn, he hadn't seen that coming. And third, he was totally fucking right... Now if only Xander would see that.

"He's seventeen years younger than me," Xander said, much to Langley's surprise.

The guy shrugged. "M-my b-b-boyfriend is f-fifteen years younger...and h-he's d-d-dominant."

Dominant? Did the guy mean what Langley thought he meant? "So you're...?"

"S-s-submissive. Y-yes. H-he's in ch-charge, and I l-l-love it. He's am-m-mazing."

How about that? Xander looked from the guy to Langley, then back. Then he put his hand on the guy's shoulder. "Thank you. I needed to hear that."

The man nodded, smiling broadly. "G-good. I n-n-need

to l-leave. He d-doesn't know I'm com-m-ming, and I c-can't wait to surp-prise him."

Before they could say another word, he'd walked out, got into a truck, and drove off. "Did he just....? Xander asked.

"Walk in here just to say that? Yeah."

"Have you seen him before?"

"Nope, never. No idea. He had a good point, though." Langley's eyes softened. "Please, Coach, let me help you. Swallow that damn pride and accept my father's loan...and then get the fuck over yourself and accept me."

"You're in love with me?"

"From the day I met you. I waited for you to be ready for this, Coach, but I'm done waiting."

Xander stared at him, but then his expression changed. He took a step forward, put his arms around Langley, and clung to him, putting his head on Langley's shoulders. "I'm so tired."

Oh god, his poor heart. Any fuller and it would explode. "I know. But I'm here now, okay? You're no longer on your own."

"This is not your problem."

"What if I want to make it mine? Make you mine?"

Xander looked up, his eyes suspiciously moist. "You'd better mean it because I don't think I could handle—"

"I love you, Xander. Always have, always will."

A deep sigh. "Okay."

It sounded like a surrender. "Yeah?"

"Mmm."

"You're not gonna tell me you love me back?"

Xander snorted. "As if you didn't know already, you cocky little shit." Then he grew serious. "Yeah, I do love you. I guess I have for a while now."

"See? I told you you'd be mine."

Xander was smiling when Langley pressed their mouths together and slipped his tongue into his boyfriend's mouth. Hmm, maybe they should close the gas station on Monday mornings...and use that time for something else. Something much more...pleasant.

He nibbled on Xander's bottom lip. "Do you want to do some more one-on-one coaching?"

The man's eyes showed nothing but love now. "I do."

I do? Hmm, that was the next step...maybe in a year or so. Because now that he finally had him, no way would Langley ever let Alexander Wingard go.

BOOKS BY NORA PHOENIX

🎧 indicates book is also available as audio book

White House Men

A romantic suspense series set in the White House that combines romance with suspense, a dash of kink, and all the feels.

- **Press** (rivals fall in love in an impossible love) 🎧
- **Friends** (friends to lovers between an FBI and a Secret Service agent) 🎧
- **Click** (a sexy first-time romance with an age gap and an awkward virgin) 🎧
- **Serve** (a high heat MMM romance with age gap and D/s play) 🎧
- **Care** (the president's son falls for his tutor; age gap and daddy kink) 🎧
- **Puzzle** (a CIA analyst meets his match in a nerdy forensic accountant)

No Regrets Series

Sexy, kinky, emotional, with a touch of suspense, the No Regrets series is a spin off from the No Shame series that can be read on its own.

- **No Surrender** (bisexual awakening, first time gay, D/s play)

Perfect Hands Series

Raw, emotional, both sweet and sexy, with a solid dash of kink, that's the Perfect Hands series. All books can be read as standalones.

- **Firm Hand** (daddy care with a younger daddy and an older boy) 🎧
- **Gentle Hand** (sweet daddy care with age play) 🎧
- **Naughty Hand** (a holiday novella to read after Firm Hand and Gentle Hand) 🎧
- **Slow Hand** (a Dom who never wanted to be a Daddy takes in two abused boys) 🎧
- **Healing Hand** (a broken boy finds the perfect Daddy) 🎧

No Shame Series

If you love steamy MM romance with a little twist, you'll love the No Shame series. Sexy, emotional, with a bit of suspense and all the feels. Make sure to read in order, as this is a series with a continuing storyline.

- **No Filter** 🎧
- **No Limits** 🎧
- **No Fear** 🎧
- **No Shame** 🎧
- **No Angel** 🎧

And for all the fun, grab the **No Shame box set** 🎧 which includes all five books plus exclusive bonus chapters and deleted scenes.

Irresistible Omegas Series

An mpreg series with all the heat, epic world building, poly romances (the first two books are MMMM and the rest of the series is MMM), a bit of suspense, and characters that will stay with you for a long time. This is a continuing series, so read in order.

- **Alpha's Sacrifice** 🎧
- **Alpha's Submission** 🎧
- **Beta's Surrender** 🎧
- **Alpha's Pride** 🎧
- **Beta's Strength** 🎧
- **Omega's Protector** 🎧
- **Alpha's Obedience** 🎧
- **Omega's Power** 🎧
- **Beta's Love** 🎧
- **Omega's Truth** 🎧

Or grab *the first box set*, which contains books 1-3 plus exclusive bonus material and *the second box set*, which has books 4-6 and exclusive extras.

Ballsy Boys Series

Sexy porn stars looking for real love! Expect plenty of steam, but all the feels as well. They can be read as stand-alones, but are more fun when read in order.

- **Ballsy** (free prequel)
- **Rebel** 🎧

- Tank 🎧
- Heart 🎧
- Campy 🎧
- Pixie 🎧

Or grab *the box set*, which contains all five books plus an exclusive bonus novella!

Kinky Boys Series
Super sexy, slightly kinky, with all the feels.

- Daddy 🎧
- Ziggy 🎧

Ignite Series
An epic dystopian sci-fi trilogy (one book out, two more to follow) where three men have to not only escape a government that wants to jail them for being gay but aliens as well. Slow burn MMM romance.

- Ignite 🎧
- Smolder 🎧
- Burn 🎧

Now also available in a *box set* 🎧, which includes all three books, bonus chapters, and a bonus novella.

Stand Alones
I also have a few stand alones, so check these out!

- **Professor Daddy** (sexy daddy kink between a college prof and his student. Age gap, no ABDL)

- **Out to Win** (two men meet at a TV singing contest) 🎧
- **Captain Silver Fox** (falling for the boss on a cruise ship) 🎧
- **Coming Out on Top** (snowed in, age gap, size difference, and a bossy twink) 🎧
- **Ranger** (struggling Army vet meets a sunshiney animal trainer - cowritten with K.M. Neuhold) 🎧

Books in German

Quite a few of my books have been translated into German, with more to come!

Indys Männer

- **Indys Flucht** No Filter)
- **Josh Wunsch** (No Limits)
- **Aarons Handler** (No Fear)
- **Brads Bedürfnisse** (No Shame)
- **Indys Weihnachten** (No Angel)

Mein Daddy Dom

- **Daddy Rhys** (Firm Hand)
- **Daddy Brendan** (Gentle Hand)
- **Weihnachten mit den Daddys** (Naughty Hand)
- **Daddy Ford** (Slow Hand)
- **Daddy Gale** (Healing Hand)

Das Hayes Rudel

- **Lidons Angebot** (Alpha's Sacrifice)
- **Enars Unterordnung** (Alpha's Submission)
- **Lars' Hingabe** (Beta's Surrender)

- **Brays Stolz** (Alpha's Pride)
- **Keans Stärke** (Beta's Strength)
- **Gias Beschützer** (Omega's Protector)
- **Levs Gehorsam** (Alpha's Obedience)
- **Sivneys Macht** (Omega's Power)
- **Lucans Liebe** (Beta's Love)
- **Sandos Wahrheit** (Omega's Truth)

Standalones

- **Mein Professor Daddy** (Professor Daddy)
- **Eingeschneit mit dem Bären** (Coming Out on Top)
- **Eine Nacht mit dem Kapitän** (Captain Silver Fox)
- **Ranger** (Ranger, cowritten with K.M. Neuhold)

Books in Other Languages

- **L'Occasione Della Vita** - Italian - The Time of my Life / Out to Win
- **Posizioni Inaspettate** - Italian - Coming Out on Top
- **L'offerta di Lidon** - Italian - Alpha's Sacrifice
- **La Sottomissione di Enar** - Italian - Alpha's Submission
- **Le Garçon du Professeur** - French - Professor Daddy
- **Une Main de Fer** - French - Firm Hand
- **Une Main de Velours** - French - Gentle Hand
- **Con Mano Firme** - Spanish - Firm Hand

MORE ABOUT NORA PHOENIX

Would you like the long or the short version of my bio?

The short? You got it.

I write steamy gay romance books and I love it. I also love reading books. Books are everything.

How was that?

A little more detail? Gotcha.

I started writing my first stories when I was a teen...on a freaking typewriter. I still have these, and they're adorably romantic. And bad, haha. Fear of failing kept me from following my dream to become a romance author, so you can imagine how proud and ecstatic I am that I finally over-came my fears and self doubt and did it. I adore my genre because I love writing and reading about flawed, strong men who are just a tad broken..but find their happy ever after anyway.

My favorite books to read are pretty much all MM/gay romances as long as it has a happy end. Kink is a plus... Aside from that, I also read a lot of nonfiction and not just books on writing. Popular psychology is a favorite topic of mine and so are self help and sociology.

Hobbies? Ain't nobody got time for that. Just kidding. I love traveling, spending time near the ocean, and hiking. But I love books more.

Come hang out with me in my Facebook Group Nora's Nook where I share previews, sneak peeks, freebies, fun stuff, and much more: https://www.facebook.com/groups/norasnook/

My weekly newsletter not only gives you updates, exclusive content, and all the inside news on what I'm working on, but also lists the best new releases, 99c deals, and freebies in gay romance for that weekend. Load up your Kindle for less money! Sign up here: http://www.noraphoenix.com/newsletter/

You can also stalk me on Twitter: @NoraFromBHR

On Instagram:

https://www.instagram.com/nora.phoenix/

On Bookbub:

https://www.bookbub.com/profile/nora-phoenix

Or become my patron on Patreon: https://www.patreon.com/noraphoenix

Printed by Amazon Italia Logistica S.r.l.
Torrazza Piemonte (TO), Italy

48091742R00227

Marvellous Mavis

LOTTE MOORE

ILLUSTRATIONS BY PHILIP HOOD

URBANE
Publications

urbanepublications.com

First published in Great Britain in 2016 by Urbane Publications Ltd
Suite 3, Brown Europe House, 33/34 Gleaming Wood Drive, Chatham, Kent ME5 8RZ
Copyright ©Lotte Moore, 2016

A CIP catalogue record for this book is available from the British Library.

ISBN 978-1-911129-94-3
EPUB 978-1-911129-95-0
MOBI 978-1-911129-96-7

Design, Typeset & Cover by Julie Martin
Cover image Copyright ©Philip Hood

Printed in Great Britain by
CPI Group (UK) Ltd, Croydon, CR0 4YY

urbanepublications.com

To dear Lavender,
whose humour and courage inspired me.

Contents

Part One

Part Two

Part One

A life less ordinary

Mavis emerged breathless from a rail of dresses, having retrieved a smart, navy-striped dress which had fallen behind the radiator.

"Phew! As it's almost closing time I'll nip into the changing room and try it on," she called out to Prue, her sparrow-like assistant in the charity shop. Mavis's tall, thick-set body struggled into the dress. "Yes, it looks chic, like the latest *Vogue* cover. I'll have that."

Mavis devoured every fashion magazine, yearning to be adorned in many of the wildly- expensive clothes. Scurrying home along Godalming High Street ten minutes later, she decided to prepare chicken fritters for her and Keith. Oh, and she mustn't forget to put out his gin and tonic before he got in. Arriving home, Mavis went to the cabinet and mixed Keith's drink in his favourite green glass and put it beside his chair.

Ambling into the kitchen she searched for the kettle. "Where can it be?" She looked out of the kitchen window at her beloved garden. "It's sitting on the lawn. Silly me, why did I leave it there?"

Five minutes later the front door opened. "Hello dear," called Keith in his neat, worn suit.

"Coming. Your drink is by your chair. I want to talk about our holiday," replied Mavis.

"Yes, I thought we'd try something new, like a week in Scarborough. The seafood is good there," replied Keith, easing himself into the chair.

"Scarborough!" exclaimed Mavis, brushing her maroon suit clear of wisteria blossom from the garden. 'Oh Keith, let's go to the Scilly Isles instead. They say the flowers there are beautiful. I love ferries don't I? Do you remem ..."

"Yes, I remember all right," Keith interrupted. "Standing on the deck with you when you got your lipstick out in a howling gale and all our holiday money blew away. What an embarrassment. No, it's not safe to take you very far."

Mavis sighed and went back into the kitchen. "Things will never change with Keith. He's getting boring," she thought. As she chopped up the chicken, she hummed a tune from last night's TV ballroom dancing. Oh, those multilayered organza dresses, sparkling shoes and taffeta stoles! How marvelous to be dressed up on TV. If only Keith liked organza.

"Would you like spinach or cauliflower tonight?" she called.

"I've got a headache," he replied.

"Have you taken your aspirin today? Keith did you hear what I said?"

Mavis walked into the sitting room and saw Keith slumped forward in his chair. She shook him urgently. "Keith!" He just stared at her. The whole house suddenly seemed empty. "Oh Keith, wake up!" she whispered into his face, her bottom lip quivering. Mavis's statuesque body moved slowly backwards, sinking deep into her armchair. She sat motionless as day dissolved into dusk, weeping intermittently.

"What shall I do with your supper?" she whispered to the dead body. "And all our future suppers?" She rose slowly, went into the kitchen and out into the garden. A full moon lit up the trees. She sank onto the garden bench and wept.

Mavis came around, shivering, as the sun rose. "Oh goodness, what am I doing here? I must go and make Keith's breakfast." She stumbled into the kitchen, wrapping an old rug round her shoulders, put the kettle on (that she'd brought in from the garden with her), then called up the stairs, "Poached eggs nearly ready. Did you hear me, Keith?"

As she walked past the sitting room door she caught sight of him slumped in his chair. "Oh my God. You've gone, haven't you? You won't need eggs now." Mavis stroked his head and shuddered at the feel of his cold body. "I've got an idea Keith, I'm going to put you to bed, all snug under the garden bench. I can talk to you there. You'll be near me." Having turned off the eggs, she took a spade from the shed and, pushing the bench aside, started digging a deep hole for Keith to rest in. It took three hours.

Mavis lowered some of Keith's favourite books down into the earth. Her aching arms rested on the spade for a few moments then she slowly dragged his body (wrapped in her best knitted blanket) outside and gently rolled him into the grave. Mavis cried softly as she waved him goodbye, then pushed the earth hurriedly onto his body, shovelling until she lost sight of him. Her arms were exhausted and her heart throbbed as she pulled the bench over the resting place. Walking sadly down to the end of the garden, she wrapped her arms round the mimosa tree which Keith had planted eight years ago. The scented blossom hung above her bowed head.

New York, New York!

Next morning Mavis woke up with a sudden thrill in her bones. "I'm free," she thought. "I can go anywhere." She rang Prue at the shop to say she'd be popping in later and set off to begin life anew. She began to bubble with excitement as she entered the travel agent and booked a ticket and hotel for New York.

"I want to fly today, please."

Ten minutes later, Mavis burst into the charity shop and gave Prue a hug. "I'm taking a break in New York. Keith's gone off to stay with his mum," she said. "Poor old dear's got cancer."

Prue was aghast at her bubbling friend.

"Order Fred's taxi to collect me from home in two hours and take me to the airport."

"Y ... yes," stuttered Prue.

Mavis swept out, almost racing down the street, her thick auburn hair sticking to her strong face as the drizzle turned into a downpour. Returning home, she slipped out onto the garden bench and whispered, "I'm going away for a bit Keith. I'll be thinking of you."

An hour-and-a-half later the doorbell rang. She stuffed some egg sandwiches into her suitcase on wheels and pulled it to the door.

"Hello Mrs Hunter," said Fred.

During the hour-long ride, they chatted about her future adventure. "I know I'm old and forgetful, but this is a dream come true."

Fred smiled into his rear-view mirror. "I'd better help you at the airport; it's very confusing there. I see you've got your hotel address round your neck. That's useful."

Fred showed her where to check in and steered her through the departure gate. Mavis waited a good two hours before the plane took off. As it finally climbed into the air she felt sick, and then looked out of the window to see flames on the wings.

"We're on fire!" she cried. "Help! I want to get out!"

A stewardess calmed her down. "It's only the exhaust from the engine. Don't worry."

Mavis was in shock. They put a blanket round her. "Could I have a brandy?" she asked and was given a miniature, which she swigged down in one and promptly fell into a snoring snooze.

~

Several hours later, having negotiated Immigration and
Customs, then being directed to a yellow cab rank, Mavis
arrived at the Bolton Hotel. She was so excited stepping
out of the cab that she almost tripped up the hotel steps.

"Hey honey, you haven't paid!" called the cab driver. "It's
eighteen bucks."

"Oh dear," said Mavis, fumbling inside her cerise jacket.
She pulled out a handful of notes from a brown envelope.
"Take what you want." Some notes dribbled down the damp
steps. The driver grabbed a $50 bill and dived back into his
cab.

Mavis was greeted by a smiling man at the reception desk.

"I'm Mrs Mavis Hunter. Do you know me?"

"Yes, madam." He smiled politely, "We'll show you to your
suite."

She followed a porter into a glass-panelled lift. They swiftly
rose twenty-four floors before getting out and walking
along a corridor to Room 2506. Mavis gasped at the
sumptuous sofa and velvet curtains. She fell onto the huge
tapestry-covered bed.

"Oh my goodness, this is splendid. And my own bathroom!
I'd like to have all my meals in my room."

"Does that mean breakfast in bed?" asked the porter.

"Yes, of course. All of it, a mug of tea, lots of jam and eggs, and oh! What am I going to do about dinner tonight?"

"Our dining room is now open in the annex," the porter informed her. As he put out his hand for a tip, Mavis shook it warmly.

After the door closed, Mavis stood staring at everything, and then caught sight of herself in the long mirror. Her hat looked rather limp, and the feathers leaned to one side in a clump. She enjoyed looking at the ripples of her red chiffon dress, the diamante sparkling in the reflection. After a few minutes preening she fell on the bed, exhausted and rather bewildered.

"I'm here and I don't know anyone or where anything is," she sighed. "But tomorrow I'm going to dress like a queen and act like a lady."

She unpacked, filling the space in each drawer with underwear and various coloured scarves. Then feeling hungry, Mavis slipped through door (leaving it open) and started wandering the thickly-carpeted corridors. On and on she went, finally coming to a vast sweeping staircase.

"Oh, I don't think I can manage that," she thought, standing on the top stair.

"Do you need the elevator?" asked a smiling, dark-skinned man in his 40s coming up the stairs towards her.

"Yes, where is it? I'm a bit too tired for the stairs."

"It's over here." The man took her arm and guided Mavis round the corner to the mirrored elevator. "What floor do you want?" he asked.

"I have no idea; I just want to find some food. I've come all the way from London and I'm lost," sighed Mavis.

"Let me take you down to the restaurant. My name's Calvin Sheet by the way."

"Oh, you're so kind. I'm Mrs Mavis Hunter," she said, expanding her chest to feel important. "Where is the best place – the most gorgeous place – to shop for a lady?"

"Definitely Bloomingdales on Fifth Avenue, it's only two blocks from here."

The elevator shuddered to a halt. "Thanks very much. Bye." Mavis waved to Calvin. She could smell roast meat and followed her nose to the noisy restaurant.

"Can I help?" asked a waiter in red trousers.

"I want to eat now please. I've come all the way from England and I'd like a lamb chop, two veg, and a ginger ale. Thank you."

The waiter bowed. Mavis shuffled the mats round the table and smelt the artificial rose. "It ought to be a real rose in this posh hotel. That was a nice man I met. 'Calvin'. An unusual name. I don't know how I'll find the way back to my room. What number was it?"

When Mavis stood up an hour later, she felt rather dizzy

and sat down fast, causing a knife to fall, stabbing her foot.

"Ouch!"

She felt someone holding her arm and looked up to see Calvin smiling at her. "Can I help you, Mrs Hunter?"

"Oh yes, Calvin. I had a dizzy moment, I don't know how to find that lift again."

"Don't worry, I'll help you back to your room."

"Do I have to pay now?" she asked.

"No, it goes on your bill."

"Tell me Calvin, what are you doing staying in this lovely hotel?" she asked.

"Oh, I'm living here for the time being, it's a relaxing place to write my novel. I have some difficult business to resolve at my apartment," he replied quietly.

They walked slowly round the table out to the elevator. Mavis didn't glance at herself this time. Calvin held her arm as the elevator shuddered to a halt and they finally found room 2506.

"Well, goodnight!" he said, and slowly walked away.

Alone in her room again, Mavis went to the loo. "Keith must be wondering where I am," she thought. "I'd better ring him." On her way out she absentmindedly pulled the red cord instead of the white one for the light. A few minutes later there was an agitated knock on the door.

"Are you all right, madam?" called the manageress.

"Yes, I'm rather sleepy."

"You pulled the emergency alarm cord so I'm checking you're O K."

"Yes, yes, sweet dreams," called Mavis as she slumped onto the bed.

Shop until you drop

Next day Mavis demolished a plateful of fried eggs and bacon then went shopping.

Dressed in her purple suit, she trotted out of the hotel onto the busy pavement. She gaped upwards in amazement at the huge towering skyscrapers, her neck craning backwards so that she almost fell over. People jostled her, rushing to work.

"Gee honey, you're in the way!" shouted a tall, whiskered man waving his arms.

As Mavis walked, she suddenly felt some hot air whooshing up her skirt. "Oh, how nice, they warm the pavements here." Plumes of steam poured out of the vents as she made her way gingerly towards Bloomingdales. The fast traffic and huge cars overawed her. The brightly lit store seem to stretch along the entire street, its windows sparkling with wonderful clothes. She had arrived.

Mavis walked slowly to the make-up department and picked up some lipsticks along with a bright blue eye-shadow kit. She plonked herself in front of an oval mirror and started trying out the lipsticks, which became blurred as each new colour mixed with the last. Then, shutting one eye, she stroked her left eyelid with pale blue eye shadow.

"Can I help, madam? You should be using the sample make-up."

Mavis was absorbed, and with one eye shut, said, "I'll buy all of these. How much?"

The assistant did some totting up. "$285 please." Mavis delved into her bag and flicked through a bunch of notes. "Would you like your purchases wrapped?"

"Yes please," smiled Mavis, forgetting that only one eye was painted and her lips glistened in several radiant reds.

Next she travelled up the escalator to 'Ladies' Wear'. Mavis stood amazed at the mass of colourful garments. After about 20 minutes she'd gathered an armful of clothes to try on and was ushered into a large, pink changing boudoir. The black and white zebra evening dress with a black cape made her look very regal. The other dresses were thrilling in their variety. A beautiful white and mauve silk coat was irresistible and made her feel young. Mavis decided to keep it on.

She bought all the clothes. "Here is the bill, madam. Would you like these items delivered?" asked a glamorous, long legged girl.

"Yes please. I'm Lady Hunter staying at the Halifax...? Leeds...? No, the Bolton Hotel," she said, counting out various notes from her bag. "This *is* a long bill. Where's the shoe department please?"

But before the girl could reply, Mavis felt a little giddy and slumped on a chair, fanning her face with a hanky. "May I have a glass of water – not fizzy – please?" she asked quietly.

"Yes, of course." The assistant returned with iced water in a long glass. Mavis sat for some time, bewildered as to why she was there, and in fact not entirely sure where she actually was. She looked up to see a large sign saying, 'Women's Shoes 3rd floor'.

"Thank you. Bye!" She waved to the girl.

~

At the top of yet another escalator her eyes lit on a shelf crowded with shiny high heels in every colour. She picked out a yellow shoe and sat down to try it on.

"Excuse me," said a decorous young man. "Shall I get your size in this style, madam?"

Meanwhile Mavis continued stuffing her right foot into the small shoe and saying, "I never know my size. It's what feels good that matters."

The assistant sighed benignly. "Perhaps I could measure your foot?" He did so and then produced a selection of beautiful shoes for her to try. She slipped them on, tottered a bit, and then put her arm out to hold the assistant.

"What's your name?" she asked, clutching both his shoulders.

"Joel. How do they feel, madam?"

"I'll try on some more when I've had a trot," breezed Mavis as she nearly toppled going towards the mirror. Her legs looked splendid. Finally, she decided on four different designs, all in bright colours. "Please send them to Lady Hunter, at the Bolton Hotel, except for this white pair which I'll wear now."

Mavis was handed the bill and gulped with surprise at the cost, but handed several notes to the assistant.

"Where is the hat department?" she asked.

"Ground floor, madam," he replied with a gentle smile.

Hundreds of hats in all shapes and sizes wobbled on stands and up the walls. She made a bee-line for a broad-brimmed creation with poppies dancing round its brim. "That would go with my spotted red," she thought.

After choosing three more, all different shapes and colours, Mavis asked for the bill and ealized there would soon be no more cash left for today. She swept up her bags and looked for the exit, where she gave the name of her hotel to the doorman as he hailed a taxi.

~

After a few more days of shopping, Mavis's wardrobe was overflowing with colourful dresses, boas, coats and stoles.

A large shelf was piled untidily with various new shoes, mainly yellow and red with matching straps, and gave her bedroom the air of a boutique. The new orange-spotted pashmina she was wearing draped round her shoulders looked gorgeous. It was perfect for meeting Calvin in the cocktail bar. Her shaky hands daubed make-up across scraggy cheeks, pale blue eye shadow smudged upper lids, and scarlet lipstick overran the allotted place. She felt great.

Her room bell rang. There was Calvin at the door, beaming. They walked to the elevator. Mavis glanced approvingly at her dress in its mirror. Calvin took one arm to steady her as both doors slid open. They walked into the long bar.

"Good evening," said a bartender showing them to a large comfy sofa. Mavis sank into it, feeling luxurious in every way.

"Shall we have bourbon?" Calvin asked.

"Yes, with all those lumps in," smiled Mavis.

"On the rocks, please," ordered Calvin.

The bowl of nuts was tempting but they often dislodged her dentures, so Mavis asked for some pitted olives instead. When her bourbon arrived on a silver platter Mavis grabbed the glass and gulped it down. "Can I have a straw next time please?"

"Yes madam!"

She sank back into the sofa and began humming 'Oh I do like to be beside the seaside...'.

"Do you like the sea Calvin? Are there any seasides in New York?"

"Lots of water but no seaside, Mavis, though there's always the hotel pool."

"Oh, I love swimming on a lilo. We could do that together tomorrow. I'll have to buy a costume mind you. Maybe a black striped one like the Queen wears on her yacht."

The second bourbon arrived with two straws. She sucked hard on one and then blew bubbles with the other. The embarrassed barman walked away.

"Would you like some olives, Mavis?" asked Calvin.

"Yes, oh yes. Green ones!"

"What are you doing tomorrow?" enquired Calvin after a pause.

"I'm going to have my hair tinted auburn and nails painted blood red like that girl on TV last night. Oh, I'm feeling beautifully happy. Where's my next iced drink?"

Calvin gave a wary glance at her increasingly scarlet face. "OK Mavis, I'll order another, but..."

"And some buttered toast too," interrupted Mavis. "I'm feeling flopsy and whoopsy."

Calvin signaled to the waiter for a small bourbon. Mavis

took her shoes off and smiling mischievously, she fiddled in her bag and brought out a wad of dollar bills, then suddenly threw a few in the air. "What shall we do with these?" she chuckled.

Calvin hushed her and collected the scattered money, putting it back in her bag.

"I think I'll have that drink by my bed," she suggested as the waiter brought her third whisky (without rocks and with one straw).

"Yes, Mrs Hunter, I'll send it up." Mavis tried to stand, but swayed as Calvin guided her to the elevator.

"Bye all," she waved to everyone in the bar. "We'll do something fun tomorrow."

Two minutes later, she slurred 'goodnight' to Calvin's blurry face and slid through the door of room 2506, catching a glimpse of her flowing dress in the process. Falling onto the bed she laughed to herself, "Ah good, I feel so, so good. Filthy pills, come on. One, two three." Mavis threw three tablets down her open mouth. "I can't be bothered to put my nightie on." A sleepy silence engulfed her.

~

Next morning the maid knocked on the door around 8am, then knocked again. No reply. She opened the door and found Mavis lying on the bed fully clothed and smiling in her sleep.

"Excuse me madam, shall I come back later?" she asked. Mavis didn't respond.

The maid gently shook her. Mavis sat bolt upright.

"Why are you shaking me? I'm in the middle of a lovely dream" she said, indignantly.

"Sorry madam, I thought you were ..." stammered the flustered maid. "I'll come back later."

At about noon, Mavis was recovering with a long squeezed orange juice in the bar when Calvin came over and sat down quietly.

"You forgot our swim this morning. Do you remember we arranged it last night?"

"Sorry," said Mavis bashfully, although she couldn't remember making the promise at all.

"Would you like a walk in Central Park? It's lovely at this time of year," suggested Calvin instead.

"Yes, I'd love to see the trees and flowers there," Mavis replied quietly, suddenly remembering England and her garden and the mimosa tree. She stared at Calvin wistfully for some time and suddenly gasped, "I must tell you I've had an idea. Would you like to come and visit England? You could stay as a guest in my house near the canal!"

Calvin took a deep breath, unable to absorb the sudden suggestion. "Oh Mavis, how kind. May I think about it?" he asked.

"Well no, not really, because when I'm full up with ideas, I can't hold on to them for long. They disappear quickly." She stared at Calvin.

"The thing is I live here and have lots of commitments and..." Calvin hesitated.

"Can't you forget here for just a *little* while," interrupted Mavis. "This is a free thought, an adventure".

The waiter walked up. "Any drinks, madam?"

"Yes, I'll have the ... what is it Calvin, on the rocks?"

The waiter smiled indulgently. "Yes, Mrs Hunter, and you Sir?"

"Are you sure that's a good idea, Mavis?" Calvin looked worried.

"Don't fret about me!" trilled Mavis "I'm thinking about England so much I can hardly breathe. I'm running out of money so I have to go home soon." She rambled on. "I'd like you to see the lovely study overlooking my beech trees."

"Perhaps I could visit for a few weeks?" suggested Calvin, to himself as much as to Mavis. She found his warm smile very beguiling. "I need to finish a novel, and I work well in a peaceful study."

"What fun! Will you write about me one day?" she asked, almost cheekily.

"Not at present, because the current novel is very serious.

Your happy personality will be for another book." Calvin stood up, and his tall, elegant frame leaned over Mavis. His glowing olive skin caught the sunlight coming through the long French windows. "Can I let you know tomorrow about your kind offer?"

After Calvin left, Mavis suddenly felt rather lonely, so she called the barman and asked him to sit beside her.

"Will you have a drink?" she asked.

"No... thank you," stuttered the barman.

"Well, talk to me then. Do you have a family? Do they pay you well? Do you like kippers? You don't seem to have them on the menu here." Mavis was rambling again. The barman tried to get up twice and go back to the bar, but Mavis had a firm hand on his arm. "Perhaps you'd like to come to England, too?" A bell rang impatiently at the bar.

"Excuse me, I must go to a customer," he said, wrenching his arm away.

"Oh dear," sighed Mavis, "Come back later for a chat."

Half-an-hour later Mavis went off to find the hotel doorman and ask where the nearest travel-agent was.

"We can book anything you require at Reception, madam. What is it you need?", he enquired.

"Well, I'm not sure how many people are coming with me to England, but I'll have to go next Monday because I'm running out of money," she sighed.

"Well Mrs Hunter, when you know what you want, just go to Reception," he stated.

Home again, home again

Three days later on the plane Calvin was recounting his friend's sudden death from an aneurysm.

"What's that?" asked Mavis.

"It's the sudden bursting of an artery. There was no warning," said Calvin gravely.

"Would you like any drinks?" interrupted a steward. "Lunch will follow in 15 minutes."

"Let's have something on the rocks like we had in New York," smiled Mavis.

"Two bourbon on the rocks, please," ordered Calvin.

The steward handed over the two drinks. "Oh how sad for you Calvin. Was he your best friend?"

"Yes, Rex was very special, we'd been together for nearly ten years. I miss him dreadfully." Calvin's voice was only a whisper. Mavis touched his right hand. They ate their plastic food in silence.

"Would you like another drink, Calvin?" she asked quietly.

"Yes please."

While waiting for the steward to return, Mavis became pensive. She'd already phoned Prue and asked her to give the cottage a quick clean, adding 'Oh and just to let you know, I'm bringing a writer friend over who's going to be my lodger. Hope the shop's going well. Please arrange a cab to meet us at Heathrow'.

~

They arrived at the cottage just after a brief downpour. Mavis took two big gulps as she unlocked the front door. She felt like a visitor coming into her own house and walked slowly into the sitting room.

"Here, Calvin sit down and make yourself comfortable."

She took a deep breath and left the room hurriedly, eager to tell Keith she was back. The back door seemed jammed, so she threw her body against it and nearly fell as it burst open. Mavis shuddered thinking of Keith in the cold under the bench. She walked over and whispered, "I'm back Keith, I'm here. Have you missed me? I've been so busy in New York. I'll sing our song."

A tear moistened her cheek as she started humming, her legs wrapped round the bench. "I've met a new friend who's coming to stay for a bit. He's very gentle and looks after me." Another tear slid down her face as she tapped the seat. Mavis felt in her pocket for the key to the kitchen door. It must have fallen out somewhere. She stumbled slightly on the uneven path. "Oh well I'll find it later," she sighed, looking up to see Calvin give a slight wave from the sitting room window. "I'd forgotten he was there for a minute." She smiled warmly, signalling him to come out and join her.

A minute later they walked under the rustling trees, on grass that was lush like a velvet carpet. Various flower beds were overflowing with poppies, foxgloves, dahlias and geraniums. Mavis walked in silence. Calvin was clearly enjoying the peaceful atmosphere.

Mavis suddenly exclaimed, "You must be hungry Calvin. Shall we have lunch in or go to the local pub? I haven't got much except the bread & milk Prue left us. I'll take you to our cosy local."

"That would be lovely," said Calvin softly.

As Mavis opened the kitchen door she half-turned to announce, "I've lost the key. We'll look for it later. Let me show you your room and the study before we go out."

Then, slamming the kitchen door, she looked down and saw the key under her left foot. "Oh silly me."

Mavis wondered whether to take the car, not having driven for a while, but decided on balance to give it a go. "I'm going to get the car out Calvin," she announced. "The pub isn't very far but we're both a bit tired." She smiled, scuttled to the garage, and heaved open its wooden door. There was Betty, her old green banger. The gears seemed stiff as she manoeuvred it slowly onto the drive, then walked back to the front door.

"Ready!" she called. Calvin came downstairs looking very smart in a new green raincoat.

Their journey was rather jerky. Mavis got muddled with the gears quite often, and stalled at a green light causing some angry hoots. Calvin was relieved when they reached the The Cock & Hen, which was adorned with masses of dangling purple fuscias.

As they walked into the pub, Mavis drew a deep sigh, suddenly recalling her last visit there with Keith. George, the ruddy faced publican, greeted her warmly.

"Hello Mavis! Welcome home. I gather from Prue you've been in the States. Had a good time?"

"Yes, lovely," replied Mavis.

"How's Keith's mum"? George queried.

"Keith's mum"? said Mavis hesitatingly.

"Yes. Prue said she's ill," explained George.

"Oh, that's right. She's terribly ill. He won't be back for a long long time, I'm afraid."

"Sorry to hear that," replied George.

"This is Calvin, a writer friend I met in America," went on Mavis hurriedly. "He's staying with me for a while to finish his novel."

"Nice to meet you." George shook hands with Calvin.

"Er, can we go into the garden for a moment?" said Calvin crossly as he guided Mavis through the open door. Then to George, "We'll be back in a minute."

Once outside, he frowned. "Now what's going on Mavis? Who's Keith? Are you married? You seem to have misled me. I can't stay in your house if your husband's away. He might suddenly return and wonder who I am." Calvin was anxious and bewildered. He looked across at Mavis cowering under an old oak tree. Her bottom lip trembled, and there were tears in her plaintive eyes.

Mavis whispered the truth about how she'd buried Keith under the bench so he could be near her after his sudden death from a heart attack. This revelation of her loss and vulnerability made Calvin realise why she'd gone straight to the bench in the garden. With great sympathy he agreed to accept her sweet deception. After all, no one need know, and they weren't hurting anyone.

"I completely understand now. Come on let's go and eat," he said, gently steering her back into the restaurant.

George showed Mavis and Calvin to a large oak table laid for lunch.

"Would you like your usual?" asked George.

"Usual what?" said Mavis.

"Your pink gin," smiled George.

"Oh no, we'll have champagne today. And the menu please," asked Mavis. She never had pink gin. That was Keith's drink. "Try the trout, Calvin it's always very good, and they do a lovely lemon sauce with it," Mavis suggested.

"Yes, I will," agreed Calvin, who suddenly found himself thinking of Rex, and how much he'd have loved this old English pub. Mavis was also quiet, recalling Keith reading the local paper when they last ate at The Cock and Hen. "I wonder how he is under the bench", she almost said out loud.

"Here we are!" George plonked their plates down. "Top up?" He filled their glasses from the champagne bucket.

"Thank you George", smiled Mavis. "Cheers to you and to our absent friends," Mavis said to Calvin warmly.

~

After lunch they drove back to the house. Mavis was feeling tipsy but managed to keep the wheel more or less under control. Then she realized the roof had leaked and that she was sitting on a very wet seat.

"Is *your* seat wet Calvin?" she asked, glancing at him. A 4 X 4 swerved to avoid her and hooted violently.

"Yes it is rather damp," said Calvin, fastening his raincoat a little tighter.

As they reached home, the rain had cleared and a glorious sunset was sparkling on the golden autumnal trees.

"So sorry Calvin. Betty's an old banger, like me. Do go and change, I'll light the drawing room fire. Or have a bath if you want. We don't have a shower. Keith thought I'd fall over in it."

"Thanks Mavis. Perhaps I will have a bath. It's quite chilly." Calvin walked upstairs saying, "Such a pleasant lunch."

Mavis strode into the sitting room, put some kindling on the fire and heaped up several logs. Then she lay on the sofa and soon nodded off. She awoke to see Calvin smiling as he said, "Are you all right, Mavis?"

"Yes, yes of course," she said, going towards the fire and giving it a prod with the poker. They both sat down to discuss the next day. "I expect you'll be hard at work in the study. I must do some gardening."

"Yes, I'll start work immediately. I have to finish the book in a couple of weeks," smiled Calvin.

"Like a cup of tea?" Mavis asked as she got up, then dithered around the kitchen opening drawers and cupboards because she'd forgotten where everything was.

"Do you take sugar?" she called.

"Yes, one please," Calvin answered as he walked into the small, cosy kitchen. A scarlet, evening sun was sinking low behind the trees.

"There we are." Mavis handed Calvin a cup and saucer with the spoon still in the cup. They both stood looking out at the garden. As he took a sip, Calvin's mouth felt very odd and he had to spit the tea out.

"Ugh! Mavis I think you've muddled the salt and sugar."

"Oh dear, silly me. Their labels have fallen off – so sorry. Have a new cup; I'll give you sweetner because I'm not sure which jar is which."

"No, I won't, thank you. May I stroll round your lovely garden?" Calvin asked,

"Yes, do. And while you do that, I'll sort out these silly old jars."

~

That evening Mavis cooked herbs and fried bread.

"This is very unusual!" exclaimed Calvin.

"Yes it's one of my inventions. I grow lots of herbs. They're very good for the stomach. Now help yourself to anything you want, I'm going shopping tomorrow. There's a spare front door key hanging by the window in the kitchen, so just feel free to roam like I did in New York." Mavis giggled remembering the fun she'd had.

Calvin stood up, "This really is a peaceful place – I'm so glad I came," he said, warming his back by the fire.

"I'm off to bed," waved Mavis, as the jet lag finally caught up with her.

~

The next morning was radiantly autumnal. "See you at lunchtime," called Mavis up the stairs. Calvin came to the top bannister, his face covered in white shaving foam. "Oh, you look like father Christmas!" she laughed. Calvin waved her off.

Mavis arrived home two hours later clutching several bags of shopping, and felt so tired that she sank into an armchair as Calvin appeared in the doorway.

"You look exhausted! Let me put some of the bags in the kitchen. I've managed to do a lot of writing," added Calvin a few moments later. "With luck I'll actually make my deadline."

"Oh good. It's rather nice to come home and chat to someone. Would you like a sandwich?" Mavis asked wearily. Then, without waiting for an answer, she walked into the kitchen, stood there for a moment, then headed into the garden.

Calvin watched through the window as she gently stroked the garden seat, curled up her legs, lay down and fell asleep. Then he went back to the study to work after making himself a sandwich. Later he heard the bath water running. Mavis must have been cold out on the seat. She appeared half-an-hour later in one of her flamboyant New York dresses – a frothy, yellow number, knee length with some matching shoes.

"Oh you look very good – that's such a lovely colour. Bloomingdales had the right styles for you," exclaimed Calvin.

"Oh, how I miss the buzz and excitement of New York," sighed Mavis. "Shall we go out for supper? That's why I dressed up. There's a little Chinese place not far from here."

"Yes, that sounds delightful. Shall I drive this time?" asked Calvin warily.

At the Golden Pagoda they chatted while Mavis played with her chopsticks, but she found the rice fell off like rain drops, scattering onto her lap. Calvin ate elegantly and avoided looking at the food carnage opposite him. Suddenly Mavis choked on a chicken bone, grew red in the face then coughed it onto the table. Calvin covered his plate with a red napkin.

"So sorry," gasped Mavis in dismay, her beautiful dress spattered with rice. "I should never have tried the chopsticks. Silly me! You manage them so naturally." She smiled, unaware of the mess she was in.

~

Two days later Mavis came in from the garden, hands dripping with compost and slumped onto a rickety kitchen chair. Calvin smiled at her.

"Well, I've had an excellent morning. Only two more chapters to finish."

They both had a snack lunch. "I'm off to see Prue at the shop now!" said Mavis once she'd finished. "Enjoy your writing. I really must hear what your novel is about sometime."

Ghost writer

Life took on a comfortable routine over the next few weeks, with Calvin writing all day and Mavis back to work part-time in the shop. She told Prue all about Bloomingdales and the lush hotel suite she'd stayed in, how she'd met the polite and attentive Calvin, and they'd ended up looking after each other in different ways like two little boats who'd lost their moorings.

"I'll bring him to the shop one day," smiled Mavis.

"Oh do! He sounds a real gentleman," said Prue.

One warm morning when Mavis had popped out to get some milk and eggs from the farm, Calvin went for a stroll round the garden. Bending down to smell one of the scarlet roses he tripped over a watering can half-hidden by overhanging foliage and fell heavily. A stabbing pain shot through his right elbow.

"OW!! It's my writing arm! What am I going to do?" He managed to dial a local taxi. When the man arrived he said, "Please could you write a note to Mrs Hunter for me, saying I've had to go to the hospital?" The driver did exactly that, then helped Calvin into the cab.

Twenty minutes later they arrived at Accident and
Emergency, and Calvin walked slowly up to the reception
desk. After a long wait he was eventually X-rayed and told
he'd cracked his elbow in several places. His arm was put
in a sling and he was sent up to the fracture ward. On the
way his mobile buzzed urgently.

"Oh Calvin, what's happened?" asked Mavis anxiously. "I've
just found your note!"

"Well, I tripped over a watering can."

"Oh, yes. I left it there to catch rainwater. Roses prefer it to
the tap variety, you see. I'm so sorry. Shall I come and get
you out?"

"No, I've got to stay in for a bit because I've damaged my
elbow, but I do need to see you about my writing. Can you
pop in?" he asked, wincing with pain.

Mavis arrived breathless an hour later carrying some
bedraggled begonias and a tin of biscuits. She looked at
Calvin's arm and gasped.

"Oh you poor thing, it's your right one. How can you finish
your book?"

"Well, that's what I want to discuss. I wondered if you
could type the last two chapters which I've already drafted
longhand? The deadline's really close now and I must get
it off to my agent. Do you think you'll be able to read my
writing?"

"Yes, of course I'll finish it for you. I'd be delighted to tinkle away on the old typewriter. It's how I write all my letters as it is. I'm a real whizz!"

"Thanks very much. Jeez, sometimes I wish I wasn't such a technophobe."

"I'll go home and start right away," said Mavis. "Here are some biscuits to keep you going. Shall I bring in a thermos of homemade soup later?"

"No, I'm not hungry." Calvin's dejected voice made Mavis sad.

As Mavis approached the study an hour later, she could see three neat piles of completed manuscript and reached out to pick up the first heap and start typing. She soon became riveted by the fascinating story line – in fact the more she typed the more involved she got, almost as if she was writing it herself.

"Oh no, I don't think that's quite right. Far too sad."

She stopped and retyped a few lines.

"Yes, now it's possible. He could do it and call for help."

She became completely absorbed. Day slid into evening. She often stopped to read out loud, smile or gasp at what was happening. She felt her alterations added greatly. At about midnight, Mavis found her head drooping onto the keyboard.

"I'll sleep here. I'm nearly halfway," she whispered, then sank onto the sofa and went straight to sleep.

~

Next morning Mavis hurriedly ate a hard boiled egg, then went upstairs to continue her work. The phone rang.

"Hello Mavis. How are you getting on?" asked Calvin.

"Marvellously. I've been working very hard – it's so interesting," Mavis replied. "How's your poor arm?"

"They're doing more tests and I've been given pain killers. I'm so relieved you're managing to type it. How far have you got?" Calvin enquired.

"I'm starting the last chapter so your 'dead time', or whatever you call it, will be alright. I'll send it off tonight if possible, if not tomorrow," Mavis enthused. "The address is already on that large white envelope, isn't it?"

"Yes. Please, please send it by registered post," Calvin insisted. "I'll pay you later."

"Don't worry. I'm good at parcels. Bye."

Two minutes later the phone rang again.

"Mavis, where are you?" asked Prue crossly. "I've had to tell Mrs Viking you're ill. You remember she was coming-in this morning to find something for her daughter's wedding, don't you?"

"Sorry. Can't possibly see anyone today. I'm *far* too busy. Tell her to come next week at the same time," said Mavis casually.

Prue was most upset. "You can't treat customers like that and just forget about them," she said.

"When I'm full steam ahead I can only do one thing at a time. I have to work now," Mavis said bluntly.

"What is happening to you, Mavis? I've never known you like this before!"

Prue put the phone down. Oblivious to her rudeness, Mavis started typing again, hurrying and correcting as she completed the last chapter. "That's a much better ending – far less sad. Sad endings aren't good for you. More laughter raises the spirits. There's no time to read the whole book, but at least I've added to it here and there. Now I must dash with it to the Post Office."

~

Next day Mavis walked into Calvin's ward but found his bed empty.

"I wonder where he is?" she said out loud.

"He's gone to physio, love," smiled the patient in the opposite bed, who was strung up like a turkey with his leg suspended from a gantry.

"Oh, thank you," said Mavis rather shyly at the sight of the rough unshaven hulk almost revealing his backside. Poor man, he looked like a gorilla. Mavis decided to lie down on Calvin's bed until he came back. She was worn out from typing late into the night. She fell asleep, snoring softly.

Half an hour later a nurse appeared with Calvin behind her, his arm in a sling.

"Excuse me, visitors aren't allowed on patient's beds. Also, you're in an all-male ward," said the nurse.

"Oh sorry, I didn't mean to nod off," apologised Mavis. "Hello Calvin, how are you? It's on it's way to America. I posted it at 9.30," she said excitedly, then got up glowering at the nurse who straightened the sheets as Calvin sat down.

"Thank you so much. You are a dear," he said warmly. "They might let me out in a couple of days."

"Oh good. I've brought you a sardine and lettuce sandwich," she said, handing him a crumpled paper bag. "I must go to the shop now. I forgot an appointment and Prue's very cross. See you tomorrow." She waved to Calvin and glided out of the ward.

As Mavis opened her shop door she saw Prue sullenly folding two dresses for a customer. The lady thanked her and swept out of the shop. "Mavis, you don't seem to care about people anymore," said Prue sighing.

"Oh things have changed now. I had to do an emergency operation on Calvin," Mavis calmly replied.

"Oh my goodness, whatever do you mean?" Prue was aghast.

"Just typing his novel. The poor man's in hospital with a

smashed elbow. He tripped over a watering can." Another customer interrupted at this point. "I'm rather tired, Prue. I'll pop in tomorrow," Mavis whispered on her way out.

~

The next day, she sat beside the phone all morning, then decided to call Calvin herself.

"Hello, it's me. Do you want a carriage home?" she laughed.

"Not sure yet," he replied. "I'll ring you after the specialist has seen me."

While she waited, Mavis wandered into the garden, deciding to dead-head some roses, and nearly tripped over the watering can herself.

"I'd better leave this on the lawn so we can see it," she muttered, then glanced at her watch. "Lunchtime. Perhaps I'll just have a plain yoghurt and drop some chives in. It's so tiresome trying to think up food when you're alone. I'll make a shepherd's pie for Calvin tonight. I wonder if he likes egg custard with a drop of brandy over it?"

She sang her old songs quite loudly with the shepherd's pie onions bouncing up and down as she tried to chop them with a blunt knife. "Where's my sharp-pointed friend?" There were onions rolling round the table and falling on the floor when the phone rang.

"Hello Mavis. Could you come to the shop later, at about 4 o'clock?" asked Prue.

"Not yet, because me and Betty are waiting to fetch Calvin."

"What?" asked Prue beginning to think Mavis was going a little mad.

"I can't explain at the moment, but I'll be in tomorrow morning."

Eventually the pie was complete and put safely in the oven to cook. Half-an-hour later Mavis returned to find smoke billowing from the oven. Opening the door she gasped to see the red and white oven gloves smouldering on top of her shepherd's pie. Mavis turned off the oven.

"Silly me. I do seem to be having a fiery time."

She slumped into a chair. The phone rang at last. "Hi Mavis. I'm being discharged around 5 pm," said Calvin.

"Right. Shall I bring a blanket to keep you warm in the car?" she asked happily.

Mavis pulled out the shepherd's pie and sprinkled some cheese onto it. " There! Calvin won't know about the oven-glovey bits. Now I'd better change into something nice before I go to the hospital." Upstairs she looked at herself in the full length mirror, remembering New York.

~

Mavis arrived at the hospital promptly, but found she couldn't remember which floor he was on. Her mind was buzzing with worry as she stood gazing at the huge notice. "It must be the 3rd floor because that arrow says 'Physio

and Limbs Unit'." Finally, a lift took her up and Mavis walked into the ward. Calvin was sitting on his bed talking to the gorilla man opposite.

"Here I am. Are you all packed up?" she asked.

"Yes," smiled Calvin, then called 'Bye, Greg' to the man opposite. Mavis took his good arm and slowly they headed to the lift. Out in the car park she helped Calvin into Betty's passenger seat and fixed his seat belt. It was a slow journey, much to the annoyance of several drivers behind. Finally, though, they pulled into the driveway.

"Oh I'm going to sneeze," Mavis spluttered. The car stopped with a jerk, then revved and shot into the garage door. There was a shattering of glass.

"Silly me! Sorry Calvin. I hope I didn't jolt your arm?"

Calvin got out to examine the damage. "The right headlamp is smashed and the number plate's half-off. Is there a garage nearby?" he asked.

"Don't worry about that. I'm sure it'll be OK. We can walk everywhere from now on. Tomorrow, I'll show you the beautiful canal a couple of fields away over there." She pointed towards a distant, gushing weir. "While you're waiting for news of your book in New York you must see some English treasures." Mavis smiled as she glanced at Calvin's tired face. Entering the house, she walked into the sitting room. " Sit by the fire. I've made a shepherd's pie for supper. I'll go and heat it up."

"Thank you, I shall enjoy some good food," said Calvin quietly.

Mavis looked into the oven and saw a few burnt bits of oven glove.

"Just going to prepare some carrots, Keith. It won't take long," Mavis called.

"That's fine," replied Calvin, choosing not to react.

Later Mavis watched him eating with one hand. "Sorry you've had to wait. I had a bit of an accident with the oven glove," she said, watching with concern as Calvin put a piece of burnt, striped material on the side of his plate. "So sorry I missed that piece. There was a small fire," said Mavis. Then in a more upbeat voice, "I've made egg custard with a dash of brandy for pudding to celebrate your return."

"Mavis you've been such a help, particularly with typing the last section of my book. What would I do without you?" Calvin smiled at her.

Life is full of surprises

The following morning Mavis gave Calvin a pair of Keith's wellingtons and they walked along the muddy path, squelching across several fields to the beautiful Wey canal. Various colourful narrowboats were moored outside the lock.

"This is very special. I've never seen such attractive boats," exclaimed Calvin.

"Yes, each is hand-painted to traditional designs. People have such fun holidaying along the canal," said Mavis animatedly. "Oh, and there's a beautiful canal shop with hand-painted item over there." Mavis pointed to a large shed.

"I'll go and have a look. Might buy a memento," Calvin laughed.

Ten minutes later, two narrow boats were jostling in a full lock. Calvin strode over with a parcel under his left arm.

"There's a great collection of artwork in there."

Mavis started to heave open the heavy lock gate but slipped as she was pulling it, and the beam passed over her.

"Whoopsie!" she cried, nearly falling headlong. The lock-keeper hauled her up.

"Haven't seen you for a long time, Mrs Hunter," he smiled.

"Just showing a friend around. He's not seen a canal before. We're going to watch the boats going through the locks," panted Mavis breathlessly. She looked for Calvin, who was walking towards her.

"That was a near miss," he laughed nervously. "Let's go home and have a coffee."

They walked back, relishing the calm sunlit day, under trees shedding their crispy russett leaves.

"Now tomorrow I thought of taking you to the local auction rooms," Mavis enthused over lunch. "You see some lovely period pieces there sometimes."

"That would be interesting," said Calvin, finishing a toasted sandwich. "This is such beautiful countryside. Those copper beech trees and the rolling hills beyond the canal are stunning."

"Yes, I'm lucky to live amongst such beauty," Mavis replied.

～

The following day was cloudless and warm.

"It's about 2 miles," said Mavis, "Is that alright?"

"That's fine. I'll take in more of the scenery on the way."

Later Mavis pointed to a large Victorian house where a bustling crowd was pushing into the auction rooms. "I'll stand this side to protect your bad arm," said Mavis, guiding Calvin into the vast hall that was buzzing with excited voices. "Let's peruse the items first." She handed Calvin a catalogue. "Oh, look at that painting of 'Skaters in Central Park'. Doesn't it remind you of home?" Mavis exclaimed.

"It certainly does," said Calvin.

"What about that antique knitting machine? I could use it to make a jumper in the winter," said Mavis.

A bell rang to signal the start of the auction. The buzzing voices went silent as a ruddy-faced man spoke to the audience.

"Who'll offer me £20 to start?" The bidders listened to the rising prices. Mavis and Calvin sat in the middle row.

"I'm just going to the toilet," whispered Calvin.

Mavis was enthralled by the electric atmosphere as the auctioneer sold off various desks, then she noticed the knitting machine being carried on. "I wonder who'll get that?" she mumbled, then put one hand up to take off her head scarf.

"How's it going?" asked Calvin as he returned to his seat.

"Very exciting," whispered Mavis.

"To you, Madam," called the auctioneer, pointing at Mavis as he brought down his hammer. A clerk approached, then stretched out a pen and paper to Mavis.

"Er, what's this for?" she asked amazed.

"You've just bid £2,000 for the antique knitting machine," he said.

"But I didn't do anything!" said Mavis indignantly.

"The auctioneer said you raised your hand, clinching the last bid."

Mavis blanched "I can't possibly afford that! I've just spent all my money in New York."

She burst into loud sobs, asking Calvin to sort everything out, which he did, quietly explaining that there must have been a mistake. Ten minutes later he led Mavis out of the hall, where, to her acute embarrassment, they passed close to the wretched machine.

~

Next morning Mavis was sweeping up leaves outside the front door when Calvin called out, "It's your friend from the shop on the phone."

"Happy birthday, Mavis," said Prue a few moments later. "Are you going out to celebrate?"

"Oh I'd forgotten it was my birthday. Can't remember how old I am," she said casually.

"'Course you can. You're 69 today. I've got a little prezzie for when you're next in," said Prue happily.

Hearing the conversation, Calvin went off to get the beautiful hand-painted bucket (still wrapped) that he'd originally bought for himself from the canal shop as a souvenir. Then he popped into the kitchen to get a tray and glasses for some sparkling wine. As Mavis finished on the phone Calvin handed her a glass.

"Right, birthday girl, let's drink to 'Marvellous Mavis'!"

She smiled, enjoying his kind words

"And this might be useful when it rains," Calvin added. Mavis took a gulp then unwrapped the parcel and gasped with delight.

"Oh, how thoughtful!" She smiled. "I'll leave it in the middle of the lawn. Thank you so much." He poured another glass. She was feeling a little woozy now.

"It was fascinating doing your novel. I did change that bit where they were arguing. So much better having a happy discussion. And I altered a few other sentences here and there so the reader could feel satisfied with how it ends," said Mavis, smiling sweetly.

"You did what!" Calvin gasped. "How could you have altered the ending! Oh my God, what have you done! I must ring my agent immediately!" The happy birthday atmosphere was ruined. Calvin dialled furiously. "Yes, it's me. I must speak to George urgently," he said as soon as he got through. "George, I'm a bit worried because ... What? Spielberg's interested? Omigosh! But hang on a minute. What about getting a publisher first?" Calvin was flushed and expectant all at once. "Two people interested in it already? Which one's offering the better deal?" Mavis could hear the agent's animated voice. "Yes I realise I'll have to come back soon if NBC want to interview me. Wow, I'm amazed! Particularly to hear you say they all love the last few chapters."

"I typed those," chipped in Mavis. Calvin looked gratefully at her for several moments.

"Er ... yeah, I'll book a flight as soon as I can. Maybe the day after tomorrow. Bye!" He put the phone down, still staring at Mavis. "Please forgive me for shouting at you. I was so afraid the novel would be spoiled, but thanks to you it sounds like it could be a huge success." He went over and pecked Mavis on the cheek. "Let's finish the sparkling wine to celebrate."

They wandered round the garden, chatting together. A huge fear entered Mavis as she realized he would have to leave soon. But she bravely said, "You must get on the next plane. So many people are waiting for you in New York."

Calvin stopped. "I don't feel right leaving you alone. I've noticed you getting tired and anxious lately," he said.

"Don't be silly. You must go. I can manage perfectly well. We'll chat on the phone. And don't forget you promised to write about *me* next," she giggled.

Next day, Fred the taxi driver rang the bell at 11:00a.m.

"I'll be back here to stay if I may one day," Calvin said, giving Mavis a hug.

"Oh do, please do." She pushed him into the taxi knowing tears were welling up, then blew a kiss as it slowly disappeared, staggered indoors sobbing, and sank into the old armchair she'd sat in after Keith died. Once again the old house was empty. "Wasn't I lucky to meet such a good friend. What shall I do with my days now? I'll pop into the shop tomorrow," she said tearfully to herself. As Mavis went upstairs she peeked into Calvin's room. There was one rose in a jam jar and a note saying, 'What fun we had together. You really are a treasure. Kind thoughts forever ... Calvin'. Her tears welled up again. "Now pull yourself together, he was never going to stay for good," she said aloud to herself. Mavis lay on her bed for a long time before finally falling asleep.

~

Next day Prue rang early. "Are you ever coming to the shop again?" she asked wearily.

"Yes, I'm popping in this morning as it happens. I've just had a rather sad farewell to deal with," murmured Mavis.

"Oh, I saw you with your handsome friend at the auction

rooms. I waved but I think you were bidding," said Prue.

"I certainly was not!" said Mavis crossly and put the phone down.

An hour later Mavis walked slowly into the shop.

"Ah! Her ladyship's arrived! Now I can go to the bank," said Prue smugly.

"Have lunch too. I'll be here for ages," sighed Mavis.

A couple of hours later Prue returned, humming. "Mavis?" she called, "Mavis, are you there?" She drew back the changing-room curtains. "Oh my God!" she cried. Mavis was sitting on a stool surrounded by beautiful dresses, gradually slicing all of them to shreds.

"They're no use any more; like me," she sighed. Prue realised that something serious was happening.

"I must call Keith," she said.

"You can't. He's gone. He's left me. I'm all alone now. Even Calvin has gone."

"Oh Mavis, I had no idea."

"Well, it's true." Mavis's shoulders began to tremble as she tossed strips of material into the air, sobbing hopelessly.

Part Two

Life goes on – sort of

It was a wet, dark November afternoon as Mavis gazed out of the window. She watched her canal bucket on the lawn slowly filling with rainwater. There was a soft knock on the bedroom door.

"Hello Mavis, will you join the others for lunch? It's spaghetti bolognaise today," said the smiling carer.

"I don't like spag bol. Can I make scrambled egg in the kitchen?" asked Mavis.

"No dear, residents aren't allowed in the kitchen," said the carer, whose name-tag said 'CATHY'.

"Well, I won't have anything in that case. I'm too sad to be hungry. Where have all the trees from my garden gone?" asked Mavis vacantly as she continued looking out of the window.

"I don't know. I have to go now to help with lunch." Cathy left.

A while later another visitor arrived.

"Coming for a potter?" asked a tall, stooping, gaunt figure with long black hair and large soulful eyes.

"Are you Anne?" asked Mavis.

"The rain's stopped. Let's look for mushrooms. We saw some last week, do you remember?"

"I think they were toadstools actually, and I'm not partial to wild mushrooms. They always have grubs crawling around them," replied Mavis quietly.

Anne was worried, having befriended Mavis, that she seemed cross and sad. She often felt the same but didn't show it like Mavis. "Oh come on, lets have a natter in the fresh air." Anne helped Mavis up and jollied her outside where they met Paula, a small, spindly, nearly bald woman who shook the whole time; and Tom, who was stone deaf and had shrunk to 5ft 4ins. The group limped and sauntered over the damp grass and came to Mavis's bucket.

"That's mine! Calvin gave me that. It collects rainwater for the roses," she announced. They all laughed. No one really listened to each other, and Tom just smiled all the time. Suddenly Paula tripped over her own twisted feet and fell flat on her face while Mavis, oblivious, walked on. Anne and Tom bent down to help her up. Paula's bleeding nose dripped everywhere so they took her across to Mavis's bucket and dipped her head in it.

"Leave my rainwater alone!" shouted Mavis crossly. "I don't want blood in it."

Luckily Cathy had seen them and ran out to rescue Paula and order everyone indoors.

~

"Christmas show coming soon Mave. Can I call you Mave?" said Anne the following day. "It's great fun. We all dress up and fool about and make our own costumes."

"I'm going to have a bath – if I'm allowed to," Mavis said, quietly drifting out of the room.

Next day at breakfast in the cold, dark dining room there were printed slips of paper on their cereal plates about preparations for the Christmas show. *'Anyone capable of making costumes most welcome'* said the notices.

"How long have we got?" Mavis asked Cathy.

"Oh, years and years hopefully," smiled Cathy busily passing round the toast.

"I mean to help for the Christmas show," queried Mavis, looking up at Cathy.

"Oh, I see. Well, the show's in six weeks' time."

Mavis rushed off to her room and rattled through her address book, loose pages falling out. "There's Prue." As she wrote the number down, Calvin's red address card fell to the floor. Stuffing the card into her pocket Mavis went up to the Manager's office. The door was half open.

"Mrs Marango, could you please call my friend Prue for me. She's got lots of bits and pieces of material. I could help with the Christmas show if she brings it over. Here's the number." Mavis handed a crumpled slip of paper to the Manager who dialled the number slowly, handing the phone back to Mavis.

"Hello Prue. Could you bring over a bag of material and bits for me. I want to make some Christmas show costumes. I think I'll be Queen Bess. Bring along some fur too. I know it's a long way but ..."

"How are you Mavis?" Prue gently interrupted. "It's so nice to hear you. Yes, I'll sort out a variety of things which might do. Will next week be alright?"

"Yes whenever you like, I'm always here."

"This mustn't happen too often, Mavis," said Mrs Marengo sternly after the call. "We don't just call people willy-nilly around here."

"How else can I get the material If I'm going to make costumes for your show?" Mavis replied leaving the office with a contemptuous look at the Manager's angry face.

Sing if you're winning

The following Friday a pianist called Mr. Bond came to 'The Brambles' to give a recital of film music. Many of the residents were dozing, a few chatting ... there was not much life in the room. Suddenly Mavis sprang to her feet.

"Let's have a sing song!" she called out.

"Sssh, sssh!" called her neighbour.

"Come on! Oh I do like to be beside the seaside ..." Mavis sang. The pianist stopped his film music, smiled at Mavis and started playing along with her. Soon a few more voices joined in and gradually the singing increased. Quiet voices got louder, someone suggested another song, but the pianist didn't know it. Mavis interrupted again by starting 'Onward Christian Soldiers' as she marched round the room. Old Paula slowly sang 'The White Cliffs of Dover'. Anne took hold of Mavis as they burst into 'The Hoki Koki'.

"Shut up!" called a grumpy old man in the corner. The pianist was doing his best to keep up with the exuberant ladies. More people hobbled up into the circle, laughing. Suddenly there was a scream and Paula tripped over her floppy feet. Mavis nearly fell on top of her.

Cathy rushed over saying, "Right, I think that's enough excitement for today. Please all clap Mr. Bond, the pianist."

"Ouch, my knee hurts!" complained Paula. Cathy heaved her up, and she hobbled out of the door.

Five minutes later the bell rang signalling cocoa time and people shuffled back to their rooms. All except Mavis. She sat in the now empty room wishing the singing hadn't finished. The fun had lifted her spirits and now she felt rather empty and began to wonder how Calvin was.

"Come along Mavis, it's bedtime," said Cathy half-an-hour later, guiding her out of the room.

~

The next day rain pounded on the windows. An air of lethargy spread round the lounge; where various wheezy objects stared vacantly into space, snuffled or slept. Mavis turned on the TV. The CNN newsreader was droning on about some elections in New York. She nodded off with boredom. A few minutes later she suddenly woke up, recognising Calvin's voice. There he was being interviewed about his new book. He smiled straight at Mavis and she waved back.

"Oh Calvin, how good to see you!" she cried triumphantly. Sadly, he soon vanished from the screen. "I must phone him!" She fiddled around in her dressing gown pocket and found the red card with his phone number on it.

"Cathy, did you see him?" she called out.

"Who?"

"My friend Calvin was on TV, smiling at me," Mavis giggled. "Please can I use the office phone? I must speak to him. Will you try this long number for me?" Mavis handed Cathy the card and a minute later they quietly closed the office door. Cathy slowly dialled the number then handed the receiver to Mavis. She almost dropped it in her excitement.

"Hello?" The soft voice was Calvin's.

"Oh, you looked so good in that nice green shirt. I was waving to you on TV. Did you see me?" burst out Mavis.

"So sorry I haven't called you Mavis, I've been incredibly busy promoting my book. The publishers are rushing it out in time for Christmas. It's all very exciting. I've had a film offer so maybe in a year or two you might see the movie released in England," said Calvin enthusiastically. Cathy was watching Mavis's animated face. "Tell me how you are. Has the bucket filled up with rainwater yet? I miss that glorious garden and the rustling trees. There's no peace here like your quiet study. Now are you being careful with the fire?" Calvin asked fondly.

"I don't know what you mean, we don't have fires here. There are no trees in the garden either," Mavis said sadly.

"Here? What do you mean? Where are you?"

"Not sure where I am. You can ask the carer, Cathy. Come over and see me one day soon. Must go, it's tea time – bye!" Mavis handed the phone to Cathy and left the office tearfully. Cathy explained to Calvin where Mavis lived now and why.

Mavis sat down for tea, rambling on about Calvin and the TV like a kettle on the boil. She nearly exploded with excitement. That evening she turned on the TV again, but there was no sign of Calvin.

"I wonder when he'll come and see me. America is such a long way away." She went on mumbling to herself, then tears overwhelmed her. Anne had been watching her trembling face. She walked over, handed Mavis a pink hankie then knelt down taking her friend's hands. Neither spoke. The utter desolation was almost tangible. It was getting dark outside when the supper bell broke their silence.

Anne slowly got up and guided Mavis off to the dining room. Balloons dangled from the ceiling and everyone was singing 'Happy Birthday' to Tom, who couldn't hear a word but kept smiling at people's jolly faces. Suddenly he stood up and started singing a wonderful song about hills. His voice was soft and resonant. Everyone listened, hushed with surprise. Cheered up by this event, Mavis mouthed "Sing some more", enunciating each word with great care. Tom nodded and broke into a saucy French song, taking Mavis by the arm and whirling her round. Everyone clapped. Laughter finished the day.

Magical mystery tour

Two days later, just after breakfast, Cathy told Mavis that Prue was on her way with some material and had asked if she could take her out for lunch.

"Not sure if I can manage that," said Mavis quietly.

"Go on, you'll love it when you're out," Cathy laughed.

Mavis was sitting on her bed gazing vacantly out at the garden when Prue arrived. She stretched her arms out almost pleadingly for a hug. Afterwards, Mavis stood gazing at her friend.

"It's good to see you Prue. Your hair is a different colour isn't it?"

"Not really, it's the same as ever, only wet from the rain." Prue put down a large bag of material and old dresses.

"Ah, I remember that lovely orange pleated dress," said Mavis, lighting up at the sight of so much colourful material. "Why is it in shreds? I must repair that for Anne at Christmas."

"I thought this maroon velvet gown could be your Queen Bess frock," smiled Prue. "Oh, and here's a feather boa." Mavis began to busy herself, wrapping the boa round her neck and strutting past a nearby mirror. Briefly she was like her old self.

"Come on Mavis, let's go for a bite. There's a little place up the road," suggested Prue.

"What shall I wear? I can't be Queen Bess yet," laughed Mavis.

Having slowly changed into a crumpled green dress and pink raincoat, Mavis let Prue guide her out past the entrance.

"See you later," called Mavis to the empty reception desk.

"How is the shop?" Mavis asked ten minutes later at the 'Copper Kettle'.

"Quite busy at present. What with Christmas coming in two weeks, we've got lots of orders. Sally, a local Mum, helps me out three days a week," said Prue.

"Oh, I'd like porridge and honey to start with please," smiled Mavis to the nearby waitress, ignoring what Prue had said about the shop.

"This is lunch Mavis. Why not have shepherd's pie and carrots. It used to be your favourite," suggested Prue.

"Alright, with lots of gravy please," Mavis smiled at the enquiring waitress.

As they ate, Prue glanced at her friend's lined face, straggly hair and slightly quivering bottom lip and fondly asked Mavis, "Have you found some new friends at The Brambles?"

"Yes, about three, but Tom is deaf. Prue, where am I? Why am I there? I can't see my trees, I miss them," Mavis said sadly.

"It's a kind place where you get looked after, Mavis. You're not alone there," Prue soothed her.

"But I want my trees back!" Mavis was getting anxious.

"Well, how about we have a little trip to the Sussex Downs after lunch?" suggested Prue.

"Oh yes, yes. Sussex. Am I in Sussex?" Mavis's eyes were sparkling at last. Some shepherd's pie was dribbling down her dress, diced carrots were sliding towards her shoes and the gravy outlined her lower lip with a shiny gloss. The waitress took her messy plate and replaced it with a large ice cream, covered with nuts and wafers.

"Oooh, how delicious!" Mavis looked vulnerable, almost childlike as she slowly licked her ice cream. "I don't like the nuts," she whispered, placing them in a row on the table.

"Here, put them on my plate," suggested Prue as she got out her money to pay the bill.

"Off we go, mustn't miss the Downs," chortled Mavis, struggling into her pink plastic raincoat. "Bye. Thank you".

They both waved to the chef at the counter.

Prue tucked Mavis into her seat belt. They drove for twenty minutes along winding country lanes and eventually stopped in a layby on a hill. Silently Prue opened Mavis's door. "Let's get out and have a look," she said quietly.

"Gosh, that must be paradise!" exclaimed Mavis. The fields stretched out forever. Trees cuddled together in groups. Paths wove through the countryside. "Just look at those beeches!" Mavis took a deep breath and stretched her arms out like a human kite. They stood in silence for some time drinking in the marvels of Nature.

"Quick, supper time soon!" Mavis suddenly cried out, looking at her watch. Prue drove slowly down the hill. Mavis chatted, always asking questions, never listening to Prue's answers. As they arrived back at the *Brambles*, Anne and Tom were standing in the doorway, Anne holding an empty flower pot.

"Thank you Prue, I've enjoyed so much just being with you." Mavis couldn't say goodbye any more. It hurt too much. She walked slowly towards Anne while Tom was waving goodbye to the car as it disappeared.

"Where *have* you been?" asked Anne anxiously.

"I've had a lovely time eating, then visiting some trees," smiled Mavis as the bell rang for supper. "I'm so full from lunch I don't think I can manage supper, but I'll come and chat."

"Yes do, I'm longing to see all the material your friend brought," replied Anne as they entered the dining room.

"Quiet please!" called Cathy. The chatter died down. "Tomorrow morning, we'll meet here after the breakfast dishes have been cleared and start planning the costumes for the Christmas show. Mavis has kindly donated lots of material, so we'll all be busy beavers. Those who can't or won't sew can paint the backcloth."

Mavis had already planned what characters some of her friends would be, but she kept quiet until after supper when she pulled Anne into what the residents called 'the wellie boot room' and sat her down on a stool.

"Now we're going to make our own costumes. Here's my list: you're going to be Florence Nightingale because you're so gentle. Paula, somebody religious. Tom's going to wear a tutu (he loves ballet so much). I'm going to be …"

Suddenly the door was opened and a huge, shocked looking Mrs Marango boomed, "I thought I heard voices. What on earth are you doing in here? You should be in the living room."

"We're discussing the Christmas show," Anne said quietly.

"You should do that in the right place." Mrs Marango shut the door firmly as Mavis and Anne scuttled off to the living room.

Cathy was pouring cocoa into mugs on the trolley. "You

both look very flushed. Here's your cocoa," said Cathy, handing them both a steaming mug.

"Let's sit over in the corner," whispered Anne. "Then we can finish the costume list."

"Yes, we got as far as Tom's tutu. I shall be Queen Bess and grumpy old Evan will be Father Christmas," laughed Mavis, her shaking hand spilling cocoa onto the carpet.

"We'll have to persuade Cathy to let us go mad," squeaked Anne.

Wardrobe roll call

Next morning, breakfast – normally a torpid affair – was buzzing with excitement about the Christmas party costumes. Some residents were shoving soggy Weetabix into their loose jaws, others were slurping tea from their saucers; another group was busy chatting. Cathy hurried everyone along.

"Come on, let's finish eating so we can start work on the costumes," she announced.

An hour later, all Mavis's material was spread out on the tables rather like a jumble sale. She couldn't contain herself.

"I'm going to be Queen Bess," she said, gathering the dress and a fur wrap around her body. Some people laughed. Paula was taken aback.

"Who's that?" she asked.

"It's the old Queen," said Mavis as she slowly walked round the table coming face to face with Cathy, "And it's who I'm going to be." People shuffled round the tables lifting up pieces of material. No one was as animated as Mavis. Four sewing machines lay waiting on the end table. Anne sat down measuring a white sheet.

"This is my nursing uniform. I'm Florence Nightingale," she said as the machine started whirring busily across the linen.

Paula sidled up to Mavis, "I'd like to be someone near to God," she said shyly.

"What about Mother Teresa?" suggested Mavis. Paula looked shocked.

"Oh I couldn't possibly."

"Of course you could," said Mavis. "You look just like her and we have a lovely tea-towel here.

Tom tiptoed up to Mavis who showed him a picture of a swan. He smiled and she shouted "Shall I make you a tutu?" Tom's face beamed as he nodded. "Could we buy some white netting for Tom's costume?" Mavis called to Cathy, who was rescuing a large piece of torn sheet ruffed up in the sewing machine.

"Yes, I expect so," she replied rather crossly as Anne watched her Florence Nightingale dress almost ripped to shreds. "We'll start again tomorrow. I'll show you how to do running stitch."

There was a sudden howl of laughter. Everyone looked round to see grumpy old Evan roaring with laughter at himself in the mirror in a fluffy white beard and a red jingle-bell hat. No one had ever seen him laugh before. Cathy was worried he might have a seizure because of his heart problems.

Things were just as frenetic two hours later when the lunch bell rang. "Come along. Please help clear the tables. We'll do some more costumes next week." Chaos continued as the floor became strewn with material. Paula nearly tripped on Anne's dangling sheet. Slowly people shuffled along with dresses, dropping them into a large suitcase. The dining room returned to normal. Silence took over as every mouth chomped the lunchtime pasta, in most cases washed down with water.

After lunch Mavis asked Cathy is she could do some sewing in her bedroom.

"Yes if it's by hand, but you can't use the machine alone." Cathy realised that Mavis was in top gear and decided to encourage her keenness. "Actually it would be a great help," she added, "Because just between you and me Mavis, I don't think the others will get everything done in time otherwise – especially the sleepy brigade. Sometimes I feel as if I can see right through them, like skeletons or shadows." The carer smiled, not realising she was confiding in Mavis, then abruptly left the room.

A few hours later, and feeling unexpectedly weary after the mornings exertions, Mavis went in search of Anne. She entered the living room where some people began emerging from their afternoon apathy, like snails stretching out of their shells. Others still sat vacant in their own silence, rigid or drooped. Mavis caught sight of Anne sitting by the window stroking a pink hankie. "That is pretty isn't it? Did you know Florence Nightingale always comforted the poor with a hankie?" Anne smiled as her friend looked at the beautifully embroidered cotton square but frowned as Mavis added "Oh, I've got a pain in my head after all the excitement," and suddenly slumped into an armchair.

"Shall I get Cathy? Or some water?" asked Anne, clutching her hankie.

"Nothing. No one. I'll just snooze," whispered Mavis, shutting her eyes as her head flopped back. Anne devotedly sat by her, finally nodding off herself.

It wasn't long before the supper bell woke everyone with a start.

"I don't feel hungry Anne, I think I'll go to my room," sighed Mavis, slowly getting up and drifting out of the door.

"I'll pop in later Mave, with something – don't know what," called Anne.

There was a soft knock on the door just after 9pm, as Cathy entered with a mug of cocoa and was surprised to find Mavis dozing fully-clothed on the floor.

"Oh, what are you doing there?" asked Cathy as Mavis slowly opened her eyes. Anne walked in with a tiny posy of weeds.

"Hello, Mave," she whispered, stroking her head before

Cathy added, "Let's get you into bed. You take her arm the other side." Together they heaved Mavis up and sat her on the bed.

"Why was I on the floor? It was rather cold down there." Mavis shuddered.

"I really don't know why you were on the floor. I hope you didn't fall." Cathy's voice was concerned.

"Can't remember. Don't know," Mavis sighed as they pulled her nightie on.

"See you in the morning." Cathy left the room while Anne stayed for a while holding Mavis's hand until she dropped off to sleep.

~

After a good night's sleep Mavis awoke to hear the pigeons cooing and without her headache. Her friends smiled as she drifted in for breakfast.

"Now you take it easy today, remember you had a little turn yesterday!" cautioned Cathy.

"Stuff and nonsense! I feel so full of life, I could build a castle," Mavis laughed.

After breakfast, as it was a damp day and they wanted some exercise, Mavis and Anne went trundling out in their wellies to move the bucket of rainwater closer to the house so Mavis could keep an eye on it. A grey squirrel shot across their path.

"I wish I could keep one as a pet and stroke its fluffy tail," said Anne.

"They're infectious and chase all the lovely red ones," Mavis told her brusquely. "Let's go back and do some sewing ready for tomorrow."

It wasn't long before only Mavis and her friends were actively sewing. Tom started splattering green paint on the backcloth and himself. Mavis helped Paula with the Mother Teresa shift, a sort of black dress with a white stripe round the collar.

"That's looking like Mother already. Now we need that white cloth for your head," Mavis said enthusiastically.

"Ow! Ow! Ow!" shrieked Anne whose finger was caught in the sewing machine. Cathy rushed over to Anne and all the old eyes swivelled to the offending sewing machine as Cathy lifted the lever, releasing the needle from Anne's finger.

"Poor thing, what a nasty accident," said Cathy, gently wrapping a tissue round the pierced finger. "Now get on with the sewing everyone, we've only got a couple of weeks to go. As for you, you silly girl, come with me and I'll get a plaster," she said guiding Anne out of the room.

Mavis was engrossed with the tutu which she was determined to finish that afternoon when Anne returned and sat beside her.

"Will you help me finish my dress?" asked Anne. "I'm not

using that horrid machine anymore."

"Yes of course, as soon as I've finished Tom's tutu. I hope the blood didn't stain your Nightingale collar," laughed Mavis. The lunch bell jangled harshly.

"Pack everything away into the suitcases," called Cathy, busily trying to lay knives and forks against the flow of the material falling off the table. Soon everyone sat down and started eating.

"Shall I cut up your cabbage?" asked Mavis, watching Anne struggle with her blunt knife which kept sliding off the leaves instead of slicing them.

"Thanks Mavis. Wasn't it silly of me to machine my finger." They both laughed.

"Let's go out for a bit after lunch," said Mavis.

The autumn sun warmed their walk. Suddenly they heard a pitiful mewing inside a low box hedge.

"Oh look, it's got a bleeding finger like you," cried Mavis picking up a forlorn tabby cat. It's got a cut on its paw. We must take it to Cathy. She's good with injuries." They cradled the now purring cat and went indoors.

Later, when Mavis lay down to rest, the cat snuggled up to her chest staring into her face. There was a soft knock on the door and Anne came in dressed as Florence Nightingale.

"Can you pin the hem for me?" she asked Mavis.

The tabby jumped off her chest as Mavis stepped off the bed and sank to the floor taking the box of pins Anne held out for her. "Stay still. Don't stroke the cat when I'm trying to level you," said Mavis as she crawled round pinning the hem. "Now take it off and I'll sew it for you."

"I can't, I've got nothing on," smiled Anne.

"Wear my dressing gown, then." Mavis handed her a long silk robe. Cathy crossly burst through the door.

"Mavis, where is the cat?" she asked.

"Under my bed, I hope," said Mavis meekly. This was met with a dismissive snort.

"There's a large poo in the passage. Please put the cat outside, we can't keep a stray that messes on the carpet."

"We all have accidents," Mavis sighed. "I'll clean it up and put him in the garden right away. Oh please don't be cruel about Twinky, I'll make sure he behaves. I love him and he loves me." Cathy left the room abruptly. "Stay still Anne, I've nearly finished the hem. Let me see it on again."

"Thanks very much Mave, I'll get some loo paper and clean up Twinky's poo. Hope it's hard – much easier to pick up!" Anne laughed.

An hour later the bell rang and Mavis gently put Twinky out in the garden. "I'll keep you some food," she whispered. At supper Mavis scooped some fish pie into her serviette and tucked it in her handbag. Then she took a paper cup and filled it so full of milk that some overflowed down her flowered shirt. No one noticed as she left the table quickly and went back to her room. Twinky's little face was blinking at the window. He loved the fish but made a mess splashing the milk on the carpet. Mavis chuckled with delight.

～

Next morning after breakfast Paula came into the room and asked Mavis to iron her Mother Teresa's dress because she'd slept in it.

"Oh dear, it does look creased and crinkled. Take it off," said Mavis, and left, carrying an untidy bundle to the utility room. In due course she returned. "Where's the tea cloth?" she asked.

"I'm sorry, I've lost it. I don't know where it's gone."

"Where did you leave it, Paula?" Mavis asked impatiently

"I think it went to the laundry by mistake. Perhaps I could put on a pillow case instead?" Paula suggested.

"Mother Teresa wouldn't wear a pillow case because she was a saint," Mavis replied. She then smelt burning, rushed back to the utility room and yelped, "Oh my God!". She found a charred hole in the Mother Teresa dress, grabbed the smoking iron and threw it in the basin, tears pouring down her cheeks.

"Silly, silly me," she choked.

Anne came in and looked at the carnage. "Bad luck Mave. Still, we can make another one before the show," she said hoping to comfort Mavis.

"Such a stupid waste," Mavis wailed. "I can't tell Paula." Then she began sweeping up the remnants.

"That bit can be saved for a skirt, so we only have to make her a top," said Anne cheerily. "Let's get some material out of the case. We'll make it today."

Paula sobbed loudly when she heard about the burnt offering. Anne was a true Florence Nightingale and comforted both crying friends. Luckily Cathy didn't smell the scorching as she was out shopping. Soon they were cutting out some brown serge and measuring Paula's chest, which was still heaving with sobs.

"Come on. You can help too," said Anne.

"I can't thread a needle because of my cataracts," Paula sobbed.

"Oh stop crying, I can't sew with that noise," said Anne crossly.

"Get into my bed and put on my nightie to keep warm," suggested Mavis, getting more absorbed in the dress making.

"Hello, are you in?" called a voice. Mavis opened the door. "How do I look?" asked Tom, beaming in his tutu glittering with sequins.

"You look wonderful" the three old ladies exclaimed, forgetting Tom was stone deaf. Mavis clapped her hands, Anne shouted to him "LOVELY!" and Paula hid under the pillow and squeaked. It was almost a pantomime scene. Laughter had returned again.

Queen Bess

That evening the pianist arrived after a bangers and mash supper to practice for the concert. It sounded dreary to Mavis who was dying to get up and sing some old lively songs. Only a few whispering voices croaked 'Good King Wenceslas' and 'The First Noel' because no one knew the words.

"Why don't you give out song sheets with the words on? Us oldies forgot most of them years ago!" suggested Mavis, staring hard at Cathy.

"Perhaps we'll try it next week for the show if we have time, but lots of people can't see well," retorted Cathy.

Mavis was frustrated and said, "OK, no fun," and walked out. Cathy followed her into the hallway.

"Mavis, you spoilt the rehearsal! You won't take part in the actual concert if you go on interfering."

Mavis went into her room and fell onto the bed face down and groaned. "I wonder where Calvin is. We did have such fun." She went on muttering to herself as Cathy retreated.

~

Party day had arrived at *Brambles*. Mrs Marengo watched as everyone in costume gathered round the Christmas tree. Mavis felt very regal dressed in a velvet robe and fur collar.

"I'm a queen," she muttered to Anne, "but I've forgotten my crown."

"Don't worry, your head is having a rest," laughed Anne, who looked calm and tranquil as Florence Nightingale. Paula trundled round in her Mother Teresa garb, complete with tea-cloths sewn together as a replacement head-dress; followed by a radiant Tom almost on tip-toes in his tutu. Some of the other residents joined the circle looking empty faced, vacant and bewildered. Mavis grabbed a piece of tinsel from the tree and wrapped it round her straggly hair, laughing, "Here's my crown!" Other people drifted into armchairs set against the wall while various wheelchairs were pushed forward by the piano.

"No song sheets, I see!" called out Mavis.

Cathy, ignored her and announced "We'll start with 'Good King Wenceslas'. The people in costume can walk round as we sing." Mavis led the way regally as Mr. Bond played very slowly. Everyone marvelled at Tom humming away in his tutu. Mrs Marango looked a little shocked at his bare, spindly, hairy legs. Next came 'The First Noel'. Mavis knew the descant and trilled several high notes in the chorus with her head tipped up, losing her tinsel crown under

Paula's feet. 'We Three Kings' was a terrible, almost silent dirge. Mavis was getting impatient with the dismal sound.

"Let's have 'Jingle Bells', it's a happy song!" she called out. "Come on Father Christmas, lead the way." The grumpy old man suddenly smiled and plodded round the tree followed by Tom at a gallop. Mavis skipped as she sang.

"Come on Anne and Paula." Cathy suddenly caught Mavis's arm.

"That's enough Mavis."

"Can we sing some of the old songs now please, please Cathy," Mavis pleaded.

"It's not really suitable at Christmas," said Mrs Marango sternly.

"You put your left leg in, your left leg out, in out in out, shake it all about. You do the Hoki Koki and you turn around ..." yelled Mavis, singing at top speed and forgetting all about her.

"That'll do," said Cathy taking hold of Mavis by the shoulders. "Come with me."

Silence and dismay followed them out. Anne wanted to go with Mavis but didn't dare. People dragged their feet as Mr Bond played 'Away in a Manger' quietly. No one sang except Tom.

"Now, let's wish Mr Bond a happy Christmas," said Mrs Marango, clapping her hands as the pianist gave a slight bow and left the room. "Time to change and get ready for supper. We did enjoy your home made costumes."

Tom sprang into the air still full of exuberance, nearly landing on Father Christmas. Anne whispered to Paula "Let's go and see poor Mavis, I bet she's cross."

As they opened Mavis's door they found her putting make up on. Bright red lipstick and some blue eye shadow.

"Where are you going Mave?" squeaked Paula.

"You look beautiful," smiled Anne.

"Sssh, shut the door, I've got a Christmas plan." Mavis had taken her top teeth out to ooze the scarlet colour round her pursed upper lip. "We're going out later to have some fun," Mavis whispered rebelliously. The supper bell rang.

"You all go and eat. Keep your clothes on and come back to me about nine. Bring Tom. Don't tell *anyone*." Mavis grinned as they went out of the door, then clicked back her upper teeth, powdered her nose and started humming.

By 9 o'clock Mavis was beginning to tremble with excitement. Anne tiptoed in followed by Paula and Tom.

"What's your idea Mave?" asked Anne enquiringly.

"We're going out tonight to have a sing song at the pub. We must creep past the washing-up people in the kitchen, then down the lane to the pub. It will cheer us up and no one will know we've gone. Come on, follow me,", whispered Mavis.

"What a surprise," murmured Paula as they crept through the kitchen door into the quiet lane. Mavis was carefree and full of laughter leading her friends on an escape trip. As they all approached the 'Royal Hen' they heard laughing voices.

"I'll go in first. We'll have a drink and start by singing 'Knees up Mother Brown'," Mavis said in a hushed voice, sweating with excitement as she opened the door and pushed past various men who were chatting amiably to each other. They instantly stopped at the sight of Mavis, Anne, Paula and Tom in his tutu.

"We'd all like double brandies," she proclaimed to the astounded barman.

"Y ... Yes," he stammered.

"We're from up the road and we're going to have a Christmas sing song."

"Whatever you say Missus. Nice to see you."

Aware of the locals amazed faces, Mavis handed each of her friends a glass, gulped hers down hastily and thirty seconds later started forming a circle with everyone nearby.

"Come on, let's sing 'Knees up Mother Brown' everyone," she cried, her fur wrap falling to the floor. Tom took her hand firmly, rather shy of all the onlookers. Anne and Paula grabbed a pair of young executive types who were rather reluctant to join in at first.

Mavis shrieked ... "Knees up Mother Brown ..." Voices stirred and soon everyone was joining in. The atmosphere was contagious. A surge of people pushed into the circle then coiled back and threw their arms in the air. The bar was vibrating with laughter. Mavis nearly fainted with the heat, her makeup pouring down her cheeks, but exuberantly went on with song after song. The pub was electric.

Suddenly a siren outside silenced everyone. The door burst open.

"Here they are," called a burly policeman over one shoulder. Mavis collapsed ecstatically into his arms.

"Hello Sarge, come and join in the the 'Hoki Koki'!" she bellowed.

"We're having such fun," added Anne.

"Come on old girl," said the sergeant, steering both women towards the door.

"Leave 'em alone, they're not doin' any 'arm," called the barman. "They're just enjoying themselves."

Mavis and her friends were shepherded out of the door, cheered by the entire pub.

"Happy Christmas to you all!" Mavis called as she was led out.

She was followed by Tom, who as ever just gave a knowing smile.

Lotte Moore is an 80-year-old writer on a mission. Her myriad children's stories have been enjoyed by primary school boys and girls around the country, particularly when they get a visit from Lotte, during which she inspires the children with her readings, and wartime stories of rationing and bombings. Lotte has written more than 16 books, including her autobiography *Snippets of a Lifetime*. Despite writing stories since her childhood, Lotte only blossomed as a writer in her 70s. She was born into an incredibly literary family. Her father, John Pudney, wrote poetry (including the popular WW2 poem '*For Johnny*'), novels and biographies. Her grandfather, Sir Alan Herbert, was a prolific writer, satirist and librettist.

As a child, Lotte lived in Kent with her parents who enjoyed entertaining, political debate and literary discussion with the likes of Charlie Chaplin, Winston Churchill, H E Bates, W H Auden and Benjamin Britten. During the war, having been evacuated, and then at school, Lotte often found herself feeling lonely and turned to writing (stories, diary, poems and letters) to express her feelings of isolation. In her early teens Lotte's commitment turned to ballet, and point shoes replaced the pen. She was selected by the Royal Ballet School to dance in the Opera Ballet. When rejected for growing 'too tall' Lotte turned to acting and intermittently to writing. She finally married aged 38 to her loyal husband Chris (who continues to support Lotte in many ways, including typing out her hand-written stories). Lotte became immersed in her stepchildren and then her own two girls. Sadly, her parents died before her writing career flourished. Lotte lives in London, on the River Thames, and at this time of year can be found entertaining young and old in her local area by putting on nativity plays with a 'real' baby performing the part of Jesus – much to the admiration of the old ladies and gents in the care homes and community centres they perform in.